CYCLOPS OF
EURIPIDES

〈

BCP Classic Commentaries on Latin and Greek Texts

Current and forthcoming titles:

CYCLOPS OF EURIPIDES

Edited with Introduction
and Commentary by
R.A.S. Seaford

Bristol Classical Press

This impression 2003
This edition published in 1998 by
Bristol Classical Press
an imprint of
Gerald Duckworth & Co. Ltd.
90-93 Cowcross Street, London EC1M 6BF
Tel: 020 7490 7300
Fax: 020 7490 0080
inquiries@duckworth-publishers.co.uk
www.ducknet.co.uk

First published by Oxford University Press, 1984
Text © Oxford University Press 1984
Editorial matter © Richard Seaford 1984

A catalogue record for this book is available
from the British Library

ISBN 1 85399 566 5

Printed and bound in Great Britain by
Antony Rowe Ltd, Eastbourne

PREFACE

This book is a somewhat unusual member of its series. Because the *Cyclops* is the only satyr-play that survives complete, my work on the play has gone hand in hand with a study of satyric drama as a whole. Reconstruction of the genre, to which much of the Introduction and some of the Commentary is devoted, has proved to be of interest for the light that it sheds not only on the *Cyclops* but also, for example, on the manner in which drama emerged from the cult of Dionysos.

The text printed is taken from the new Oxford Classical Text of Euripides, volume I, edited by Dr. J. Diggle. The places in which I disagree with the editor were never very numerous, and have been reduced, though not of course entirely eliminated, by a detailed exchange of views.

The κάματος of several years' work has been made εὐκάματος by five institutions: Brasenose College and Queen's College in Oxford, the University of Berlin, the Fondation Hardt in Geneva, and the University of Exeter. I am grateful also for the assistance of colleagues too numerous to mention, and in particular to Professor Hugh Lloyd-Jones and Professor George Thomson for their interest and encouragement, to Professor R. Kassel for what I learnt in discussion of numerous textual problems, and to Professor M. D. Reeve and Professor P. T. Stevens, who examined the doctoral thesis on which this book is based. My greatest debts are to two scholars whose influence on the Commentary is invisibly ubiquitous: Mr. T. C. W. Stinton, who supervised my thesis, and Dr. J. Diggle, who as well as providing the text read the Commentary in its final form.

The University of Exeter   R.A.S.S.
March 1984

CONTENTS

LIST OF PLATES

ABBREVIATIONS

ABV	J. D. Beazley, *Attic Black-Figure Vase-Painters* (Oxford, 1956).
ARV[2]	J. D. Beazley, *Attic Red-Figure Vase-Painters* (Oxford, 1963).
Denniston, *GP*	J. D. Denniston, *The Greek Particles* (2nd ed., revised by K. J. Dover, Oxford, 1954).
K-B, K-G	R. Kühner, *Ausfuhrliche Grammatik der Griechischen Sprache* (3 Aufl.), Teil i, besorgt von F. Blass; Teil ii, besorgt von B. Gerth (Hanover, 1890–1904).
LSJ	Liddell and Scott, *Greek–English Lexicon* (9th ed., revised by H. S. Jones, Oxford, 1940).
PMG	*Poetae Melici Graeci*, ed. D. L. Page (Oxford, 1962).
Tr. 1, Tr. 2, Tr. 3	see Introduction §VIII.

In general abbreviations are those in LSJ and (for periodicals) *L'Année Philologique*. Plays and fragments cited without the author's name are by Euripides. Verse numbers cited alone are from *Cyclops*.

The dramatic fragments are normally cited in the following editions.

Aeschylus	A. Nauck, *Tragicorum Graecorum Fragmenta* (2nd ed., Leipzig, 1889; reprinted with suppl. by B. Snell, Hildesheim, 1964). H. Lloyd-Jones, appendix to vol. ii of H. Weir Smyth, *Aeschylus* (Loeb Classical Library, 1957).
Sophocles	S. Radt, *TrGF* iv (Göttingen, 1977).
Euripides	Nauck (as Aeschylus).
Minor Tragedians	B. Snell, *TrGF* i (Göttingen, 1971).
Trag. adespota	R. Kannicht and B. Snell, *TrGF* ii (Göttingen, 1981).
Comedy	T. Kock, *Comicorum Atticorum Fragmenta* (Leipzig, 1880–8); F. H. Sandbach, *Menandri Reliquiae Selectae* [OCT, 1972].

The fragments of Pindar are cited in the edition of Snell, of Sappho and Alcaeus in the edition of Lobel and Page, of the remaining lyric poets in *PMG*.

I refer by author's name only to the following commentaries.

V. De Falco, *Il Ciclope* (Naples, 1936).
J. Duchemin, *Le Cyclope d'Euripide* (Paris, 1945).
F. A. Paley, *Euripides*, vol. iii (London, 1860).
R. G. Ussher, *Euripides Cyclops* (Rome, 1978).

An extensive bibliography of the play and of the satyric genre is to be found in Ussher. The fullest bibliography of the genre is to be found in N. C. Hourmouziades, *Satyrika* (Athens, 1974). The most important items are referred to in the course of my Introduction and Commentary.

INTRODUCTION

A. SATYRIC DRAMA

I. PLAYFUL TRAGEDY

IN Aeschylus' Oresteian trilogy the sufferings of the house of
Atreus were brought to a joyful and spectacular conclusion in
the finale of the third play. A torchlit procession accompanied
the Eumenides to their new home in Athens. But that was not
the end of the performance. There followed a light-hearted
afterpiece, the satyr-play *Proteus*: we move to the island of
Pharos, where another member of the house of Atreus,
Menelaos, is becalmed on his way home from Troy, and
where there happens to be a chorus of satyrs. Menelaos successfully extracts from the Old Man of the Sea the secret of
how to restore the wind, as related in the fourth book of the
Odyssey, and leaves for home. The satyrs probably leave with
him.

But the *Proteus* is lost, like almost every other satyr-play.
The ancient selections to which we owe most surviving
tragedy had no room for satyric drama. Only the *Cyclops* was
passed on to the medieval tradition, in a section preserved by
good fortune from the alphabetically-ordered collection of
the plays of Euripides. This relative lack of interest is not
surprising. It is easier to see the point of tragedy and comedy.
In order to understand and appreciate satyric drama we have
to make an effort of informed imagination.

The *Cyclops* is not our only evidence. We have titles of other
satyr-plays from theatrical records, titles and fragments
quoted by ancient authors, a certain amount of ancient comment (notably in Horace's *Ars Poetica*), visual evidence (notably Athenian vase-painting), and, most importantly of all,
discoveries made this century of papyri, notably of about half
of Sophocles' *Ichneutai* ('The Trackers').

It seems that in the classical period (cf. §III 2) a satyr-play (cατυρικὸν δρᾶμα, or just cάτυροι) on a mythical theme was generally performed after each set of three tragedies at the City Dionysia.[1] A known exception is the 'prosatyric' *Alcestis*, which was performed fourth in Euripides' tetralogy of 438 BC: having no chorus of satyrs, it cannot be called a satyr-play, although the theme, and to some extent the mood, is characteristic of the genre. There is nothing in the satyric fragments to suggest that *Cyc.*, with 709 lines, was of abnormal length. Aeschylus' *Diktyoulkoi* ('the Net-pullers') seems to have been a little longer; and the prosatyric *Alcestis*, with 1163 lines, is, if we disregard the lacunose *Heracleidae* and the probably spurious *Rhesus*, the shortest of Euripides' extant plays apart from *Cyc.* Comparison of the fragments of Aeschylus and Sophocles with *Cyc.*, which was probably performed about 408 BC (§VI), suggests that in the course of the fifth century satyric drama tended to lose its specific qualities (§III) and allows a glimpse of the basis on which Aeschylus was regarded in antiquity as the best satyric dramatist.[2]

Vase-paintings were often inspired by satyric drama, and sometimes show satyrs wearing recognizably theatrical costumes.[3] An example is provided by the theme of Prometheus. In a line preserved by Plutarch from Aeschylus' *Prometheus Pyrkaieus* (472 BC) Prometheus warns a satyr who is trying to embrace the fire that he will burn himself. We now also possess a papyrus fragment[4] containing what is almost certainly part of the satyrs' song celebrating Prometheus' gift. Furthermore a number of vase-paintings (e.g. Plate I) dating from about 430 to 410 BC show the satyrs either dancing around Prometheus, who holds one or two torches, or holding the torches themselves: clearly they are inspired by a satyr-

---

[1] The terms τριλογία and τετραλογία may have been applied to drama no earlier than the 3rd century BC: see P. Wiesmann, *Das Problem der tragischen Tetralogie* (Zurich, 1939). There were apparently no satyr-plays at the Lenaia: *IG* ii[2] 2319.

[2] Pausan. 2.13.6; D.L. 2.133.

[3] F. Brommer, *Satyrspiele*[2] (1959), 2–18.

[4] *P. Oxy.* 2245 (fr. 278 Lloyd-Jones); cf. frr. 206, 207 (Nauck).

play, perhaps by a revival of Aeschylus'.[5] Again, the Lucanian 'Richmond Crater' (Plate II),[6] on which two satyrs hover around the blinding of Polyphemos, is no doubt inspired by a satyric *Cyclops*, perhaps Euripides'.

Of particular interest is the frequently depicted Attic 'Pronomos Vase' (Plate III),[7] which shows the cast of a satyr-play from about 400 BC. In the centre the artist has imagined Dionysos and his bride Ariadne. On either side of the divine pair are three figures—representing Herakles, and perhaps Laomedon and Hesione—carrying masks and dressed in the gorgeous costumes of tragic actors. The chorus is composed of young beardless men, each carrying an identical bearded, slightly balding satyr-mask with its characteristic pointed ears and snub nose. Most of them are garlanded, and they are all wearing an apparently equine tail and a furry περίζωμα (loin-cloth) with phallus, except that one is apparently wearing the smooth περίζωμα found also on some other depictions of theatrical satyrs, and another, no doubt the chorus-leader, is wearing an ornamented chiton and a himation. The painter seems to have a specific chorus in mind, for most of the satyrs are labelled with ordinary Athenian names. Next to Herakles is the satyrs' father, Silenos, played by an older, bearded man, carrying in one hand a staff, in the other a white-bearded mask, and over his shoulder a leopard-skin. A white-tufted, tightly-fitting costume covers his whole body. The remaining figures are the αὐλός-player Pronomos, the lyre-player Charinos, and the poet Demetrios. To judge from other vase-paintings, the appearance of the cast of a satyr-play in the classical period never differed much from their appearance on the Pronomos vase, except that the satyrs

[5] Brommer, op. cit. n. 3, figs. 42–6 (*ARV*[2] 1056.86, 1334.19, 1104.6; Berlin F2578).

[6] A. D. Trendall, *The Red-Figured Vases of Lucania, Campania and Sicily* i p. 27 n. 85; reproduced by Brommer, op. cit. n. 3, fig. 11.

[7] *ARV*[2] 1336; frequently reproduced, e.g. A. Pickard-Cambridge, *The Dramatic Festivals of Athens* (2nd ed., revised by J. Gould and D. M. Lewis, Oxford, 1968), fig. 49.

might sometimes wear in addition the costume of a particular
occupation, as they do in *Cyc.* (see note on 80); and they might
also be older than usual, as apparently in Aeschylus' *Sphinx*.[8]
The greater variety of mask and costume listed in the second
century AD by Pollux (*Onom.* 4.118) includes post-classical
innovations (see note on 80).

Silenos occupies an ambiguous position between chorus
and actors. In *Cyc.* he speaks the prologue, conducts a conversation with the chorus-leader (82–95), and leaves the stage
at will (174). On the other hand he is the father of the satyrs
and very much part of the θίαcoc. On the Pronomos vase there
are only eleven satyrs, which suggests that he was in some
sense part of a chorus of twelve. True, we are told that
Sophocles raised the number of the chorus from twelve to
fifteen; but whether this applied to all, or indeed any, subsequent satyric drama is uncertain: the tragic chorus (τραγωιδοί) may not have formed the satyric (cάτυροι) as well.[9]
The actors of satyric drama, on the other hand, who seem to
have been tragic in appearance and to some extent also in
utterance (§V), may well have acted also in the preceding
tragedies. Did one of them play Silenos? It appears very likely
from the titles and fragments of Aeschylus' satyr-plays that
most of them required two actors as well as Silenos; and most
of his satyr-plays were written before the introduction of the
third actor. This suggests that Silenos, however independent,
was a member of the chorus. On the other hand neither the
prosatyric *Alcestis* nor any scene of extant satyric drama requires three actors (as well as Silenos). Although this latter
consideration is not decisive (*Medea* needs only two actors,
and the Cyclopeia could hardly be dramatized for three),
it may be that when three actors became available one of
them tended to be assigned the part of Silenos, so that the role

---

[8] See the newly published Hydria Fujita: Simon (in *SHAW* 1981/5)
explains their age by Dionysos coming earlier in the Theban genealogy than
Oedipus. She points to elderly satyrs also in A. *Dion. Trophoi* (cf. note on 3–4),
rejuvenated perhaps as boy-satyrs (cf. *ARV*[2] 1660 Altamura painter n. 71).

[9] Despite Hor. *Ars. P.* 221 (see Brink ad loc., and §III (1) below).

of κορυφαῖοc devolved onto the spokesman of the satyrs.[10]

In its obscenity, hilarity, and joyful endings satyric drama resembles comedy, from which it is at the same time sharply distinct: in form it appears to resemble tragedy; its content, like tragedy's, is mythological; and it was written by tragedians as part of the tetralogy. Horace compares the effect with a matron who has to dance among satyrs at a festival (*Ars Poetica* 232–3):

> Ut festis matrona moveri iussa diebus
> intererit satyris paulum pudibunda protervis.

In the same vein, a fifth-century Attic cup in the Ashmolean Museum in Oxford (Plate IV) is painted with a satyr creeping up with obviously erotic intentions on a sleeping maenad labelled τραγωιδία. 'Nobody would think of writing a playful tragedy' remarked Demetrius (*De Elocutione* 169), 'for if so, he will write a satyr-play' (ἐπεὶ cάτυρον γράψει ἀντὶ τραγωιδίαc). But why would anybody write a satyr-play? What was the relationship of this curious *Mischgattung* with tragedy on the one hand and comedy on the other? These questions can be properly answered only after an inquiry into the origins of satyric drama, which must in turn be preceded by a brief account of the nature and activities of satyrs outside the theatre.

II. SATYRS

Throughout recorded antiquity people held beliefs about satyrs, dressed up as satyrs, and made images of satyrs. For example, it was believed that when Sulla's army was preparing to sail from Greece to Italy in 83 BC a satyr was captured while sleeping in a nearby grove of the Nymphs and brought

---

[10] So Collinge in *PCPhS* 5 (1958–9), 30–3; cf. Sutton in *CQ* 24 (1974), 19–23. There is no archaeol. evidence for Sil. as *Urschauspieler*: Buschor, 'Satyrtänze und frühes Drama', in *SBAW* 1943/5, 57–8, 80–1. On the Pronomos Vase there appear to be three actors as well as Sil.; but we should in this particular allow for the painter's imagination: see Brommer in *Arch. Anzeig.* 79 (1964), 109–14.

to Sulla.[11] There were satyrs in the great procession arranged by Ptolemy Philadelphus in Alexandria; and in 692 AD the Christian authorities in Constantinople saw fit to forbid the wearing of satyr-masks.[12] Satyrs are a common theme not only of Attic vase-painting but also, for example, of funerary art of the Imperial period. Consequently they exhibit considerable variety of appearance. Suffice it here to note that they are in general more human than animal, and that the animals they tend to resemble are the horse and (largely after the classical period) the goat. As a creature of the imagination, the satyr inevitably came to be an amalgam of various local traditions.

Even their association with Dionysos is not universal, and may not be very ancient: the archaeological evidence suggests that it was consolidated in the course of the sixth century BC. In the same century it appears that the somewhat equine (Attic-Ionian) cιληνοί were amalgamated with the (Peloponnesian) cάτυροι, so that the terms began to be used interchangeably.[13] And so the creatures I will call 'satyrs' might be more accurately called 'satyr-silens'. In fifth-century satyric drama, in keeping with the ancient belief in individual cιληνοί,[14] a distinctive member of the *thiasos* with the name Σιληνόc has emerged as father of the other satyrs.[15]

Belief about satyrs presents a paradox. From the beginning they are worthless hedonists. The first mention in literature of

[11] Plut. *Sulla* 27 (mythical model: Sil. captured and brought to Midas: Theopomp. 115 *FGH* 75 (b)); see also, e.g., Philostr. *Apoll. Tyan.* 6.27.

[12] Athen. 197–200; *Patr. Gr.* 137, p. 727; see also D.H. 7.72.10; Plut. *Ant.* 24; Lucian *De Salt.* 79; Theodoret. *Affect. Cur.* 7.12.

[13] F. Brommer in *Philol.* 94 (1941), 222–8; Plato *Symp.* 222d; Xen. *Symp.* 4.19; cf. Hdt. 7.26; Plato *Symp.* 215b, 216d, 221d; Lys. fr. 34. Brommer, *Satyroi* (Würzburg, 1937), and Buschor (art. cit. n. 10) discuss the extensive early archaeol. evidence.

[14] Pi. frr. 156, 157; Hdt. 7.26, 8.138; Pausan. 1.23.6, 3.25.2, 6.24.8; D.S. 3.72; Apollod. 2.5.4; Clem. Alex. *Protr.* 24. Individual satyr: Apollod. 2.1.2.

[15] S. *Ichn.* 153; *Cyc.* 539; V. *Ecl.* 6.14; etc. The chorus of *Cyc.* are called cάτυροι (100). See note on 590. Sil., perhaps as a result of his fatherhood, is generally old (παππocιληνόc).

ειληνοί is as making love to nymphs in caves (*h. hom. Aphr.* 262–3); of cάτυροι it is as οὐτιδανοὶ καὶ ἀμηχανοεργοί (Hes. fr. 123). And yet king Midas sought a more than human wisdom by catching a silen (or 'satyr') in his garden, just as Virgil's shepherds extract a song of great wisdom and beauty from Silenos by catching him in a cave.[16] The satyr is an ambiguous creature, cruder than a man and yet somehow wiser, combining mischief with wisdom and animality with divinity.[17] The ambiguity is exploited in Alcibiades' comparison of Socrates with a satyr in Plato's *Symposium*. And despite the cowardice and low hedonism of the satyrs in the theatre, Ion of Chios could say (ap. Plut. *Perikl.* 5) that virtue, like a performance of tragedies, should not be without a satyric element.

Of the practice of dressing up as satyrs a well documented example is provided by the ancient Attic spring festival of Dionysos, the Anthesteria. The second day of the festival was named Χόες after the festal use of wine-jugs. Many of these jugs have survived, painted with scenes from the celebrations. And although there is no doubt much in the scenes that is artistic fantasy, the many pictures of satyrs suggest that men and boys dressed up as satyrs for the occasion.[18] Beliefs about the mischievous and frolicsome nature of the satyrs derive no doubt from the actual behaviour of the satyrs on this and similar occasions.[19]

[16] Hdt. 8.138; Arist. fr. 44 Rose (ap. Plut. *Mor.* 115b); etc.; V. *Ecl.* 6. The paradox is certainly not just a result of the fusion of silen and satyr. It is there in the ancient silen, and even Hesiod's satyrs are, together with the Nymphs and Κουρῆτες θεοί, the grandsons of Phoroneus the inventor of fire.

[17] In this respect, as in others (παιδοτροφία, forced by man to reveal secrets, associated with τέχναι, harvesting, assisting men at work, etc.), he resembles many of the 'wild men' of European folk-belief: Seaford in *Maia* 28 (1976), 213–14.

[18] G. van Hoorn, *Choes and Anthesteria* (Leiden, 1951), esp. p. 53 (and fig. 84 shows a silen-mask). Humans and satyrs perform the same kind of frolics.

[19] The same relationship between practice and belief obtains for many other similar 'wild men' (n. 17), as for the satyrs' descendants, the *kallikántzaroi* (J. C. Lawson, *Modern Greek Folklore and Ancient Greek Religion* (1910), 221–32).

It appears that the Χόες culminated in a ceremony in which the wife of the Archon Basileus (the βαcίλιννα), in association with a group of fourteen women (γεραιραί), performed a secret sacrifice, saw something secret, and was given in a sacred marriage to Dionysos.[20] What she saw were probably sacred objects (ἱερά), which were later handled by the γεραιραί.[21] These are all features of the Dionysiac mysteries. In this way the Anthesteria combined general public festivity with the mystic ritual of a band of women. And there is evidence for the same arrangement in other festivals of Dionysos: e.g. the Attic Lenaia, and at Delphi, Miletos, and Pergamon.[22] It also seems likely that at the Anthesteria Dionysos was escorted to his sacred marriage by men dressed as satyrs,[23] who although part of the public celebrations may have formed a distinct group or *thiasos*.

Satyrs participated not only in public festivals but also in mystic ritual. Plato refers to a kind of dancing in which people dress up as nymphs, pans, silens, and satyrs in order to perform certain purifications (καθαρμοί) and initiations (τελεταί).[24] And there is plenty of evidence in the visual art of the Hellenistic and Roman periods for people dressing up as satyrs and silens in order to enact mystic initiations.[25] Furthermore, the few surviving inscriptions relating to the members of Dionysiac associations include the titles

[20] L. Deubner, *Attische Feste*[2], 100–101, 108.

[21] Deubner, op. cit. n. 20, 108; [Dem.] *Neair.* 78.

[22] P-Cambridge, op. cit. n. 7, 30–6; Deubner, op. cit. n. 20, 130; *RE* vi A s. Thyiades 686 (cf. D.S. 4.3.3); Henrichs in *HSCP* 82 (1978), 121–60; cf. *Ba.* 35–6 with 1109; Strabo 14.1.20 (640); Sokolowski, *Lois Sacr. As. Min.*, n. 48; etc.

[23] Refs. in P-Cambridge, op. cit. n. 7, 12; contra, W. Burkert, *Homo Necans* (de Gruyter, 1972), 223 (but even the Attic Anthesteria is called Διονύcια: Thuc. 2.15.4), 263 (cf. P-Cambridge, op. cit. n. 7, 17). Satyrs are also sometimes present at the ritual depicted on the 'Lenäenvasen'.

[24] *Leg.* 815c: the passage is corrupt but the general sense is clear. Cf. §III (3). Bacchic τελεταί are initiations: Seaford in *CQ* 31 (1981), 253.

[25] M. P. Nilsson, *The Dionysiac Mysteries of the Hellenistic and Roman Age* (Lund, 1957); E. Simon in *Röm. Mitt.* 69 (1962), 145–6; the participants are sometimes clearly wearing satyr-masks.

Σειληνόκοϲμοϲ, Σειληνόϲ, and ἅππαϲ Διονύϲου.[26] To be initiated into the mysteries might be to join a *thiasos* consisting
partly at least of satyrs.[27] And so, inasmuch as the *thiasos* is a
community of this world and the next, a dead initiate may be
imagined as a satyr.[28] It seems then that the ambiguity of
belief about satyrs is associated with a similar ambiguity of
satyrs in festival and ritual. On the one hand they are men
and boys, dressed up for frolics at the festival; and on the other
hand they are, within the *thiasos*, the attendants of the god and
the initiated custodians of a solemn and secret tradition.

The two kinds of celebration, though distinct, may occur
together. That is to say, the mystic ritual may be celebrated
within a public festival; and in such cases it must tend to be
performed for the well-being not so much of its initiates as
of the community as a whole, as was the case in the 'more
ancient' (Thuc. 2.15) of the Attic festivals of Dionysos, the
Anthesteria.[29] Another spring festival of Dionysos, the City
Dionysia, seems to have been organized in the time of
Peisistratus in such a way that the division between the mystic
ritual of the *thiasos* on the one hand and the public celebration

[26] Cumont in *AJA* 37 (1933), 232–63; Nilsson, op. cit. n. 25, 56; *SIG*[3]
1115; n. 118 below.

[27] E.g. Keil-Premerstein i 28 n. 42 (2nd cent. AD Philadelphia), where the
Dionysiac μύϲτηϲ is represented as a satyr. With his obvious respectability cf.
e.g. Luc. *De Salt.* 79 (εὐγενέϲτατοι καὶ πρωτεύοντεϲ as satyrs), and the personal
names Σάτυροϲ and Σειληνόϲ.

[28] Hence the popularity of satyrs in funerary art from the archaic period
onwards: Webster in A. Pickard-Cambridge, *Dithyramb, Tragedy and Comedy*
(2nd ed., Oxford, 1962), 103; A. B. Cook, *Zeus* iii 382–6; Roscher *Lex. Myth.*
iv s. Satyros, 446; Schauenburg in *JDAI* 68 (1953), 67; A. Bruhl, *Liber Pater*,
64; Nilsson, op. cit. n. 25, 126; C. Picard, *L'Art Romain*, pl. 36; F. Matz, *Die
Dionysische Sarkophage* (Berlin, 1968–75), *passim*; cf. *AP* 7.37; Pausan. 6.24.8
(cf. E. Ohlemutz, *Die Kulte und Heiligtümer der Götter in Pergamon* (1968), 111).
In *CIL* III 686 (Philippi) the dead boy is imagined as a satyr welcomed by a
Dionysiac company into Elysium: cf. esp. *Arch. Anzeig.* 1950, 170–1 (dead
woman becoming maenad among satyrs).

[29] ὑπὲρ τῆϲ πόλεωϲ, [Dem.] *Neair.* 73; cf. Henrichs, art. cit. n. 22, 148–9
(Miletus). In such cases the mysteries may be celebrated without the initiation of a novice.

on the other was dissolved. Because the essential prerequisite
of drama, action in an alien identity, is inherent in the mysteries, this dissolution was a crucial stage in the evolution of
drama, to which we must now turn our attention.[30]

III. THE ORIGINS, HISTORY, AND FUNCTION
OF SATYRIC DRAMA

(1) *Origins.* In §4 of his *Poetics* Aristotle remarked that tragedy
took time to acquire its elevated tone and to discard 'small'
plots and ridiculous diction, 'because it developed from the
satyr-play-like' (διὰ τὸ ἐκ σατυρικοῦ μεταβαλεῖν). In the pro-
lific debate about the origins of tragedy this has been a central
and controversial passage. The tendency to dismiss it as evidence has been based, firstly, on an apparent contradiction
with the Alexandrian view, preserved in Horace's *Ars Poetica*,
that satyric drama was a later addition to tragedy; secondly,
on an apparent contradiction with Aristotle's own observation, earlier in the same chapter, that tragedy arose from
the leaders of the dithyramb; and thirdly, on a preconceived
unwillingness to believe that tragedy could originate in
crudity, as for example in the bizarre but influential contribution of G. F. Else,[31] who, having thrust aside the obstacles
presented by Aristotle and others to modern preconceptions
of literary development as engineered by men of genius, feels
free to regard tragedy as 'not the end product of a gradual
development but the product of two successive *creative acts* [his
italics] by two men of genius'.

The preconceptions of Aristotle, on the other hand, were
controlled by a knowledge of early drama much greater than
our own.[32] And he does indeed state in the next chapter that
the stages of tragedy's development, unlike those of comedy,

---

[30] Dithyramb and mystic initiation: Seaford in *Maia* 29 (1977–8), 88–92.
See also Seaford, art. cit. n. 24, 263–75.

[31] *The Origin and Early form of Greek Tragedy* (Camb. Mass., 1965).

[32] D. W. Lucas, *Aristotle Poetics*, 79–80; Kranz in *NJA* 43 (1919) 148–50;
Seaford, art. cit. n. 24, 269.

are known. In fact of course the derivation ἐκ cατυρικοῦ would be curious as a mere hypothesis,[33] not least because it cuts across the framework set up earlier in the chapter, in which there is an early historical division between serious and trivial poetry. cατυρικόν here means neither 'satyr-play', which would probably have been expressed by ἐκ τῶν cατυρικῶν, nor merely 'boisterous', but 'satyr-play-like', just as by τραγικόν Aristotle can mean a quality appropriate to tragedy (*Rhet.* 1406b8). Whether he thought of the dithyramb from which tragedy evolved as actually performed by satyrs or merely like satyr-play in some other respects is uncertain. Certainly, the likelihood of sixth-century satyrs performing dithyrambs, and the similarity between satyric drama and early dithyramb, are both much greater than is generally supposed, and possibly greater even than Aristotle knew.[34] Notably, the remains of both satyric drama and of dithyramb betray traces of an origin in the mystic ritual of the Dionysiac *thiasos*, in which there are independent reasons for seeing the origins of tragedy (see n. 44 below). A stage in the evolution of tragedy out of ritual was the performance by the *thiasos* (satyric or not) of a Dionysiac hymn, the dithyramb.

As for the account of events in Horace, this complements rather than contradicts Aristotle. Neither account is complete. How, on the one hand, if tragedy developed ἐκ cατυρικοῦ, do we explain the continued performance of satyric drama alongside tragedy? And why, on the other hand, as Horace maintains, did the Athenians decide to introduce a novelty, the satyr-play, to be an integral part of the tragic διδαcκαλία? The answer to both questions is that satyric drama was formally instituted in the Dionysia to preserve what had been lost in the development of tragedy described by Aristotle. This hypothesis is supported by two considerations. Firstly, it appears that the Peripatetic Chamaileon, in his

[33] As believed by H. Patzer. *Die Anfänge der Griechischen Tragödie* (Wiesbaden, 1962), 70–85.

[34] Seaford in *Maia* 29 (1977–8). 88–94, and in art. cit. n. 24, 269–70; also Webster, op. cit. n. 28, 20, 34.

monograph on Thespis (fr. 38), gave the following explanation of the proverb οὐδὲν πρὸς τὸν Διόνυσον: when Σατυρικά about Dionysos began to be replaced by tragedies on other themes, people shouted 'nothing to do with Dionysos'. Zenobius (5. 40) adds that this led to the institution of satyric drama. It is true that all this accords with Aristotle's account of early tragedy. But it seems unlikely to have derived entirely from it; and nobody has challenged the authenticity, or given a better explanation, of the proverb. Here then, perhaps, is a trace of the traditionalist popular opinion by which satyric drama was ensured a place in the Dionysia. Secondly, we find strikingly similar developments elsewhere, unknown to Aristotle. For example, the Japanese Kyogen, farcical interludes performed between the serious Nō plays, 'preserved the comic elements characteristic of early Sarugaku when that entertainment turned its attention to the serious pursuit of Nō'.[35] Similarly, the grotesque, comic element was gradually excluded from the English Court Masque, only to return to it in the form of a conventional attachment, the Antimasque.[36] The details of the similar process which seems to have occurred in Athens are largely irrecoverable, and so the following reconstruction must contain an element of hypothesis.

In the second half of the sixth century BC the Athenian public cult of Dionysos seems to have been open to influences from earlier innovations in the northern Peloponnese. It seems that in Sikyon the tyrant Kleisthenes had incorporated hero-lamentations (described as τραγικοὶ χοροί by Herodotus, 5.67) into a public festival of Dionysos; and a few miles away, in Corinth, Arion had turned the traditional, processional dithyramb into a stationary performance of a text.[37] In a similar but more far-reaching development in Athens the dithyramb abandoned its Dionysiac content and style, and assumed the characteristics of tragedy. And so

[35] P. G. O'Neill, *Early Nō Drama* (London, 1958), 5, 87.

[36] See further Seaford, art. cit. n. 17, 210–11.

[37] *Suda* s. Ἀρίων; Hdt. 1.23: Seaford, art. cit. n. 24, 269–70.

Greek tradition associates the birth of tragedy not only with Epigenes of Sikyon and with Arion, but also with the Athenian Thespis, who is said to have first produced tragedy at the Athenian Dionysia in about 534 BC.[38] Arion's dithyramb at Corinth was probably performed by satyrs.[39] At Athens too satyrs accompanied Dionysos in the kind of festal procession likely to have been accompanied by a dithyramb.[40] But whether the *thiasos* of Attic satyrs actually contributed to the development of tragedy, it is impossible to say.

The first writer of satyric drama is said to have been Pratinas of Phleius.[41] The statement is not above suspicion, but may well reflect a genuine association of Pratinas with the formal introduction of satyric drama into the City Dionysia. Of his career we know only that thirty-two of his fifty plays were satyric, and that he competed in Athens during the 70th Olympiad (499–496 BC) and was perhaps dead by 467 BC, when his son Aristias produced one of his satyr-plays. It is in the years after 520 BC that Attic vase-painting, which had long depicted satyrs (or 'silens'), begins to show them in scenes apparently influenced by drama.[42] This change, if not a result of fashion in painting or accidents of survival, suggests that satyric drama evolved at this time, perhaps under the influence of the newly arrived Pratinas.

Had the Athenians not been already familiar with satyrs in their public cult of Dionysos,[43] it seems unlikely that they would have admitted Pratinas' compositions. What then was

[38] *Suda* s. Ἀρίων and s. Θέσπις; Solon fr. 30a; *Marm. Par.* A 43; etc.

[39] A. Lesky, *Die Tragische Dichtung der Hellenen* (3rd ed., Göttingen, 1972), 39. But the etymology of τραγωιδία probably has nothing to do with satyrs: see Burkert in *GRBS* 7 (1966), 87-121.

[40] Probably at the Anthesteria: n. 23 and n. 18 above; cf. also Boardman in *JHS* 78 (1958), 6. Satyrs are sometimes included in the 'Lenäenvasen' (showing ritual at Lenaia? P-Cambridge, op. cit. n. 7, 30–4). For the City Dionysia we do not have such good visual documentation (though cf. Frickenhaus in *JdAI* 27 (1912), 61-88).

[41] *Suda* s. Πρατίνας; *AP* 7.707 (n. 58 below).

[42] Buschor, art. cit. n. 10, 74, 83.

[43] See e.g. Buschor, art. cit. n. 42, 29-33, 39-58.

new about Pratinas? If he arrived in Athens in about 520 BC, he might well have found as the central attraction of the new City Dionysia tragedy at the ὀρχήϲτρα, developing from the dithyramb and losing its ϲατυρικόϲ quality. He would also have found, at the Anthesteria, and perhaps also at the City Dionysia, the traditional, disorganized ϲιληνοί, celebrating perhaps the same story every year about their god. And so his importance as an innovator may have consisted in introducing from Phleius, which is a few miles from Corinth, the practice of writing texts (cf. *Suda* s. Arion) for the satyric element at the Dionysiac celebrations. He would thereby have brought the Attic ϲιληνοί from the disorganized periphery of the festival into its stationary centre, the ὀρχήϲτρα, where, being acceptable to the Athenians as restoring the Dionysiac element, they were at some point integrated into the tragic διδαϲκαλία.

Had satyric drama been essentially alien, this integration could not have occurred. Indeed, it is clear from the vase-painting that the theatrical satyrs are from the very beginning not Peloponnesian (ϲάτυροι), but of the Attic variety (ϲιληνοί).[42] And if satyric drama was an essentially Attic product instituted to preserve what was being lost from Attic tragedy, it should be called as a witness in the investigation of tragedy's origins. And in fact certain features of tragedy which, it has been argued without consideration of satyric drama, derive from tragedy's origin in the ritual of the Dionysiac *thiasos*, are found in a more pronounced form in the scanty remains of mature satyric drama.[44] The unfashionable view that the performance of tragedy originated in the practice of ritual is thereby confirmed.

This does not mean that Pratinas brought nothing more from Phleius than the idea of extending the writing of dramatic texts to the Attic satyrs. The Dorian name ϲάτυροι, by

---

[44] George Thomson, *Aeschylus and Athens*, chs. 7–11; Seaford, art. cit. n. 17; and in the dithyramb: Seaford, art. cit. n. 47.

which the Attic cιληνοί were generally known in the theatre, may reflect his influence. It is possible also that some of the themes of the very earliest satyr-plays, as reflected in vase-painting, may derive from the northern Peloponnese.[45]

This earliest period of satyric drama probably preceded the rule of the tetralogy, which is thought to have been instituted in the reorganization of the City Dionysia which seems to have occurred in about 502–1 BC.[46] That would make sense of the remark in the *Suda* to the effect that of Pratinas' fifty plays thirty-two were satyric. Indeed the only substantial fragment of Pratinas, which is almost certainly satyric,[47] seems to come from this early period. The satyrs enter the ὀρχήcτρα with a vigorous attack, in a parody of a certain dithyrambic style, on the χορεύματα that have just taken place there; the αὐλός, they claim, should not dominate the song. At about the same time as the Athenian satyric celebrations were raised to a new level from abroad by Pratinas, another alien, Lasos from pre-Dorian Hermione in the Argolid, appears to have breathed new life into the dithyramb. Not only is he associated with the institution of dithyrambic contests at the City Dionysia; he is also said to have 'changed pre-existing music by altering the rhythms to the dithyrambic ἀγωγή and adjusting it to the polyphony of αὐλοί' (Ps. Plut. *De Mus.* 1141C). This is surely the tendency attacked by Pratinas' satyrs. Satyric choruses and dithyrambs are associated in cult (see n. 34 above), and had begun to be performed at the Dionysia around the same θυμέλη. Whether or not the style of the Lasian dithyramb had infected the satyric choruses, Pratinas' satyrs are making the claim of their Dorian song (ἄκουε τὰν ἐμὰν Δώριαν χορείαν, v. 17) for the Διονυcιάδα πολυπάταγα θυμέλαν (v. 2).

The resemblance of Pratinas' song is not so much with the fifth-century mythological afterpiece as with Old Comedy,

---

[45] Brommer, art. cit. n. 13, 227; Buschor, art. cit. n. 10, 84, 87–8.

[46] P-Cambridge, op. cit. n. 7, 102–3.

[47] See Seaford in *Maia* 29 (1977–8), 81–94, for the detailed argument on which this summary is based.

both in form (an anapaestic entrance followed by an invocation) and in content (verbal and physical agression, self-presentation, 'literary' invective and reference to the theatre rather than dramatic illusion and plot). In Old Comedy these elements of the parodos, agon and parabasis are 'predramatic' relics of the recent transition from choral performance to drama. Indeed, it has been plausibly argued that parodos, agon, and parabasis have differentiated out of a single choral performance.[48] This hypothesis, which was constructed without consideration of Pratinas, is confirmed by the combination in his song of the various predramatic elements scattered about Old Comedy: the fragment is precisely the kind of undifferentiated choral performance required by the hypothesis. This does not mean, of course, that comedy derives from satyric drama, rather that the Dorian roots of comedy may include the agonistic choruses of which another offshoot was the kind of satyr-play that seems to have flourished briefly in the hands of Pratinas in the last two decades of the sixth century. The fragment, which owes its preservation paradoxically to historians of music, is then the oldest surviving European dramatic text. It is perhaps this period of transition from choral performance to drama that is dimly reflected in Athenaeus' remark (630c) that in ancient times all satyric poetry consisted, like the tragedy of the same period, of choruses.

(2) *History*. Satyric drama was instituted in the Dionysia to preserve something of what tragedy had ceased to be. But this does not mean that it was itself immune to change. Indeed, precisely because it was the specific by-product of a unique transition, it was unlikely to retain its original character once that transition had been forgotten. And in fact we can trace significant changes that occurred both (*a*) in satyric drama itself and (*b*) in its relation to tragedy.

   (*a*) The structure of *Cyc.* is tragic, with a prologue, parodos,

[48] F. M. Cornford, *The Origins of Attic Comedy* (1914).

four episodes (one containing an agon, 285–346) each followed by a choral song, and an exodos. And as in tragedy, the choral songs are accompanied by the exits and entrances of actors. Turning to the fragments, we find that in Sophocles' *Ichneutai* it seems unlikely that there was a formal agon, and, more importantly, the passages of choral lyric (9 in about 450 lines) are apparently unrelated to exits and entrances,[49] more frequent than in *Cyc.*, and in general more agitated: it is impossible to resist the impression that the chorus of satyrs is at any moment ready to burst into vigorous action expressed in dance and song. What remains of Pratinas, Aeschylus' *Theoroi* and Sophocles' *Inachos*[50] suggests that in this respect these plays resemble *Ichneutai* rather than *Cyc.* We do not know the date of the Sophoclean plays; but the *Theoroi* was written before 456 BC (Aeschylus' death), and fr. 3 of Pratinas (see above) is likely to be much earlier. *Cyc.* is very probably one of Euripides' last plays (§VI). Now Aristotle tells us that tragedy had its origin in improvisation (ἀπ᾽ ἀρχῆc αὐτοcχεδιαcτικῆc), as well as that it developed ἐκ cατυρικοῦ. And so it seems very likely that satyric drama too had its origin in an improvisatory performance. We may therefore suggest that the *Inachos* and the *Ichneutai* were either early or, in keeping with the nature of the genre, conservative, and that the tragic structure of *Cyc.* represents a degeneration: frequent, agitated choral passages, the relics of an improvisatory performance preserved in the literary creation by an ever-dwindling feeling for tradition, were eventually eliminated by an inevitable process of assimilation to tragedy. Or perhaps they were merely attenuated to such exclamations by the satyrs as ἆ ἆ ἆ, ἰού ἰού, and ὠή: these are frequent in the choral passages of *Ichneutai* and *Inachos*, and in *Cyc.* occur three times in choral

[49] O. Taplin, *The Stagecraft of Aeschylus* (Oxford, 1977), 57–8.

[50] From the other frr. there is nothing to be gained on this point, except perhaps from the agitated, partly dochmiac reaction to the gift of fire in A. *Prom. Pyrk.* fr. 278 Lloyd-Jones. *Inachos* as satyric: Seaford in *CQ* 30 (1980), 28; D. F. Sutton, *Sophocles' Inachus*, (Beitr. Klass. Phil. 97 (Meisenheim am Glan, 1979)).

passages (49, 51, 656) and twice isolated, *extra metrum*, and probably accompanied by dance-steps, in passages of spoken iambic (157, 464). It seems then that by the end of the fifth century, if *Cyc.* is anything to go by, satyric drama had lost most of its specific form. The result is a comparative marginalization of the chorus, as in Euripidean tragedy. Nevertheless, even in *Cyc.* the chorus, albeit marginal to the action, has not sunk to the merely decorative role of some tragic choruses. In the parodos they accompany their own action with a pastoral song, and all their subsequent songs are to some slight extent functional (see 361, note on 511–18, 616–18, 655).

Just as satyric drama tended to lose its specific form, so also it tended to lose its specific content. In the fragments of Pratinas, Aeschylus, and Sophocles it seems that the various themes are taken up into a specifically satyric world, rustic, self-sufficient, and still very much alive. The πόλιϲ does not impinge. Here, for example, from Aeschylus' *Diktyoulkoi*, is Silenos imagining the future of the baby Perseus:

> ἴξηι παιδοτρόφουϲ ἐμάϲ,
> ὦ φίλοϲ, χέραϲ εὐμενοῦϲ.
> τέρψηι δ' ἰκτίϲι καὶ νεβροῖϲ
> ὑϲτρίχων τ' ὀβρίχοιϲι,
> κοιμήϲηι τὲ τρίτοϲ ξὺν
> μητρὶ καὶ πατρὶ τῶιδε.

In the remains of Euripidean satyric drama, on the other hand, in a development analogous to the development of tragedy, the traditional, vibrant activities of the satyrs have yielded ground to the concerns of the contemporary πόλιϲ. The figure of Polyphemos in *Cyc.* parodies a sophisticated contemporary type (§VIII), and the long fragment of his satyric *Autolykos* (fr. 282) is a polemic about the uselessness to the πόλιϲ of athletes.[51] His satyric *Skiron* contained a joke

---

[51] And A. Dihle (in *Hermes* 105 (1977), 28–42) argues that the philosophical fr. attributed to Critias (fr. 19) comes in fact from E.'s satyric *Sisyphos*.

at the expense of Corinthian courtesans (fr. 675); and in Achaios' *Alkmeon* (fr. 12) the satyrs made fun of the Delphians. This ridicule of contemporaries suggests the influence of Old Comedy; and so does the frequency in *Cyc.* of paratragedy, which, without approaching the scale of Aristophanes, appears to be greater than in the fragments of Aeschylus and Sophocles.[52]

Later we find ridicule of contemporaries extended, in the manner of Old Comedy, to named individuals. Python's *Agen*, produced in 324 BC (or 326)[53] in Alexander's camp on the river Hydaspes, ridiculed Harpalus, Alexander's rebellious satrap, and his relationship with his courtesans, in trimeters characteristic in their licence of Old Comedy (cf. §V). Personal references are also found in the fragments of Timokles' *Ikarioi Satyroi*, which is however so entirely comic in spirit that the play is generally taken to be one of Timokles' comedies, and a similar doubt attaches to fr. 4 of the younger Astydamas,[54] preserved by Athenaeus as from Ἡρακλῆc cατυρικόc, in which the view is expressed, in the comic Eupolidean metre, that a good poet will provide the spectators with variety like that of a rich dinner. And so if, as it seems, in the latter half of the fourth century BC satyric drama aroused little interest, this was perhaps because through partial assimilation to both of the major dramatic genres it had lost much of its old specific appeal. At this period only one was performed at the City Dionysia (see below); and although the Peripatetic Chamaileon devoted one of his numerous monographs to satyric drama, the genre was ignored by Aristotle in his *Poetics*.

---

[52] This may though be only an accident of survival. *Cyc.* 2, 41, 80, 86, 89, 186–7, 206, 218, 222, 314, 424, 683, 687, 706–7; cf. only S. fr. 331.

[53] B. Snell, *Scenes From Greek Drama* (California and Cambridge, 1964), 113–17; D. F. Sutton, *The Greek Satyr Play* (Meisenheim am Glan, 1980), 77–81.

[54] Timokl.: Constantinides in *TAPA* 100 (1969), 49–61; cf. Sutton, op. cit. n. 53, 83–5. Astyd.: Sutton, op. cit. n. 53, 82: the rupture of dramatic illusion is probably unparalleled in satyric drama: see note on 8.

The assimilation to comedy continues into third century Alexandria.[55] Lycophron wrote a satyr-play about the contemporary philosopher Menedemos. The few surviving verses display the metrical looseness of comedy; one of them, nevertheless, is reminiscent of Sophocles: Silenos calls the satyrs παῖδες κρατίστου πατρὸς ἐξωλεστάτοι (fr. 2.1; cf. *Ichn.* 153 τοιοῦδε πατρός, ὦ κάκιστα θηρίων). A more substantial resemblance to fifth-century satyric drama is to be found in the only other[56] satyric remains from Alexandria, from the *Daphnis or Lityerses* by Lycophron's colleague in the Pleiad, Sositheos. The play appears to represent a reaction against the fourth-century assimilation of satyric drama to comedy, both metrically—the twenty-three surviving trimeters contain no resolutions at all—and thematically: an ogre who molests wayfarers is finally defeated in a contest (in reaping) by Herakles, who thereby frees the ogre's captives (Daphnis, and perhaps the satyrs).[57] The appearance of archaizing is in fact confirmed by the epitaph for Sositheos put into the mouth of a satyr guarding his tomb: Sositheos, says the satyr, by reverting to ancient practice had caused him (the satyr), ἐν καινοῖς τεθραμμένον ἤθεσιν ἤδη, to remember his native place (i.e. Phleius, the home of Pratinas).[58]

Although classical satyric drama is not without a pastoral element (e.g. the parodos of *Cyc.*), the presence in Sositheos' *Daphnis or Lityerses* of Daphnis, the inventor of bucolic song, suggests that Sositheos' attempt to revive the pristine satyrplay derived not simply from Alexandrian interest in classical drama, but also perhaps from that new, urban interest in

[55] cf. D.L. 9.110 on the satyr-plays said to have been written by the contemporary philosopher Timon of Phleius, and Sositheos fr. 4 (satyric?).

[56] Unless Sositheos fr. 4 is satyric, or the asigmatic Atlas fr. P. Bodmer xxviii satyric and Alexandrian (Turner in *MH* 33 (1976), 1–23).

[57] frr. 1a, 2, 3; cf. §IV below. E. *Theristai* may also have been about Lityerses. Sositheos' *Krotos* (fr. 5) may also have employed a traditional theme (P. Guggisberg, *Das Satyrspiel* (Diss. Zurich, 1947), 143).

[58] By the Alexandrian Dioscurides: *AP* 7.707.3–6, reading πατρίδος ἀρχαΐcαc (Gow and Page, *Hellenistic Epigrams*, ii 256).

nature and its creatures which accompanied the elevation of bucolic poetry to a literary genre. Horace, who in his *Ars Poetica* reproduces Alexandrian views on satyric drama,[59] emphasizes that the satyric style must not sink to the level of the comic (229, 234–8, 244–7), because the satyrs belong to the country and not to the town, are *silvis deducti* rather than *velut innati triviis ac paene forenses*. And Horace's contemporary, Vitruvius, again probably drawing on Alexandrian material, distinguishes the rustic satyric scenery from the palaces of tragedy and the houses of comedy (5.6.9).

(*b*) Horace also assumes a close relationship between the satyr-play and tragedy (226, 231–2), and seems to be aware that originally it was written by the tragedian to be performed after his tragedies (220–4). And in this respect too the very fragmentary evidence allows us to detect a gradual change, in which satyric drama separated itself from tragedy.

We know of the following combinations of satyr-play (or 'prosatyric' play; see below) with tragedy:

Aeschylus

(1) 472 BC: *Phineus, Persai, Glaukos Potnieus, Prometheus* (DID C 2).[60]

(2) 467 BC: *Laios, Oedipus, Seven Against Thebes, Sphinx* (DID C 4).

(3) Between 465 and 459 BC: *Suppliants, Aigyptioi, Danaids, Amymone* (DID C 6) (virtually certain).

(4) 458 BC: *Agamemnon, Choephoroi, Eumenides, Proteus* (DID C 7).

(5) Of unknown date: *Edonians, Bassarids, Neaniskoi, Lykourgos* (schol. Ar. *Thesm.* 135).

Euripides

(6) 438 BC: *Cretans, Alkmeon, Telephos, Alkestis* (DID C 11).

[59] C. O. Brink, *Horace on Poetry* (Cambridge, 1971), ii 273–4, i 149. There is no real evidence for satyr-play in Rome: Brink, ii 274–5.

[60] References are to B. Snell, *Tragicorum Graecorum Fragmenta* (Göttingen), vol. i.

(7) 431 BC: *Medea, Philoctetes, Diktys, Theristai* (DID C 12).
(8) 415 BC: *Alexander, Palamedes, Troades, Sisyphos* (DID C 14).

Minores

(9) 467 BC: *Perseus, Tantalos, Palaistai* (Pratinas) (DID C 4).
(10) 415 BC: *Oedipus, Lykaon, Bacchae, Athamas* (Xenocles) (DID C 14).

We may also guess with confidence at

(11) *Phorkides, Polydektes, Diktyoulkoi* (Aeschylus),

and with rather less confidence at

(12) *Psychagogoi, Ostologoi, Penelope, Kirke* (Aeschylus)[61]

A thematic link between tragedy and satyr-play is clearly apparent in (2), (3), (4), (5), (11) and (12). And in all these cases the tragedies too cohere with each other thematically.[62] In (1) and (6) there is clearly no thematic link between the tragic trilogy and the fourth play, and here the trilogies too are thematically incoherent. There is then no clear case of a coherent trilogy in an incoherent tetralogy, nor any clear case of a satyr-play cohering with part of an incoherent tetralogy.

In (7), (8), (9), and (10) we cannot entirely rule out a thematic link between tragedy and satyr-play. The story of Daphnis and Lityerses, containing as it does a reaping contest (see above), has been proposed as the plot of the *Theristai*

[61] H. J. Mette, *Der verlorene Aischylos* (1963), 127–9; T. Gantz in *AJP* 101 (1980), 149–53. There have of course been other, less likely guesses: e.g. I leave out of account the 'Argonauten-tetralogie' (Mette, 130–2), and possible combinations under Sophocles and Mesatos in the lacerated DID C 6. For a detailed general account see N. Hourmouziades, *Satyrika* (Athens, 1974), ch. 1.

[62] Other possible exx. of thematically coherent tetralogies are Polyphrasmon's Λυκούργεια τετραλογία (DID C 4), Philokleon's Πανδιονίς τετραλογία (schol. Ar. *Av.* 281), Meletus' Οἰδιπόδεια (DID C 24). On τετραλογία see Wiesmann, op. cit. n. 1, 28–31. for S. Τελέφεια see Sienkewicz in *ZPE* 20 (1976), 109–12.

I. Prometheus (?) and the satyrs (late fifth century).

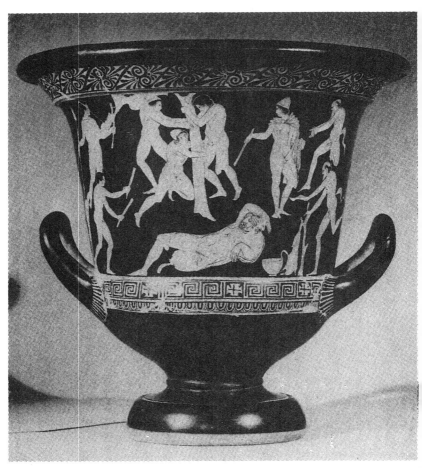

II. Calyx-krater in the British Museum (late fifth century).
The blinding of Polyphemos, with satyrs.

('Reapers') (7). If so, the play was thematically unconnected with the preceding (thematically incoherent) trilogy. In (8)[63] the three tragedies all belong to the Trojan cycle; the satyric *Sisyphos*, about which we know almost nothing, may conceivably have included the origins of the crafty Odysseus, who had of course been prominent in the trilogy, in the seduction of Anticleia by Sisyphos (cf. note on 104). As for (9) and (10), the tragedies do not cohere with themselves, and there is no evidence for coherence between the tragedies and the satyr-play.[64]

It is of interest that all the clear cases of closely coherent tetralogies—(2), (3), (4), (5), and perhaps (11) and (12)—are Aeschylean, whereas in all the cases from the second half of the fifth century—(6), (7), (8), and (10)—it is either likely or certain that there was no *close* connection between the trilogy and the fourth play. This leaves (1), an incoherent Aeschylean tetralogy, and (9), a presumably incomplete list of plays produced after the playwright's death.

Looking more closely at the clear cases of thematically coherent tetralogies (all Aeschylean), we find immediately that the satyr-play does not have to continue the story of the trilogy. Its theme is chosen rather for its suitability for the genre: the story of the Sphinx (2), for example, which is ideal for a satyr-play (cf. §IV), belongs chronologically between the first and second tragedies. Yet the connection between satyr-play and tragedy may have been closer than at first appears from the scanty evidence. In the Homeric model for the *Proteus* (4) Proteus relates to Menelaos the fate of his brother Agamemnon (*Od.* 4.512–37). Whether or not this narrative was reflected in any form in the satyr-play, it was surely not without thought for the *Proteus* that Aeschylus wrote *Ag.* 674–9: the 'hope' for Menelaos (679 ἐλπίϲ τιϲ αὐτὸν πρὸϲ

[63] See most recently R. Scodel, *The Trojan Trilogy of Euripides* (*Hypomnemata* 60, Göttingen, 1980), who presents a highly speculative case for coherence of treatment in the tetralogy.

[64] Except that in myth both Athamas and Lykaon killed children, and Athamas harboured the young Dionysos. The theme of *Palaistai* is unknown.

δόμους ἥξειν πάλιν) resides in the defeat of Proteus, which was to be, as presumably the culmination of the satyr-play, the prelude to a happier homecoming than Agamemnon's.

In the *Amymone* (3) the Danaid Amymone rejected the violent attentions of a satyr, just as the Danaids rejected those of their cousins in the *Suppliants*. In the *Amymone* it seems that Amymone then yielded to Poseidon, and in the trilogy that Hypermnestra was seen to be *una de multis face nuptiali digna*. It has therefore been suggested[65] 'that Aeschylus had taken up and translated into suitable satyric terms the theme of the contrast between rape and courtship which had already been developed in the trilogy'. Similarly, in (11), the attempt on Danae in the satyr-play was no doubt thwarted in a happier manner than the attempt on Danae in the trilogy.[66] Furthermore, it is probable that the *Amymone* began with Amymone's search for water and ended with the creation for her by Poseidon of the stream named after her.[67] And so if, as seems not unlikely, the *Danaids* ended with the institution of the Thesmophoria, then the trilogy ended with the *collective*, the satyr-play with an *individual* Danaid contribution to the fertility of the Argolid.[68] As for (12), all we can say is that Telegonus, Odysseus' son by Kirke, is mentioned in *Psychagogoi* (fr. 275), and that an erotic theme is likely enough in the satyric *Kirke*.

The post-Aeschylean separation of satyr-play from tragedy is manifest in more than just the thematic incoherence of the tetralogy. By 438 BC the satyr-play had become dispensable, for in that year Euripides wrote the *Alcestis* in place of a satyr-

---

[65] Winnington-Ingram in *JHS* 81 (1961), 147 (cf. 151).

[66] M. Werre-de Haas, *Aeschylus Dictyulci* (Leiden, 1961); cf. *Lykourgos* (5), where the satyrs were probably slaves of Lyk. (§IV), like Dionysos in *Edonoi*, and Lyk. may have been converted to wine (cf. fr. 124; Strabo 10.3.16 (471); etc.): the connection between trilogy and satyr-play seems particularly close: Deichgräber in *NGG* 1938, 273–6.

[67] Apollod. *Bibl.* 2.1.4; Hygin. *Fab.* 169a; *Pho.* 188; §IV.

[68] Refs. in A.F. Garvie, *Aeschylus' Supplices: Play and Trilogy* (Cambridge, 1969), 227 n. 6. Further possible similarities: Hourmouziades, op. cit. n. 61, 27–30.

play as the fourth play in the tetralogy.[69] And in the same decade a contest of tragedy was instituted in the Lenaia without satyric drama.[70] Moving on to the fourth century we find, in an inscription concerning the Dionysia in 341–339 BC, that the only mention of satyric drama is a single play at the beginning of the list, performed apparently therefore as a preliminary and certainly not as part of the tragic contest (*IG* ii² 2320). In the 320s (see note 53 above) Python's satyric *Agen*, admittedly a special case, was produced in Alexander's camp on the river Hydaspes, it seems without any accompanying tragedy. Our next evidence is an Athenian inscription[71] of the mid-third century BC recording separate actors' contests, with old plays, for each of the three dramatic genres. Then an inscription[72] from Magnesia-on-the-Maiander of the latter half of the second century BC records separate contests for each of the three dramatic genres, with each poet competing with one play. This is the pattern repeated in most of the remaining records of performance of satyric drama: from mid-second century BC Samos, late-second century BC Delos, post-Sullan Boiotia, Teos, and (the latest record) second century AD Thespiai.[73] Given the post-classical versatility of poets,[74] the late Hellenistic evidence of tragedy and

[69] Sutton (op. cit. n. 53, ch. 12) argues that *Helen* and *IT* were also 'prosatyric'. Cf. A. Pippin Burnett, *Catastrophe Survived* (Oxford, 1971), index s. satyr play.

[70] P-Cambridge, op. cit. n. 7, 40–1.

[71] *Hesperia* 7 (1938), 116–18; Dionysia or Lenaia? See P-Cambridge, op. cit. n. 7, 41 n. 11.

[72] *SIG*³ 1079.

[73] Samos: *JHS* 7 (1886), 148. Delos: G. M. Sifakis, *Studies in the History of Hellenistic Drama* (London, 1967), 26–7. Boiotia: *IG* vii 416, 419–20, 540 (with *SEG* xix 335), 1760–1, 2727, 3197. Teos; (date unknown) Le Bas-Waddington, *Voyage Archéologique en Grèce et Asie Mineure* (Paris, 1869), iii 91. Thespiae: *IG* vii 1773; *SEG* iii 334. Other refs. in V. Steffen, *De Graecorum Fabulis Satyricis* (1979), 91–3. Sat-masks in the 3rd cent. AD (T. B. L. Webster, *Monuments illustrating Tragedy and Satyr Play* (*BICS* suppl. 20, 1967), AT 28, FM 1, FS 3) barely count as evidence for performances.

[74] E.g. Callim. according to the *Suda* wrote tragedy and s-drama (doubted by Snell, op. cit. n. 60, p. 327); and the 1st. cent. BC Aminias wrote s-drama and epic (op. cit. n. 60, p. 36).

satyr-play being written by the same poet[75] does not indicate
a persistence of the ancient close association of the genres,
which were apparently now performed separately and in
separate contests.

(3) *Function.* Why did the tragedian write a satyr-play to
follow his tragedies? The first extant answer to this question is
in Horace's *Ars Poetica* (220–4):

> Carmine qui vilem tragico certavit ob hircum,
> mox etiam agrestes satyros nudavit, et asper
> incolumi gravitate iocum temptavit, eo quod
> illecebris erat et grata novitate morandus
> spectator, functusque sacris et potus et exlex.

Satyr-plays were to detain the spectator who had performed
the rituals and was drunk and disorderly. This passage was
paraphrased in the fourth century AD by the grammarian
Diomedes as 'ut spectator inter res tragicas seriasque saty-
rorum iocis et lusibus delectaretur', and by Marius Victorinus
in much the same way. Victorinus however has not *delectaretur*
but *relaxetur*; and this tiny shift of sense prefigures the observation of A. W. Schlegel that the purpose of satyric drama was
'mental relaxation after the engrossing severity of tragedy'.[76]
This view has never been challenged. For example, the pro-
fessed 'theme' of Sutton's recent *The Greek Satyr Play* is that
'the purpose of classical satyr play was to supply comic relief
after tragedy'.

There is in fact no evidence that the audience was, or
expected to be, affected by satyric drama in this way. It is
a plausible inference from the nature of the plays. But it
cannot constitute a satisfactory answer to the question why
tragedians wrote satyr-plays. The institution and specific
character of the genre were not determined by this factor

[75] See e.g. Sifakis, op. cit. n. 73, 93; the Magnesian inscr. (n. 72); DID B 12
and 13 Snell (op. cit. n. 60).

[76] *Lectures on Dramatic Art and Literature* (transl. 1846), 142.

alone. 'Comic relief' might be provided just as well by comedy. Furthermore, we have seen the gradual separation of satyric drama from tragedy, a process that had begun already in the fifth century BC. Sutton, noticing that by 341 BC satyric drama was being produced separately, infers that 'the original purpose of satyric drama was therefore obviated'; but he fails to ask what the reason might have been for such a perverse change, or what new purpose satyric drama contrived to acquire during its performance as a separate genre over the next five centuries.

A third obstacle to the orthodox view is that however natural it seems to us, it conflicts with the earliest accounts of the appeal of drama. According to Aristotle's *Poetics* emotional relief is provided by the *tragedies*; and according to Horace's *Ars Poetica* the drunken spectator, so far from requiring theatrical relaxation after tragedy, has to be detained (223, *grata novitate morandus*) by a satyr-play from leaving the theatre. *Grata novitate* may refer to the change of mood or theme after the tragedies, or, as Brink argues in his commentary, to the novelty of the genre at its institution. But there is no mention of the emotions caused by tragedy. Whereas for Horace the reason for satyric drama is to be found in the nature of the *festival*, Victorinus in his paraphrase unconsciously adopts the natural explanation that has prevailed ever since: it is to be found in the nature of tragedy.

According to Horace the drunk and disorderly spectator is to be detained by satyric drama. Why? For Sutton this means that 'a certain kind of spectator, caught up in the festive spirit of the Dionysia, is to be more or less seduced into sitting through the trilogy by the expectation of the pleasures to be offered by the following satyr-play'. But it is improbable that Horace, or his source, believed that in the earliest phase of the tetralogy a significant section of the audience watched the tragedies in a state of intoxicated impatience. And it is in fact clear from the preceding passage that Horace regarded the practice of drinking at the festival in the *daytime* as a later development (209). Perhaps what underlies 223-4 is no

more than the possibly erroneous idea that the fourth drama
of the day had to reckon with the evening drinking.[77] The
fact is that Horace reproduces the limitations as well as the
sophistication of Alexandrian theory. The institution of
satyric drama cannot be explained by a decision to detain
the drunken spectator any more than by a decision to relax
the sober one. It cannot be explained from any exclusively
synchronic perspective. As we have seen (§III (1)), satyr-
choruses were instituted to preserve what was being lost from
tragedy. Horace may be right in thinking of this as a concession to the audience. But if so, it was a concession not to
their drunkenness but to their conservatism.

This account has the additional advantage of explaining
the specific nature and development of the genre. In satyric
drama, according to Horace, the tragedian, *incolumi gravitate*,
must not sink to the level of comedy. The gods and heroes
whom we have seen in the tragedies must not reappear, in the
satyr-play, in *obscurae tabernae* (227–9). Like a matron who has
to dance among satyrs at a festival (231–3), tragedy must
preserve her dignity among the satyrs, who are themselves
superior in utterance to the low, urban characters of comedy
(237–9, 244–5). Despite the appearance of Peripatetic con-
ceptualization, this account of satyric drama as of a specific
kind of middle style between tragedy and comedy accords
well with the fifth-century remains (§V). How did the style
come into being? Tragedy, according to Aristotle, ὀψὲ ἀπ-
εσεμνύνθη (*Poetics* 1449a21); but it had presumably never
been as vulgar in tone as Old Comedy. And so if the satyric
performances were designed to preserve what was being lost
from tragedy, they could not but be distinct in mood from Old
Comedy on the one hand and from mature (σεμνός) tragedy
on the other—at least in the utterances of the satyrs. But the
satyrs, however conservative their performance, could not be
limited every year to the old Dionysiac stories. In the interest

[77] Cf. P-Cambridge, op. cit. n. 7, 272.

of novelty, and under the influence of tragedy, they find themselves in various mythical plots, which may have nothing to do with Dionysos. They inevitably consort with the non-Dionysiac heroes of mature tragedy. This then is the process giving rise to the specific ingredients of the style prescribed by Horace: satyric utterance is superior to comic, and consorts in the satyr-play with tragic utterance.

In this way the tendency in early tragedy for the Dionysiac element to disappear occurred also in satyric drama, though in a form limited by the essential conservatism of the genre. As the process continues, the original function of satyric drama cannot but be gradually forgotten. Inasmuch as the poet no longer feels compelled to breathe the spirit of the extra-theatrical satyric celebrations into his tetralogy, there will be little to prevent either the assimilation of satyric drama to tragedy and comedy or the loosening of its paradoxical association with tragedy (see above). Nevertheless, satyric drama retained for centuries the constituent of its identity: the ancient Dionysiac nucleus, the *thiasos* of satyrs, who even when separated from him belong to their god (*Cyc.* 1–40, 67–81, etc.).

But if satyric drama, in contrast to the general appeal of tragedy and comedy, was an *Übergangsphänomen*, the specific solution to a transient problem, why did it last so long? Certainly, it seems to have possessed its own specific humour in the confrontation between the satyrs and the solemn figures of tragedy, *vertere seria ludo*.[78] Humour of this kind was perhaps most effective in the thematically coherent Aeschylean tetralogy, particularly where characters from the trilogy reappeared in the satyr-play. But to judge from the few known titles after 200 BC (see n. 72 above) it may have been a permanent ingredient of the genre. For although alien to most of comedy, it has an obvious and ubiquitous appeal. Nevertheless, satyric drama has remained virtually exclu-

[78] Hor. *Ars. P.* 226. See e.g. notes on 101, 104.

sively Greek.[79] Unlike so many others, the tradition could not
be transplanted successfully to an alien soil, no doubt because
it depended on the persistence of one of the factors in its
creation: the importance of the *thiasos* of satyrs in the religious
imagination of the Greeks and in their public and private
religious celebrations (§II).

What was the nature of this importance? The earliest references to satyric drama, in Aristophanes (*Thesm.* 157), Plato
(*Symp.* 222d) and Xenophon (*Symp.* 4.19), tell us little. But the
passage of Plato's *Laws* (815c) already cited (§II) contains a
remark of great interest. Bacchic dancing, he says, in which
people imitate nymphs, pans, satyrs, and silens, and perform
purifications and initiations, constitutes a special type, which
is οὐ πολιτικόν. It does not belong to the πόλις.

As we have seen, initiation into the *thiasos* of satyrs continues into the imperial period (§II). There are two closely
related senses in which it is outside the city-state. Such creatures as satyrs are at home in the wild, outside the confines of
the civilized community. And, secondly, they represent a
community which is antithetical to the πόλις, because representative of more ancient social relations. To be initiated
into a satyric *thiasos* is to enter a group united by a strong sense
of solidarity based on mystic ritual and on the fictions of
kinship and a shared animality.[80] It was at the time of the
rapid development of Athens as an urban centre (Peisistratus)
and the elimination of an ancient, anachronistic set of
kinship-relations as an organizing principle of the democratic, centralized πόλις (Cleisthenes) that the satyric celebrations were raised to a new level.

Even the festival of Dionysos is urbanized. The satyrs
were no doubt a traditional feature of the ancient Anthesteria
(Thuc. 2.15 τὰ ἀρχαιότερα Διονύσια); but in the spring festival

---

[79] For the few imitations after antiquity see Sutton, op. cit. n. 53, ch. 13.
[80] L. Gernet and A. Boulanger, *Le génie grec dans la religion* (Paris, 1932),
122–6; Thomson, op. cit. n. 44, ch. 7; Seaford, art. cit. n. 17.

of Dionysos established by Peisistratus in the city[81] their celebrations were raised to the level of drama. Just as literary pastoral poetry was a product of unprecedentedly urban Alexandria, so satyric drama was created out of the urbanization of Athens and then recreated in Alexandria (see above). In an urban culture the pre-urban *thiasos* acquires a sharper symbolic significance. Nevertheless, the satyrs are progressively humanized. Just as satyric drama fails to resist gradual assimilation to tragedy and comedy, so in the satyrs themselves the element of animality (for example the equine proportions of their phalli) on the whole gradually diminishes from the sixth to the third century BC. It is not before the fifth century that we find evidence of the satyr-family, with three generations like the human, its younger members beardless but still balding.

The original Dionysiac themes of tragedy, though involving a death (Pentheus), or perhaps a death and rebirth (Dionysos), probably concluded with a joyful reunification of the *thiasos* with their god, in keeping with the mood of the festival. But as tragedy developed it adopted non-Dionysiac death and suffering. This tended to exclude the komastic ending,[82] which was restored by the institution of satyric drama. Furthermore, the tension between the Dionysiac and the non-Dionysiac, which had been a feature of the Dionysiac dramatic themes (Pentheus, Lykourgos), was extended in satyric drama to incorporate the contradiction between the satyric *thiasos* and non-Dionysiac myths. In this way the

---

[81] Thuc. 5.20 ἀστικὰ Διονύσια. The urbanization, probably of a pre-existing celebration, may have consisted partly in the transference of the emergent drama to the city-centre (Seaford in art. cit. n. 24, 270 n. 164). Perhaps even the satyrs could become tainted by urban values (n. 93 below). Some of the changes in the *thiasos* noted in vase-painting by M. W. Edwards (*JHS* 80 (1960), 78–87) may reflect the (new) realities of an urban festival.

[82] Although something similar reappears, apparently under the influence of satyric drama, in *IT* and *Hel*: A. Pippin Burnett, *Catastrophe Survived* (Oxford, 1971), 72, 81; cf. n. 69.

isolated sufferings of tragedy were reabsorbed, in the final
play, into the ancient social relations of the Dionysiac *thiasos*.
This is the truth half-expressed in Nietzsche's remark on the
comfort provided by the satyr-play: 'the Greek *Kulturmensch*
in the presence of the chorus of satyrs felt his civilization
dissolve'.[83]

This means that the reassurance provided by satyric drama
consisted neither in 'debunking that which is taken seriously
in tragedy, by showing that it is really rather silly' (Sutton),
nor in just the contrast of an 'uncomplicated, optimistic view
of human life, after the tragic world-view' (Seidensticker).[84]
The first of these aims would have been best achieved by
satyr-plays on the same themes as tragedy; whereas in fact
satyr-plays concentrate rather on folk-tale elements. And
both of them could have been achieved without a satyric
thiasos; indeed paratragedy is more common in Aristophanes
than in what survives of satyric drama.

The key to the problem is in the paradoxical nature of the
satyrs (§II). In the urban dramatic festival this is of particular
significance: their vulgar hedonism, in which they outdo even
the πολῖται of Old Comedy, derives nevertheless from a source
which sets them above the royal personages of tragedy. They
are δαίμονες, implicitly immortal,[85] the intimate companions
of a god, and unconcerned with any distinction between
human and divine (see note on 495–502)—even to the extent
of attempting to rape Hera (*ARV²* 370.13) without, we can be
sure, suffering the fate of Ixion. In this way the absolute
division between tragedy and comedy created by the urban
festival is transcended by creatures whose performance is still
in a sense οὐ πολιτικόν. Horace was careful to distinguish *custos*

---

[83] F. Nietzsche, *Die Geburt der Tragödie aus dem Geist der Musik*, §7.

[84] Sutton, *The Date of Euripides' Cyclops* (Ann Arbor, 1974), 192; B.
Seidensticker in *Das Griechische Drama* (ed. G. A. Seeck, Darmstadt, 1979),
255.

[85] E.g. Sil. θεοῦ μὲν ἀφανεστέρος τὴν φύσιν, ἀνθρώπου δὲ κρείττων, ἐπεὶ καὶ
ἀθάνατος ἦν (Theopomp. 115 *FGH* 75). Though they may grow old (*Cyc.* 2,
and n. 8 above). And dead humans may be imagined as satyrs (n. 28 above).

famulusque dei Silenus alumni and the satyrs *silvis deducti* on the one hand from the low urban characters of comedy on the other (*Ars. P.* 236–47). The satyrs belong to the wild, and to the very point indeed at which culture is created out of nature: when wine is for the first time ever extracted by a god from the grapes, or the sound of the lyre from a dead tortoise, they are there as the first to enjoy the invention (§IV). This position gives them a special perspective on mankind. Silenos despises the mortal preoccupations of Olympus (probably his pupil on the αὐλός, Pi. fr. 157): ὦ τάλας ἐφάμερε, νήπια βάζεις χρήματά μοι διακομπέων. And it was in the gardens of Midas, where miraculous roses grew uncultivated (Hdt. 1.138), that the wealthy king hunted and caught Silenos, who called him an ἐφήμερον σπέρμα and reluctantly revealed that for men the best thing of all would have been never to have been born, the second best to die as quickly as possible (Aristotle fr. 44 Rose). It is in the same spirit, but with necessarily less detachment, that the Theban chorus sing to Oedipus ἰὼ γενεαὶ βροτῶν ὡς ὑμᾶς ἴσα καὶ τὸ μηδὲν ζώσας ἐναριθμῶ (S. *OT* 1186–8; cf. 1391–2, *OC* 1225).

IV. THE THEMES OF SATYRIC DRAMA

It is generally recognized that satyric drama is a genre of typical recurrent themes,[86] of which the most common are as follows.

(a) *The Captivity, Servitude and Liberation of the Satyrs*

This theme is not unlikely in any play in which satyrs appeared in an alien and uncongenial context, and in particular in those many plays in which it seems that a persecutor of mankind is defeated (e.g. A. *Kerkyon*; S. *Amykos*; E. *Bousiris*).

---

[86] See Guggisberg, op. cit. n. 57, 60–74; I. M. Fischer, *Typische Motive im Satyrspiel* (Göttingen, 1958); Seidensticker, op. cit. n. 84, 243–7. I have resisted the temptations (1) to list plays which are not certainly or very likely satyric (for this problem see Sutton in *HSCP* 78 (1974), 107–43); (2) to include much speculation on the themes of lost plays.

There is reference to servitude in the scanty fragments of E. *Bousiris* and *Eurystheus* as well as in the papyrus hypothesis of *Skiron*.[87] In S. *Herakles* the satyrs were described as Helots.[88]

The captivity of the satyrs was no doubt frequently useful as explaining the satyrs' presence, as in *Cyc.* (23–6). But this was not always the case. In S. *Ichneutai* the *thiasos* arrives freely, in response to a public proclamation by Apollo, who then promises them freedom as well as gold (63, 78, 162–4, 457) if they can find his cattle. So far as we can judge from the surviving first half of the play, the satyrs' servitude is not required by the plot, and it is referred to so briefly that it seems to be introduced as a traditional element expected by the audience.

The satyrs were also slaves of Dionysos (*Cyc.* 709). In *Cyc.* (76–7n.) they bitterly compare the service of Polyphemos with the lost service of Dionysos. But in the fragments of A. *Theoroi* the satyrs are apparently attempting to *escape* from the service of Dionysos, in order to adopt the τέχνη (92) of athletics, which Dionysos (?) describes resentfully as τρόπουc και[νοὺc (34). In *Ichneutai* the new tracking activity of the satyrs is described in similar terms both by Silenos (124 τίν' αὖ τέχνην cὺ τήν[δ' ἄρ' ἐξ]ῆυρεc ... τίc ὑμῶν ὁ τρόποc;) and by Kyllene (223–4 τίc ἥδε τέχνη; τίc μετάcταcιc πόνων | δὺc πρόc-θεν εἶχεc δεcπότηι χάριν φέρων κτλ;). But in this case, although the previous πόνοι are Dionysiac revels (cf. *Ba.* 66), the unnamed δεcπότηc is probably not Dionysos,[89] but some person in his entourage (227 ἀμφὶ τὸν θεόν), most likely the lord of

---

[87] frr. 313, 375 (the διάκονοc might however be Herakles): see note on 31; cf. S. fr. 1130.2.

[88] Perhaps also suppliants in the temple of Poseidon at Taenarum, which, as 'shaped like a cave' (see note on 292), would suit a satyr-play. Cf. A. *Theoroi* 79–84; Thuc. 1.128; schol. Ar. *Ach.* 510; Plut. *Pomp.* 24. (temple as ἄcυλον); W. H. D. Rouse, *Greek Votive Offerings*, 336–7 (temple slaves there in 5th. cent. BC).

[89] Unless, with Maas and Robert, we suppose a lacuna after 224. But cf. E. Siegmann, *Untersuchungen zu Sophokles' Ichneutai* (Hamburg, 1941), 46; εὐίαζεc in 227 is an emendation in the papyrus for εὐιάζετ'.

Arcadia, Pan.[90] In the lost second half of the play it seems certain that Apollo received the newly invented lyre from Hermes. If he also detached the satyrs from the pipe and syrinx player Pan,[91] this might have provided the aetiology for the satyrs' use of (relatively civilized)[92] stringed instruments in addition to their wind instruments. In the same way the satyrs' rejection of Dionysos in the *Theoroi* may reflect a novel interest in athletics outside as well as inside the theatre (see below); and their fragmentary complaint about poor accommodation[93] may accordingly reflect a newly acquired and somewhat ridiculous contempt for the old Dionysiac ὀρειβαςία arising from experience of the civilized festival complete with athletics.

In short, the contrast between the old service of Dionysos and some newly adopted activity seems to have been a feature of the genre, although the attitude of the satyrs to the new activity may have varied greatly from play to play. In *Cyc.* the satyrs, as slaves of Polyphemos, work unwillingly as shepherds. Captivity may have meant work, uncongenial and unaccustomed rather than unsuitable, in other plays too: e.g. S. *Herakles* (fr. 225: collecting wood), *Inachos* (herdsmen), *Pandora or the Hammerers* (fr. 482); E. *Theristai*, *Autolykos* (frr. 283, 284); Sositheos *Daphnis* (reapers).[94] On the other hand

---

[90] An unpopular suggestion by Siegmann, op. cit. n. 89, 53-4, on the basis of *Ichn.* 438, *Aj.* 694-700, *OT* 1098-1109; 887 *PMG*; *h. hom.* 19.3, 19. Cf. also Pi. frr. 85, 89 Bowra. Pan is at home on Kyllene, and already in the 5th. cent. seen in the Dionysiac *thiasos*: F. Brommer, *Satyroi* (Würzburg, 1937), 12.

[91] Cf. Ov. *Met.* 11.146-71; Mythogr. Vat. 1.90.

[92] Buschor, op. cit. n. 10, 28, 71-3. On *ARV*[2] 1172.8 the satyrs with lyres at the Panathenaia seem unusually self-conscious. Satyrs played cύριγγεc as well as αὐλοί: Brommer, op. cit. n. 13, 2-3.

[93] 43 κακ]ῶι τε κο[ί]τωι καὶ κακαῖc δ[υc]αυλίαιc. Similar in spirit perhaps is Dionysos apparently removing a cloak from a satyr on *ARV*[2] 613.6.

[94] Cf. the European 'wild men' (n. 17 above). To judge from *Cyc.* and *Ichn.* the work-song may have been a feature of the genre; other possibilities: A. *Dikt.* (Pfeiffer in *SBAW* 1938/2, 18); S. *Pandora or the Hammerers*; E. *Theristai*; Sosith, *Daphnis or Lityerses* (Latte in *Hermes* 60 (1925), 10).

certain practices were probably adopted by the satyrs voluntarily, like athletics in A. *Theoroi*: e.g. in Pratinas' *Palaistai*; A.
Kerykes, *Trophoi*; Iophon's *Auloidoi*; Python's *Agen* (μάγοι?);
Anon. *Mathetai* (Snell DID A 4a14). In A. *Diktyoulkoi* ('Net-
pullers') they seem to have answered a public appeal, as in S.
Ichneutai and perhaps also in his *Oineus* (? fr. 1130, as suitors).
Finally, vase-painting shows the satyrs in various unlikely
roles, not necessarily derived from the drama, such as aged
councillors, warriors, athletes, a suppliant, even as Herakles,
or a maenad.[95] As the satyrs themselves boast (S. fr. 1130.
8–9), πᾶσα δ' ἥρμοσται τέχνη πρέπουϲ' ἐν ἡμῖν.

(b) Marvellous Inventions and Creations

(1) *Musical Instruments*. Trag. adesp. 381 is from a play in
which Athena invented the αὐλός and then gave it to a satyr.
In the *Ichneutai* the satyrs dance and sing their consternation,
and then their delight, at the sound of the lyre invented by the
infant Hermes. And such is their consternation in S. *Inachos* at
the sound of the invisible Hermes' syrinx that it seems not
unlikely that it has just been invented.[96]

(2) *Other Artefacts*. In A. *Theoroi* the satyrs express both
delight at certain likenesses of themselves and perplexity at
certain νεοχμὰ ἀθύρματα newly made with adze and anvil.[97]
S. *Daidalos*, *Kedalion* and *Kophoi* (fr. 364) may have had to do
with metal-working.[98] In E. *Eurystheus* an old man, perhaps
Silenos, was frightened by some speaking and moving ἀγ-
άλματα made by Daidalos (fr. 372). Sositheos seems to have

[95] Hydria Fujita (n. 8 above); *ARV*[2] 70.3, 221.14, 835.1, 776.2; Brommer,
op. cit. n. 3, fig. 69.

[96] R. J. Carden, *The Papyrus Fragments of Sophocles* (de Gruyter, 1974), 81;
Ov. *Met.* 1. 687–8; *h. hom. Herm.* 512; Euphorion fr. 182 van Groningen; cf.
Sutton, op. cit. n. 50, 4.

[97] 85–91 Lloyd-Jones; Snell suggests javelins (in *Hermes* 84 (1956), 8). A
metal foundry has recently been discovered within the precincts of Poseidon's
temple at Isthmia, where the play was set: see Sutton in *GRBS* 22 (1981), 337.
Cf. T. Hadzisteliou Price in *GRBS* 13 (1972), 239–45.

[98] Cf. Anth. Planud. 15, 15b (cf. S. *Ach. Erast.* frr. 152, 156?); Buschor,
op. cit. n. 10, 88 (Dionysos with the tools of Hephaistos and satyrs).

written a satyr-play containing the invention of archery (fr. 5).

(3) *Fire.* Vase-paintings, together with the fragments of A. *Prometheus Pyrkaieus*,[99] make it virtually certain that in that play the novelty of fire was greeted by the satyrs with vigorous delight. Fire may have been revealed in satyr-plays by S. (fr. 362) and Aristias (fr. 8).

(4) *Negative Creations.* There is evidence (Schol. Hes. *Op.* 89) for a satyr-play in which Prometheus received the πίθος κακῶν from the satyrs. S. *Pandora or the Hammerers* presumably concerned the creation (fr. 482) or first appearance of Pandora. No less disastrously, in his *Kophoi* it seems that the satyrs bartered a φάρμακον ἀγηρασίας, which they had received from Zeus as a reward for revealing Prometheus' gift of fire, for a drink of water (fr. 362).

(5) *Wine.* Silenos in *Cyc.* seems to refer to a satyr-play in which Dionysos gave to Oineus the εὕρημα of wine (see note on 39). In S. *Dionysiskos* the satyrs expressed their delight at wine, newly invented by the infant Dionysos (fr. 172): πόθεν ποτ' ἄλυπον ὧδ' ηὗρον ἄνθος ἀνίας; It has been suggested that Nemesianus' third eclogue (see esp. 36–55) reflects the contents of this play.

(6) Fertility. A. *Amymone* probably ended with the creation of a stream (see n. 67 above) in which, in a later depiction of the scene,[100] it seems that a satyr is taking pleasure. S. *Inachos* may well have culminated in the creation of the river Inachos.[101]

(c) *Emergence from the Underworld*

This seems to have occurred in A. *Sisyphos*, S. *Herakles* and *Inachos*,[102] E. *Alcestis* (prosatyric), Python's *Agen* (fr. 1.5–8),

---

[99] See nn. 4 and 5 above.

[100] Athens NM 12596 (Brommer, op. cit. n. 3, fig. 16).

[101] Seaford, art. cit. n. 50; cf. also Buschor, op. cit. n. 10, 102–4.

[102] A. fr. 227 (cf. 228–30) (see below); Pearson, *Sophocles Fragments*, i 167–8 (the temple led to the underworld: see note on 292); Seaford, art. cit. n. 50.

perhaps also in Aristias' *Keres* (fr. 3) and *Orpheus*,[103] Achaios'
Aithon (fr. 11), E. *Eurystheus* (fr. 371) and *Sisyphos*.[104] And in a
number of fifth-century vase-paintings the satyrs react vigorously to a female (Persephone?) emerging from the
ground.[105] The theme is clearly more frequent than in the
much more extensive remains of tragedy.[106]

(d) The care of divine or heroic infants

In A. *Diktyoulkoi* Silenos holds out to the infant Perseus the
prospect of growing up under his care in the wild: ἵξηι παιδοτ-
ρόφους ἐμάς, ὦ φίλος, χέρας εὐμενοῦς κτλ. And his *Trophoi* (or
Dionysou Trophoi) is generally thought to have been satyric.[107]
Sophocles wrote a satyric *Dionysiskos* (see esp. fr. 171) and a
satyric *Herakleiskos*; and the infant Hermes was at the centre of
the *Ichneutai*. Other plays which may have contained satyric
παιδοτροφία are S. *Amphiaraos*,[108] Xenocles' *Athamas*, and
Timesitheos' *Zenos Gonai*. The way in which the theme is
introduced even into *Cyc.* suggests that it was a familiar
feature of the genre (see note on 142). One might also compare the satyr-plays about the education of a hero (see note on
521).

(e) Sex

Vase-painting is full of the unrestrained sexual activity of

---

[103] Satyric? See Sutton, art. cit. n. 86, 115.

[104] The hypoth. *P. Oxy.* 2455 fr. 7 ...]φυγὼν δ' ἐντεῦθε[ν....]μαχόμ[ε]νος
σὺν α[ὐ]τῶι[... ἐπι]φανεὶς δὲ τοῖς σατύροις παρ[εξέπ]ληξεν αὐτοὺς may be from
Sisyphos: C. Austin, *Nova Fragmenta Euripidea* (de Gruyter, 1968), p. 93.

[105] E. Buschor, 'Feldmäuse', *SBAW* 1937/1; trag. adesp. 8h; cf. n. 124.

[106] For this point, and in general, see Seaford, art. cit. n. 50, 29 (add E.
Protes.). As for *HF*, cf. the greater importance of Hades in prosatyric *Alc.* Sen.
Phaedra 835–49 is no evidence for S. *Phaidra*. (cf. Sen. *Oed.* 530–659!). Other
possible satyr-plays on underworld: *Omphale* (Ion, Achaios): cf. *RE* xviii 1 s.
Omphale, 394; Harmodius *Protes.*

[107] Sutton, art. cit. n. 86, 127.

[108] Pearson, op. cit. n. 102, i 72; conceivably also S. *Iambe*: Sutton, op. cit.
n. 53, 42–3.

satyrs, and so are the dramatic fragments.[109] No doubt their desires were usually frustrated,[110] particularly perhaps in those plays which seem to have culminated in the γάμος of a god or hero,[111] a theme which appears to have been much less significant in tragedy.[112]

(f) Athletics

Plays including this theme seem to have been Pratinas' *Palaistai*, A. *Theoroi*, *Kerkyon* (fr. 102), *Proteus* (?); S. *Amykos*, (fr. 112), fr. 1130; E. *Autolykos* (fr. 282), *Bousiris* (? Dio Chrys. 8.32); Achaios' *Athla* (fr. 4). A fine specimen of the many vase-paintings of satyrs as athletes is ARV^2 221 n. 14 (Brommer, op. cit. n. 3, figs. 59–60).

The typicality of these themes has been recognized, but never explained, perhaps because it cannot be explained in purely theatrical terms. We have to look rather at the ambiguous nature of the satyr in ritual and in popular belief (§II). Their high spirits and low hedonism, both typical features of the genre, are manifest in numerous vase-paintings of extra-theatrical satyric celebrations. For example, satyrs stealing food or wine are found in depictions of pre-theatrical satyric choruses and of the Anthesteria (§II), as well as in *Cyc*.[113] Can

---

[109] E.g. A. *Amym.* (fr. 15), *Dikt.*; S. *Hel. Gamos, Momos* (fr. 421), *Pandora* (? frr. 483–4), fr. 1130 (?); Achaios *Moirai* (fr. 28; cf. fr. 52); E. *Skiron* (Austin, op. cit. n. 104, p. 94). Homosexuality: S. *Ach. Erast.* (frr. 149, 153), fr. 756; Ach. *Linos* (fr. 26).

[110] As in A. *Amym.*, *Dikt.*; cf. S. *Ach. Erast.* fr. 153; ARV^2 370.13 (Brygos painter); cf. Edwards, art. cit. n. 81, 82.

[111] A. *Amym.*, *Kirke* (?); S. *Hel. Gamos* (same play as *Krisis*? see fr. 361 II), *Inachos* (Seaford, art. cit. n. 50); E. *Syleus*; also perhaps A. *Dikt.* (Diktys?); S. *Momos, Eris*, frr. 1130–3; E. *Sisyphos* (or *Autolykos*?); Achaios *Moirai, Omphale*; Ion *Omphale*; Demetrius *Hesione*; Iophon *Dexamenos*; Sosith. *Daphnis*; anon. *Althaia* (?: note on 39). for the γάμος of Polyphemos see note on 511–18, 581–3.

[112] Seaford, art. cit. n. 50, 28.

[113] Buschor, art. cit. n. 42, 24, 32, 84; van Hoorn, op. cit. n. 18, e.g. figs. 1, 210, 211; *Cyc.* 545–65.

our six listed recurrent themes be related to the activities of the satyrs in ritual and popular belief? They will be taken now in reverse order.

(f) It is conceivable that the surprising association of the theatrical satyrs with athletics derives from the participation in the athletic contests at the Anthesteria of men or boys dressed as satyrs.[114]

(e) The evening of the second day of the Anthesteria culminated in a ἱερὸc γάμοc of Dionysos with the wife of the ἄρχων βαcιλεύc. Dionysos may have been escorted there in a ship-cart by men dressed as satyrs.[115] It is remarkable that the theatrical satyrs on the Pronomos vase (§I), like the famous Mysteries at Pompeii, are centred around a ἱερὸc γάμοc of Dionysos and his bride (Ariadne).

(d) Silenos' education of the infant Dionysos[116] may be the individualization of an ancient popular belief in Silenos as a protector and educator of children.[117] Silenos and the satyrs appear with children in later celebrations of the Dionysiac mysteries.[118] And satyrs may have been imagined in a paedagogic role even in the public celebrations of the Anthesteria.[119]

(c) Belief in the dead as satyrs occurred in the *thiasos*

---

[114] Athletics at Anthesteria (L. Deubner, *Attische Feste*[2] (1969), 116; van Hoorn, op. cit. n. 18, 33–5) included torch-races: cf. satyr-boys in torch-race depicted on Beazley, *Paralipomena*, 394.71 (Berlin 1962.33).

[115] Deubner, op. cit. n. 114, 100–107; n. 23 above; cf. *Cyc.* 37–40; satyrs and ἱερὸc γάμοc in 6th cent. v-painting: Buschor, art. cit. n. 10, 84; satyrs escorting bride: Simon in *AntK* 6 (1963), 16.

[116] This idea persists: e.g. Eus. *Praep. Ev.* 53d; Firm. Mat. *Err. Prof. Relig.* 6.4.

[117] Furtwängler in *Archiv.f. Relig.* 10 (1907), 331; Seaford in art. cit. n. 17, 213–4; cf. n. 17 above.

[118] Nilsson, op. cit. n. 25, esp. ch. 7, and p. 56 (ἄππαc Διονύcου in the mysteries).

[119] Van Hoorn, op. cit. n. 18, n. 636; there are numerous satyr-children on the χόεc. Anthesteria as rite of passage for children: Deubner, op. cit. n. 114, 115.

(§II).[120] More will be said about emergence from the underworld under (b).

(b) In the *Ichneutai* the satyrs are startled by the newly invented lyre, which they cannot see, being played from within the cave of the nymph Kyllene. She exhorts them to secrecy, and then reveals the nature of the instrument—not directly, but through a riddle (300; cf. *h. hom.* 4.38): πιθοῦ· θανὼν γὰρ ἔσχε φωνήν, ζῶν δ' ἄναυδος ἦν ὁ θήρ. The satyrs then approach the answer (the χέλυς) by a series of conjectures, one of which is (307) ἀλλ' ὡς κεράςτης κάνθαρος δῆτ' ἐςτὶν Αἰτναῖος φυήν; Compare the (clearly satyric) fragments from A. *Sisyphos*, which have been joined thus: X. ἀλλ' ἀρουραῖος τίς ἐςτι ϲμίνθος ὧδ' ὑπερφυής; / Y. ⟨πῶς λέγεις;⟩ Αἰτναῖός ἐςτι κάνθαρος βίαι πονῶν. Whether this arrangement is precisely right or not, it appears that the satyrs have been startled by Sisyphos' emergence from the ground, just as in vase-painting they are startled by the ἄνοδος of a female (Persephone?), and are attempting to guess what the τέρας is.

Thirdly, in a papyrus fragment of S. *Inachos* it appears that the satyrs are startled by an invisible syrinx-player emerged from the underworld,[121] and make guesses (one of them expressed in a riddling etymology) at his identity. These three passages appear to represent a τόπος of the genre, which reappears even in *Cyc.*[122]

How do we explain the existence of this τόπος? I have argued in detail elsewhere that (1) it derives, in keeping with

[120] In Aristias' Κῆρες were the satyrs identified with the Κῆρες of the Anthesteria (see esp. fr. 3)? See Deubner, op. cit. n. 114, 111–4; cf. Burkert, op. cit. n. 23, 250–3. The dead have of course often been imagined in partly animal form, inside and outside Europe.

[121] Fr. 269c. Seaford, art. cit. n. 50, 25.

[122] Argued in art. cit. n. 17, 216–19; see note on 464–5. Cf. also S. fr. 162 (*Daidalos*), and the perplexity of Admetus at the end of prosatyric *Alc.* Further exx. of riddling language in s-drama referring to εὑρήματα or θαυμαστά: A. *Dikt.* 8–9, *Theor.* 20; S. *Inach.* fr. 269a 42–3 (cf. Pfeiffer in *SBAW* 1958/6, 25), *Ichn.* 124–30; see also A. *Sphinx*; S. *Amph.* fr. 121; Achaios *Omph.* fr. 33; Seaford, art. cit. n. 17, 219.

the conservatism of satyric drama (§III), from a pre-dramatic celebration by the Dionysiac *thiasos* of revelations associated with their cult (musical instruments? mask? wine? ἄνοδος?); (2) this celebration derives in turn from initiation into the satyric *thiasos*, in which the initiand is confused and stimulated, before the completion of the revelation, by riddling language; (3) this ritual has left its traces in both the Dionysiac genres associated with the origins of tragedy: dithyramb and satyric drama.[123]

To complete the argument, one further point remains to be made here. In the τόπος both ἄνοδος and εὕρημα amaze the satyrs. And in fact the εὕρημα and the ἄνοδος may be combined. In the *Ichneutai* the newly-invented lyre is not seen, and is perhaps played from below the stage.[124] In the *Inachos* the invisible syrinx has been brought from the underworld, and may be newly invented. Both sounds have a devastating effect on the satyrs. We find the same sort of thing in the mysteries. A fragment of Aeschylus' *Edonians* refers to terrifying bull-bellowings ἐξ ἀφανοῦς, and the terrifying sound of a drum as of subterranean thunder, in the ritual of the Dionysiac *thiasos*.[125] And in the Eleusinian mysteries the initiands experienced in some form the emergence of Persephone (Κόρη) from the underworld, apparently with joy and thanksgiving after perplexity and grief.[126] We are told that τῆς Κόρης

[123] And in an attenuated form even in tragedy: n. 44 above. Cf. now also the Fackelmann papyrus (Old Comedy?), in which it appears that a Dionysiac μύςτης is created by drinking the newly invented wine (Kramer in *ZPE* 34 (1979), 11). Satyrs are also associated with musical inventions in myth: *Ba.* 120–34; Athen. 184a; etc. And on a χοῦς (cf. n. 18) a satyr appears amazed at the discovery of a lyre (van Hoorn, op. cit. n. 18, n. 952; cf. n. 991).

[124] C. Robert in *Hermes* 47 (1912), 537–9; Jane Harrison in *Essays and Studies presented to W. Ridgeway* (Cambridge, 1913), 136–40; Buschor, art. cit. n. 105, 32–4; Taplin, op. cit. n. 49, 447–8.

[125] Fr. 57. The bull-noise was produced probably by the ῥόμβος, known as a sacred object in the Dionysiac mysteries: Kannicht on *Hel.* 1362–3.

[126] Clem. *Protr.* 2.12; Lactant. *Div. Inst. epit.* 23; etc.; Burkert, op. cit. n. 23, 316; N. J. Richardson, *The Homeric Hymn to Demeter* (Oxford, 1974), 24–5; G. E. Mylonas, *Eleusis and the Eleusinian Mysteries* (Princeton, 1961), 264.

ἐπικαλουμένης the hierophant sounded a gong—not I think as an invocation, but rather in order to frighten the initiands, before the final transition to joy, with a chthonic sound unseen.[127] Central to the experience of the Eleusinian initiands were also the announcement of the birth of a child, and the revelation of the gift of corn.[128]

(a) In the *Bacchae* Pentheus imprisons Dionysos and threatens his *thiasos* (the chorus) with slavery (509-14). There is no attempt to carry out the threat; but the imprisonment of their protector Dionysos throws the chorus into despair for themselves (610-12). The *Theban* maenads *are* imprisoned (226-7) and miraculously liberated (443-8), an event which is briefly related and serves no purpose in the play--it seems rather to be included as a traditional element in the story, and had indeed been more important apparently in Aeschylus' *Lykourgeia*.[129] Apollodorus (3.5.1) says that Lykourgos in his conflict with Dionysos imprisoned the maenads and the satyrs, a detail which may derive from Aeschylus, but is I suspect independent of the theatre (Apollodorus mentions the satyrs as a group nowhere else).

I have argued in detail elsewhere[130] that the *Bacchae* dramatizes a sacred story (ἱερὸς λόγος) of the Dionysiac mysteries, in which the imprisonment and miraculous liberation of Dionysos (perhaps also of his followers), comparable to the Eleusinian loss and reappearance of Κόρη, was an important element. Here, I believe, is the pre-theatrical origin of the theatrical theme of the captivity and liberation of the *thiasos* of satyrs, perhaps also of their wretched but temporary separation from Dionysos.

---

[127] Apollod., *FGH* 244.110; cf. the role of the χαλκοῦ αὐδὰν χθονίαν during the loss of Κόρη at *Hel.* 1346, and Vell. Pat. 1.4.1 *nocturno aeris sono, qualis Cerealibus sacris cieri solet*; Schol. Ar. *Ach.* 708; Burkert, op. cit. n. 23., 315.

[128] Richardson, op. cit. n. 126, 26-30; Burkert, op. cit. n. 23, 318-21.

[129] E. R. Dodds, *Euripides Bacchae*² (1960), xxxii, and his note on 443-8. Cf. also the miraculous liberation of Sil., captured by his inferior in wisdom, King Midas (Theopomp. 115 *FGH* 75 (b)).

[130] Art. cit. n. 24.

The combination of diverse and yet typical themes in the genre is explained in this way as deriving from the activities of the satyrs both in the mysteries of the *thiasos* and in the public festival, two kinds of celebration which, once the division between them had been dissolved at the Great Dionysia, gave birth to drama.[131]

Though essentially conservative (§III (1)), satyric drama had no less than tragedy to meet the demands of annual novelty by exploring myths which had nothing to do with Dionysos. And yet, unlike tragedy, satyric drama retained its Dionysiac content. This it achieved not only through retaining a chorus of satyrs, but also by virtue of its choice and adaptation of non-Dionysiac myths. To take an example not already mentioned: the choice of the arrival at Seriphos of Danae and the infant Perseus by sea in the chest as the central event of a satyr-play (A. *Diktyoulkoi*) allowed scope for a typical satyric scene (see above): initial perplexity (such as has survived in the fragments) at the strange object, and then, after the amazing revelation of mother and child saved from the sea, vigorous delight and the prospect of a γάμος. But of all the themes inherited from the pre-dramatic celebrations it appears that the most adaptable, and useful, was the captivity of the satyrs. In *Cyc.* for example, they are captives, though not (as almost certainly in A. *Lykourgos*) to a traditional enemy of Dionysos. Still, Polyphemos is introduced to wine for the first time, as Lykourgos probably was, and he is also subjected to a mock initiation into the Dionysiac mysteries, like Pentheus in the *Bacchae*.

V. METRE AND LANGUAGE

The difference in mood between Tragedy and Old Comedy is expressed partly by differences in language and in the

---

[131] See §II. Although (masked) satyrs are the obvious case of predramatic action in an alien identity, we cannot affirm that the *thiasos* from which tragedy originated was satyric (§III (1). Of the dissolution there are hints even at the Anthesteria: van Hoorn, op. cit. n. 18, 36–7 (but not fully-fledged s-plays); P-Cambridge, op. cit. n. 7, 11 nn. 1 and 8); cf. D.H. 7.72.10 (imitative satyrs in procession).

metrical technique of the spoken iambic trimeter. Where does satyric drama stand in relation to these differences?

(1) *The Iambic Trimeter*[132]

Aristophanes exhibits certain licences not enjoyed by Tragedy. In most such cases—frequency of resolution, resolution of the tenth element after a long ninth,[133] word-ending after the first syllable of resolved *longa*,[134] the 'split anapaest',[135] the caesura,[136] crasis, synizesis, elision, and lengthening by position—*Cyc.* behaves like tragedy. But in three respects—'comic anapaests',[137] Porson's Law,[138] and three consecutive tribrachs (203, 210)—*Cyc.* deviates from tragedy, without however (in the first two categories) approaching the degree of licence exhibited by Old Comedy.[139] As for the extant satyric fragments, there is nothing in them to

[132] I have discounted cases where there are good independent reasons for suspecting the text.

[133] This does not occur at all in *Cyc.* or in tragedy, and is rare in tragedy even where the ninth is short: 10 occurrences in A., 9 in S., 37 in E. (J. Descroix, *Le Trimètre Iambique* (1931), 112–15); the 5 in *Cyc.* (173, 240, 348, 597, 677) do not represent a frequency greater than later E. (Ceadel in *CQ* 35 (1941), 72).

[134] P. Maas, *Greek Metre* (transl. H. Lloyd-Jones, Oxford, 1962), §104, §110; see notes on 144 and 343.

[135] Exx. are transmitted in *Cyc.* at 235, 334, 343, 410, but are all suspect for other reasons (except 334?—see note) and all easily emended. And we should probably discount μὰ Δι' (154, etc.), which is not found in tragedy, and is proclitic in comedy: J. W. White, *The Verse of Greek Comedy* (London, 1912), 46; Arnott in *CQ* 7 (1957), 189).

[136] See note on 7.

[137] I.e. a resolved *breve* or *anceps* outside the first foot and not accommodating a proper name: in *Cyc.* there are 17 certain exx.: 154, 232, 234, 242, 272, 274, 546, 558, 560, 562, 566, 582, 588, 637, 646, 647, 684. Only at 234 is the second *anceps* resolved, as sometimes in comedy.

[138] The infringements which would certainly be illegitimate in tragedy are 210, 681, 682: on 304 see note.

[139] In Ar. there is on average one comic anapaest every 2.3 trimeters (White, op. cit. n. 135, 44), and an infringement of Porson's law about every 5 trimeters (Maas, op. cit. n. 134, §110). Three consec. tribrachs in Ar. are not common: White, op. cit. n. 135, 49.

suggest that *Cyc.* was in any of these respects untypical of the genre.[140]

It is worth noting that no certain cases of deviation from tragic practice occur in Odysseus' trimeters. Nor do any occur in the agon (285–346). It appears indeed that the humorous contrast between the satyrs and the elements more appropriate to tragedy was expressed even in the metre. In the farcical scene 519–89 Odysseus has one resolution in 18.5 lines, whereas Silenos and Polyphemos, who have both been drinking have 16 in 16 lines and 17 in 34.5 respectively. Similarly, of the three untragic licences in *Cyc.* two are confined to scenes of agitated movement redolent of comedy (203, 210, 681, 682), and the third (comic anapaests) is particularly common in such scenes.

(2) *The Songs*

A little needs to be added here to what has already been said on this subject in §III (2). The choral songs of *Cyc.*, although five in number as in tragedy, resemble the songs of Old Comedy in their shortness, metrical simplicity, and tendency to accompany action. And the last two songs are astrophic. In the satyric fragments the choral songs appear to be more frequent than in *Cyc.*, and in the *Ichneutai* we find both *astropha* and strophic pairs divided by spoken lines. In these respects the fragments resemble Old Comedy more closely than does *Cyc.* But the regularity and simplicity of rhythm characteristic of *Cyc.* is found in the fragments only at A. *Dikt.* 806–20; the other surviving songs tend to express agitated action or reaction, notably with dochmiacs, runs of short syllables, and rapid alternation of metres. According to Marius Victorinus

---

[140] Except the apparently unique synizesis τοῦ ἱεροῦ at A. *Theoroi* 80 (cf. 50). And I leave aside Python's *Agen*, which is entirely exceptional. Porson's law is infringed at A. *Theoroi* fr. 276.23 (Lloyd-Jones); S. *Ichn.* 341, 353; Lycophron fr. 2.2, 10. Comic anap.: Achaios fr. 11.2; Lycophron fr. 2.7 (possible: A. fr. 205; S. *Ichn.* 128, fr. 756). In all other respects, including frequency of resolution, s-drama behaves like tragedy. At S. *Ichn.* 45 and 230 mute and liquid make position after an augment, which is rare even in tragedy (see Denniston-Page on A. *Ag.* 536).

(*Ars. Gramm.* 2.11) proceleusmatic rhythm was characteristic of the old satyric choruses.

(3) *Language*

Colloquialism in Euripides, defined as 'the kind of language that in a poetic or prosaic context would stand out however slightly as having a distinctly conversational flavour', has been investigated by P. T. Stevens.[141] From *Cyc.* he lists thirty-two instances[142] which reappear in tragedy. To these must be added a further twenty or so which are not found in tragedy.[143] In all, *Cyc.* contains considerably more colloquialisms per spoken line than any Euripidean tragedy, and twice as many per spoken line than the average for Euripidean tragedy (Stevens, 64–5).

However, it is in this respect much closer to tragedy than to Old Comedy. Furthermore it contains, even in passages referring to sex (e.g. 169–72), no Aristophanic vulgarisms such as πέος, πρωκτός, βωμολοχεύματα. And of those colloquialisms that are not found also in tragedy only one is spoken by Odysseus: κλαίειν c' ἄνωγα (701).[144] This exception proves the rule: Odysseus is referring to the blood dripping from Polyphemos' eye (cf. 174) in such a way as to echo cruelly Polyphemos' use of the same colloquial expression (340).

The picture presented by the fragments of fifth-century satyric drama is broadly similar. Colloquialisms[145] are not as frequent as in Aristophanes. The most vulgar expression is

---

[141] 'Colloquial Expressions in Euripides', *Hermes Einzelschrift* 38 (1976). This supersedes Amati in *SIFC* 9 (1901), 125–48 and Stevens in *CQ* 31 (1937), 182–91.

[142] 8, 37, 124, 131, 149, 152, 153, 168, 217, 220, 222, 241, 247, 259, 319, 336, 439, 450, 474, 492, 510, 520, 536, 542, 552, 557, 558, 562, 568, 595, 631, 705.

[143] E.g. diminutives at 185, 266, 267, 316, μὰ Δία at 9, 154, etc.; see also 104, 153, 156, 169, 174, 175, 270, 340, 558, 564, 572, 643, 677, 683–4, 686, 701.

[144] Unless one adds διεκάναξε in 158; two colloquialisms not found in tragedy are spoken by Pol. in the *agon* (316, 340).

[145] E.g. S. *Ichn.* 118 (μὰ Δία), 120 (τουτί), 197 (μιαρός abusive), 381, frr. 120, 329, 1130.16; A. *Dikt.* 812; Achaios frr. 12, 28.

nothing worse than ὡς ποcθοφίληc ὁ νεοccόc (A. *Dikt.* 795).
And there is nothing non-tragic known to be spoken by a
relatively serious character. At the same time, in keeping with
the relative humility of satyric subject matter, there is nothing
in extant satyric drama to approach the most high-flown
passages in tragedy.

To conclude, the language and metrical technique of the
spoken lines present a remarkably similar picture. Odysseus'
lines, and to a large extent Polphemos' lines in the agon, are
virtually indistinguishable in these respects from tragedy.
Horace was then right in describing *tragoedia* among the satyrs
as *effutire leves indigna ... versus* (*Ars. P.* 231). He goes on to
require that the speech of Silenos, though distinct from the
tragic, should not sink to the level of the slaves of (new)
comedy. And certainly the speech of Polyphemos outside the
agon, of Silenos, and of the satyrs, though clearly distinct in its
licence from tragedy, is much closer to it than to Old Comedy
at least.

B. THE CYCLOPS

VI. THE DATE OF THE PLAY

The *Cyclops* was probably written after 411 BC, in the last five
years of Euripides' life. The most likely year of its production
is 408 BC. No more than a summary can be offered here of the
argument I have set out in detail in *JHS* 102 (1982), 163–72.

Almost all the attempts to date the play by similarities with
passages of plays of known date are unconvincing:[146] in
general it has not been appreciated that a dramatist, when
treating a situation identical or similar to one in a previous
play either by himself or another, is not always concerned to
devise a structure or diction that is entirely original, but will
draw, consciously or unconsciously, and even after a lapse of

---

[146] See, most recently, Sutton, op. cit. n. 53, 114–20, who argues for 424
BC on the basis of similarities with *Hecuba*; cf. Seaford in *JHS* 102 (1982),
170–2.

years, on a pattern of utterance and a stock of metrical phrases that are not the private property of any one individual.[147]

However, a very few passages do not fall into this category, and so can perhaps be used to date the play. Perseus' first words in Euripides' *Andromeda* (of 412 BC) were ἔα τίν' ὄχθον τόνδ' ὁρῶ περίρρυτον κτλ. (fr. 125). This was parodied in the following year by Aristophanes: ἔα τίν' ὄχθον τόνδ' ὁρῶ καὶ παρθένον κτλ. (*Thesm.* 1105). In *Cyc.* Polyphemos' first words on seeing the Greeks are ἔα τίν' ὄχλον τόνδ' ὁρῶ πρὸς αὐλίοιϲ κτλ. (222). Milman Parry's suggestion that 'Euripides is here answering Aristophanes' mockery by mocking himself[148] is I think correct. There is *not* enough similarity of situation to demand the stock phrase, but there is enough to make the self-parody recognizable. And the similarity of phrase seems to be too elaborate to be unconscious, partly because it is achieved largely by coincidence of *sound* (ὄχθον and ὄχλον). The point is clinched by the parody in Aristophanes. Here then is a deliberate echo. If so, it seems unlikely that E. would introduce a ridiculous echo of a satyr-play into the tragic *Andromeda*. It must be the other way around (see also notes on 203, 225).

Secondly, Polyphemos declares that in order to pelt the departing Greeks he will go up to the hilltop δι' ἀμφιτρῆτοϲ τῆϲδε (707). The omission of a noun is surprising, particularly as there has been no previous mention[149] of this feature of the cave ('pierced through', i.e. with another entrance at the back). And so A. M. Dale[150] saw here a parodic allusion to the only other occurrence of the adjective, in Sophocles' *Philoktetes*, δι' ἀμφιτρῆτοϲ αὐλίου (19), of the

---

[147] Cf. e.g. A. *Ag.* 1343–5, S. *El.* 1415–16, E. *Hec.* 1035–7, *Cyc.* 663–5.

[148] In *HSCP* 41 (1930), 140–1, reprinted in *The Making of Homeric Verse* (Oxford, 1971), 319.

[149] Except perhaps at 60 (see note).

[150] In *WS* 69 (1956), 106, reprinted in *Collected papers* (Cambridge, 1969), 129; cf. Sutton, op. cit. n. 53, 102–3. One might add that αὔλιον and μέλαθρον referring to a cave occur outside S. *Phil.* only at *Cyc.* 345, 491, except perhaps *AP* 6.334.

cave of Philoktetes, lovingly presented (cf. 16–18, 159, 952) to the audience of 409 BC.

These apparent allusions may be thought insufficient by themselves to date the play. But no help can be offered either by vase-painting or by supposed reflections in the drama of historical events.[151] We must therefore turn to the criteria which have been used successfully to date Euripides' tragedies— the increasing frequency of resolutions in the spoken iambic trimeter, and in particular of certain kinds of resolution and word-shape at various points in the line. These numerous and subtle criteria[152] have never been properly applied to *Cyc.*, no doubt because a satyr-play might be expected to behave more freely in these respects than does tragedy. However, the trimeters spoken by Odysseus (and those spoken by Polyphemos in the agon) are, in contrast to the others, virtually indistinguishable from tragedy (§V). There is therefore a case for using them to date the play.

If it is objected here that Euripides may have accepted the tendencies in question in the 'tragic' lines in *Cyc.* earlier than in tragedy, and that a wedge must after all be maintained between these lines and tragedy, it can legitimately be replied that the tendencies in question are hardly a deliberate expression of licence or mood, but rather are embedded deep within the poet's half-conscious conception of the trimeter, and that if in composing the 'tragic' lines of *Cyc.* Euripides had consciously or unconsciously adopted a mood sufficiently distinct from tragedy as to exaggerate half-conscious metrical tendencies, then we would expect *a fortiori* this mood to be manifest also in the *style* of utterance generally, and especially in an untragic looseness of vocabulary. But it is not, except for two mild instances in Polyphemos' lines in the agon (§V). Let

[151] A recent detailed study is L. Paganelli, *Echi Storicho-Politici nel 'Ciclope' Euripideo* (*Proagones* 18, Padova, 1979).

[152] Formulated by T. Zielinski, *Tragodoumenon* II, *De Trimetri Euripidei Evolutione* (Cracow, 1925); Ceadel, art. cit. n. 133, 66; A. M. Dale, *Euripides Helen* (Oxford, 1967), xxiv–xxviii. Cf. Devine and Stephens in *TAPA* 110 (1980), 63–79 and 111 (1981), 43–64.

us then exclude the latter group and take only Odysseus' lines. Indeed, much of the humour of the play requires Odysseus to have stepped straight out of tragedy. When applied to his lines the metrical criteria cohere among themselves, as well as with the indications already discussed, in dating *Cyc.* to within three or four years of 410 BC.

VII. THE *Cyclops* AND HOMER

'La materia è morta nelle mani del poeta.' Momigliano's judgement[153] on *Cyc.* is not untypical. This section is concerned to lay a basis for challenging it. Comparison with Euripides' model, book nine of the *Odyssey*, is of great interest.[154] The major discrepancies can be assigned to the differences of (*a*) medium, (*b*) intellectual and social environment, and (*c*) genre.

(*a*) In Homer the cave is sealed by a great stone, whereas in the drama Odysseus has to be allowed to emerge from it on to the stage before the blinding. No longer do the Greeks have to be tied under the sheep in order to escape. The time-scale has to be condensed. And inasmuch as the fabulous Homeric giant has to be represented by an actor, he must appear much closer to a mere man than he is imagined in Homer. Then, to anticipate (c), there are Silenos and the chorus of satyrs. And inasmuch as they must be there against their will, Polyphemos must be an owner of slaves (cf. §IV).

(*b*) And so we find the human slave-owner's slaves cleaning his cave of its Homeric dung and preparing him a meal while he is out hunting with his hounds.[155] He is a man of some sophistication. And so whereas in Homer he eats the Greeks 'like a mountain lion', it is in keeping with his dietary fastidiousness in Euripides (247–8) that he should sacrifice (in

---

[153] In *Atene e Roma* 10 (1929), 156.

[154] For a detailed treatment in Latin see W. Wetzel, *De Euripidis Fabula Satyrica Quae Cyclops Inscribitur, Cum Homerico Comparata Exemplo* (Wiesbaden, 1965).

[155] See note on 29, 214 (cf. Prince Hippolytus at *Hipp.* 109 τερπνὸν ἐκ κυναγίας τράπεζα πλήρης).

a sense) the Greeks and cook them with elaborate care.[156] In fact Polyphemos seems to have appeared as a glutton and gourmet already in the comedies of Epicharmos and Cratinus.[157] Euripides' contribution may have been to extend the cannibal's sophisticated Hellenism into the realm of the intellect. His first words to the Greeks characterize him as a man of the πόλις (275–6), and he then (283–4) displays a disconcerting familiarity with the fashionable τόπος condemnatory of the Trojan expedition. More remarkable still is the manner in which he is soon rejecting Odysseus' plea in the agon.

The giant implicitly claims a superior intellect (316), by virtue of which he is able to replace traditional deity (*a*) as the right object of reverence, by wealth (316), food, and drink (336); (*b*) as the source of man's sustenance, by ἀνάγκη (332); (*c*) as the source of νόμοι, by mankind; νόμοι can then be dismissed as an unnecessary complication (338–40). It has been generally recognized that this passage parodies certain contemporary intellectual developments (see commentary). We are reminded in particular of Kallikles in Plato's *Gorgias*,[158] who argues that strong individuals have a duty, based on φύσις, to satisfy their desires at the expense of νόμοι, which are to be despised as the creation of the weak majority.

Kallikles is a wealthy and aristocratic young man of oligarchic connections, profoundly hostile to democracy, and just entering public life in the troubled last years of the fifth century.[159] In the *Laws* (890a) Plato refers to certain views

---

[156] See notes on 244–6, 345–6, 395, 402, 404.

[157] Epich. *Cyc.* fr. 82; Cratin. *Odysseis* fr. 143; another known early dramatization is Aristias' satyric *Cyc.*; cf. note on 213–14.

[158] See W. K. Guthrie, *A History of Greek Philosophy* iii (Cambridge, 1969), 101–7; ἀναγκή is associated with φύσις (Guthrie, 100), and at fr. 433 is opposed to νόμος; cf. fr. 920, *Tro.* 886, *Ba.* 895–6; etc.

[159] Guthrie, op. cit. n. 158, 102; E. R. Dodds, *Plato Gorgias* (Oxford, 1959), 12–14; Paganelli, op. cit. n. 151, 52; cf. e.g. Ps. Xen. *Ath. Resp.* 3.2 Cf. also the ideas and career of Kritias.

which he believes give rise to civil conflict: that the gods are not such as νόμος prescribes, and that one should live κατὰ φύσιν, which consists in dominating others rather than being subservient to them κατὰ νόμον.

It is clear that in general Euripides was a supporter of νόμος and of democracy, though not of ochlocracy.[160] *Cyc.* was almost certainly written shortly after 411 BC (§VI), in a period of fierce conflict in Athens between democrats and oligarchs. In the same period he wrote the *Phoinissai*, in which Polyneikes' appeal to δίκη, and Jokasta's attempt to avert the fratricide by appealing to the principle of equality, are both rejected by Eteokles (469–592) in terms reminiscent in their brutal realism of Polyphemos' rejection of Odysseus' plea. One aspect of the figure of Polyphemos in *Cyc.* is a caricature of a certain contemporary anti-democratic ideology.[161] He is a man of substance, equipped with slaves, cattle in addition to his Homeric sheep, and a sophisticated ideology. And yet he is still the Homeric savage. Indeed, his intellectual, sacrificial, and culinary sophistication is actually employed in the service of his cannibalism.[162]

The force of this caricature derives from the combination of these apparent opposites. But there is more to it than a *reductio ad absurdum* of selfish hedonism to cannibalism. One of the arguments in favour of respect for νόμος was a historical one: the first men lived like animals, in caves, without laws or agriculture, and even ate each other.[163] In the famous dramatic fragment variously attributed to Critias (fr. 19) and to

[160] See esp. Theseus in *Su.*; and e.g. Paganelli, op. cit. n. 151, 53–6;

[161] This will seem to mean that *Cyc.* is an intellectual or political tract only to those who regard all politics in literature as contrived and want their poetry and their humour autonomous. Cf. the dismissal by Sutton, op. cit. n. 53, 121.

[162] Rather as his refined statement of sexual preference (see note on 583–4) has as object the grotesque figure of Sil.

[163] Guthrie, op. cit. n. 158, 60–8; A. *PV* 442–68, 478–506; E. *Su.* 201–13; Critias fr. 19; Moschion fr. 6; Isocr. *Paneg.* 32–42; D.S.1.8.1–7, 13.26.3; etc.; cf. Orph. fr. 292 Kern.

Euripides, it is said by someone that laws were originally invented by men as a remedy for the disorderly and beastlike nature of their lives. Euripides' Theseus, a champion of νόμος and of democracy, praises the god who brought men out of beastlike confusion. And Plato's Protagoras maintains that in order to prevent men being wiped out by wild beasts Zeus gave them αἰδώς and δίκη, which allowed them to combine in πόλεις.

The race of Cyclopes, as described in Homer, is remarkably similar to this 'progressive' image of primitive man. They have neither assemblies nor laws (θέμιστες), and live in caves, without concern for each other or for Zeus (9.112–5, 275). And Polyphemos eats like a lion, leaving nothing (9.292–3). But there is one detail in Homer which suggests the opposed image of the past as a 'golden age'. Although the Cyclopes do not practise agriculture, cereals and vines grow spontaneously (108–11). Now in *Cyc.* Silenos tells Odysseus about the Cyclopes (115–28): they have no πόλεις, they live in caves, they are μονάδες (see note on 120). Because agriculture requires có-operation, Odysseus is prompted to ask whether they grow corn or live on something else. Silenos replies that they live on pastoral products, and soon reveals that they also enjoy human flesh. As in Homer, the Cyclopes have no agriculture, but the spontaneous growth of cereals and vines has been omitted. Of this omission there are two consequences. Firstly, in contrast to Homer, wine will be a novelty for Polyphemos. And secondly the Cyclopean life appears as unmitigatedly horrible as the 'progressive' image of the distant past.

One of the recurrent constituents of this image is the beastlike (θηριώδης) quality of human life. The opposed notion, that animals should actually serve as a model for human behaviour, had its full flowering in Cynical philosophy, but was clearly already a point of controversy in late-fifth-century Athens.[164] For example, Kallikles compares the admirable

[164] Guthrie, op. cit. n. 158, 104, 114 n. 4, 308, 368; for the Cynical Golden Age see Vidal-Naquet in *JHS* 98 (1978), 135.

III. The Pronomos vase (late fifth century): a satyric chorus with actors, Dionysos and Ariadne.

IV. Oinochoe in Oxford (last third of the fifth century): a satyr creeps up on a sleeping maenad named Tragodia.

individual to a lion whom society fails to tame. According to
Aristotle, he who cannot live in society, or does not need to
through self-sufficiency (αὐτάρκεια), is either a beast or a
god.[165] The self-sufficiency[166] of the Homeric Cyclopes, in
which they were perhaps more super-human (276) than subhuman, has acquired in Euripides a hedonistic dimension
(323–41). His Polyphemos calls himself a god (231, 345) but
is called by others a beast (θήρ: 402, 602, 658) as well as an
ἀνήρ (591, 605), and, like the Cynic Diogenes,[167] transgresses
not only dietary norms by his approbation of cannibalism
(341), as in Homer, but also sexual norms by his approbation
of masturbation (327–8). Precisely because of man's advantages over the animals, Aristotle goes on to say, he is, if
without ἀρετή, ἀνοσιώτατον καὶ ἀγριώτατον and πρὸς
ἀφροδίcια καὶ ἐδωδὴν χείριcτον. Euripides' Polyphemos, in
contrast to Homer's, is ἀνόcιοc (see note on 26).

The location of the Cyclopes in Sicily, near Aitna, is not
Homeric. Euripides did not invent it (see note on 20), but he
refers to it no less than fifteen times in the course of a very short
play. It is certainly fanciful to see Polyphemos as deliberately
equipped with qualities associated with Sicily: an 'almost
Gorgianic rhetoric', gourmandise, despotism, and Hellenism
mixed with barbarism.[168] But if, as argued in §VI, the play
was written not long after the Athenian disaster in Sicily of
413 BC, then the audience may have been reminded, as they
saw the Greeks trapped in the Aitnaian cannibal's cave, of
their fellow-citizens imprisoned in the Syracusan quarries
with the growing pile of bodies.[169]

The Sicilian setting also lends a humorous poignancy to
Odysseus' desperate appeal to Polyphemos: 'we saved Greece

[165] *Pol.* 1253a 27–9; αὐτάρκεια as an ideal in the fifth century among
enemies of νόμος: Antisthenes? see Guthrie, op. cit. n. 158, 308; Hippias? see
Guthrie, 119, 283.

[166] *Od.* 9.114–5, quoted in note on 118.

[167] At least according to Diog. Laert. 6.69, 73.

[168] Paganelli, op. cit. n. 151, 121–2.

[169] Argued by Seaford, art. cit. n. 146, 173; see Thuc. 7.87; Xen. *Hell.*
1.2.14; Plut. *Nik.* 29; Cic. *Verr.* 2.5.68.

from the Trojans' (290–8). This is both false and inept. What gives it point is a stock element of Athenian propaganda— 'we saved Greece from the Persians'—used (according to Thucydides) to justify their empire in answer to the Syracusans in 415–14 BC, and even by the Syracusan Nikolaos (according to Diodorus Siculus) in a plea for mercy for the Athenian captives in 413 BC.[170] Odysseus is of course no heroic representative of νόμος, humanity, and Athenian democratic values. He is in Euripidean tragedy so associated with crafty self-interest that the audience of *Cyc.* must have regarded his rhetorical plea as an example of the πολλῶν λόγων εὑρήμαθ' ὥστε μὴ θανεῖν (*Hec.* 250) with which he once saved his life when recognized in Troy by Hecuba, only to treat her without thanks or pity after the Greek victory. They may well have enjoyed his unexpected rhetorical defeat by Polyphemos. Silenos at any rate has no illusions, designating him immediately on his arrival as κρόταλον δριμύ, Σισύφου γένος (104; cf. 313–15). The victory at Troy, in which Odysseus expresses great pride (178, 198–202, 290–8, 603, 694–5), is seen by the satyrs only as an opportunity for the collective rape of Helen (179–81). Against such deflation of tragic pretension Odysseus must maintain his dignity, like Horace's matron forced to dance, *paulum pudibunda,* among satyrs.

Any serious thought that the play contains derives from the compatibility of Polyphemos' modern sophistication with his savagery, and much of the humour from their incompatibility. For example, the fastidiousness of his concern with his (barbarous) milk (see notes on 216–17, 218, 326, 328) and the Hellenic modernity of his cannibalism invest the old story with a sense of unreality (see note on 376). This sense is reinforced by the presence of the satyrs. We are faced in fact with a multiple incongruity, between the Homeric folk-tale, the loftiness of tragedy, the rhetorical expression of contemporary intellectual debate characteristic of Euripidean tragedy, and the Dionysiac world of the *thiasos.*

[170] Thuc. 6.82–3; D.S. 13.25.2; see further note on 297.

(c) It is in a sense Dionysos who prevails (454, etc.). Despite his sophistication Polyphemos knows nothing of wine or of Dionysos, is disdainful of the *thiasos* (204–5, 220–1), and has to be instructed in the manners of the symposium. A remarkably detailed similarity can be traced here with the 'conversion' of Pentheus in the *Bacchae*. That is because both cases are based on the process of initiation into the mysteries of Dionysos.[171] Alone of extant drama, *Cyc.* and *Bacchae* represent the original type, in which the chorus is a Dionysiac *thiasos* and the theme expresses in the refractive medium of myth the ritual of mystic initiation into the *thiasos* (§II). But *Bacchae* expresses it more closely than *Cyc.* For the theme of *Bacchae* is the traditional myth of the *thiasos*, the ἱερὸς λόγος of their mysteries, and the sufferings of Pentheus reflect the sufferings of the initiand: form and content cohere inasmuch as the form is merely an expression of the story. In *Cyc.*, on the other hand, we can see the persistence of the traditional form fused, sometimes with humorous results, with a novel and somewhat incongruous content. Similarly, certain passages of the play stand out from their context in such a manner as to appear to represent traditional τόποι of the genre adapted to the story of Polyphemos.[172] In these ways *Cyc.* exemplifies that tension between the Dionysiac and the non-Dionysiac which, as we have seen (§III), lies at the heart of satyric drama, and which is resolved by the victory of Dionysos, to whose service the departing satyrs proclaim their return (709).

J-P. Vernant has argued that in Sophocles' *Oedipus Tyrannus* the complementary opposition within the figure of Oedipus between the τύραννος and the φαρμακός, the combination and confusion of the superhuman and the subhuman, obliterates the upper and lower boundaries within which man is contained by his νόμοι, and thereby calls into question the

[171] See Seaford, art. cit. n. 24. A model for *Cyc.* may have been Aeschylus' satyric *Lykourgos*, in which Lyk., who belongs to the same type as Pentheus, may have been introduced to wine (see n. 66 above).

[172] See notes on 37–40, 76–7, 142, 169, 464–5, 477, art. cit. n. 24, and index s. τόποι.

polar structure inherent in Greek institutions and political theory. 'When man decides, like Oedipus, to carry the enquiry into what he is as far as it can go, he discovers himself to be enigmatic, without consistency . . . with no defined essence, oscillating between being the equal of the gods and the equal of nothing at all.'[173] The point is suggestive. Pentheus, the τύραννος of the *Bacchae*, is also at once superhuman (319–21) and subhuman (988–90, etc.). But the Dionysiac drama is in a sense less negative in its conclusions than the tragedy which evolved out of it. Whereas the discovery and annihilation of Oedipus gives rise to his departure, like a φαρμακός, from the πόλις, the discovery (924, etc.) and annihilation of Pentheus is effected by his absorption, despite himself, into an association outside of and antithetical to the πόλις, the Dionysiac *thiasos*.

The downfall of Polyphemos, in the only other extant drama of the ancient Dionysiac type, is similar. But because this is a satyr-play (§III), the tension between the Dionysiac and the non-Dionysiac, inherent in the ancient Dionysiac myths of Pentheus and Lykourgos, has been extended to a story which has nothing to do with Dionysos. Furthermore, the story brings with it the poignant complication that the enemy of the *thiasos* is also the enemy of the πόλις. In this way the various non-Homeric elements cohere. The combination in the Homeric Polyphemos of the superhuman and the subhuman has been expressed by Euripides as a positive, intellectualized hostility to the basis of the contemporary πόλις, with the paradoxical result that the same combination in his enemies, the satyrs, does not place them entirely outside the life of the πόλις.[174] The μονάς (120) who defined god as his own wealth and pleasure (316, 334–8) is brought to see the

[173] In *Tragedy and Myth in Ancient Greece* (Vernant and Vidal-Naquet, transl. by Janet Lloyd, 1981), 110. Cf. Sil.'s words to Midas (Arist. fr. 44 Rose): μετ' ἀγνοίας γὰρ τῶν οἰκείων κακῶν ἀλυπότατος ὁ βίος, and §III (3) above.

[174] See note on 483–518; D. Konstan in *Ramus* 10 (1981), 87–103 explores the similarities between Pol. and the satyrs as opposed to the (human) Od. For urbanized satyrs cf. pp. 31 n. 81, 35 above.

throne of Zeus and all the δαιμόνων ἁγνὸν cέβαc (580), and has
to be dissuaded from going out on a κῶμοc to share his wine
with his brothers (530–42). The mock-initiation and blinding
of the enemy of *thiasos* and πόλιc concludes the tetralogy with
the triumph of Dionysos, the god of *thiasos* and City Dionysia.

VIII. THE TEXT OF THE CYCLOPS

Cyc. is one of nine Euripidean plays preserved only in a single
fourteenth-century manuscript in the Laurentian library in
Florence ('L': Cod. Laur. plut. 32.2). These 'alphabetical'
plays appear to have survived by chance from an ancient
collection of Euripidean plays arranged alphabetically. They
appear in another fourteenth-century manuscript ('P': Laur.
Conv. Soppr. 172 and Palat. gr. 287), which is now generally
agreed to derive from L.[175]

The 'alphabetical' plays in L have no scholia. But they do
contain corrections, made apparently in three stages by the
Byzantine scholar Demetrius Triclinius. It is on the whole
possible, though often very difficult or quite impossible, to
distinguish the stages by inspection of the colour of the ink
used;[176] and this I have in a number of cases attempted to
do. It is generally accepted that P was copied from L after the
first stage of Triclinius' corrections. Diggle's apparatus distinguishes between corrections made at the first stage (Tr. 1)
and all subsequent ones (Tr. 2). I have also distinguished the
third stage (Tr. 3). It must however be admitted that these
distinctions have little bearing on the establishment of the
text. One of the conclusions of Zuntz's study is that Triclinius'
'first spell amounted to doing the *ex-officio*-corrector's job; for
this purpose he would naturally have referred to the manuscript (Λ) from which L had been copied. His final effort,

---

[175] G. Zuntz, *An Inquiry into the Transmission of the Plays of Euripides* (1965).
On the application of his conclusions to individual 'alphabetical' plays see R.
Kannicht, *Euripides Helena* (1969) i 97–104; C. Collard, *Euripides Supplices*
(1975) i 31–47.
[176] Zuntz, op. cit. n. 175, *passim*; cf. the warnings of Sansone in *GGA* 230
(1978), 238–41.

on the other hand, centred on the correction, according to
his lights, of the metres in lyric passages, where evidently
he relied on his own devices.' This factor should be taken
into account when considering the merits of, for example,
ἐξαποξύνας (Tr. 1, 456) on the one hand and ἐγὼ (Tr. 3, 13)
on the other. But even this consideration is of limited value,
inasmuch as Zuntz himself has to admit that 'actually there
are authoritative readings as well as sheer inventions among
every type and stage of Triclinius' alterations'. As for P, apart
from some emendations made by a later hand (P²), it is for
this play worth citing only as a witness to the reading of L as it
was before one of Triclinius' later corrections, as at 604.

CODICES ET CODICUM SIGLA

L.	Laurentianus plut. 32.2	saec. xiv in.
L¹ᶜ	L post correctionem a prima manu factam	
Lᵘᵛ	L ut videtur	
Lˢ	in L supra scriptum a prima manu	
Tr	Demetrius Triclinius codicis L emendator	
Tr¹	prior Triclinii emendatio	
Tr²	altera vel tertia Triclinii emendatio	

Apographa codicis L

P	Palatinus gr. 287 (uu. 1-243, 352-709)	saec. xiv in.
P²	codicis P manus secunda (sive in textu sive supra lineam)	
Pˢ	in P supra scriptum a prima manu	
apogr. Par.	Parisinus gr. 2887	saec. xv ex.
	vel Parisinus gr. 2817	saec. xvi in.
apogr. Flor.	Laurentianus 31.1	saec. xv

SIGLA ET NOTAE

Σ	scholiasta, scholia
*	littera erasa vel obliterata
∼	lectio cum ceteris codicibus consentit contra lectionem vel coniecturam modo memoratam

ΥΠΟΘΕCΙC ΚΥΚΛΩΠΟC

Ὀδυccεὺc ἀναχθεὶc ἐξ Ἰλίου εἰc Cικελίαν ἀπερρίφη, ἔνθα ὁ Πολύφημοc· εὑρὼν δὲ δουλεύονταc ἐκεῖ τοὺc Cατύρουc οἶνον δοὺc ἄρναc ἤμελλε λαμβάνειν καὶ γάλα παρ' αὐτῶν. ἐπιφανεὶc δ' ὁ Πολύφημοc ζητεῖ τὴν αἰτίαν τῆc τῶν ἰδίων ἐκφορήcεωc. ὁ 5 Cιληνὸc δὲ τὸν ξένον λῃcτεύοντα καταλαβεῖν φηcιν...

τὰ τοῦ δράματοc πρόcωπα· Cιληνόc, χορὸc Cατύρων, Ὀδυc-cεύc, Κύκλωψ.

personarum indicem add. Tr¹: om. L

fabula incertum quo tempore acta

ΚΥΚΛΩΨ

CIΛΗΝΟC

'Ω Βρόμιε, διὰ cὲ μυρίους ἔχω πόνους
νῦν χὦτ' ἐν ἤβηι τοὐμὸν εὐcθένει δέμας·
πρῶτον μὲν ἡνίκ' ἐμμανὴς "Ηρας ὕπο
Νύμφας ὀρείας ἐκλιπὼν ὦιχου τροφούς·
ἔπειτά γ' ἀμφὶ γηγενῆ μάχην δορὸς   5
ἐνδέξιος cὦι ποδὶ παραcπιcτὴς βεβὼς
'Εγκέλαδον ἰτέαν ἐς μέcην θενὼν δορὶ
ἔκτεινα—φέρ' ἴδω, τοῦτ' ἰδὼν ὄναρ λέγω;
οὐ μὰ Δί', ἐπεὶ καὶ cκῦλ' ἔδειξα Βακχίωι.
καὶ νῦν ἐκείνων μείζον' ἐξαντλῶ πόνον.   10
ἐπεὶ γὰρ "Ηρα cοι γένος Τυρcηνικὸν
ληιcτῶν ἐπῶρcεν, ὡς ὁδηθείης μακράν,
⟨ἐγὼ⟩ πυθόμενος cὺν τέκνοιcι ναυcτολῶ
cέθεν κατὰ ζήτηcιν. ἐν πρύμνηι δ' ἄκραι
αὐτὸς λαβὼν ηὔθυνον ἀμφῆρες δόρυ,   15
παῖδες δ' ⟨ἐπ'⟩ ἐρετμοῖς ἥμενοι γλαυκὴν ἅλα
ῥοθίοιcι λευκαίνοντες ἐζήτουν c', ἄναξ.
ἤδη δὲ Μαλέας πληcίον πεπλευκότας
ἀπηλιώτης ἄνεμος ἐμπνεύcας δορὶ
ἐξέβαλεν ἡμᾶς τήνδ' ἐς Αἰτναίαν πέτραν,   20
ἵν' οἱ μονῶπες ποντίου παῖδες θεοῦ
Κύκλωπες οἰκοῦc' ἄντρ' ἔρημ' ἀνδροκτόνοι.
τούτων ἑνὸς ληφθέντες ἐcμὲν ἐν δόμοιc
δοῦλοι· καλοῦcι δ' αὐτὸν ὦι λατρεύομεν
Πολύφημον· ἀντὶ δ' εὐίων βακχευμάτων   25
ποίμνας Κύκλωπος ἀνοcίου ποιμαίνομεν.

Inscriptio εὐ- κ- Tr¹: om. L   1ⁿ cιληνόc add. Tr¹: om. L   2 ηὐ-
θένει L. Dindorf   5 δ' Heath   6 βεβὼc Kassel (Maia 25 [1973]
100): γεγὼc L: cf. Ph. 1073–4   13 ⟨ἐγὼ⟩ Tr², ⟨εὐθὺc⟩ Diggle
15 λαβὼν] βεβὼc Diggle   ηὔθυνον Heath: εὔθ- L   16 δ' add. Tr¹:
om. L   ⟨ἐπ'⟩ Seidler

παῖδες μὲν οὖν μοι κλειτύων ἐν ἐσχάτοις
νέμουσι μῆλα νέα νέοι πεφυκότες,
ἐγὼ δὲ πληροῦν πίστρα καὶ σαίρειν στέγας
μένων τέταγμαι τάσδε, τῶιδε δυσσεβεῖ   30
Κύκλωπι δείπνων ἀνοσίων διάκονος.
καὶ νῦν, τὰ προσταχθέντ', ἀναγκαίως ἔχει
σαίρειν σιδηρᾶι τῆιδέ μ' ἁρπάγηι δόμους,
ὡς τόν τ' ἀπόντα δεσπότην Κύκλωπ' ἐμὸν
καθαροῖσιν ἄντροις μῆλά τ' ἐσδεχώμεθα.   35
ἤδη δὲ παῖδας προσνέμοντας εἰσορῶ
ποίμνας. τί ταῦτα; μῶν κρότος σικινίδων
ὅμοιος ὑμῖν νῦν τε χῶτε Βακχίωι
κῶμος συνασπίζοντες Ἀλθαίας δόμους
προσῆιτ' ἀοιδαῖς βαρβίτων σαυλούμενοι;   40

ΧΟΡΟΣ

παῖ γενναίων μὲν πατέρων   [στρ.
γενναίων δ' ἐκ τοκάδων,
πᾶι δή μοι νίσηι σκοπέλους;
οὐ τᾶιδ' ὑπήνεμος αὔ-
ρα καὶ ποιηρὰ βοτάνα,   45
δινᾶέν θ' ὕδωρ ποταμῶν
ἐν πίστραις κεῖται πέλας ἄντρων, οὗ σοι βλαχαὶ τεκέων;

ψύττ'· οὐ τᾶιδ', οὔ;   [μεσωιδ.
οὐ τᾶιδε νεμῆι κλειτὺν δροσεράν;   50
ὠή, ῥίψω πέτρον τάχα σου·

27 κλειτύων Wackernagel: κλιτ- L   32 ἔχει Tr¹ uel Tr² (et P): -οι
Lᵘᵛ (et Pˢ)   37 σικιννίδων Barnes   39 κῶμος Diggle: κῶμοι L:
κώμοις Dobree, Bothe, -ωι Porson   41ⁿ χορὸς σατύρων L   41 παῖ
Dindorf: πᾶ δή μοι L   42 δ' L. Dindorf: τ' L   μὲν...τε in
anaphora non testatur Denniston, GP 374–6   44 αὐλὰ Musgrave
47 πίστροις Boissonade   48 οὐ Casaubon: οὗ Tr¹: •• L   50 νεμῆι
Matthiae: νέμη L   κλειτὺν Wackernagel: κλιτ- L

ὕπαγ' ὧ ὕπαγ' ὧ κεράστα
⟨πρὸς⟩ μηλοβότα cταcιωρὸν
Κύκλωποc ἀγροβάτα.

cπαργῶνταc μαcτοὺc χάλαcον·   [ἀντ.
δέξαι θηλὰc πορίcαc'   56
οὓc λείπειc ἀρνῶν θαλάμοιc.
ποθοῦcί c' ἀμερόκοι-
    τοι βλαχαὶ cμικρῶν τεκέων.
εἰc αὐλὰν πότ' †ἀμφιβαίνειc†   60
ποιηροὺc λιποῦcα νομοὺc
Αἰτναίων εἴcω cκοπελῶν;

οὐ τάδε Βρόμιοc, οὐ τάδε χοροὶ   [ἐπωιδ.
Βάκχαι τε θυρcοφόροι,
οὐ τυμπάνων ἀλαλαγμοί,   65
οὐκ οἴνου χλωραὶ cταγόνεc   67
κρήναιc παρ' ὑδροχύτοιc·   66
οὐδ' ἐν Νύcαι μετὰ Νυμ-   68
    φᾶν ἴακχον ἴακχον ὠι-
    δὰν μέλπω πρὸc τὰν Ἀφροδί-   70
    ταν, ἃν θηρεύων πετόμαν
Βάκχαιc cὺν λευκόποcιν.
†ὧ φίλοc ὧ φίλε Βακχεῖε
ποῖ οἰοπολεῖc
ξανθὰν χαίταν cείειc;†   75

52 ὕπαγ' ὧ ὕπαγ' ὧ apogr. Par.: ὑπάγω ὑπάγω L   53 ⟨πρὸς⟩ Wecklein   cταcιωρὲ post Stephanum Wilamowitz   54 ἀγροβάτα Tr²: -βότα L   56 θηλὰc πορίcαc' Broadhead: θηλαῖcι cποράc L   57 οὓc Diggle: ἆc L: cf. 224, 234, 256   63 τάδε...τάδε Aldina: τᾶδε...τᾶδε L τάδε alterum del. Headlam, sed cf. Hyps. 1.ii.9   66 post 67 trai. Hermann   68 Νύcαι Musgrave: νύccα ⟨L⟩P   69 ἴακχον ἴακχον ὠιδᾶι Kassel (ὠιδαῖc Seaford)   70 πρὸc del. Wecklein   73–4 βακχεῖε Tr²: aut -εῖε aut -ῖε L   [ὧ φίλοc] ὧ φίλε Βάκχιε, ποῖ ⟨δ'⟩ Paley, ὧ φίλοc [ὧ φίλε Βακχεῖε], ποῖ ⟨δ'⟩ Diggle (ad δέ uide Denniston, GP 174) ποῦ Wecklein   οἰοπολῶν Nauck   75 ⟨ποῦ⟩ ξανθὰν Conradt   cείων Tr²

ἐγὼ δ' ὁ cὸc πρόπολοc
Κύκλωπι θητεύω
τῶι μονοδέρκται δοῦλοc ἀλαίνων
cὺν τᾶιδε τράγου χλαίναι μελέαι   80
cᾶc χωρὶc φιλίαc.

Ci.   ciγήcατ', ὦ τέκν', ἄντρα δ' ἐc πετρηρεφῆ
      ποίμναc ἀθροῖcαι προcπόλουc κελεύcατε.
Χο.   χωρεῖτ'· ἀτὰρ δὴ τίνα, πάτερ, cπουδὴν ἔχειc;
Ci.   ὁρῶ πρὸc ἀκταῖc ναὸc Ἑλλάδοc cκάφοc   85
      κώπηc τ' ἄνακταc cὺν cτρατηλάτηι τινὶ
      cτείχονταc ἐc τόδ' ἄντρον· ἀμφὶ δ' αὐχέciν
      τεύχη φέρονται κενά, βορᾶc κεχρημένοι,
      κρωccούc θ' ὑδρηλούc. ὦ ταλαίπωροι ξένοι·
      τίνεc ποτ' εἰcίν; οὐκ ἴcαcι δεcπότην   90
      Πολύφημον οἷόc ἐcτιν ἄξενόν τε γῆν
      τήνδ' ἐμβεβῶτεc καὶ Κυκλωπίαν γνάθον
      τὴν ἀνδροβρῶτα δυcτυχῶc ἀφιγμένοι.
      ἀλλ' ἥcυχοι γίγνεcθ', ἵν' ἐκπυθώμεθα
      πόθεν πάρειcι Cικελὸν Αἰτναῖον πάγον.   95

ΟΔΥCCΕΥC
      ξένοι, φράcαιτ' ἂν νᾶμα ποτάμιον πόθεν
      δίψηc ἄκοc λάβοιμεν εἴ τέ τιc θέλει
      βορὰν ὁδῆcαι ναυτίλοιc κεχρημένοιc;
      ⟨ἔα·⟩
      τί χρῆμα; Βρομίου πόλιν ἔοιγμεν ἐcβαλεῖν·
      Cατύρων πρὸc ἄντροιc τόνδ' ὅμιλον εἰcορῶ.   100
      χαίρειν προcεῖπα πρῶτα τὸν γεραίτατον.
Ci.   χαῖρ', ὦ ξέν', ὅcτιc δ' εἶ φράcον πάτραν τε cήν.
Οδ.   Ἴθακοc Ὀδυccεύc, γῆc Κεφαλλήνων ἄναξ.

77 Κύκλωπι θητεύω Fritzsche: θ- κ- L: ad numeros cf. Alc. 401 ∼ 413,
Su. 781 ∼ 789, IT 400 ∼ 415, Or. 1447   86 ἄνακταc Tr²: -τα L
91 τε γῆν Jacobs: cτέγην L   93 τὴν apogr. Par., Bothe: τήνδ' L
ἀνδροβρῶτα P²: -βῶτα L   u. interrogationis nota dist. F. J. Williams
99 ⟨ἔα⟩ Wecklein   101 προcεῖπον Fix

Ci.   οἶδ' ἄνδρα, κρόταλον δριμύ, Cιcύφου γένοc.

Οδ.   ἐκεῖνοc αὐτόc εἰμι· λοιδόρει δὲ μή.   105

Ci.   πόθεν Cικελίαν τήνδε ναυcτολῶν πάρει;

Οδ.   ἐξ Ἰλίου γε κἀπὸ Τρωϊκῶν πόνων.

Ci.   πῶc; πορθμὸν οὐκ ἤιδηcθα πατρώιαc χθονόc;

Οδ.   ἀνέμων θύελλαι δεῦρό μ' ἥρπαcαν βίαι.

Ci.   παπαῖ· τὸν αὐτὸν δαίμον' ἐξαντλεῖc ἐμοί.   110

Οδ.   ἦ καὶ cὺ δεῦρο πρὸc βίαν ἀπεcτάληc;

Ci.   ληιcτὰc διώκων οἳ Βρόμιον ἀνήρπαcαν.

Οδ.   τίc δ' ἥδε χώρα καὶ τίνεc ναίουcί νιν;

Ci.   Αἰτναῖοc ὄχθοc Cικελίαc ὑπέρτατοc.

Οδ.   τείχη δὲ ποῦ 'cτι καὶ πόλεωc πυργώματα;   115

Ci.   οὐκ ἔcτ'· ἔρημοι πρῶνεc ἀνθρώπων, ξένε.

Οδ.   τίνεc δ' ἔχουcι γαῖαν; ἦ θηρῶν γένοc;

Ci.   Κύκλωπεc, ἄντρ' ἔχοντεc, οὐ cτέγαc δόμων.

Οδ.   τίνοc κλύοντεc; ἢ δεδήμευται κράτοc;

Ci.   μονάδεc· ἀκούει δ' οὐδὲν οὐδεὶc οὐδενόc.   120

Οδ.   cπείρουcι δ'—ἢ τῶι ζῶcι;—Δήμητροc cτάχυν;

Ci.   γάλακτι καὶ τυροῖcι καὶ μήλων βορᾶι.

Οδ.   Βρομίου δὲ πῶμ' ἔχουcιν, ἀμπέλου ῥοάc;

Ci.   ἥκιcτα· τοιγὰρ ἄχορον οἰκοῦcι χθόνα.

Οδ.   φιλόξενοι δὲ χὤcιοι περὶ ξένουc;   125

Ci.   γλυκύτατά φαcι τὰ κρέα τοὺc ξένουc φορεῖν.

Οδ.   τί φήιc; βορᾶι χαίρουcιν ἀνθρωποκτόνωι;

Ci.   οὐδεὶc μολὼν δεῦρ' ὅcτιc οὐ κατεcφάγη.

Οδ.   αὐτὸc δὲ Κύκλωψ ποῦ 'cτιν; ἦ δόμων ἔcω;

Ci.   φροῦδοc, πρὸc Αἴτνηι θῆραc ἰχνεύων κυcίν.   130

Οδ.   οἶcθ' οὖν ὃ δρᾶcον, ὡc ἀπαίρωμεν χθονόc.

Ci.   οὐκ οἶδ', Ὀδυccεῦ· πᾶν δέ cοι δρώιημεν ἄν.

104 u. dist. Kirchhoff   γόνον Σ S. Ai. 190   105 αὐτόc L. Dindorf: οὗτοc L   107 τε Hermann: uide Denniston, GP 133   108 ἤιδηcθα Matthiae: ἤδειcθα L   112 διώκων ⟨γ'⟩ Wecklein   116 ἔcτ' Schenk: εἴc' L   117 ἢ Kirchhoff: ἦ L   120 μονάδεc V. Schmidt (Maia 27 [1975] 291): νομάδεc L   123 πῶμ' Tr¹: πόμ' L   ῥοάc Reiske: ῥοαῖc L   129 ἦ Kirchhoff: ἢ L   130 Αἴτνην Reiske   131 δρᾶcον Canter: δράcειc L   ἀπάρωμεν Wecklein

Οδ. ὅδηcον ἡμῖν cῖτον, οὗ cπανίζομεν.
Cι. οὐκ ἔcτιν, ὥcπερ εἶπον, ἄλλο πλὴν κρέαc.
Οδ. ἀλλ' ἡδὺ λιμοῦ καὶ τόδε cχετήριον.   135
Cι. καὶ τυρὸc ὀπίαc ἔcτι καὶ βοὸc γάλα.
Οδ. ἐκφέρετε· φῶc γὰρ ἐμπολήμαcιν πρέπει.
Cι. cὺ δ' ἀντιδώcειc, εἰπέ μοι, χρυcὸν πόcον;
Οδ. οὐ χρυcὸν ἀλλὰ πῶμα Διονύcου φέρω.
Cι. ὦ φίλτατ' εἰπών, οὗ cπανίζομεν πάλαι.   140
Οδ. καὶ μὴν Μάρων μοι πῶμ' ἔδωκε, παῖc θεοῦ.
Cι. ὃν ἐξέθρεψα ταῖcδ' ἐγώ ποτ' ἀγκάλαιc;
Οδ. ὁ Βακχίου παῖc, ὡc cαφέcτερον μάθηιc.
Cι. ἐν cέλμαcιν νεώc ἐcτιν ἢ φέρειc cύ νιν;
Οδ. ὅδ' ἀcκὸc ὃc κεύθει νιν, ὡc ὁρᾶιc, γέρον.   145
Cι. οὗτοc μὲν οὐδ' ἂν τὴν γνάθον πλήcειέ μου.
⟨Οδ.   ⟩
⟨Cι.   ⟩
Οδ. ναί· δὶc τόcον πῶμ' ὅcον ἂν ἐξ ἀcκοῦ ῥυῆι.
Cι. καλήν γε κρήνην εἶπαc ἡδεῖάν τ' ἐμοί.
Οδ. βούληι cε γεύcω πρῶτον ἄκρατον μέθυ;
Cι. δίκαιον· ἦ γὰρ γεῦμα τὴν ὠνὴν καλεῖ.   150
Οδ. καὶ μὴν ἐφέλκω καὶ ποτῆρ' ἀcκοῦ μέτα.
Cι. φέρ' ἐγκάναξον, ὡc ἀναμνηcθῶ πιών.
Οδ. ἰδού. Cι. παπαιάξ, ὡc καλὴν ὀcμὴν ἔχει.
Οδ. εἶδεc γὰρ αὐτήν; Cι. οὐ μὰ Δί', ἀλλ' ὀcφραίνομαι.
Οδ. γεῦcαί νυν, ὡc ἂν μὴ λόγωι 'παινῆιc μόνον.   155
Cι. βαβαί· χορεῦcαι παρακαλεῖ μ' ὁ Βάκχιοc.
       ἆ ἆ ἆ.
Οδ. μῶν τὸν λάρυγγα διεκάναξέ cου καλῶc;
Cι. ὥcτ' εἰc ἄκρουc γε τοὺc ὄνυχαc ἀφίκετο.
Οδ. πρὸc τῶιδε μέντοι καὶ νόμιcμα δώcομεν.   160
Cι. χάλα τὸν ἀcκὸν μόνον· ἔα τὸ χρυcίον.

136 βοὸc] Διὸc Athen. 658 C   139 πῶμα Tr¹: πόμα L   144 cέλμαcιν Aldina: -cι L   145 ἀcκόc Radermacher: ἀ- L   146 post h.u.
lac. indic. Nauck, Kirchhoff   148 τ' Reiske: γ' L   152 ἐγκάναξον
Valckenaer, Pierson: ἐκπάταξον L

Οδ. ἐκφέρετέ νυν τυρεύματ' ἢ μήλων τόκον.
Ci. δράςω τάδ', ὀλίγον φροντίςας γε δεςποτῶν.
　　　ὡς ἐκπιών γ' ἂν κύλικα μαινοίμην μίαν,
　　　πάντων Κυκλώπων ἀντιδοὺς βοςκήματα　　　165
　　　ῥίψας τ' ἐς ἅλμην Λευκάδος πέτρας ἄπο
　　　ἅπαξ μεθυςθεὶς καταβαλών τε τὰς ὀφρῦς.
　　　ὡς ὅς γε πίνων μὴ γέγηθε μαίνεται·
　　　ἵν' ἔςτι τουτί τ' ὀρθὸν ἐξανιςτάναι
　　　μαςτοῦ τε δραγμὸς καὶ †παρεςκευαςμένου†　　　170
　　　ψαῦςαι χεροῖν λειμῶνος ὀρχηςτύς θ' ἅμα
　　　κακῶν τε λῆςτις. εἶτ' ἐγὼ ⟨οὐ⟩ κυνήςομαι
　　　τοιόνδε πῶμα, τὴν Κύκλωπος ἀμαθίαν
　　　κλαίειν κελεύων καὶ τὸν ὀφθαλμὸν μέςον;

Χο. ἄκου', 'Οδυςςεῦ· διαλαλήςωμέν τί ςοι.　　　175
Οδ. καὶ μὴν φίλοι γε προςφέρεςθε πρὸς φίλον.
Χο. ἐλάβετε Τροίαν τὴν 'Ελένην τε χειρίαν;
Οδ. καὶ πάντα γ' οἶκον Πριαμιδῶν ἐπέρςαμεν.
Χο. οὔκουν, ἐπειδὴ τὴν νεᾶνιν εἵλετε,
　　　ἅπαντες αὐτὴν διεκροτήςατ' ἐν μέρει,　　　180
　　　ἐπεί γε πολλοῖς ἥδεται γαμουμένη,
　　　τὴν προδότιν, ἣ τοὺς θυλάκους τοὺς ποικίλους
　　　περὶ τοῖν ςκελοῖν ἰδοῦςα καὶ τὸν χρύςεον
　　　κλωιὸν φοροῦντα περὶ μέςον τὸν αὐχένα
　　　ἐξεπτοήθη, Μενέλεων ἀνθρώπιον　　　185
　　　λῷςτον λιποῦςα; μηδαμοῦ γένος ποτὲ
　　　φῦναι γυναικῶν ὤφελ', εἰ μὴ 'μοὶ μόνωι.
Ci. ἰδού· τάδ' ὑμῖν ποιμνίων βοςκήματα,
　　　ἄναξ 'Οδυςςεῦ, μηκάδων ἀρνῶν τροφαί,

164 ἐκπιών Kirchhoff: -πιεῖν L, quo seruato μαιοίμην F. W. Schmidt
166 ῥίψας Kirchhoff: ῥίψαι L　　　169 τ' ὀρθὸν Seidler: τοὐρθὸν L
171 ὀρχηςτύς Canter: -ςτύος L　　　172 ⟨οὐ⟩ Matthiae (et fort. apogr.
Par.)　　　⟨οὐ⟩κ ὠνήςομαι Tyrwhitt　　　175ⁿ Χο. Tyrwhitt: om. L
177ⁿ et 179ⁿ Χο. Tyrwhitt: ci. L　　　181 ἥδεται Pᵃ pot. qu. P: ἥδετε L
184 κλωιὸν Dindorf: κλοιὸν L　　　187 'μοὶ Bothe: μοι L　　　188ⁿ Ci.
apogr. Par., Tyrwhitt: om. L　　　188 ποιμνίων Scaliger: ποιμένων L

πηκτοῦ γάλακτός τ' οὐ σπάνια τυρεύματα.   190
φέρεσθε· χωρεῖθ' ὡς τάχιστ' ἄντρων ἄπο,
βότρυος ἐμοὶ πῶμ' ἀντιδόντες εὐίου.
οἴμοι· Κύκλωψ ὅδ' ἔρχεται· τί δράσομεν;

Οδ.   ἀπολώλαμέν τἄρ', ὦ γέρον· ποῖ χρὴ φυγεῖν;
Ci.   ἔσω πέτρας τῆςδ', οὗπερ ἂν λάθοιτέ γε.   195
Οδ.   δεινὸν τόδ' εἶπας, ἀρκύων μολεῖν ἔσω.
Ci.   οὐ δεινόν· εἰσὶ καταφυγαὶ πολλαὶ πέτρας.
Οδ.   οὐ δῆτ'· ἐπεί τἂν μεγάλα γ' ἡ Τροία στένοι,
εἰ φευξόμεσθ' ἕν' ἄνδρα, μυρίον δ' ὄχλον
Φρυγῶν ὑπέστην πολλάκις σὺν ἀσπίδι.   200
ἀλλ', εἰ θανεῖν δεῖ, κατθανούμεθ' εὐγενῶς
ἢ ζῶντες αἶνον τὸν πάρος συσσώσομεν.

ΚΥΚΛΩΨ
ἄνεχε πάρεχε· τί τάδε; τίς ἡ ῥαιθυμία;
τί βακχιάζετ'; οὐχὶ Διόνυσος τάδε,
οὐ κρόταλα χαλκοῦ τυμπάνων τ' ἀράγματα.   205
πῶς μοι κατ' ἄντρα νεόγονα βλαστήματα;
ἢ πρός τε μαστοῖς εἰσι χὐπὸ μητέρων
πλευρὰς τρέχουσι, σχοινίνοις τ' ἐν τεύχεσιν
πλήρωμα τυρῶν ἐστιν ἐξημελγμένον;
τί φάτε, τί λέγετε; τάχα τις ὑμῶν τῶι ξύλωι   210
δάκρυα μεθήσει. βλέπετ' ἄνω καὶ μὴ κάτω.
Χο.   ἰδού· πρὸς αὐτὸν τὸν Δί' ἀνακεκύφαμεν
καὶ τἄστρα καὶ τὸν Ὠρίωνα δέρκομαι.
Κυ.   ἄριστόν ἐστιν εὖ παρεσκευασμένον;
Χο.   πάρεστιν· ὁ φάρυγξ εὐτρεπὴς ἔστω μόνον.   215
Κυ.   ἦ καὶ γάλακτός εἰσι κρατῆρες πλέωι;

193 Sileno contin. L. Dindorf: Ulixi trib. L   194 τἄρ' Hartung:
γὰρ L   198 στένοι P²: -ει L   202 συσσώσομεν Schenk: εὖ σώσομεν L
πάροιθε σώσομεν Hartung   203ⁿ Κυ. Tyrwhitt: ci. L   204 οὐχὶ
Διόνυσος Musgrave: οὐ διώνυσος L (διόν- P)   207 ἢ Hermann: ἦ L
τε L. Dindorf: γε L   212ⁿ, 215ⁿ, 217ⁿ, 219ⁿ Χο. Tyrwhitt:
ci. L   213 τά τ' ἄστρα Choerob. in Theod. i. 272 (∼ anecd. Par. iv. 194)
216 ἢ Tr¹: ἦ L

Xo. ὥcτ' ἐκπιεῖν γέ c', ἢν θέληιc, ὅλον πίθον.

Kυ. μήλειον ἢ βόειον ἢ μεμειγμένον;

Xo. ὃν ἂν θέληιc cύ· μὴ 'μὲ καταπίηιc μόνον.

Kυ. ἥκιcτ'· ἐπεί μ' ἂν ἐν μέcηι τῆι γαcτέρι   220
πηδῶντεc ἀπολέcαιτ' ἂν ὑπὸ τῶν cχημάτων.
ἔα· τίν' ὄχλον τόνδ' ὁρῶ πρὸc αὐλίοιc;
ληιcταί τινεc κατέcχον ἢ κλῶπεc χθόνα;
ὁρῶ γέ τοι τούcδ' ἄρναc ἐξ ἄντρων ἐμῶν
cτρεπταῖc λύγοιcι cῶμα cυμπεπλεγμένουc   225
τεύχη τε τυρῶν cυμμιγῆ γέροντά τε
πληγαῖc μέτωπον φαλακρὸν ἐξωιδηκότα.

Cι. ὤμοι, πυρέccω cυγκεκομμένοc τάλαc.

Kυ. ὑπὸ τοῦ; τίc ἐc cὸν κρᾶτ' ἐπύκτευcεν, γέρον;

Cι. ὑπὸ τῶνδε, Κύκλωψ, ὅτι τὰ c' οὐκ εἴων φέρειν.   230

Kυ. οὐκ ἦιcαν ὄντα θεόν με καὶ θεῶν ἄπο;

Cι. ἔλεγον ἐγὼ τάδ'· οἱ δ' ἐφόρουν τὰ χρήματα,
καὶ τόν γε τυρὸν οὐκ ἐῶντοc ἤcθιον
τούc τ' ἄρναc ἐξεφοροῦντο· δήcαντεc δὲ cὲ
κλωιῶι τριπήχει, κατὰ τὸν ὀφθαλμὸν μέcον   235
τὰ cπλάγχν' ἔφαcκον ἐξαμήcεcθαι βίαι,
μάcτιγί τ' εὖ τὸ νῶτον ἀπολέψειν cέθεν,
κἄπειτα cυνδήcαντεc ἐc θἀδώλια
τῆc ναὸc ἐμβαλόντεc ἀποδώcειν τινὶ
πέτρουc μοχλεύειν, ἢ 'c μυλῶνα καταβαλεῖν.   240

Kυ. ἄληθεc; οὔκουν κοπίδαc ὡc τάχιcτ' ἰὼν
θήξειc μαχαίραc καὶ μέγαν φάκελον ξύλων
ἐπιθεὶc ἀνάψειc; ὡc cφαγέντεc αὐτίκα
πλήcουcι νηδὺν τὴν ἐμὴν ἀπ' ἄνθρακοc

219 ὧν Kaibel   'μὲ Matthiae: με L   220 μ' Seidler: γ' L
227 μέτωπον Tyrwhitt: πρόcωπον L: cf. Ar. Equ. 631 (πρόcωπ' pro μέτωπ'
Crates ap. Athen. 367 A), Xen. Cyn. 4. 8   233 τῶν...τυρῶν Markland   ἐῶντοc P²: ἐόντοc L   234 ἐξεφροῦντο Musgrave   cὲ Nauck:
cε L   235 κατὰ Canter: κᾶτα L: cf. El. 910, Rh. 421, fr. 410. 3
236 ἐξαμήcεcθαι Duport: -cαcθαι L   237 ἀπολέψειν Ruhnken:
ἀποθλίψειν L   238 θἀδώλια Seidler: τἀδ- L   239 ναὸc Blaydes:
νηὸc L   240 ἢ 'c μυλῶνα Ruhnken: ἢ πυλῶνα L   243 ὡc apogr. Par.: ὣ L

θερμὴν διδόντες δαῖτα τῶι κρεανόμωι,   245
τὰ δ' ἐκ λέβητος ἐφθὰ καὶ τετηκότα.
ὡς ἔκπλεώς γε δαιτός εἰμ' ὀρεσκόου·
ἅλις λεόντων ἐστί μοι θοινωμένωι
ἐλάφων τε, χρόνιος δ' εἴμ' ἀπ' ἀνθρώπων βορᾶς.

Ci.   τὰ καινά γ' ἐκ τῶν ἠθάδων, ὦ δέσποτα,   250
ἡδίον' ἐστίν. οὐ γὰρ οὖν νεωστί γε
ἄλλοι πρὸς ἄντρα σοὐσαφίκοντο ξένοι.

Οδ.   Κύκλωψ, ἄκουσον ἐν μέρει καὶ τῶν ξένων.
ἡμεῖς βορᾶς χρήιζοντες ἐμπολὴν λαβεῖν
σῶν ἆσσον ἄντρων ἤλθομεν νεὼς ἄπο.   255
τοὺς δ' ἄρνας ἡμῖν οὗτος ἀντ' οἴνου σκύφου
ἀπημπόλα τε κἀδίδου πιεῖν λαβὼν
ἑκὼν ἑκοῦσι, κοὐδὲν ἦν τούτων βίαι.
ἀλλ' οὗτος ὑγιὲς οὐδὲν ὧν φησιν λέγει,
ἐπεὶ κατελήφθη σοῦ λάθραι πωλῶν τὰ σά.   260

Ci.   ἐγώ; κακῶς γ' ἄρ' ἐξόλοι'.   Οδ. εἰ ψεύδομαι.

Ci.   μὰ τὸν Ποσειδῶ τὸν τεκόντα σ', ὦ Κύκλωψ,
μὰ τὸν μέγαν Τρίτωνα καὶ τὸν Νηρέα,
μὰ τὴν Καλυψὼ τάς τε Νηρέως κόρας,
μὰ θαἱερὰ κύματ' ἰχθύων τε πᾶν γένος,   265
ἀπώμος', ὦ κάλλιστον ὦ Κυκλώπιον,
ὦ δεσποτίσκε, μὴ τὰ σ' ἐξοδᾶν ἐγὼ
ξένοισι χρήματ'. ἦ κακῶς οὗτοι κακοὶ
οἱ παῖδες ἀπόλοινθ', οὓς μάλιστ' ἐγὼ φιλῶ.

Χο.   αὐτὸς ἔχ'. ἔγωγε τοῖς ξένοις τὰ χρήματα   270
περνάντα σ' εἶδον· εἰ δ' ἐγὼ ψευδῆ λέγω,
ἀπόλοιθ' ὁ πατήρ μου· τοὺς ξένους δὲ μὴ ἀδίκει.

---

245 διδόντες Heath: ἔδοντος L (fort. ⁵δοντος L, ἔ- L¹ᶜ uel Tr¹)
247 εἰμ' ὀρεσκόου Stephanus: ἱμεροσκόου L   251 ἡδίον' Tr¹: ἤδιον L
οὖν Reiske: αὖ L   252 σοὐσαφίκοντο Murray: τὰ σ' ἀφίκοντο L: cf. 288,
561   258 τούτων Barnes: -τω L   260 γ' ἐλήφθη Heath, sed cf. 304
261 γ' ἄρ' Kirchhoff: γὰρ L: nisi mauis γ' ἄρ' (uide Lowe, Glotta 51
[1973] 34–64)   265 θαἱερὰ Franke: θ' ἱερὰ L: ad rhythmum uide 334
(θαἱρὰ scribere nolim)

Κυ.　ψεύδεσθ'· ἔγωγε τῷδε τοῦ 'Ραδαμάνθυος
　　μᾶλλον πέποιθα καὶ δικαιότερον λέγω.
　　θέλω δ' ἐρέσθαι· πόθεν ἐπλεύσατ', ὦ ξένοι;　　　275
　　ποδαποί; τίς ὑμᾶς ἐξεπαίδευσεν πόλις;
Οδ.　'Ιθακήcιοι μὲν τὸ γένος, 'Ιλίου δ' ἄπο,
　　πέρcαντες ἄcτυ, πνεύμαcιν θαλαccίοις
　　cὴν γαῖαν ἐξωcθέντες ἥκομεν, Κύκλωψ.
Κυ.　ἦ τῆς κακίcτης οἳ μετήλθεθ' ἁρπαγὰς　　　280
　　'Ελένης Cκαμάνδρου γείτον' 'Ιλίου πόλιν;
Οδ.　οὗτοι, πόνον τὸν δεινὸν ἐξηντληκότες.
Κυ.　αἰcχρὸν cτράτευμά γ', οἵτινες μιᾶς χάριν
　　γυναικὸς ἐξεπλεύcατ' ἐς γαῖαν Φρυγῶν.
Οδ.　θεοῦ τὸ πρᾶγμα· μηδέν' αἰτιῶ βροτῶν.　　　285
　　ἡμεῖς δέ c', ὦ θεοῦ ποντίου γενναῖε παῖ,
　　ἱκετεύομέν τε καὶ λέγομεν ἐλευθέρως·
　　μὴ τλῇς πρὸς ἄντρα coὐcαφιγμένους φίλους
　　κτανεῖν βοράν τε δυccεβῆ θέcθαι γνάθοις·
　　οἳ τὸν cόν, ὦναξ, πατέρ' ἔχειν ναῶν ἕδρας　　　290
　　ἐρρυcάμεcθα γῆς ἐν 'Ελλάδος μυχοῖς·
　　ἱερᾶς τ' ἄθραυcτος Ταινάρου μένει λιμὴν
　　Μαλέας τ' ἄκρας κευθμῶνες ἥ τε Cουνίου
　　δίας 'Αθάνας cῶς ὑπάργυρος πέτρα
　　Γεραίcτιοί τε καταφυγαί· τά θ' 'Ελλάδος　　　295
　　†δύcφρον' ὄνειδ†† Φρυξὶν οὐκ ἐδώκαμεν.
　　ὧν καὶ cὺ κοινοῖ· γῆς γὰρ 'Ελλάδος μυχοὺς
　　οἰκεῖς ὑπ' Αἴτνηι, τῆι πυριcτάκτωι πέτραι.
　　νόμος δὲ θνητοῖς, εἰ λόγους ἀποcτρέφηι,
　　ἱκέτας δέχεcθαι ποντίους ἐφθαρμένους　　　300

273 τῷδε Canter: τοῦδε L　　　274 μᾶλλον Kirchhoff: πολλὰ L
288 coὐcαφιγμένουc Radermacher: coὐc ἀφιγμένουc L: cf. 252　　290 ναῶν
Canter: νεῶν L　　　291 ἐρρυcάμεcθα Matthiae: εἰρυc- L　　　292 ἱερᾶc
Kassel: ἱερεύc L: ἱερός apogr. Par.　　　ἄθραυcτος Tr¹: ἄθαυcτος L
293 ἄκρας Seaford: ἄκροι L　　　ἦ apogr. Par.: οἳ L　　　295 post
h.u. lac. indic. Hermann　　　296 δύcφορά γ' apogr. Par. (-φρονά γ' Tr²)
δύcφορον ὄνειδος per parenthesin Diggle　　　297 κοινοῖ Seidler: κοινοῦ L
298 Αἴτνης Hermann　　　299 νόμος Musgrave: νόμοις L　　　εἰ Reiske:
εἰc L

ξένιά τε δοῦναι καὶ πέπλους ἐπαρκέσαι,
οὐκ ἀμφὶ βουπόροισι πηχθέντας μέλη
ὀβελοῖσι νηδὺν καὶ γνάθον πλῆσαι σέθεν.
ἄλις δὲ Πριάμου γαῖ' ἐχήρωσ' Ἑλλάδα
πολλῶν νεκρῶν πιοῦσα δοριπετῆ φόνον   305
ἀλόχους τ' ἀνάνδρους γραῦς τ' ἄπαιδας ὤλεσεν
πολιούς τε πατέρας. εἰ δὲ τοὺς λελειμμένους
σὺ συμπυρώσας δαῖτ' ἀναλώσεις πικράν,
ποῖ τρέψεταί τις; ἀλλ' ἐμοὶ πιθοῦ, Κύκλωψ·
πάρες τὸ μάργον σῆς γνάθου, τὸ δ' εὐσεβὲς   310
τῆς δυσσεβείας ἀνθελοῦ· πολλοῖσι γὰρ
κέρδη πονηρὰ ζημίαν ἠμείψατο.

Cι. παραινέσαι σοι βούλομαι· τῶν γὰρ κρεῶν
μηδὲν λίπηις τοῦδ'· ἢν δὲ τὴν γλῶσσαν δάκηις,
κομψὸς γενήσηι καὶ λαλίστατος, Κύκλωψ.   315

Κυ. ὁ πλοῦτος, ἀνθρωπίσκε, τοῖς σοφοῖς θεός,
τὰ δ' ἄλλα κόμποι καὶ λόγων εὐμορφία.
ἄκρας δ' ἐναλίας αἷς καθίδρυται πατὴρ
χαίρειν κελεύω· τί τάδε προυστήσω λόγωι;
Ζηνὸς δ' ἐγὼ κεραυνὸν οὐ φρίσσω, ξένε,   320
οὐδ' οἶδ' ὅτι Ζεύς ἐστ' ἐμοῦ κρείσσων θεός.
οὔ μοι μέλει τὸ λοιπόν· ὡς δ' οὔ μοι μέλει
ἄκουσον· ὅταν ἄνωθεν ὄμβρον ἐκχέηι,
ἐν τῆιδε πέτραι στέγν' ἔχων σκηνώματα,
ἢ μόσχον ὀπτὸν ἤ τι θήρειον δάκος   325
δαινύμενος, εὖ τέγγων τε γαστέρ' ὑπτίαν,
ἐπεκπιὼν γάλακτος ἀμφορέα, πέπλον
κρούω, Διὸς βρονταῖσιν εἰς ἔριν κτυπῶν.
ὅταν δὲ βορέας χιόνα Θρήικιος χέηι,
δοραῖσι θηρῶν σῶμα περιβαλὼν ἐμὸν   330

301 πέπλους Blaydes: -οις L   305 δοριπετῆ Nauck: δορυπ- L
314 δὲ Lenting: τε L   316 τοῖς Tr²: τοῖ L   317 εὐμορφία Nauck:
-ίαι L   318 αἷς Paley: ἆς L   324 στεγάν' Blaydes   ἔχων Reiske:
ἔχω L, quo seruato καὶ μόσχον 325 Boissonade   326 εὖ τέγγων τε
Reiske: ἐν στέγοντι L   327 πέδον Musgrave   330 περιβαλὼν Tr¹:
-λαβὼν L

καὶ πῦρ ἀναίθων, χιόνος οὐδέν μοι μέλει.
ἡ γῆ δ' ἀνάγκηι, κἂν θέληι κἂν μὴ θέληι,
τίκτουca ποίαν τἀμὰ πιαίνει βοτά.
ἀγὼ οὔτινι θύω πλὴν ἐμοί, θεοῖcι δ' οὔ,
καὶ τῆι μεγίcτηι, γαcτρὶ τῆιδε, δαιμόνων.   335
ὡc τοὐμπιεῖν γε καὶ φαγεῖν τοὐφ' ἡμέραν,
Ζεὺc οὗτοc ἀνθρώποιcι τοῖcι cώφροcιν,
λυπεῖν δὲ μηδὲν αὑτόν. οἳ δὲ τοὺc νόμουc
ἔθεντο ποικίλλοντεc ἀνθρώπων βίον,
κλαίειν ἄνωγα· τὴν ⟨δ'⟩ ἐμὴν ψυχὴν ἐγὼ   340
οὐ παύcομαι δρῶν εὖ, κατεcθίων γε cέ.
ξένια δὲ λήψηι τοιάδ', ὡc ἄμεμπτοc ὦ,
πῦρ καὶ πατρῶιον τόνδε χαλκόν, ὃc ζέcαc
cὴν cάρκα διαφόρητον ἀμφέξει καλῶc.
ἀλλ' ἕρπετ' εἴcω, τοῦ κατ' αὔλιον θεοῦ   345
ἵν' ἀμφὶ βωμὸν cτάντεc εὐωχῆτέ με.

Οδ.   αἰαῖ, πόνουc μὲν Τρωϊκοὺc ὑπεξέδυν
θαλαccίουc τε, νῦν δ' ἐc ἀνδρὸc ἀνοcίου
ὠμὴν κατέcχον ἀλίμενόν τε καρδίαν.
ὦ Παλλάc, ὦ δέcποινα Διογενὲc θεά,   350
νῦν νῦν ἄρηξον· κρείccονac γὰρ Ἰλίου
πόνουc ἀφῖγμαι κἀπὶ κινδύνου βάθρα.
cύ τ', ὦ φαεννᾶc ἀcτέρων οἰκῶν ἕδραc
Ζεῦ ξένι', ὅρα τάδ'· εἰ γὰρ αὐτὰ μὴ βλέπειc,
ἄλλωc νομίζηι Ζεὺc τὸ μηδὲν ὢν θεόc.   355

333 φύουca Athenag. leg. 25. 2 (~ Plut. mor. 435 B)   334 οὔτι
Hermann: cf. 265, Men. Asp. 219   336 τοὐμπιεῖν Reiske: τοῦ πιεῖν L
κἀμφαγεῖν Reiske   338 λυπεῖν Tr²: λιπεῖν L   340 ⟨δ'⟩ Barnes
341 γε Hermann: τέ L   cέ Fix: ce L   342 δὲ Fix: τε L   ἄμεμπτοc
Aldina: ἄμεπτοc L   343 χαλκόν Jackson: λέβητά γ' L   344 διαφόρητον Scaliger: δυcφόρητον L: δυcφόρητοc Seaford   345 τοῦ...θεοῦ
Blaydes: τῶ...θεῶ L   346 βωμὸν Stephanus: κῶμον L   349 ὠμὴν
Reiske: γνώμην L   352 βάθη Musgrave   353 φαεννᾶc Kassel:
-ῶν L   354 ζεῦ Tr¹: ζεὺc Lᵘᵛ

Χο. Εὐρείας φάρυγος, ὦ Κύκλωψ,   [στρ.
  ἀναστόμου τὸ χεῖλος· ὡς ἕτοιμά σοι
  ἐφθὰ καὶ ὀπτὰ καὶ ἀνθρακιᾶς ἄπο ⟨θερμὰ⟩
  χναύειν βρύκειν
  κρεοκοπεῖν μέλη ξένων
  δασυμάλλωι ἐν αἰγίδι κλινομένωι.   360

  μὴ 'μοὶ μὴ προσδίδου·   [μεσωιδ.
  μόνος μόνωι γέμιζε πορθμίδος σκάφος.
  χαιρέτω μὲν αὖλις ἅδε,
  χαιρέτω δὲ θυμάτων
  ἀποβώμιος †ἃν ἔχει θυσίαν†   365
  Κύκλωψ Αἰτναῖος ξενικῶν
  κρεῶν κεχαρμένος βορᾶι.

  †νηλὴς ὦ τλᾶμον ὅςτις δωμάτων†   [ἀντ.
  ἐφεστίους ἱκτῆρας ἐκθύει δόμων,   371
  ἐφθά τε δαινύμενος μυσαροῖσί τ' ὀδοῦσιν   373
  κόπτων βρύκων   372
  θέρμ' ἀπ' ἀνθράκων κρέα   374
  ⟨   ⟩.

Οδ. ὦ Ζεῦ, τί λέξω, δείν' ἰδὼν ἄντρων ἔσω   375
  κοὐ πιστά, μύθοις εἰκότ' οὐδ' ἔργοις βροτῶν;

356 φάρυγος Hermann: -γγος L   357 ἀναστομοῦ Wilamowitz
358 ἄπο ⟨θερμὰ⟩ χναύειν praeeunte Musgrave (ἄπο χν-) Hermann: ἀπο-
χναύειν L   βρύκειν Casaubon: βρύχ- L   359 κρεοκοπεῖν apogr. Par., L.
Dindorf: κρεω- L   360 κλινομένωι Reiske: καινόμενα L (-ό- Tr¹,
-ού- Lᵘᵛ)   361 'μοὶ Conradt: μοι L   362 γέμιζε Wecklein: κόμιζε L
363 ἅδε Dindorf: ἥδε L   365 ἃν ἀνάγει Jackson (CQ 35 [1941] 37)
θυσία Hartung   370 aut δωμάτων delendum (Murray) aut 371 ξένους
pro δόμων scribendum (Kirchhoff)   371 ἐφεστίους Bothe: ἐφεστίους
ξενικοὺς L   373 ante 372 trai. Hermann   μυσαροῖσί τ' Kirchhoff:
-οῖσιν L (fort. -οῖς** L, -οῖσιν L¹ᶜ)   372 βρύκων Casaubon: βρύχ- L
374 θέρμ' Hermann: ἀνθρώπων θέρμ' L   post h.u. ⟨δασυμάλλωι ἐν αἰγίδι
κλινόμενος⟩ Haupt   376 μύθοις ⟨δ'⟩ Dawe

Χο.   τί δ' ἔcτ', 'Οδυccεῦ; μῶν τεθοίναται cέθεν
      φίλουc ἑταίρουc ἀνοcιώτατοc Κύκλωψ;
Οδ.   διccούc γ' ἀθρήcac κἀπιβαcτάcαc χεροῖν,
      οἳ cαρκὸc εἶχον εὐτραφέcτατον πάχοc.   380
Χο.   πῶc, ὦ ταλαίπωρ', ἧτε πάcχοντεc τάδε;
Οδ.   ἐπεὶ πετραίαν τήνδ' ἐcήλθομεν †χθόνα†,
      ἀνέκαυcε μὲν πῦρ πρῶτον, ὑψηλῆc δρυὸc
      κορμοὺc πλατείαc ἐcχάραc βαλὼν ἔπι,
      τριccῶν ἁμαξῶν ὡc ἀγώγιμον βάροc,   385
      καὶ χάλκεον λέβητ' ἐπέζεcεν πυρί.   392
      ἔπειτα φύλλων ἐλατίνων χαμαιπετῆ   386
      ἔcτρωcεν εὐνὴν πληcίον πυρὸc φλογί.
      κρατῆρα δ' ἐξέπληcεν ὡc δεκάμφορον,
      μόcχουc ἀμέλξαc, λευκὸν ἐcχέαc γάλα,
      cκύφοc τε κιccοῦ παρέθετ' εἰc εὖροc τριῶν   390
      πήχεων, βάθοc δὲ τεccάρων ἐφαίνετο,   391
      ὀβελούc τ', ἄκρουc μὲν ἐγκεκαυμένουc πυρί,   393
      ξεcτοὺc δὲ δρεπάνωι τἆλλα, παλιούρου κλάδων,
      †Αἰτναῖά τε cφαγεῖα πελέκεων γνάθοιc†.   395
      ὡc δ' ἦν ἕτοιμα πάντα τῶι θεοcτυγεῖ
      Ἅιδου μαγείρωι, φῶτε cυμμάρψαc δύο
      ἔcφαζ' ἑταίρων τῶν ἐμῶν, ῥυθμῶι θ' ἑνὶ
      τὸν μὲν λέβητοc ἐc κύτοc χαλκήλατον
      ⟨   ⟩
      τὸν δ' αὖ, τένοντοc ἁρπάcαc ἄκρου ποδόc,   400
      παίων πρὸc ὀξὺν cτόνυχα πετραίου λίθου

377 τεθοίναται Reiske: γε θοινᾶται L   379 cταθμήcαc Pierson
380 εὐτραφέcτατον Scaliger: ἐντρεφ- L: εὐτρεφ- P²   381 ἧcτε Nauck
382 cτέγην Musgrave   392 huc trai. Paley (post 395 Hartung)
387 ἔcτρωcεν Pierson: ἔcτηcεν L.   389 ἐγχέαc Herwerden
390 cκύφον Blaydes   392. uide post 385   394 τἆλλα Scaliger: γ'
ἀλλὰ L   κλάδων Scaliger: -δω L et Athen. 650 A: -δουc Kirchhoff
395 ante h.u. lac. indic. Boissonade, post h.u. Fix   u. delere malit
Diggle   397 Ἅιδου Stephanus: δίδου L   δύο apogr. Par.,
Matthiae: δύω L   398 θ' ἑνὶ Wilamowitz: τινί L
399 κύτοc Aldina: cκύτοc L   post h.u. lac. indic. Diggle   401 cτόνυχα Scaliger: γ' ὄνυχα L

78 ΕΥΡΙΠΙΔΟΥ

ἐγκέφαλον ἐξέρρανε· καὶ †καθαρπάσας†
λάβρωι μαχαίραι σάρκας ἐξώπτα πυρί,
τὰ δ' ἐς λέβητ' ἐφῆκεν ἕψεσθαι μέλη.
ἐγὼ δ' ὁ τλήμων δάκρυ' ἀπ' ὀφθαλμῶν χέων   405
ἐχριμπτόμην Κύκλωπι κἀδιακόνουν·
ἄλλοι δ' ὅπως ὄρνιθες ἐν μυχοῖς πέτρας
πτήξαντες εἶχον, αἷμα δ' οὐκ ἐνῆν χροΐ.
ἐπεὶ δ' ἑταίρων τῶν ἐμῶν πλησθεὶς βορᾶς
ἀνέπεσε, φάρυγος αἰθέρ' ἐξανεὶς βαρύν,   410
ἐσῆλθέ μοί τι θεῖον· ἐμπλήσας σκύφος
Μάρωνος αὐτῶι τοῦδε προσφέρω πιεῖν,
λέγων τάδ'· Ὦ τοῦ ποντίου θεοῦ Κύκλωψ,
σκέψαι τόδ' οἷον Ἑλλὰς ἀμπέλων ἄπο
θεῖον κομίζει πῶμα, Διονύσου γάνος.   415
ὁ δ' ἔκπλεως ὢν τῆς ἀναισχύντου βορᾶς
ἐδέξατ' ἔσπασέν ⟨τ'⟩ ἄμυστιν ἑλκύσας
κἀπήινεσ'· ἄρας χεῖρα· Φίλτατε ξένων,
καλὸν τὸ πῶμα δαιτὶ πρὸς καλῆι δίδως.
ἡσθέντα δ' αὐτὸν ὡς ἐπηισθόμην ἐγώ,   420
ἄλλην ἔδωκα κύλικα, γιγνώσκων ὅτι
τρώσει νιν οἶνος καὶ δίκην δώσει τάχα.
καὶ δὴ πρὸς ὠιδὰς εἷρπ'· ἐγὼ δ' ἐπεγχέων
ἄλλην ἐπ' ἄλληι σπλάγχν' ἐθέρμαινον ποτῶι.
ἄιδει δὲ παρὰ κλαίουσι συνναύταις ἐμοῖς   425
ἄμουσ', ἐπηχεῖ δ' ἄντρον. ἐξελθὼν δ' ἐγὼ
σιγῆι σὲ σῶσαι κἄμ', ἐὰν βούληι, θέλω.
ἀλλ' εἴπατ' εἴτε χρήιζετ' εἴτ' οὐ χρήιζετε

402 διαρπάσας uel διαρταμῶν Paley   404 τὰ δ' Heath: τάδ' L
406 κἀδιακόνουν Dindorf: καὶ διηκ- L   407 ἄλλοι Kirchhoff: ἄλλοι L
410 φάρυγος Scaliger: -γγος L et Athen. 23 E   ἐξανεὶς Porson: ἐξιεὶς
L: ἐξανιεὶς Athen.   411 σκύφον Blaydes   412 αὐτῶι τοῦδε
L. Dindorf: αὐτοῦ τῶδε L   413 ὦ παῖ Aldina, sed cf. IT 1230, Ion
1619   417 ⟨τ'⟩ Barnes   419 καλῆ Tr²: -ὸν L: -ῆ Lˢ uel Tr¹
422 οἶνος post Herwerden (ὤινος) Murray: οἰ- L   425 συνναύταις
Aldina: σὺν ν- L   426 ἐπηχεῖ Barnes: ἐπήχει L

φεύγειν ἄμεικτον ἄνδρα καὶ τὰ Βακχίου
ναίειν μέλαθρα Ναΐδων νυμφῶν μέτα.   430
ὁ μὲν γὰρ ἔνδον còς πατὴρ τάδ' ᾔνεσεν·
ἀλλ' ἀсθενὴс γὰρ κἀποκερδαίνων ποτοῦ
ὥсπερ πρὸς ἰξῶι τῆι κύλικι λελημμένοс
πτέρυγας ἀλύει· cὺ δέ (νεανίας γὰρ εἶ)
cώθητι μετ' ἐμοῦ καὶ τὸν ἀρχαῖον φίλον   435
Διόνυсον ἀνάλαβ', οὐ Κύκλωπι προσφερῆ.

Χο. ὦ φίλτατ', εἰ γὰρ τήνδ' ἴδοιμεν ἡμέραν
Κύκλωπος ἐκφυγόντες ἀνόсιον κάρα.
ὡς διὰ μακροῦ γε †τὸν сίφωνα τὸν φίλον
χηρεύομεν τόνδ' οὐκ ἔχομεν καταφαγεῖν.†   440

Οδ. ἄκουε δή νυν ἣν ἔχω τιμωρίαν
θηρὸς πανούργου сῆς τε δουλείας φυγήν.

Χο. λέγ', ὡς 'Ἀсιάδος οὐκ ἂν ἥδιον ψόφον
κιθάρας κλύοιμεν ἢ Κύκλωπ' ὀλωλότα.

Οδ. ἐπὶ κῶμον ἕρπειν πρὸς κασιγνήτους θέλει   445
Κύκλωπας ἡсθεὶς τῶιδε Βακχίου ποτῶι.

Χο. ξυνῆκ'· ἔρημον ξυλλαβὼν δρυμοῖсί νιν
сφάξαι μενοινᾶιс ἢ πετρῶν ὦсαι κάτα.

Οδ. οὐδὲν τοιοῦτον· δόλιος ἡ προθυμία.

Χο. πῶс δαί; сοφόν τοί с' ὄντ' ἀκούομεν πάλαι.   450

Οδ. κώμου μὲν αὐτὸν τοῦδ' ἀπαλλάξαι, λέγων
ὡς οὐ Κύκλωψι πῶμα χρὴ δοῦναι τόδε,
μόνον δ' ἔχοντα βίοτον ἡδέως ἄγειν.
ὅταν δ' ὑπνώссηι Βακχίου νικώμενος,
ἀκρεμὼν ἐλαίας ἔсτιν ἐν δόμοιсί τις,   455
ὃν φασγάνωι τῶιδ' ἐξαποξύνας ἄκρον

429 ἄμεικτον Murray: ἄμικτον L   430 Ναΐδων Casaubon: δαναίδων L
436 ἀνάλαβ' οὐ apogr. Par.: ἀναλαβοῦ L   439–40 τὸν φίλον χηρεύομεν
(uel -ομαι) / сίφωνα τόνδε Diggle (de seqq. despero)   440 οὐκ Tr¹:
ἐκ L   καταφυγεῖν apogr. Par., καταφυγήν Hermann   445 ἐπίκωμος
Wecklein   447 δρυμοῖсί Tyrwhitt: ῥυθμοῖсί L   448 κάτα apogr.
Par., Nauck: κάτω L   449 ἡ προθυμία Musgrave: ἡ 'πιθυμία L
453 βίοτον Tr¹: βίοντον L   454 ὑπνώсσηι Hermann: -ώсη L: -ωθῆι
(-ωсθῆι) Dobree   456 ἐξαποξύνας Tr¹: ἀποξ- L, quo seruato
φασγάνωι ⟨'γὼ⟩ Murray

ἐc πῦρ καθήcω· κᾆθ' ὅταν κεκαυμένον
ἴδω νιν, ἄρας θερμὸν ἐc μέcην βαλῶ
Κύκλωπος ὄψιν ὄμμα τ' ἐκτήξω πυρί.
ναυπηγίαν δ' ὡcεί τις ἁρμόζων ἀνὴρ   460
διπλοῖν χαλινοῖν τρύπανον κωπηλατεῖ,
οὕτω κυκλώcω δαλὸν ἐν φαεcφόρωι
Κύκλωπος ὄψει καὶ cυναυανῶ κόρας.

Χο. ἰοὺ ἰού·
γέγηθα μαινόμεcθα τοῖc εὑρήμαcιν.   465

Οδ. κἄπειτα καὶ cὲ καὶ φίλους γέροντά τε
νεὼc μελαίνης κοῖλον ἐμβήcας cκάφος
διπλαῖcι κώπαιc τῆcδ' ἀποcτελῶ χθονός.

Χο. ἔcτ' οὖν ὅπως ἂν ὡcπερεὶ cπονδῆc θεοῦ
κἀγὼ λαβοίμην τοῦ τυφλοῦντος ὄμματα   470
δαλοῦ; πόνου γὰρ τοῦδε κοινωνεῖν θέλω.

Οδ. δεῖ γοῦν· μέγας γὰρ δαλός, οὗ ξυλληπτέον.

Χο. ὡc κἂν ἁμαξῶν ἑκατὸν ἀραίμην βάρος,
εἰ τοῦ Κύκλωπος τοῦ κακῶc ὀλουμένου
ὀφθαλμὸν ὥσπερ cφηκιὰν ἐκθύψομεν.   475

Οδ. cιγᾶτέ νυν· δόλον γὰρ ἐξεπίcταcαι·
χὥταν κελεύω, τοῖcιν ἀρχιτέκτοcιν
πείθεcθ'. ἐγὼ γὰρ ἄνδρας ἀπολιπὼν φίλους
τοὺς ἔνδον ὄντας οὐ μόνος cωθήcομαι.
[καίτοι φύγοιμ' ἂν κἀκβέβηκ' ἄντρου μυχῶν·   480
ἀλλ' οὐ δίκαιον ἀπολιπόντ' ἐμοὺς φίλους
ξὺν οἵcπερ ἦλθον δεῦρο cωθῆναι μόνον.]

Χο. ἄγε, τίς πρῶτος, τίς δ' ἐπὶ πρώτωι
ταχθεὶς δαλοῦ κώπην ὀχμάcαι

458–9 βαλῶ...ὄμμα τ' Pierson: βαλὼν...ὄμματ' L   462 κυκλήcω
Musgrave   464 ἰοῦ ἰοῦ Hermann   468 ἀποcτελῶ Tr¹ˢ pot. qu. Tr²ᵃ:
-cτέλλω L   469 ὡcπερεὶ Reiske: ὥcπερ ἐκ L   471 πόνου Nauck:
φόνου L   472 οὗ Reiske: ὃν L   473 ἀραίμην Matthiae: ἀροίμην L
475 ἐκθύψομεν Hertlein: ἐκθρύψ- L   480–2 del. nescioquis (Phil.
Anz. 4 [1872] 332), denuo Conradt   481 ἐμοὺς apogr. Par.: ἐμοῦ L
484 δαλοῦ Stephanus: -ῶ L   ὀχμάcαι Musgrave: -cαc L

Κύκλωπος ἔσω βλεφάρων ὤσας   485
λαμπρὰν ὄψιν διακναίσει;
[*ὠιδὴ ἔνδοθεν.*]
σίγα σίγα. καὶ δὴ μεθύων
ἄχαριν κέλαδον μουσιζόμενος
σκαιὸς ἀπωιδὸς καὶ κλαυσόμενος   490
χωρεῖ πετρίνων ἔξω μελάθρων.
φέρε νιν κώμοις παιδεύσωμεν
τὸν ἀπαίδευτον·
πάντως μέλλει τυφλὸς εἶναι.

μάκαρ ὅστις εὐιάζει   [στρ. α
βοτρύων φίλαισι πηγαῖς   496
ἐπὶ κῶμον ἐκπετασθεὶς
φίλον ἄνδρ' ὑπαγκαλίζων,
ἐπὶ δεμνίοις τε †ξανθὸν†
χλιδανᾶς ἔχων ἑταίρας   500
μυρόχριστος λιπαρὸν βό-
στρυχον, αὐδᾶι δέ· Θύραν τίς οἴξει μοι;

Κυ.   *παπαπαῖ· πλέως μὲν οἴνου,*   [στρ. β
    γάνυμαι ⟨δὲ⟩ δαιτὸς ἥβαι,
    σκάφος ὁλκὰς ὣς γεμισθεὶς   505
    ποτὶ σέλμα γαστρὸς ἄκρας.
    ὑπάγει μ' ὁ φόρτος εὔφρων
    ἐπὶ κῶμον ἦρος ὥραις
    ἐπὶ Κύκλωπας ἀδελφούς.
    φέρε μοι, ξεῖνε, φέρ', ἀσκὸν ἔνδος μοι.   510

487 hanc παρεπιγραφήν in textu habet L   490 κατακλαυσόμενος Hermann, τάχα κλ- Fix   491 χωρεῖ Tr²: χωρεῖ γε L   492 νυν Diggle 495 μάκαρ Hermann: μακάριος L   497 ἐπίκωμος Wilamowitz 500 χλιδανᾶς Diggle: -ῆς L   501 λιπαρὸν Scaliger: -ὸς L, quo seruato μυρόχριστον Musgrave   502 τίς Aldina: τις L   503 παπαπαῖ Hermann: πα πα πᾶ L   504 ⟨δὲ⟩ Tr²   ἥβαι post Lobeck (-ηι) Diggle: -ης L   507 φόρτος Seymour: χόρτος L   508 ἐπίκωμον Wecklein 510 ξεῖνε φέρ' Tr²: φέρε ξέν' ⟨L⟩P

Χο.　καλὸν ὄμμασιν δεδορκὼς　　　　　　　　　　　[στρ. γ
　　　καλὸς ἐκπερᾶι μελάθρων.
　　　⟨　　　　⟩ φιλεῖ τίς ἡμᾶς;
　　　λύχνα δ' †ἀμμένει δαῖα σὸν
　　　χρόα χὼς† τέρεινα νύμφα　　　　　　　　　　　515
　　　δροσερῶν ἔςωθεν ἄντρων.
　　　στεφάνων δ' οὐ μία χροιὰ
　　　περὶ σὸν κρᾶτα τάχ' ἐξομιλήςει.

Οδ.　Κύκλωψ, ἄκουσον· ὡς ἐγὼ τοῦ Βακχίου
　　　τούτου τρίβων εἴμ', ὃν πιεῖν ἔδωκά σοι.　　　520
Κυ.　ὁ Βάκχιος δὲ τίς; θεὸς νομίζεται;
Οδ.　μέγιστος ἀνθρώποισιν ἐς τέρψιν βίου.
Κυ.　ἐρυγγάνω γοῦν αὐτὸν ἡδέως ἐγώ.
Οδ.　τοιόςδ' ὁ δαίμων· οὐδένα βλάπτει βροτῶν.
Κυ.　θεὸς δ' ἐν ἀσκῶι πῶς γέγηθ' οἴκους ἔχων;　　525
Οδ.　ὅπου τιθῆι τις, ἐνθάδ' ἐστὶν εὐπετής.
Κυ.　οὐ τοὺς θεοὺς χρὴ σῶμ' ἔχειν ἐν δέρμασιν.
Οδ.　τί δ', εἴ σε τέρπει γ'; ἢ τὸ δέρμα σοι πικρόν;
Κυ.　μισῶ τὸν ἀσκόν· τὸ δὲ ποτὸν φιλῶ τόδε.
Οδ.　μένων νυν αὐτοῦ πῖνε κεὐθύμει, Κύκλωψ.　　530
Κυ.　οὐ χρή μ' ἀδελφοῖς τοῦδε προσδοῦναι ποτοῦ;
Οδ.　ἔχων γὰρ αὐτὸς τιμιώτερος φανῆι.
Κυ.　διδοὺς δὲ τοῖς φίλοισι χρησιμώτερος.
Οδ.　πυγμὰς ὁ κῶμος λοίδορόν τ' ἔριν φιλεῖ.
Κυ.　μεθύω μέν, ἔμπας δ' οὔτις ἂν ψαύσειέ μου.　535
Οδ.　ὦ τᾶν, πεπωκότ' ἐν δόμοισι χρὴ μένειν.
Κυ.　ἠλίθιος ὅστις μὴ πιὼν κῶμον φιλεῖ.

512 καλὸς Scaliger: -ὸν L　　　　ἐκπερᾶις Heath, ἐκπέρα Scaliger
513 τις Aldina　　514–15 desperati (uide Maia 24 [1972] 345–7, JHS
97 [1977] 138–9)　　ἀμμένει Tr¹ uel Tr² et P: ἀμμέν•• L (-ον teste Prinz;
fort. pot. -ει)　　517 χροιὰ Barnes: χρόα L　　520 οὐ Lenting　　πιεῖν
apogr. Par.: πιὼν L　　521 u. dist. Nauck: ad rhythmum cf. Med. 701
525 οἴκους Canter: οἴνους L　　526 τιθῆι Porson: τιθεῖ L　　527 οὗτοι
Herwerden　　δῶμ' Pierson　　534 πληγὰς...θ' ὕβριν φέρει Athen.
36 D　　535 μεθύω μέν Reiske: μεθύωμεν L

Οδ. ὃς δ' ἂν μεθυσθείς γ' ἐν δόμοις μείνηι σοφός.
Κυ. τί δρῶμεν, ὦ Cιληνέ; coὶ μένειν δοκεῖ;
Cι. δοκεῖ· τί γὰρ δεῖ cυμποτῶν ἄλλων, Κύκλωψ;   540
Οδ. καὶ μὴν λαχνῶδές γ' οὖδας ἀνθηρᾶς χλόης.
Cι. καὶ πρός γε θάλπος ἡλίου πίνειν καλόν.
    κλίθητί νύν μοι πλευρὰ θεὶς ἐπὶ χθονός.
Κυ. ἰδού.
    τί δῆτα τὸν κρατῆρ' ὄπισθ' ἐμοῦ τίθης;   545
Cι. ὡς μὴ παριών τις καταβάληι. Κυ. πίνειν μὲν οὖν
    κλέπτων cὺ βούληι· κάτθες αὐτὸν ἐς μέcον.
    cὺ δ', ὦ ξέν', εἰπὲ τοὔνομ' ὅτι cε χρὴ καλεῖν.
Οδ. Οὖτιν· χάριν δὲ τίνα λαβών c' ἐπαινέcω;
Κυ. πάντων c' ἑταίρων ὕcτερον θοινάcομαι.   550
Cι. καλόν γε τὸ γέρας τῶι ξένωι δίδως, Κύκλωψ.
Κυ. οὗτος, τί δρᾶις; τὸν οἶνον ἐκπίνεις λάθραι;
Cι. οὔκ, ἀλλ' ἔμ' οὗτος ἔκυcεν ὅτι καλὸν βλέπω.
Κυ. κλαύcηι, φιλῶν τὸν οἶνον οὐ φιλοῦντα cέ.
Cι. οὐ μὰ Δί', ἐπεί μού φηc' ἐρᾶν ὄντος καλοῦ.   555
Κυ. ἔγχει, πλέων δὲ τὸν cκύφον δίδου μόνον.
Cι. πῶς οὖν κέκραται; φέρε διαcκεψώμεθα.
Κυ. ἀπολεῖc· δὸς οὕτως. Cι. οὐ μὰ Δί', οὐ πρὶν ἄν γέ cε
    cτέφανον ἴδω λαβόντα γεύcωμαί τ' ἔτι.
Κυ. οἰνοχόος ἄδικος. Cι. ⟨οὐ⟩ μὰ Δί', ἀλλ' οἶνος
    γλυκύς.   560
    ἀπομακτέον δέ coὐcτὶν ὡς λήψηι πιεῖν.

541[n] Οδ. Mancini: κυ. L   541 γ' οὖδας Porson: τοὖδας L   ἀνθηρᾶι
χλόηι Kirchhoff   544 ἰδού add. Tr[1]: om. L   545 ὄπισθ' ἐμοῦ
Diggle: -θέ μου L   τίθης Tr[2]: τιθεὶς L   546 παριών Reiske: παρών L
καταβάλη P[2]: -λάβη L   550 ὕcτατον Hermann   551[n] Cι. Lenting:
ὀδ. L   553[n] cι. L[1c] uel Tr[1]: ὀδ. L   554 cέ Diggle: cε L   555 οὐ
Diggle: ναὶ L   φηc' Florens Christianus: φὴc L   558 οὐ (prius)
Wecklein: ναὶ L: ceterum οὐ μὰ Δία πρὶν Blaydes, Kaibel, νὴ Δί' οὐ πρὶν
Diggle   559 τέ τι Nauck   560 οἰνοχόος Canter (ὦιν-): ὦ οἰν- L
⟨οὐ⟩ Hermann: rasura in L: ⟨ναὶ⟩ Aldina   οἶνος Canter (ὦιν-):
ὦνος L: hoc seruato scribendum ὠινοχόος   561 ἀπομακτέον Cobet:
-μυκτέον L   coὐcτὶν ὡς Wilamowitz: coι ὡς L: coί γ' ὅπως Tr[1]

Κυ.　ἰδού, καθαρὸν τὸ χεῖλος αἱ τρίχες τέ μου.
Ci.　θές νυν τὸν ἀγκῶν' εὐρύθμως κᾆτ' ἔκπιε,
　　ὥσπερ μ' ὁρᾶις πίνοντα χὤσπερ οὐκ ἐμέ.
Κυ.　ἆ ἆ, τί δράςεις; Ci. ἡδέως ἡμύςτιςα.　　565
Κυ.　λάβ', ὦ ξέν', αὐτὸς οἰνοχόος τέ μοι γενοῦ.
Οδ.　γιγνώςκεται γοῦν ἄμπελος τῆμῆι χερί.
Κυ.　φέρ' ἔγχεόν νυν. Οδ. ἐγχέω, ςίγα μόνον.
Κυ.　χαλεπὸν τόδ' εἶπας, ὅςτις ἂν πίνηι πολύν.
Οδ.　ἰδού, λαβὼν ἔκπιθι καὶ μηδὲν λίπηις·　　570
　　ςυνεκθανεῖν δὲ ςπῶντα χρὴ τῶι πώματι.
Κυ.　παπαῖ, ςοφόν γε τὸ ξύλον τῆς ἀμπέλου.
Οδ.　κἂν μὲν ςπάςηις γε δαιτὶ πρὸς πολλῆι πολύν,
　　τέγξας ἄδιψον νηδύν, εἰς ὕπνον βαλεῖ,
　　ἢν δ' ἐλλίπηις τι, ξηρανεῖ ς' ὁ Βάκχιος.　　575
Κυ.　ἰοὺ ἰού·
　　ὡς ἐξένευςα μόγις· ἄκρατος ἡ χάρις.
　　ὁ δ' οὐρανός μοι ςυμμεμειγμένος δοκεῖ
　　τῆι γῆι φέρεςθαι, τοῦ Διός τε τὸν θρόνον
　　λεύςςω τὸ πᾶν τε δαιμόνων ἁγνὸν ςέβας.　　580
　　οὐκ ἂν φιλήςαιμ'; αἱ Χάριτες πειρῶςί με.
　　ἅλις· Γανυμήδη τόνδ' ἔχων ἀναπαύςομαι
　　κάλλιον ἢ τὰς Χάριτας. ἥδομαι δέ πως
　　τοῖς παιδικοῖςι μᾶλλον ἢ τοῖς θήλεςιν.
Ci.　ἐγὼ γὰρ ὁ Διός εἰμι Γανυμήδης, Κύκλωψ;　　585
Κυ.　ναὶ μὰ Δί', ὃν ἁρπάζω γ' ἐγὼ 'κ τῆς Δαρδάνου.
Ci.　ἀπόλωλα, παῖδες· ςχέτλια πείςομαι κακά.
Κυ.　μέμφηι τὸν ἐραςτὴν κἀντρυφᾶις πεπωκότι;

564 οὐκ ἐμέ] οὐκέτι Nauck　　566 λάβ' ὦ...τέ μοι Dobree: λαβὼν...
γέ μου L　　569 πίηι Fix　　571 ςπῶντα Casaubon: ςιγῶντα L
573 ςπάςηις Dobree: -ςη L　　574 βαλεῖ Musgrave: -εῖς L　　575 ἐλλίπηις Herwerden: ἐκλ- L　　576 ἰοὺ ἰού Hermann　　577 μόλις Nauck
581 interrogationis notam add. Wilamowitz　　582 post ἅλις dist.
Wecklein　　　Γανυμήδη Elmsley: -δην L　　583 κάλλιον ἢ Spengel:
κάλλιςτα νὴ L　　586 τῆς Hermann: τοῦ L: cf. Hcld. 140, Ion 1297
588 κἀντρυφᾶις Casaubon: -αῖς L　　πεπωκότι Scaliger: -ότα L

Κι.   οἴμοι· πικρότατον οἶνον ὄψομαι τάχα.

Οδ.   ἄγε δή, Διονύcου παῖδεc, εὐγενῆ τέκνα,   590
      ἔνδον μὲν ἀνήρ· τῶι δ' ὕπνωι παρειμένοc
      τάχ' ἐξ ἀναιδοῦc φάρυγοc ὠθήcει κρέα.
      δαλὸc δ' ἔcωθεν αὐλίων †ὠθεῖ† καπνὸν
      παρευτρέπιcται, κοὐδὲν ἄλλο πλὴν πυροῦν
      Κύκλωποc ὄψιν· ἀλλ' ὅπωc ἀνὴρ ἔcηι.   595
Χο.   πέτραc τὸ λῆμα κἀδάμαντοc ἔξομεν.
      χώρει δ' ἐc οἴκουc πρίν τι τὸν πατέρα παθεῖν
      ἀπάλαμνον· ὥc coι τἀνθάδ' ἐcτὶν εὐτρεπῆ.
Οδ.   "Ηφαιcτ', ἄναξ Αἰτναῖε, γείτονοc κακοῦ
      λαμπρὸν πυρώcαc ὄμμ' ἀπαλλάχθηθ' ἅπαξ,   600
      cύ τ', ὦ μελαίνηc Νυκτὸc ἐκπαίδευμ', "Υπνε,
      ἄκρατοc ἐλθὲ θηρὶ τῶι θεοcτυγεῖ,
      καὶ μὴ 'πὶ καλλίcτοιcι Τρωϊκοῖc πόνοιc
      αὐτόν τε ναύταc τ' ἀπολέcητ' 'Οδυccέα
      ὑπ' ἀνδρὸc ὧι θεῶν οὐδὲν ἢ βροτῶν μέλει.   605
      ἢ τὴν τύχην μὲν δαίμον' ἡγεῖcθαι χρεών,
      τὰ δαιμόνων δὲ τῆc τύχηc ἐλάccονα.

Χο.   λήψεται τὸν τράχηλον
      ἐντόνωc ὁ καρκίνοc
      τοῦ ξενοδαιτυμόνοc· πυρὶ γὰρ τάχα   610
      φωcφόρουc ὀλεῖ κόραc.
      ἤδη δαλὸc ἠνθρακωμένοc
      κρύπτεται ἐc cποδιάν, δρυὸc ἄcπετον   615
      ἔρνοc. ἀλλ' ἴτω Μάρων, πραccέτω,
      μαινομένου 'ξελέτω βλέφαρον

589[n] Κι. apogr. Par.: om. L   590[n] ὀδ. Tr[1]: [L]   590 διονύcου P:
διων- L   591 ἀνήρ Matthiae: ἀν- L   τῆιδ' Blaydes   592 φάρυγοc
Barnes: -γγοc L   593 καπνὸν ⟨πνέων⟩ uel ⟨πνέων⟩ κ- (del. ὠθεῖ)
Diggle, καπνούμενοc Murray   594 κοὐδὲν Kirchhoff: δ' οὐδὲν L
598 ἀπάλαμνον Canter: ἀπαλλαγμὸν L   604 ναύταc Tr[2]: ναῦc ⟨L⟩P
αὐτοῖcι ναύταιc Pierson, sed uide ICS 6.1 (1981) 92   610 ξενοδαιτυμόνοc
Hermann: ξένων δαιτυμόνοc L   617 μαινομένου 'ξελέτω Hermann:
μαινόμενοc ἐξελέτω L

Κύκλωπος, ὡς πίηι κακῶς.
κἀγὼ τὸν φιλοκιссοφόρον Βρόμιον   620
ποθεινὸν εἰcιδεῖν θέλω,
Κύκλωπος λιπὼν ἐρημίαν·
ἆρ' ἐc τοcόνδ' ἀφίξομαι;

Οδ. cιγᾶτε πρὸς θεῶν, θῆρες, ἡcυχάζετε,
  cυνθέντεc ἄρθρα cτόματος· οὐδὲ πνεῖν ἐῶ, 625
  οὐ cκαρδαμύccειν οὐδὲ χρέμπτεcθαί τινα,
  ὡc μὴ 'ξεγερθῆι τὸ κακόν, ἔcτ' ἂν ὄμματοc
  ὄψιc Κύκλωπος ἐξαμιλληθῆι πυρί.
Χο. cιγῶμεν ἐγκάψαντεc αἰθέρα γνάθοιc.
Οδ. ἄγε νυν ὅπωc ἅψεcθε τοῦ δαλοῦ χεροῖν 630
  ἔcω μολόντεc· διάπυρος δ' ἐcτὶν καλῶς.
Χο. οὔκουν cὺ τάξειc οὕcτιναc πρώτουc χρεὼν
  καυτὸν μοχλὸν λαβόνταc ἐκκαίειν τὸ φῶc
  Κύκλωπος, ὡc ἂν τῆς τύχηc κοινώμεθα;
Χο.ᵃ ἡμεῖc μέν ἐcμεν μακροτέρω πρὸ τῶν θυρῶν 635
  ἐcτῶτεc ὠθεῖν ἐc τὸν ὀφθαλμὸν τὸ πῦρ.
Χο.ᵝ ἡμεῖc δὲ χωλοί γ' ἀρτίωc γεγενήμεθα.
Χο.ᵃ ταὐτὸν πεπόνθατ' ἆρ' ἐμοί· τοὺς γὰρ πόδαc
  ἐcτῶτεc ἐcπάcθημεν οὐκ οἶδ' ἐξ ὅτου.
Οδ. ἐcτῶτεc ἐcπάcθητε; Χο.ᵃ καὶ τά γ' ὄμματα 640
  μέcτ' ἐcτὶν ἡμῖν κόνεος ἢ τέφρας ποθέν.

626 χρέμπτεcθαί Tr²: χρίμπτ- L 633 καυτὸν post Scaliger (καυcτὸν)
Hermann: καὶ τὸν L   ἐκκαίειν Aldina: -κάειν L   635–41 hos
uu. duobus tantum choreutis distribuendos esse censeo (sunt qui tribus
uel quattuor distribuant): uidelicet ab eodem choreuta pronuntiatos esse
uu. 635–6 et 638–9 e uocabulo ἐcτῶτεc repetito, uu. 637 et 640b–641 e
particulis καί…γε colligas 635ⁿ Χο.ᵃ] χο. L; 'Ημιχ. Brodaeus
635 μακροτέρω Matthiae: -ότεροι L: -οτέραν Cobet, -ότερον Musgrave
637ⁿ Χο.ᵝ] ἡμιχ. L   637 χωλοί Tr²: χολοί ⟨L⟩P
638ⁿ Χο.ᵃ] ὀδ. L: 'Ημιχ. Musgrave 638 ἆρ' Tr²: ἄρ' L ante τοὺς
notam χο. habet L, del. Barnes   640ⁿ Χο.ᵃ] χο. Tr¹ et fort. L
641 μέcτ' ἐcτὶν Scaliger: μέτεcτιν L ἡμῖν Barnes: ἡμῶν L κόνεοc
Musgrave: -εωc L

Οδ. ἄνδρες πονηροὶ κοὐδὲν οἴδε σύμμαχοι.

Χο. ὁτιὴ τὸ νῶτον τὴν ῥάχιν τ' οἰκτίρομεν
καὶ τοὺς ὀδόντας ἐκβαλεῖν οὐ βούλομαι
τυπτόμενος, αὕτη γίγνεται πονηρία;   645
ἀλλ' οἶδ' ἐπῳδὴν 'Ορφέως ἀγαθὴν πάνυ,
ὥςτ' αὐτόματον τὸν δαλὸν ἐς τὸ κρανίον
ςτείχονθ' ὑφάπτειν τὸν μονῶπα παῖδα γῆς.

Οδ. πάλαι μὲν ἤιδη c' ὄντα τοιοῦτον φύςει,
νῦν δ' οἶδ' ἄμεινον. τοῖcι δ' οἰκείοιc φίλοιc   650
χρῆcθαί μ' ἀνάγκη. χειρὶ δ' εἰ μηδὲν cθένειc,
ἀλλ' οὖν ἐπεγκέλευέ γ', ὡς εὐψυχίαν
φίλων κελευcμοῖc τοῖcι cοῖc κτηcώμεθα.

Χο. δράcω τάδ'· ἐν τῶι Καρὶ κινδυνεύcομεν.
κελευcμάτων δ' ἕκατι τυφέcθω Κύκλωψ.   655

ἰὼ ἰώ· γενναιότατ' ὠ-
θεῖτε cπεύδετ', ἐκκαίετε τὰν ὀφρὺν
θηρὸς τοῦ ξενοδαίτα.
τύφετ' ὦ, καίετ' ὦ
τὸν Αἴτνας μηλονόμον.   660
τόρνευ' ἕλκε, μή c' ἐξοδυνηθεὶς
δράςηι τι μάταιον.

Κυ. ὤμοι, κατηνθρακώμεθ' ὀφθαλμοῦ cέλας.

Χο. καλός γ' ὁ παιάν· μέλπε μοι τόνδ' αὖ, Κύκλωψ.

Κυ. ὤμοι μάλ', ὡς ὑβρίcμεθ', ὡς ὀλώλαμεν.   665
ἀλλ' οὔτι μὴ φύγητε τῆcδ' ἔξω πέτρας
χαίροντες, οὐδὲν ὄντεc· ἐν πύλαιcι γὰρ
cταθεὶς φάραγγος τῆcδ' ἐναρμόcω χέρας.

647 ὥcτ' Blaydes: ὡc L: uide Studies 8   649 ἤιδη Heath: ἤδειν L
650 οἰκείοιc P²: οἰκίοιc L   653 κελευμοῖc P   654 κινδυνευτέον Σ Pl.
Lach. 187 B   655 κελευμάτων ed. Heruag.   656–7 numeri incerti
sunt   ἰὼ ἰώ· / ὠθεῖτε γενναιότατα, / cπεύδετ', ἐκκαίετ' ὀφρὺν Diggle (τὰν
iam del. Hermann)   τὰν Hermann: τὴν L   659 τύφετ' ὦ, καίετ' ὦ
Musgrave: τυφέτω καιέτω L   660 Αἴτνας Victorius: ἔτνας L
661 numeri incerti sunt   μὴ 'ξοδυνη-/θεὶς apogr. Par., Groeppel
664 αὖ Markland: ὦ L   668 τῆcδ' Nauck: τάcδ' L: ταῖcδ' Kirchhoff

Χο.　τί χρῆμ' αὐτεῖς, ὦ Κύκλωψ;　Κυ. ἀπωλόμην.

Χο.　αἰσχρός γε φαίνηι.　Κυ. κἀπὶ τοῖσδέ γ' ἄθλιος.　670

Χο.　μεθύων κατέπεσες ἐς μέσους τοὺς ἄνθρακας;

Κυ.　Οὖτίς μ' ἀπώλεσ'.　Χο. οὐκ ἄρ' οὐδείς ⟨c'⟩ ἠδίκει.

Κυ.　Οὖτίς με τυφλοῖ βλέφαρον.　Χο. οὐκ ἄρ' εἶ τυφλός.

Κυ.　†ὣς δὴ cύ†.　Χο. καὶ πῶς c' οὖτις ἂν θείη τυφλόν;

Κυ.　σκώπτεις. ὁ δ' Οὖτις ποῦ 'στιν;　Χο. οὐδαμοῦ,

　　　　Κύκλωψ.　675

Κυ.　ὁ ξένος ἵν' ὀρθῶς ἐκμάθηις μ' ἀπώλεσεν,

　　　　ὁ μιαρός, ὅς μοι δοὺς τὸ πῶμα κατέκλυσεν.

Χο.　δεινὸς γὰρ οἶνος καὶ παλαίεσθαι βαρύς.

Κυ.　πρὸς θεῶν, πεφεύγασ' ἢ μένουσ' ἔσω δόμων;

Χο.　οὖτοι σιωπῆι τὴν πέτραν ἐπήλυγα　680

　　　　λαβόντες ἑστήκασι.　Κυ. ποτέρας τῆς χερός;

Χο.　ἐν δεξιᾶι σου.　Κυ. ποῦ;　Χο. πρὸς αὐτῆι τῆι

　　　　πέτραι.

　　　　ἔχεις;　Κυ. κακόν γε πρὸς κακῶι· τὸ κρανίον

　　　　παίσας κατέαγα.　Χο. καί σε διαφεύγουσί γε.

Κυ.　οὐ τῆιδέ πηι, τῆιδ' εἶπας;　Χο. οὔ· ταύτηι λέγω.　685

Κυ.　πῆι γάρ;　Χο. περιάγου κεῖσε, πρὸς τἀριστερά.

Κυ.　οἴμοι γελῶμαι· κερτομεῖτέ μ' ἐν κακοῖς.

Χο.　ἀλλ' οὐκέτ', ἀλλὰ πρόσθεν οὖτός ἐστι σοῦ.

Κυ.　ὦ παγκάκιστε, ποῦ ποτ' εἶ;　Οδ. τηλοῦ σέθεν

　　　　φυλακαῖσι φρουρῶ σῶμ' Ὀδυσσέως τόδε.　690

Κυ.　πῶς εἶπας; ὄνομα μεταβαλὼν καινὸν λέγεις.

Οδ.　ὅπερ μ' ὁ φύσας ὠνόμαζ' Ὀδυσσέα.

　　　　δώσειν δ' ἔμελλες ἀνοσίου δαιτὸς δίκας·

　　　　καλῶς γὰρ ἂν Τροίαν γε διεπυρώσαμεν

　　　　εἰ μή σ' ἑταίρων φόνον ἐτιμωρησάμην.　695

672 ἀπώλεσ' Matthiae: -εσεν L　　　⟨c'⟩ Battierius　　　674 c' οὖτις
Canter: cύ· τίς c' L　　　u. del. Dindorf　　　677 κατέκλυσεν Canter:
κατέκαυσε L　　　678ⁿ Χο. Reiske: om. L　　　678 οἶνος Camper (ὠιν-):
οἶνος L　　　679ⁿ Κυ. Reiske: om. L　　　685 τῆιδέ πηι Blaydes: τῆδ' ἐπεί L
686 περιάγου κεῖσε Nauck: περιάγουσί σε L　　　688 σοῦ Diggle: cου L
690 σῶμ' Canter: δῶμ' L　　　692 μ' Nauck: γ' L: μ' post φύσας apogr.
Par., sed uide El. 264, Ion 324, 671　　　694 καλῶς Dobree: κακῶς L:
ἄλλως Cobet　　　διεπυρώσαμεν Fix: -σάμην L

Κυ. αἰαῖ· παλαιὸς χρησμὸς ἐκπεραίνεται·
     τυφλὴν γὰρ ὄψιν ἐκ σέθεν σχήσειν μ' ἔφη
     Τροίας ἀφορμηθέντος. ἀλλὰ καὶ σέ τοι
     δίκας ὑφέξειν ἀντὶ τῶνδ' ἐθέσπισεν,
     πολὺν θαλάσσηι χρόνον ἐναιωρούμενον.   700
Οδ. κλαίειν σ' ἄνωγα· καὶ δέδραχ' ὅπερ λέγω.
     ἐγὼ δ' ἐπ' ἀκτὰς εἶμι καὶ νεὼς σκάφος
     ἥσω 'πὶ πόντον Σικελὸν ἔς τ' ἐμὴν πάτραν.
Κυ. οὐ δῆτ', ἐπεί σε τῆσδ' ἀπορρήξας πέτρας
     αὐτοῖσι συνναύταισι συντρίψω βαλών.   705
     ἄνω δ' ἐπ' ὄχθον εἶμι, καίπερ ὢν τυφλός,
     δι' ἀμφιτρῆτος τῆσδε προσβαίνων ποδί.
Χο. ἡμεῖς δὲ συνναῦταί γε τοῦδ' Ὀδυσσέως
     ὄντες τὸ λοιπὸν Βακχίωι δουλεύσομεν.

701 λέγεις Paley   703 ἔς τ'] εἰς Schumacher   704 σε Tr¹: γε L
705 συνναύταισι Barnes: σὺν ν- L   707 ποδί] πέτρας Kirchhoff
post h.u. lac. indicare paene malit Diggle

COMMENTARY

Hypothesis

This is an ancient summary of the plot, incomplete and of no great interest. Since the discussion of Euripidean hypotheseis by G. Zuntz, *The Political Plays of Euripides* (1955), 129–46, several more, including some satyric ones, have been discovered in a fragmentary state on papyri: C. Austin, *Nova Fragmenta Euripidea* (1968), Appendix II.

Scene

The whole action of the play takes place outside the cave of Polyphemos under Mt. Aitna in Sicily. On either side of the (central) entrance to the cave there is probably painted a background of rocks and grass (43, 45; N. Hourmouziades, *Production and Imagination in Euripides*, 48–9), and in front of it there are buckets of water (46) and a cauldron (343). From the cave there emerges, rake in hand (33), the grotesque, familiar figure of Silenos.

Prologue (1–40)

Like most Euripidean prologues, this is a monologue which informs the audience of what nowadays they might read in their programme. Here, of course, no self-identification is required (cf. e.g. *Hel.* 22), the necessary background information is relatively simple (cf. e.g. *Hec.*), and the monologue is fairly well motivated (cf. e.g. *Alc.*): well might Sil. as he goes about his menial work grumble at his god as the cause both of previous adventures (3–9) and of the satyrs' present plight as Pol.'s slaves in Sicily (10–35).

1. The opening words, as in E.'s satyric *Skiron* (Austin, *Nova Fragmenta Euripidea*, p. 94; see also *Su.*; A. *Su.*, *Ag.*, *Cho.*, *Eum.*), are those of a prayer, perhaps in this case to the image of Dionysos which stood in the theatre (Ar. *Eq.* 536; Pickard-Cambridge, *The Dramatic Festivals of Athens²*, 60). **Βρόμιε:** later derivations of this title from βορά (*Suda* s. βρόμιος) or from the thunder at Dionysos' birth (D.S. 4.5.1; *EM* s. βρόμιος) do not help us to understand its original significance. In early poetry the god himself is ἐρίβρομος (*h. hom.* 7.56; Anacr. 365 *PMG*) and Ἐριβόας (Pi. fr. 75.10). He turns into a lion and roars (*h. hom.* 7.45 μέγα δ' ἔβραχεν). The music of his worship is βαρύβρομος (*Ba.* 156; Ar. *Nu.* 313). And when he passes with his train, the mountains and valleys βρέμονται (Ar. *Thesm.* 997–8), and the wood is filled with βρόμος (*h. hom.* 26.10). Like κελαδεινός of Artemis (*Il.* 16.183, 21.511), βρόμιος is found both alone and with another title (Ar. *Thesm.* 991). διὰ cὲ creates the expectation of praise of the deity (cf. Hes. *Op.* 3; *h. hom.* 20.5; Aristid. *Or.* 43.29; of Dionysos *Ba.* 285 ὥcτε διὰ τοῦτον τἄγαθ' ἀνθρώπους ἔχειν and Timoth. 794 *PMG* διὰ cὲ καὶ τεὰ δῶρα). But between Dionysos and his satyric followers there is a peculiar intimacy. Sil. is no happier in his servile occupation than Klytaimnestra's watchman (A. *Ag.* 1). And so rather than praising his god, he grumbles at him (for irony in a prayer after διὰ cὲ cf. Ar. *Av.* 1546; Timokr. 731 *PMG*; in general: W. Horn, *Gebet und Gebetsparodie in den Komödien des Aristophanes* (1970)). πόνους: πόνοι in the service of Dionysos are elsewhere pleasurable: S. *Ichn.* 223–8; *Ba.* 65, 1053; cf. *Ion* 131, *Hyps.* fr. 1.V 21; Ar. *Eccl.* 972 and 975 (a lover to his girl) διά τοι cὲ πόνουc ἔχω. But Sil. is claiming heroic status: cf. Herakles' ἀτὰρ πόνων δὴ μυρίων ἐγευcάμην (*HF* 1353). His boasting of his youthful exploits will be belied by the audience's knowledge of the γιγαντομαχία (cf. 5–9n., 8n.), just as in S. *Ichn.* it is belied by his subsequent abject cowardice (153–8, 205–9). So too the satyrs' confidence at *Cyc.* 596 is deceptive (635–55n.).

2. The point is not just that an old man will refer to the exploits of his youth. Vase-painting suggests that Sil. may have become older in the course of the fifth century *after* various stories about cιληνοί were already known; and so the exploits of his relative youth would be remembered by others beside himself. (The same is true of Nestor if his reminiscences in the *Iliad* reflect a lost epic.) Cf. Sil. at S. *Ichn.* 154–5 οὐ πόλλ' ἐφ' ἥβηc μνήματ' ἀνδρείαc ὕπο | κεῖται παρ' οἴκοιc νυμφικοῖc ἠcκημένα. εὐcθένει: although εὐθενεῖν is probably to be restored for εὐcθενεῖν at A. *Eum.* 895, and also perhaps at D.C. 53.8.2 (cf. Arist. *EN* 1100a6, *GA* 775a29), and despite the ambiguity of δέμαc (see below: εὐθενεῖν suits the mysterious flourishing of nature), L's εὐcθένει should be retained; cf. S. *OC* 501 οὐ γὰρ ἂν cθένοι τοὐμὸν δέμαc. Against ηὐcθένει see O. Lautensach, *Grammatische Studien zu den griechischen Tragikern und Komikern* (Leipzig, 1899), 146–9. δέμαc: Eustathius (ad *Il.* 22.499) explains δέμαc at Pl. Com. fr. 173.10 τὸ γὰρ δέμαc ἀνέρος ὀρθοῖ as a synonym used by οἱ cεμνότεροι for ψωλή (cf. Hsch. s. δέμαc; Athen. 621b5). δέμαc at Pratinas fr. 3.14 (almost certainly satyric: Seaford in *Maia* 29 (1977–8), 81–94), of an αὐλός, probably has an obscene secondary reference (Garrod in *CR* 34 (1920), 135). On the Pronomos vase (intro., n. 7) the only θιαcώτηc whose phallus is *not* erect is Sil.; indeed at *Cyc.* 169 he relishes the *prospect*. This distinction from the satyrs seems to be recent, and may be a consequence of his ageing. If οὐ γὰρ ἂν cθένοι τοὐμὸν δέμαc (S. *OC.* 501) had predecessors in tragedy, then the humour may contain an element of paratragedy.

3–4. Hera's infliction of madness on Dionysos (Apollod. 3.5.1; Nonnus 32.98–152) was probably invented to explain the (originally cultic) 'frenzy' of Dionysos (*Il.* 6.132; Dodds on *Ba.* 120–34; cf. Pl. *Leg.* 672b), and motivated no doubt by that resentment of Zeus' extramarital affairs (cf. Nonn. 20.182–4) which caused her to contrive the death of Dionysos' mother Semele and to madden Herakles and Io. As for the consequent πόνοι of Sil., the briefness of the allusion suggests that they were already known to the audience. Were they then the theme of a previous satyr-play (cf. 5–9n., 11–17n., 39n.)? There have been three suggestions: (a) A. *Dionysou Trophoi* (Kaibel in *Hermes* 30 (1895), 88–9), in which Medea τὰc Διονύcου τροφοὺc μετὰ τῶν ἀνδρῶν αὐτῶν ἀνεψήcαcα ἐνεοποίηcε (Arg. E. *Med.*; cf. Schol. Ar. *Eq.* 1321). In this there is only a slight inconsistency with ἐν ἥβηι (2), which seems part of a humorous τόποc (2n.). In fact Sil. as παιδότροφοc Διονύcου in vase-painting is never young (H. Heydemann, *Dionysos' Geburt und Kindheit* (1885), 25, 53; Brommer, *Satyrspiele²*, 53). Kaibel imagines that Dionysos returned from his wanderings to rejuvenate a θίαcοc which had aged in his absence. (b) Achaios *Iris*. Drago (*Dioniso* 5 (1936), 231–42) cites Phld. *Piet.* p. 36 Gomp. (Achaios fr. 20), which appears to refer (cf. Sutton in *Eos* 62 (1974), 209) to Dionysos as ἀκατάcχετοc in Achaios' *Iris*. Iris was sent by Hera to madden Herakles in *HF*, and may have had a similar mission in S.'s satyric *Inachos* (fr. 272). (c) S. *Dionysiskos* (Sutton, art cit.), which we know contained the invention of wine (intro., §IV). But the two supports for this view, Pl. *Leg.* 672b, in which the introduction of Dionysiac frenzy and of wine are ascribed to the madness sent by Hera, and Apollod. 3.5.1, in which the god's madness and wandering are mentioned immediately after the invention of wine, are slight as well as inconsistent. It may after all be a mistake to seek a specific play. At Apollod. 3.5.1 Dionysos, made mad by Hera, enters on his wanderings, in the course of which he suffers at the hands of (among others) Lykourgos and Pentheus. Perhaps a stage in the god's travels had been introduced in the prologue of a satyr-play, by an exasperated Sil., as a consequence of his madness. E.g. in A. *Lykourgos* it seems that the satyrs were, as in

Apollod., the slaves of Lykourgos; such πόνοι would of course be
appropriately remembered here. If there were several such plays,
E. may not have had a particular one in mind here.

3. ἐμμανὴς: ἐκμανεὶς Scaliger; but cf. e.g. *Ba.* 1094 θεοῦ πνοαῖσιν
ἐμμανεῖς. ὗπο: for the preposition following its noun see K-G i 554,
Schwyzer, *Griech. Gramm.*, ii 426–7, Denniston on *El.* 574. For the
consequent anastrophe of the accent see K-B i 333–5, Schwyzer i
387 anm. 3.

4. Sil., the satyrs, and the nymphs are all associated, in both literature and art, with κουροτροφία in general and the nurture of
Dionysos in particular: e.g. *h. hom.* 5.262, 273; 26.3–5;
Heydemann, op. cit. 3–4n.; see esp. the Vatican crater (Brommer,
Satyrspiele,[2] 53; *ARV*[2] 1017). ὀρείας: in Hes. fr. 123 the satyrs'
nymph sisters are οὔρειαι. Hes. may have had no specific mountain in mind, but here the audience would probably think of Nysa
(68n.).

5–9. Of the new situations in which the satyrs appear in Attic vase-
painting towards the end of the 6th century, probably as a result of
the development of the satyric drama, the γιγαντομαχία is one of
the earliest. Five paintings from the penultimate decade (*ARV*[2]
70.3, 168.15, 170.3, 170 (middle); Beazley, *Campana Fragments*,
pl.4.28) of armed or trumpeting satyrs are taken by Buschor
(*SBAW* 1943/5, 89) as inspired by a specific play: Dionysos' well-
known involvement in the battle would make it an obvious choice
(probably the epic Γιγαντομαχία had no mention of satyrs; but cf.
ps. Eratosth. *Cat.* 11.2., where Dionysos, Hephaistos and the satyrs
arrive on asses, whose terrifying braying routs the giants). There
are about twenty more vase-paintings, extending into the fourth
century, of satyric warriors, some of them ἀμφὶ γηγενῆ μάχην (see
F. Brommer, *Satyroi* (Würzburg, 1937), 55; M. Mayer, *Die
Giganten und Titanen in der Antiken Sage und Kunst* (1887), 322–25; F.
Vian, *La Guerre des Géants*, 83–90; Caskey and Beazley, *Attic Vase
Paintings in Boston*, ii 70–2). Never do the satyrs (or Sil.) engage in
serious combat. In the apparent exception (*ARV*[2] 1338 (middle))
the satyr's opponent is in fact caught in a vine—Dionysos' trick in
overcoming his giant opponent. After about 480 BC, the date of
ARV[2] 121.23, in which the satyr is clearly wearing stage-costume,
there is no definite evidence for any satyr-play on the same theme.
For although vase-paintings are frequently inspired by satyr-plays
(Brommer, op. cit. 3–4n.) the satyric warrior might have lived on
in the vase-painter's repertoire independently of the theatre.
Indeed, from the titles of lost satyr-plays it seems that themes
involving Dionysos himself had been exhausted well before the

middle of the 5th century (intro., §III (3)) — though they could of
course be repeated. Perhaps Hegemon's comedy Γιγαντομαχία,
produced shortly before *Cyc.* (Ath. 407a), contained satyrs (cf. also
Hermipp. *Theoi* frr. 31, 34; Ar. *Av.* 824-5). Anyway Sil.'s real part
in the incident (cf. 1n., 8n.) was probably well known to the
audience. (It would probably not occur to the audience here that
Pol. was himself a παῖc γῆc, 648.)

5. γε: ὅτε Hermann; δὲ Heath. But for exx. of πρῶτον μέν ... ἔπειτά γε
in Plato (admittedly spanning intervention by another speaker)
see Denniston, *GP*, 145-6, 376-7. It may suit a rambling complaint. ἀμφὶ: ἐν μάχηι is frequent in E. (e.g. fr. 1109.4 ἐν μάχηι
δορὸc). Why then ἀμφὶ here? Temporal ἀμφὶ is rare, and not found
in E.; though its vagueness would suit a reference to πόνοι *before*,
during and after the battle. More likely it is spatial, the vagueness
(*Andr.* 215; Jebb on S. *Aj.* 1064 ἀμφὶ χλωρὰν ψάμαθον ἐκ-
βεβλημένοc) implying mobility (*Il.* 13.806 πάντηι δ' ἀμφὶ φάλαγγαc)
rather than peripherality! **μάχην δορὸc** appears also in the satyr-
suitors' list of their skills at S. fr. 1130.9-10 (further exx. in R. J.
Carden, *The Papyrus Fragments of Sophocles*, 143).

6. Sil. inflates his part in the battle (cf. 5-9n.): the hoplite shelters
behind the shield of the man to the right of him in the rank (Thuc.
5.71). Perhaps Lucian was thinking of this or a similar passage
when he wrote that in Dionysos' battle against the Indians his
right wing was led by Sil. (*Bacch.* 4). The right wing was the most
prestigious position in the τάξιc: Hdt. 9.26.6, 28.2. **βεβὼc:** Kassel
(in *Maia* 25 (1973), 100); cf. *Pho.* 1073-4, *Su.* 850. γεγὼc (L) here
would mean much the same as πεφυκὼc, which is inept.

7. Ἐγκέλαδον: Enceladus' usual victor is Athena (*HF* 908, *Ion* 209;
Hor. *Odes* 3.4.56-7; etc.; for vase-painting see Mayer, op. cit.
5-9n., 309-16). He seems to have been the most fearsome of the
giants, later their leader (Ov. *Tr.* 2.2.11; Aristid. *Or.* 2.11;
Philostr. *Her.* 31, p. 138; Claud. *Rapt. Pros.* 3.351), and in some
versions is killed by Zeus (*Batr.* 284; Q.S. 5.641-2; Nonnus 48.70).
And so Sil.'s claim is particularly implausible; slightly less implausible would have been Rhoitos or Eurytos, Dionysos' traditional enemies in the battle (Mayer, 200-201). In the later tradition at least it is Enceladus, rather than Typhoeus, who is imprisoned under Aetna (Mayer, 214; V. *Aen.* 3.578-9; etc.), that is
to say under Sil.'s feet. **ἰτέαν ἐc μέcην** makes good sense (cf. 229,
458, *El.* 841, *Ba.* 704). Disyllabic ἰτέαν is unique, but to delete ἐc
(Elmsley) would leave the verse without a normal caesura. Verses
in E. transmitted without a normal caesura are *Andr.* 397, *Su.* 303,
699, *Hec.* 355, 1159, *El.* 546, *Hel.* 86, *Ba.* 1125. fr. 495.6 (on the

spuriousness of *IA* 630, 1578, 1593 see Page, *Actors' Interpolations in Greek Tragedy*, 166, 196). But in all these cases either a simple emendation will remove the anomaly, or there are independent grounds for suspecting the paradosis (cf. Diggle in *GRBS* 14 (1973), 263–4). Certainly E. allowed himself less licence in this respect than A. or S. (J. Descroix, *Le Trimètre Iambique* (1931), 262–3; P. Maas, *Greek Metre* (transl. Lloyd-Jones, 1962), § 103). And so although 'absence of caesura is not a fatal objection to the text' (Denniston on *El.* 545–6), to introduce the anomaly by emendation is unjustified even in a satyr-play (see intro., § V). For rare synizesis see 144n., and K-B i 227, for synizesis of -εα- e.g. A. *Sept.* 327, *Eum.* 959; S. *Ant.* 95, *Aj.* 104; *IA* 1341, *Rhes.* 977. **θενών δορὶ ἔκτεινα:** cf. fr. 282. 20–1 (from the satyric *Autolykos*): δι' ἀσπίδων χερὶ / θείνοντες ἐκβαλοῦσι πολεμίους πάτρας.

8. φέρ 'ἴδω. The boast is so unlikely that even Sil. momentarily doubts it (cf. Ar. *Ran.* 51; Plaut. *Men.* 1047). If such humility in Sil. seems oddly untypical, one might read φέρε δή, which is used to reproach the audience at Ar. *Thesm.* 788. However, there is no undisputed instance of audience-address in satyric drama: see Bain in *CQ* 25 (1975), 23–5. **ὄναρ** is either the object of ἰδὼν (cf. Ar. *Eq.* 1090; Pl. *Ap.* 40d) or attached to it adverbially (cf. *IT* 518, *HF* 495). In the latter case ἰδὼν is to be taken more closely with τοῦτο the object of λέγω. On the perception of dreams see G. Björck in *Eranos* 44 (1946), 306–14.

9. Sil. boasts of the μνήματα of his youthful bravery at S. *Ichn.* 154–5. Where the human practice is dedication, **ἔδειξα** suggests a delightful intimacy with the god; cf. 69–70n. In *ARV*² 598.2 a satyr presents a breastplate to a Maenad (E. Roos, *Die Tragische Orchestik im Zerrbild der Altattischen Komödie* (1951), 225, fig. 34). **καὶ:** see Denniston, *GP*, 297. **Βακχίωι** shows that Sil. is no longer addressing his god.

10. ἐξαντλῶ: this emphatic word occurs also at 110 and 282, and elsewhere in E. only at *Med.* 79 and *Su.* 838 (and fr. 454, if by E.). This disproportion is attributable not just to overdramatization of their sufferings by Od. and Sil., but also to a tendency in E. to repeat a rare word, though in a different context, at short intervals (98n.).

11–17. The sea-voyaging of Dionysos, associated by the 5th cent. comedian Hermippus with the spread of his blessings (fr. 63.2), was already implicit in those apparently ancient festivals, such as the Attic Anthesteria, in which it seems that Dionysos moved through the streets in a ship-cart overshadowed with vines (L. Deubner, *Attische Feste*², 102; Boardman in *JHS* 78 (1958), 6–7; cf.

ABV 146.21). And in the ancient seventh Homeric Hymn a vine and ivy sprout from the pirates' ship when (like Pentheus and Lykourgos) they fail disastrously to recognize the divinity of their captive. The story may also have been told by Pindar (fr. 236). The part of Hera in it and the satyrs' quest, on the other hand, may have been relatively recent inventions by a satyric dramatist. Hera's malice is an obvious (3n.) and unnecessary explanation, and does not occur in any other extant version. In the black-figure vase-paintings of the Anthesteria (?) satyrs accompany Dionysos' ship-cart. On either side of a b–f. amphora in Tarquinia (inv. n. 678) they row Dionysos in a ship. On the choregic monument of Lysicrates (334 BC) they fight the pirates on the shore while Dionysos sits on a rock. In a picture described by Philostratus (*Im.* 1.19) they are no doubt the *comites* whose music, according to Aglaosthenes (ap. Hyg. *Astr.* 2.17), caused the pirates to jump into the sea with delight. But their quest occurs only in what Sil. says here. P. Waltz (in *Acropole* 6 (1931), 289–91) argues that this quest must have been the subject of a previous satyr-play, observing (1) the detail of 14–17, (2) that *Ichn.* is a satyr-play based on a Homeric Hymn, and (3) the absurdity of satyr-rowers: unusual roles for the chorus are typical of the genre. This overstates the case. E. is fond of picturesque detail in his prologues (e.g. *Hel.* 17–20), not all of of which refers to previous plays. The pirate episode may have been employed to explain the satyrs' presence overseas in any of a number of plays (e.g. A. *Kirke*, Aristias *Cyclops*, Ion *Omphale*, E. *Bousiris*): like the madness of Dionysos (3–4n.) it may have been described by Sil. in the prologue of a previous satyr-play, just as it is here, as the origin of his present plight. It is after all hard to imagine even the satyrs rowing a ship in the theatre, although at A. *Theoroi* 93–5 they are perhaps about to go on a sea voyage, as of course they are at the end of the *Cyclops* (708 cυvvαῦται). Satyr-rowers do appear, with Dionysos, on the amphora mentioned above, which is perhaps too early to be inspired by a satyr-play. Cf. also a satyr rowing a boat in a Campanian vase-painting (Trendall n. 139), and *ARV*² 134.3; Slater in *AJA* 81 (1977), 556. γένος Τυρϲηνικὸν ληϲτῶν. The ambiguity of γένος between 'class, sort, kind' (LSJ V.1: e.g. fr. 282.2 ἀθλητῶν γένος) and 'race' creates the impression that all Τυρϲηνοί are pirates, which as far as the Greek seafarer was concerned they no doubt were. To the extent that 'sort' is meant there is *hypallage*, which there is no need to remove by reading Τυρϲηνικῶν.

12. ὁδηθείης: this verb occurs elsewhere (apart from in Hsch. and Phot.) only at 98 and 133, the compound ἐξοδᾶν only at 267: see

98n. **μακράν**: we need not supply ὁδόν or suppose that a sense of movement is preserved in the verb: see Fraenkel on A. *Ag.* 916, and *IT* 629 μακρὰν γὰρ βαρβάρου ναίει χθονός.

13. ἐγώ is Tr. 3 and so may well be a guess (intro., § VIII). But it is no worse than Diggle's εὐθὺς or πυθόμενος αὐτὸς (Kalinka).

14. Cf. S. *Trach.* 55 ἀνδρὸς κατὰ ζήτησιν.

14–17. In distinguishing between himself and his rowers Sil. follows epic practice (e.g. *Od.* 9.177–180). On the amphora mentioned 11–17n. Sil. is in one of the pictures holding the rudder.

15. **δόρυ** cannot mean (as Wilamowitz, Duchemin, *et al.*) 'rudder': (1) it has that meaning nowhere else; (2) at 19 it means 'ship'; (3) one steers a ship but turns a rudder (despite Ar. *Av.* 1739 ἡνίας εὔθυνε); (4) the phrase δόρυ (ship) εὐθύνειν occurs at *Hel.* 1611, A. *Pers.* 411; (5) with ἀμφῆρες δόρυ cf. Thuc. 4.67.3 ἀκάτιον ἀμφηρικόν; Hsch. s. ἀμφήρεις· νῆες ἀμφοτέρωθεν ὁρμώμεναι ἢ ἐρεσσόμεναι (Bond on *HF* 243). But since δόρυ means 'ship', **λαβὼν** is suspect. Kassel (*RhM* 98 (1955), 280) defends it with Sen *ad Marc.* 6.3 *at ille vel in naufragio laudandus quem obruit mare navem (clavum* Erasmus) *tenentem*. But the context is too different to allow this as a parallel. More to the point is *Od.* 15.269–70 τοὔνεκα νῦν ἑτάρους τε λαβὼν καὶ νῆα μέλαιναν / ἤλθον πευσόμενος πατρὸς δὴν οἰχομένοιο, where Telemachus, like Sil. here, is beginning a quest for a missing φίλος. Sil. here clearly imagines himself as an epic hero, and the whole passage is heavily influenced by such passages of *Od.* (14–17n. 16–17n., 18–20n.). Ussher compares S. *Ant.* 1163 λαβών τε χώρας παντελῆ μοναρχίαν / ηὔθυνε. But λαβὼν here could be omitted without detriment to the syntax; and in such cases it usually means actually taking hold of something (exx. given by Stinton in *PCPhS* 21 (1975), 84–5), a possible exception being Ar. *Thesm.* 212 ἐμοὶ δ᾽ ὅτι βούλει χρῶ λαβών. Diggle (*PCPhS* 15 (1969), 30) therefore may well be right to substitute βεβὼς, comparing *Tro.* 690 ὁ μὲν παρ᾽ οἴαχ᾽, ὁ δ᾽ ἐπὶ λαίφεσιν βεβώς. Cf. also *Od.* 9.177–80 Ὣς εἰπὼν ἀνὰ νηὸς ἔβην, ἐκέλευσα δ᾽ ἑταίρους / αὐτούς τ᾽ ἀμβαίνειν κτλ.

16–17. **δ᾽** before **ἐρετμοῖς** is Tr. 1 (see intro., § VIII), and is anyway entirely apt: cf. the passages of *Od.* mentioned below. With the resultant text we may take ἐρετμοῖς (1) with ἥμενοι, 'sitting at the oars'; but this dative is difficult, and *Ba.* 38 ἀνορόφοις ἧνται πέτραι (*on* the rocks), *El.* 315 θρόνωι καθῆνται count against it; (2) as instrumental and qualified by ῥοθίοισι (Franke in 1829, Ussher). With ἥμενοι by itself cf. Od. 9.177–80 Ὣς εἰπὼν ἀνὰ νηὸς ἔβην ... οἱ δ᾽ αἶψ᾽ εἴσβαινον ... ἑξῆς δ᾽ ἑζόμενοι πολιὴν ἅλα τύπτον ἐρετμοῖς, 12.180 (cf. 14–17n., 15n., 18–20n.). Certainly in tragedy the adjective from ῥόθος (a confused or rushing sound) occurs usually as the noun ῥόθιον meaning a wave. But at *IT* 407 and 1133 (cf. also *Hel.* 1117) it seems to be an adjective describing *oars*. However, all three of these passages are textually suspect. Further, the resulting word order is odd, and we expect to be told *where* the satyrs are sitting, in contrast to Sil., who is ἐν πρύμνηι δ' ἄκραι (see *Od.* 9.179 again, and 12.171). (3) Best is δ' ἐπ' ἐρετμοῖς (Seidler); cf. *Od.* 12.171–2 οἱ δ' ἐπ' ἐρετμὰ / ἑζόμενοι λεύκαινον ὕδωρ ξεστῆις ἐλατῆισιν; Ar. *Ran.* 197 καθίζ' ἐπὶ κώπην (cf. 199). **ἅλα ῥοθίοισι λευκαίνοντες**: cf. *Od.* 12.172; 'in ridiculum detorquet satyricus epica verba' (W. Wetzel, *De Euripidis Fabula Satyrica Quae Cyclops Inscribitur, Cum Homerico Comparata Exemplo* (Wiesbaden, 1965), 42) goes too far: cf. *IT* 1387. In fact the phrase is a subtle combination of the heard and the seen: the ῥόθος implied by ῥόθιον 'wave' is often merely the sound of the surf (e.g. S. *Phil.* 688; Hsch. s. ῥόθιον· κῦμα τὸ μετὰ ψόφου γενόμενον), but in this context must suggest the splash of the oars (cf. *IT.* 407–8; Schol. on Thuc. 4.10); see further Diggle on *Phaeth.* 80–1.

18–20. The story of the capture of Dionysos is usually set in the Aegean: the god asks the Tyrrhenians for passage to Naxos (Hyg. *Astr.* 2.17; Servius on *Aen.* 1.67; Apollod. 3.5.3; Ov. *Met.* 3.636). However, and despite the 'Pelasgian' Τυρσηνοί living in the Chalkidike (Thuc. 4.109) and in Argos (S. fr. 270.4 and Pearson's note), E. probably meant westerners here, for Sil. sails westwards after them. These western Tyrrhenians were not unknown in the Aegean. Strabo (5.2.2) refers to their μακραὶ στρατεῖαι early in their history; they stole a statue of Hera from Samos (Menodot. ap. Athen. 672b = *FGH* 541.1); and precautions against them are recorded on an inscription from Athens of 325 BC and one from Delos of 299 BC (*Bibl. écol. Franc. Ath.* 49 (1887), 68). Where were the satyrs going? Duchemin takes the emphatic ἤδη in 18 to mean that they had almost returned home, after a trip westwards along the north coast of Africa. However, Od. in Homer arrives at the land of the Cyclopes by being blown off course as he rounds Malea (293n.) from the *east*; he says that he would have arrived home safely, ἀλλά με κῦμα ῥόος τε περιγνάμπτοντα Μάλειαν, / καὶ Βορέης ἀπέωσε κτλ. (*Od.* 9.80–1). So too surely Sil. rounds Malea from the east, and because the Cyclopes are now located in Sicily, the east wind (19) is substituted for the north. ἤδη, implying proximity to the goal after a long journey, is of course less appropriate to Sil.'s voyage than it would have been to Od.'s; but this is entirely consonant with the light absurdity of Sil.'s epic pretensions. (The proverb Μαλέας δὲ κάμψας ἐπιλάθου τῶν οἴκαδε (Strabo 8.6.20) applies more naturally to westward voyages. Cf. also Hdt. 4.179.2, 7.168.4, and the later Κάβο Μαλία, Κάβο Μαλία, / Βόηθε Χριστὲ κὶ Παναγία.)

20. The location of the giants in Sicily, as in V. *Aen.* 3, is not Homeric; but nor is it the dramatist's fantasy: Thuc. 6.2 παλαίτατοι μὲν λέγονται ἐν μέρει τινι τῆc χώρac Κύκλωπεc καί Λαιcτρυγόνεc οἰκῆcαι. Strabo (1.2.9) says that the Cyclopes and the Laestrygonians were lords of the region about Aitna and Leontini. **Αἰτναίαν:** Αἰτναῖον Wecklein, comparing 295; cf. Kannicht on *Hel.* 335, Diggle in *Illinois Class. Stud.* 2 (1977), 123. But the feminine form is transmitted also at *Tro.* 220 and A. *PV.* 365.

21. Cf. 286, 413, 648n. **μονῶπεc:** cf. 78, 174, 235, 648. That the Cyclopes are one-eyed is stated by Hesiod (*Th.* 143–5), but not by Homer (although it is required by the story). Both he (*Od.* 9.389) and E. (463, 470, 511, 611) sometimes seem to assume that Pol. had two eyes, rather as in *War and Peace* Tolstoy refers to the one-eyed Kutuzov's 'eyes'. The reason for the ambiguity is not, as the scholiast on *Od.* 9.383 thought, that Pol. was already blind in one eye, rather that the anomaly of Pol.'s one eye was as difficult to accommodate in poetic language as it was in art: see O. Touchefeu-Meynier, *Thèmes Odysséens dans l'art antique* (1968), ch. 1, esp. 73–4. Before the 5th cent. BC he usually seems to have two eyes. But as the face is often in profile, we cannot be sure that what appears to be a normally placed eye was not imagined as central. On later vases and masks he tends to have one large central eye above his nose (as here: 174, 235), sometimes as well as two normal ones, which are usually shut (as on the Richmond vase: Plate II).

22. **ἄντρ' ἔρημα:** cf. *Od.* 9.113–15, 182–9. **ἀνδροκτόνοι:** cf. 92–3, 127–8. In Homer we are given no such warning. But E.'s prologues characteristically describe the situation fully. And cf. the description of the cruelty of Lityerses in what is probably the prologue of Sositheos' satyric *Daphnis or Lityerses* (fr. 2).

23. **ἑνὸc** seems to go with δόμοιc, with δοῦλοι, and (as genitive of agent: e.g. S. *OC* 1323 τοῦ κακοῦ πότμου φυτευθείc, E. Schwyzer in *APAW* 1942/10) with ληφθέντεc. In e.g. Hdt. 2.91.3 cανδάλιον αὐτοῦ πεφορημένον the genitives of possession and agency merge.

24. **δοῦλοι** is in emphatic position. For the enslavement and menial labour (λατρεύομεν) of the satyrs in s-drama see intro., § IV. **αὐτόν:** αὐτόc as antecedent to a relative clause is unusual, and tends to be emphatic (e.g. *Tro.* 667, K-G i 654); but here it has the connotation 'master' (Ar. *Nub.* 219 with Dover's note).

25. Cf. *Andr.* 164 δεῖ c' ἀντὶ τῶν πρὶν ὀλβίων φρονημάτων / πτῆξαι ταπεινήν ... / cαίρειν τε δῶμα τοὐμόν; S. *OT* 1491. **εὐίων** does not mean 'Bacchic' (LSJ, Ussher): cf. *Ba.* 608 εὐίου βακχεύματος, and *Tro.* 451 (of *Apolline* cτέφη). It refers rather to the cry εὐοῖ.

26. **ἀνοcίου** is used of human sacrifice by Plato (*Min.* 315b.), and frequently in this play of Pol. or his meal (31, 348, 378, 438, 693). Cf. also δυccεβής at 30, 289. In Homer, although Od. claims the protection of Zeus (9.270, cf. 479), Pol. and his crime are described in more secular terms (295 cχέτλια ἔργα, 352, 428, 477). Cf. Seaford in *CQ* 31 (1981), 272.

27. For transitional **μὲν οὖν** see Denniston, *GP*, 470–4. **μοι** implies both that the παῖδες are Sil.'s and that their work is somehow under his supervision. **κλειτύων** (κλιτύων L): see Diggle in *CQ* 21 (1971), 42; Wackernagel, *Spr. Unt. z. Hom.*, 74–5. **ἐcχάτοις:** see Gow on Theocr. 13.25.

28. **νέα νέοι:** juxtaposition of the same or similar words in E. may express a logical link (e.g. *Alc.* 799 ὄντας δὲ θνητοὺς θνητὰ καὶ φρονεῖν χρεών; see D. Fehling, *Die Wiederholungsfiguren und ihr Gebrauch bei den Griechen vor Gorgias* (Berlin, 1969), 218), a mutual relationship (e.g. *Ba.* 470 ὁρῶν ὁρῶντα, Fehling, 221), and a paradox (e.g. *IA* 466 οὐ cυνετά cυνετός). But sometimes the point is simply the intensifying effect of repetition (e.g. *Ba.* 160–1 λωτὸς ὅταν εὐκέλαδος ἱερὸς ἱερὰ παίγματα βρέμηι). νέα νέοι falls into this category – the youth of the sheep seems arbitrary (cf. 55), but this is no objection to the text (νεανίαι Pierson), as the same arbitrariness appears at *HF* 126–8 δι ξύνοπλα δόρατα νέα νέωι ... ξυνῆν ποτε; cf. also *Alc.* 471 (with Dale's note), *Ion* 712; S. *Ichn.* 359 κιν]ῶν ἐν νέωι νέον λόγον.

29. **πίcτρα:** 'drinking troughs', occurs only here as neuter, and elsewhere only at 47, Strabo 8.3.31, and in the lexica. **cαίρειν:** the reduction of royalty to sweeping was a τόπος in E.: *Andr.* 166 (quoted 25n.), *Hec.* 363, *Hyps.* fr. 1.ii.17. And so the joke is that Sil. is implicitly claiming a previously royal status (as the satyrs do later: 80n.). Along with this there is perhaps the absurd suggestion in cτέγας of the royal palace of tragedy. (The price of this joke is a slight inconsistency with 118.) In *Od.* (9.330) there is a lot of dung in Pol.'s cave, which would be unacceptable to E.'s civilized Pol. (intro., §VII). In a humorous version of the story, perhaps by Philoxenos Cyth., Od. suggests that Pol. sweep out his cave to make it ready for the nymph Galatea (818 *PMG*).

30. **μένων** has been suspected (γέρων Pierson), but makes perfect sense. Probably Sil. often entered alone to speak the prologue, and this separation from the chorus may more than once have been rationalized as a division of labour: cf. 31n. τάϲδε, τῶιδε: for the juxtaposition cf. S. *Trach.* 716. Here it expresses Sil.'s exasperated resentment, like the alliteration at 29 and the repetition of 29 in 33. With τῶιδε of the absent Pol. cf. Klytaimnestra's τῆϲδε at S. *El.* 540 expressing the vividness of the dead Iphigeneia in her thoughts (and e.g. *Hipp.* 48, *IA* 72: Lloyd-Jones in *CR* 15 (1965), 241–2). τῶι τε (Hermann) derives from a correction (apparently Tr. 3) in L of τῶδε, is unnecessary, and has the drawback of making us supply τέταγμαι with διάκονοϲ.

31. There is no real inconsistency here with 249; cf. the γε in 251. **δείπνων:** for the genitive see Schwyzer, *Griech. Gramm.*, ii 121: διακονεῖν can take the accusative (e.g. Hdt. 4.154). **ἀνοϲίων:** cf. 26n.; S. *Aj.* 1293 δυϲϲεβέϲτατον / προθέντ᾿ ἀδελφῶι δεῖπνον οἰκείων τέκνων. **διάκονοϲ:** cf. 406; S. *Ichn.* 150; E. fr. 375 (satyric *Eurystheus*); *P. Oxy.* 2455 fr. 6 (Hypoth. to E.'s satyric *Skiron* = fr. 18 Austin, 81–2): (Skiron) [ἔχων δὲ πρόϲκο]πον καὶ διάκονον τῆϲ ὑβ[ρέωϲ Ϲιληνόν].

32. **καὶ νῦν** is the usual expression for the transition, in a prologue, from a generalization to the present instance: cf. 10; S. *Aj.* 3, *Ant.* 7. **τὰ προϲταχθέντα** is in apposition to what follows it: cf. A. *Ag.* 550 ὡϲ νῦν, τὸ ϲὸν δή, καὶ θανεῖν πολλὴ χάριϲ; *HF* 323. Duchemin makes it the subject of ἔχει, with ϲαίρειν ... με κτλ. appositional. But ἀναγκαίωϲ ἔχει is almost always followed by an infinitive (real or understood): e.g. *HF* 859 εἰ δὲ δή μ᾿ Ἥρα θ᾿ ὑπουργεῖν ϲοί τ᾿ ἀναγκαίωϲ ἔχει, 502, *Hel.* 512, 1399, *Or.* 715, *Pho.* 358, *Ba.* 1351, fr. 757.5.

33. **ἁρπάγηι** refers elsewhere only to a hook for drawing buckets from a well, and to a grappling iron. And so Duchemin thought that the joke is that Sil. is trying to sweep the place with a hook. But ἁρπάγη here must mean 'rake', and the joke is that Sil. is using a farmyard instrument, rather than a broom (κόρημα), to clean δόμοι (in *Od.* there is much dung in Pol.'s cave: 29n.). To judge from the Pronomos vase (intro., n. 7) Sil. usually carried a staff, for which the ἁρπάγη here is a humorous substitute, indicating Sil.'s changed circumstances (8on.). **δόμουϲ** of the cave: cf. 29n., 129, 455, etc.; *h.hom.Herm.* 27, 246.

34–5. There is bathos, after the honorific reference to Pol., in the postponement of μῆλα, and the irony is sustained in ἄντροιϲ ... ἐϲδεχώμεθα (cf. S. *OT.* 818 δόμοιϲ δέχεϲθαι).

36. E. has the prologist introducing, in effect, chorus to audience at *Hipp.* 54, *Su.* 8, *IT* 63, *Or.* 132, *Ba.* 55. **προϲνέμοντϲϲ** occurs in this sense here only: -νέμονταϲ refers to the driving of the sheep (cf. Pol.

at *Od.* 9.233 ἦοc ἐπῆλθε νέμων), and προc- adds the idea that the satyrs are approaching the cave.

37–40. A festal entry for the chorus seems out of place (cf. 63). Why then does Sil. so describe it? Perhaps because it was a traditional feature of the genre: cf. the pap. hypoth. *P. Oxy.* 2455 fr. 6 (Austin, p. 94): ... cάτυ[ρ]οι εἰcκ[ωμαcάντεc μετὰ] ἑταιρῶν ...; cf. 30n., 31n., Seaford in *CQ* 31 (1981), 268–71.

37. μῶν expresses not disapproval but surprise: 377n. **cικινίδων:** relics of Peripatetic scholarship on this dance are preserved in Athenaeus, Pollux, and the lexicographers (C. Bapp, *de fontibus quibus Athenaeus in rebus musicis lyricisque enarrandis usus sit* (*Leipzig. Stud.* 8 (1885)); E. Rohde, *de Julii Pollucis in apparatu scenico enarrando fontibus* (Leipzig, 1870), 39–40; V. Festa, *Sikinnis* (*MAAN* 1918, 2), 37). Satyrs on red-figure vases are called ΣΙΚΙΝΟΣ and ΣΙΚΙΝΝΟΣ (Ch. Fraenkel, *Satyr und Bakchennamen auf Vasenbildern* (Halle, 1912), vases β, γ, δ, R, (= *ARV*[2] 1184.1, 1608, 1214.1, 61)), but the spelling cίκιννιc occurs only here and may be haplography (though we cannot say that the second iota is short). According to Aristoxenos the cίκιννιc was the characteristic dance of satyric drama, as the ἐμμέλεια of tragedy and the κόρδαξ of comedy (frr. 104, 106 Wehrli). Athenaeus records the tradition that the inventor of the dance was a barbarian and that he was Cretan (630b). And according to Eustathius the dance was in origin Phrygian (ad *Il.* 16.617). Most recent opinion (see the etymological dictionaries of Fick, Boisacq, and Frisk s. κηκίω or κηκίc) gives the word a Thraco-Phrygian origin and compares it to κηκίω and to the Lithuanian *szókti* meaning dance or leap. The dance was called by Aulus Gellius (20.3) a *genus veteris saltationis*, and the satyrs themselves are associated with leaping (*Cyc.* 221; Moschus 6.2; Lucian *Deor. Conc.* 4; Sositheos *AP* 7.707; Nonnus 14.111). And yet Athenaeus numbers the dance (along with ἐμμέλεια and κόρδαξ) among the cταcιμώτερα καὶ πυκνότερα (Kaibel, ποικιλώτερα MSS.) καὶ τὴν ὄρχηcιν ἁπλουcτέραν ἔχοντα, 'the more stationary dances, in closer formation and with simpler dance-movement'. The antithesis is with such dances as the πυρρίχη, which however the cίκιννιc resembles in its fast pace (630d); Scamon derived the word cίκιννιc from cείω, others from κίνηcιc, the latter derivation being based on the great speed of the dance; and because it never slows down it has no πάθοc (630b–c). In Hsch. (s. cίκιννιc) the dance is cύντονοc, 'intense', (opposed, as a musical term, to ἀνειμένοc and μαλακόc at Arist. *Pol.* 1342b21). Later apparent evidence (e.g. D.H. 7.72.10) may be based on an extension of the term to cover all dancing by satyrs. But one might add the kind of αὐλόc-playing called Σικιννοτύρβη (Athen. 618c₎: τύρβη is a tumult (cf. Pausan. 2.24.6). Further evidence is in the words κρότοc and cαυλούμενοι (40n.) here, which is the only certain reference in satyric drama to the dance (although it is probably what is meant by the κτύποc πέδορτοc, the πηδήματα κραιπνά, and the λακτίcματα of S. *Ichn.* 218–19). The Pronomos vase (intro., n. 7) shows a satyr standing on the toes of his right foot, with his left leg bent at the knee and raised to his left, his left arm thrust out to his left, the palm turned upwards and outwards, his right hand on his hip, and his head turned towards his right. Because this painting is of the *cast* of a satyr-play, rather than of a satyric scene, one expects the dancing to be typical of satyric drama, i.e. the cίκιννιc. Festa (art. cit., 51) collects vase-paintings of similar movements by satyrs, from which he constructs a dance consisting of the alternate raising of each leg accompanied by corresponding alternate movements of the opposite arm and hand, and a semicircular movement of the body. Cf. Pratinas fr. 3.15 (intro., §III (1)): ἦν ἰδού· ἅδε cοι δεξιᾶc καὶ ποδὸc διαρριφά. The hand positions Festa plausibly identifies with the χεὶρ cιμή and the χεὶρ καταπρηνήc (Athen. 630a; cf. Poll. 4.105). Less plausibly associated with the cίκιννιc are the κονίcαλοc (Hsch. s. κονίcαλοc; cf. Roos, op. cit. 9n., 168), the cκώψ (Photius s. cκώπευμα; cf. Poll. 4.103; Hsch. s. cκωπεύματων; Athen. 391a, 629f), the cόβαc (Athen. 629f), and the cκέλοc ῥίπτειν (Schol. Ar. *Vesp.* 1530); the connection of these latter two cχήματα with the cίκιννιc depends on the erroneous (Roos, 167–83) idea that the cίκιννιc is danced in the exodos of the *Wasps*. For satyric dancing in general see Buschor, art. cit. 5–9n. The cίκιννιc was not confined to the theatre: see e.g. G. van Hoorn, *Choes and Anthesteria* (1951), ns. 337, 352, 375; Keil-Premerstein i 28 n. 42 (2nd cent. AD Dionysiac mysteries).

39. κῶμοc: L's κῶμοι must mean 'bands of revellers'. But the satyrs form a *single* band (and cf. *Ba.* 1167; Ar. *Ran.* 218; Dem. *Meid.* 10). κώμοιc (Dobree, Bothe) meaning 'with revels' or 'with revel-songs' (cf. 492, Ar. *Thesm.* 989 ἐγὼ δὲ κώμοιc cὲ φιλοχόροιcι μέλψω) would be a feeble anticipation of ἀοιδαῖc (40), and anyway can hardly be the instrument of cυναcπίζοντεc (*pace* Duchemin). κώμωι (Porson) would give the sense 'standing in the line with Bacchos in the κῶμοc' (Βακχίωι must be a noun: 73–4n.): cf. Thuc. 3.54 μάχηι ... παρεγενόμεθα ὑμῖν. But this would create 'an intolerably unstylish collocation of independent datives' (Diggle in *CQ* 21 (1971), 42). κῶμοc (Diggle) would have been easily corrupted. Satyrs called

ΚΩΜΟΣ appear in vase-painting (e.g. *ARV*² 1031.40, 1269.3, 1253.57; more exx. in Ch. Fränkel, op. cit. 37n.; *RE* xi. s. κῶμος, 1298). In Epicharmos' Κωμασταί ἢ Ἅφαιστος the κωμασταί were no doubt satyrs (Lloyd-Jones, Appendix to *Loeb Aeschylus* ii, 548). **cυναcπίζοντεc:** at 6 Sil. is the god's παραcπιcτήc. Here the satyrs are, metaphorically, his cυναcπιcταί. The metaphor may have been suggested by the sometimes bellicose nature of the amorous κῶμος (Headlam-Knox on Herod. 2.34; F. O. Copley, *Exclusus Amator*, ch. 1; cf. Pratinas fr. 3.7–9, where the satyrs call the αὐλόc a cτρατηλάτας in the κῶμος and in brawls of drunk young men at the front door), perhaps by the connection of the satyrs with the war-dance called πυρρίχη (Roos, op. cit. 37n., 129, 226–7). It occurs in reverse at *Pho.* 791 and *Su.* 390, where an army is called a κῶμος (cf. A. *Ag.* 1189). **Ἀλθαίαc:** as the guest of Oeneus, King of Calydon, Dionysos fell in love with his wife Althaia. Oeneus sensitively withdrew from the palace for a time, and was consequently rewarded with the gift of the vine (Hyg. *Fab.* 129; the fruit of the encounter was Deianeira: Apollod. 1.8.1). Why does Sil. single out this episode? Unlike the events described in 11–17, it is, though a rare story, merely mentioned rather than described, and has no function save the evocation of a mood. Almost certainly (*pace* Ussher) E. has in mind a previous satyr-play (Waltz, art. cit. 11–17n., 292). Apart from the probability that Oeneus appears in S. fr. 1130 (Carden, op. cit. 5n., 137), there is no evidence for the appearance of Oeneus or Althaia in satyric drama. But the story could hardly be better suited to the genre, combining as it does sex (cf. esp., for a god's affair with a mortal woman, A. *Amymone* and S. *Inachos*), the home of a strange king, and wine, and culminating in a marvellous εὕρημα (cf. intro., §IV), at which the satyrs would have danced their delight no less vigorously than at the coupling of their god with Althaia (or with Ariadne in 6th-cent. vase-painting: Buschor, art. cit. 5–9n., 45–6; cf. the Pronomos vase, intro. n. 7). A comedy in which the satyrs accompanied Dionysos in an illicit amorous adventure, this time with Helen, was Cratinus' comedy *Dionysalexandros* (see hypoth. in *P. Oxy.* 663). **δόμουc προcῆιτε:** a form of secular κῶμος would seek entrance to the house of a lover (Copley, op. cit. 39n., ch. 1 and p. 145). Religious κῶμοι were of course particularly appropriate to the worship of Dionysos: e.g. *Ba.* 1167; Ar. *Ran.* 218; Dem. *Meid.* 10; *RE* xi. s. κῶμος, 1291–4 (for vase-painting see Deubner, op. cit. 11–17n., 238–47; van Hoorn, op. cit. 37n.). This is at once secular and religious, a combination symptomatic of the satyrs' position between man and god (9n., 69–70n., 81n., 495–502n.).

40. ἀοιδαῖc means songs (sung to the βάρβιτα: cf. e.g. *Med.* 424 λύρας
... θέσπιν ἀοιδάν), as it always does (except just possibly *Hel.* 358:
cf. T. C. W. Stinton, *Euripides and the Judgement of Paris* (*JHS* suppl.
vol. 1965), 76. ἀείδειν is used of a bowstring at *Od.* 21.411), rather
than mere sounds (cf. S. *Phil.* 213 μολπὰν cύριγγος). But cf. 65n.
βαρβίτων: the βάρβιτος or βάρβιτον, the 'Dionysiac lyre', was a
stringed instrument deeper in tone and longer than the lyre, and
associated with good cheer (Snyder in *CJ* 67 (1972), 331–40). The
convivial Anakreon was called φιλοβάρβιτος (Kritias fr. 1 D-K 4);
and Admetos in mourning for Alkestis renounces κῶμοι and the
βάρβιτον (*Alc.* 343–5). It appears frequently, sometimes along
with the αὐλός, in vase-paintings of κῶμοι, of satyrs, and of
Dionysiac scenes generally (M. Wegner, *das Musikleben der Griechen*
(1949), 44). In one vase-painting it is carried by a satyr in stage-
costume (*ARV*² 591.20 = Brommer, *Satyrspiele*², fig. 20). On the
Pronomos vase (intro., n. 7) there are, as well as the double αὐλός,
two stringed instuments which seem to be lyres. Sil. mentions only
βάρβιτα here, not because it was the only or the primary instrument of the *thiasos*, but perhaps because the αὐλός was too commonplace to mention (Roos, op. cit. 37n., 216.15). Cf. Pratinas fr.
3. **cαυλούμενοι** connotes lasciviousness: Anacr. fr. 458 *PMG* cαῦλα
βαίνειν is of a ἑταίρα (cf. fr. 411 Διονύcου cαῦλαι βαccαρίδες); Ar.
Vesp. 1173 cαυλοπρωκτιᾶν.

41–81. *Parodos.* The Parodos is the earliest extant pastoral song. At
Od. 9.315 Pol. whistles as he drives his sheep; and appears later in
bucolic poetry (Philoxenos 815–824 *PMG*; Theocr. 6 and 11).
This pastoral element fits nicely into the rustic satyric drama. In S.
Inachos, in which Argos sang a βουκολικὸν μέλος (Schol. A. *PV* 575;
Pfeiffer in *SBAW* 1938/2, 29), the satyrs looked after the king's
cattle (Pfeiffer, 27); and in A. *Kirke* they may well have looked
after Kirke's pigs. The theft of cattle was a theme of S. *Ichneutai* and
E. *Autolykos*. E. had a taste for the bucolic even in tragedy (*El.*
493–6, *Andr.* 274–94, *IA* 573–81, 1283–1309, *Hel.* 357–9; Stinton,
op. cit. 40n., ch. 2). Furthermore, the land of the Cyclopes, Sicily,
seems to have been associated with the origins of bucolic poetry
(Dover, *Theocritus*, lxiii–lxv). The Sicilian cowherd said to have
invented βουκολιασμός, Diomos, featured in the Sicilian
Epicharmos' plays *Alkyoneus* and *Odysseus Nauagos*. Epicharmos
also wrote an *Agrostinos* and a *Cyclops*, may well have been the first
to write a bucolic song for drama, and was known in late-5th-cent.
Athens (*RE* vi s. Epicharmos, 39). For work-songs in general in
satyric drama see intro., p. 35 n. 94.

Were the sheep (36–7) real? The view of P. D. Arnott (*Greek*

Scenic Conventions, 179) that they were left to the imagination of the audience is based on the absence from the play of the Homeric method of escape under the sheep, and on the necessity for the satyrs to be dancing. But the Homeric escape would be unpractical on stage; and he forgets the πρόϲπολοι (83), whose presence is difficult to explain unless the sheep were real. The transference of sacrifices to backstage at Ar. *Pax* 1018, *Av.* 850, 1057 suggests the presence of real animals on stage (*pace* Arnott, 54). And cf. Handley on Men. *Dysk.* 393–4. But of course men dressed as animals were familiar enough in comedy, and 49–54 demand an obediently errant ram. Perhaps the sheep were real, except for a man dressed as a ram: so it would have been in the Oxford production of 1976, had it been possible to keep the sheep in Magdalen College overnight.

Metre. The song is made up largely of choriambic dimeters. Its metrical simplicity is characteristic of the play. Wilamowitz (*Griech. Versk.*, 223) and Schroeder (*Euripides Cantica*, 1–2) divide so as to give blunt close with word overlap at 44 (αὖ / ρα = -κοι / τοι in 58), 65, 68, 69 and 70. This seems correct (Maas, *Greek Metre*, §59; Dale, *The Lyric Metres of Greek Drama*[2], 145–7; cf. the same choice at *Hcld.* 377–80). It leaves 69 as glyconic and all the other affected verses as choriambic, of the kinds represented by e.g. 42, 46, 48. Individual metrical points are discussed in the notes on 49–50, 53, 56, 61, 63, 73–4, 76–81. For the heptasyllable in 42 cf. e.g. *Hel.* 1339 = 1355. For the discrepancy *in ancipiti* at 44 = 58 cf. e.g. the same colon at *Ion* 1057 = 1070.

The strophe is followed in L by a few lines (49–54) on which responsion with 63 ff. cannot be forced. Three solutions have been suggested: to print a lacuna after 62 (Paley), to reprint 49–54 after 62 as a refrain (e.g. Murray, Ussher), and to leave the text unchanged, taking the verse as a mesode (Wilamowitz, Behrens). The parallels for refrain and for mesode are discussed at 365–74n., where we have the same choice. They do not (*pace* Duchemin and Ussher) support the case for a refrain here, for they suggest that a refrain in drama nearly always has the nature of a prayer. Further, repetition here would be dramatically worse than useless, importing as it does regularity to the ram's meandering; and presumably the antistrophe turns to the ewe because the ram has been persuaded to come to the cave.

Metrical Scheme. 'X' is a choriambic dimeter type B (the terminology is Dale's, op. cit., ch. 9). 'Y' is a blunt choriambic heptasyllable. Z is a choriambic enoplian B.

41–8 = 55–62	— — — — — ⏑ ⏑ —	X
	— — — — ⏑ ⏑ —	Y
	— — — — — ⏑ ⏑ —	X
	— — ⏑ — ⏑ ⏑ —	Y
45 = 59	— — — — — ⏑ ⏑ —	X
	— — — ⏑ — ⏑ ⏑ —	X
	— — — — — ⏑ ⏑ —	X
	— — — — — ⏑ ⏑ —	X
49	— — ⏑· —	anapaestic monometer
	— — ⏑ ⏑ — / — — ⏑ ⏑ —	anapaestic dimeter
	— — — — / — — ⏑ ⏑ —	anapaestic dimeter
	⏑ ⏑ — ⏑ ⏑ — ⏑ — —	enoplian
	— — ⏑ ⏑ — ⏑ ⏑ — —	enoplian (paroemiac)
	≍ — ⏑ — ⏑ ⏑ —	Y
63	— ⏑ ⏑ / ⏑ ⏑ ⏑ / — ⏑ ⏑ / ⏑ —	iambic dimeter
	— — ⏑ — ⏑ ⏑ —	Y
65	— — ⏑ — ⏑ ⏑ — —	Z
67	— — — — — ⏑ ⏑ —	X
66	— — ⏑ — ⏑ ⏑ —	Y
	— — — — ⏑ ⏑ —	Y
	— ⏑ — ⏑ ⏑ — ⏑ —	glyconic
70	— — — — — ⏑ ⏑ —	X
	— — — — — ⏑ ⏑ —	X
	— — — — ⏑ ⏑ —	Y
	— ⏑ ⏑ — ⏑ ⏑ — ⏑ —	ibycean (?73n.)
	— — ⏑ ⏑ —	anapaestic monometer (?74n.)
75	⟨—⟩ — — — — — —	spondaic paroemiac (?75n.)
	⏑ — ⏑ — ⏑ ⏑ —	Y
	≍ — ⏑ — / · — · —	iambic dimeter with spondaic contraction (76–81n.)
	— ⏑ ⏑ — — / — ⏑ ⏑ — —	anapaestic dimeter
80	— — ⏑ ⏑ — / — — ⏑ ⏑ —	anapaestic dimeter
	— — — ⏑ ⏑ —	anapaestic colarion

41–8. To whom is the strophe addressed, the ram of 49–54 (52 κεράστης) or the ewe of the antistrophe? Two considerations decide for the ram. 41–54 contain a sequence of flattery, enticement and, when they fail (cf. 43 and 49), threat. And secondly, in Homer the ram under which Od. escapes, μήλων ὄχ᾽ ἄριστος ἁπάντων, is addressed in a memorable passage by Pol. (9.443–60), who tells him that he was always the first of the flock to pasture, the first to the river, and the first back home in the evening to the sheepfold (πρῶτος δὲ σταθμόνδε λιλαίεαι ἀπονέεσθαι / ἑσπέριος). E. combined the reminiscence with a parody of the elaborate form of address in tragedy exemplified by S. *El.* 129 ὦ γενέθλα γενναίων πατέρων, *Phil.* 96; *Ion* 262, *Hyps.* fr. 8/9. 11; although no doubt the satyrs, themselves noble animals (590, 624), mean it seriously. Even for this touch there is inspiration in Homer: Pol. calls the ram μακρὰ βιβάς (450), a phrase associated with the noble stride of heroes (e.g. *Il.* 7.213, 15.307). One suspects also the influence of literary or actual bucolic: in Theocritus shepherds address their animals individually (1.151, 4.45, 5.102, 8.49), as real Greek shepherds do today. Cf. also J. K. Campbell, *Honour, Family and Patronage* (1964), 26, 30–1, on solidarity between modern Greek shepherds and their sheep.

41. παῖ (Dindorf; πᾶ δή μοι L) restores responsion with 55, explains the genitives, and unlike other conjectures (e.g. πᾶ μοι, γέννα γενναίων κτλ. Hermann) requires no addition to the antistrophe (in 55 μοι τοὺς between σπαργῶντας and μαστοὺς was added (Tr. 3) to create responsion with L's πᾶ δή μοι κτλ.). The corruption was caused probably by assimilation to 43.

42. δ᾽ἐκ (Dindorf; τ᾽ ἐκ L): see apparatus. **τοκάδων:** more often of animals than of women (e.g. Theocr. 8.63 of goats). But that does not mean that it is bathetic here: of E.'s three other uses of the word, two are of women (*Hipp.* 559, *Hec.* 1157; cf. *Med.* 187).

43. The ram wanders or leaps towards the rocks, which are probably painted on either side of the cave. The satyrs then tempt him back to the grass (cf. 541) and the drinking troughs (cf. 29). **νίσῃ** is perhaps future (*Il.* 23.76), but more likely present (*Hel.* 1483; Hes. *Op.* 237). For the simple accusative σκοπέλους cf. *Pho.* 1234 χθόνα νίσεσθε.

44. ὑπήνεμος αὔρα: Ussher takes ὑπο- as diminutive. But does diminutive ὑπο- ever combine with a noun to form an adjective? In the only two possible cases (ὕπαφρος and ὕπομβρος) it is doubtful that ὑπο- is diminutive (Pisani in *Rend. Acad. Linc.* 1932, 340). ὑπήνεμος elsewhere describes a relationship with the ἄνεμος, usually meaning 'sheltered' from it. And so the passages cited by Kassel (in *Maia* 25 (1973), 100: S. *Tr.* 953 ἀνεμοέccα . . . αὔρα; *Hel.* 1455; Alc. fr. 319 L-P) are not in fact parallel. Tempting therefore is ὑπήνεμοc αὐλά (Musgrave): cf. 60. But an αὔρα tends to be more gentle than an ἄνεμοc. And so ὑπήνεμοc αὔρα can mean an αὔρα sheltered from the ἄνεμοc, i.e. a gentle breeze. A gentle breeze is a τόποc of the *locus amoenus* (*Med.* 839–40; Pl. *Phdr.* 230c; *AP* 16.228.2; Hor. *Od.* 3.4.6–8; G. Schönbeck, *der locus amoenus von Homer bis Horaz* (diss. Heidelberg, 1962)).

46. At Theocr. 11.44–8 Pol. tempts Galatea to his cave with a *locus amoenus*, like the satyrs here: ἔcτι ψυχρὸν ὕδωρ κτλ. **δινᾶέν:** a Homeric epithet for rivers (*Il.* 5.479, *Od.* 6.89; cf. Simon. 564.2).

47. πίcτραιc: at 29 the neuter form is guaranteed by the metre. Elsewhere it is feminine (*EM*, Strabo 8.3.31). We should allow E. the inconsistency (390n.).

48. οὐ: οὔ (Tr.1) may be influenced by 44 and 49. But οὐ τᾶιδε in 44 may justify οὔ here: τᾶιδε is understood in the second limb of the anaphora, just as *hic* is understood at V. *Aen.* 1.461–2 *sunt hic etiam sua praemia laudi, sunt lacrimae rerum*, where admittedly the anaphora is easier. See Kenney in *CR* 14 (1964), 13.

49–50. There are some obscured letters above the line before κλιτὺν in L, representing it seems two syllables. They served as the basis for conjectures by Hermann and Bothe, but are in fact nothing more than a misguided attempt (Tr. 3) to create responsion with 64. Perhaps Tr. observed that in L 49 and 63 are metrically equivalent. In fact the obvious similarities of wording between 49 and 63, together with the responsion of the preceding lines, may have inspired an ancient κωλίζων to create responsion by adjusting 63 (n.), perhaps also 49 (to delete the third οὐ would give the kind of expression exemplified by *Phaeth.* 219, S. *OT* 430–1, *El.* 1430). **ψύττα:** this is the onomatopoeic -st-, common to many languages and still uttered by Greek shepherds. The -α is phonetic rather than etymological (Schwyzer in *ZVS* 58 (1931), 170): then as now the Greeks found it difficult to end a word with a consonant other than c, ν, or ρ. That being the case, Wilamowitz is wrong to see synizesis between ψύττα and οὐ rather than elision (L has ψύττα οὐ). cίττα is used by Theocritean shepherds to get animals to move, and at 4.45 and 5.100 it is certainly elided (cf. 4.46, 5.3, 8.69; Rossi in *SIFC* 1971, 8). Cf. ψ at S. *Ichn.* 176. **νεμῆιc** is future.

51. At *Ion* 158 Ion threatens a bird: μάρψω c' αὖ τόξοιc κτλ. For the construction cf. *Ba.* 1096 αὐτοῦ χερμάδαc . . . ἔρριπτον. **ὠή** is used to attract attention, as always elsewhere (*pace* Carden, op. cit. 5n., 87, on S. fr. 269c. 25), except for *Pho.* 269: cf. A. *Eum.* 94; *HF* 1106 (probably), *Ion* 907 (Apollo's), *IT* 1304, *Pho.* 1067, 1069, *Hel.* 435, 1180.

52. If it is legitimate to distinguish ὤ in exclamations from ὦ before a vocative or imperative (LSJ s. 4; Fraenkel on A. *Ag.* 22), then here we should read ὦ. Even at 658 τύφετ' ὦ, καίετ' ὦ (where, as here, L fails to isolate the ὦ), the ὦ can be taken with the preceding imperative: cf. Ar. *Pax* 461 ὦ εἶα with 468 εἶα ὦ; also *Tro.* 335; A. *Cho.* 942; Ar. *Lys.* 350. And here, as at *Alc.* 234 βόασον ὦ στέναξον ὦ Φεραία χθών, at least the second ὦ may go also with the following vocative. Cf. Ar. *Vesp.* 290 ὕπαγ' ὦ παῖ ὕπαγε.

53. μηλοβότα refers to Pol. (cf. 660). στασιωρὸν means guardian of the στάσις (= σταθμός; cf. fr. 442): cf. πυλωρός, κηπωρός, etc. Murray refers it to the πέτρον (presumably as the great stone that bars the entrance to the cave in Homer: 9.243), Wilamowitz (στασιωρὲ) to the ram, Paley to the satyr who utters the words. But the best candidate is Sil. (Musgrave), for it is he who is guardian of the fold (29–35). This requires the addition of **πρὸς** which if placed before μηλοβότα (Wecklein) gives an enoplian (paroemiac): Dale, *The Lyric Metres of Greek Drama* (2nd ed.; 1968), 172.

54. ἀγροβότα (L) makes no sense, for in all other -βότης compounds the first half refers to what is fed (e.g. μηλοβότης, ἱπποβότης: Buck and Peterson, *Reverse Index*, 561). ἀγροβάτα (Tr. 3) is correct (same corruption at S. *Phil.* 214). Cf. *Tro.* 436 ὀρειβάτης Κύκλωψ. It means that Pol., the ram's accustomed master, is out hunting. Sil. is offered as his deputy (35). Conceivably μηλοβότα (53) is an intrusive gloss on ἀγροβότα, but much more likely caused the corruption. For μηλοβότα .. ἀγροβάτα cf. *El.* 169–70 γαλακτοπότας ἀνὴρ Μυκηναῖος οὐριβάτας.

55–62. Having addressed the strophe to a ram, the satyrs now address the antistrophe to a ewe. At *Od.* 9.244–5 Pol. milked the ewes and goats, then ὑπ' ἔμβρυον ἧκεν ἑκάστηι.

55. Cf. 41n.

56. Wilamowitz (*Griech. Versk.*, 223) retained L's σποράς. -ι before στ- must be long (Bond on *Hyps.* fr. 64.66). Can – – ◡ – respond with the choriamb in 42? 499, adduced by Murray, is irrelevant because suspect on other grounds. 'A choriamb rarely, if ever, answers anything except a choriamb' (Denniston in *Greek Poetry and Life, Essays Presented to Gilbert Murray*, 142): of the possible exceptions (to Denniston's list add S. *Phil.* 1138 = 1161; Ar. *Lys.* 326 = 340) only Ar. *Lys.* 324 = 338 is – – ◡ –, but the reading is unsure. Denniston's survey was of dramatic 'iambo-choriambic'. But I know of no exception in the (closely related: Dale, op. cit. 53n., ch. IX) 'purely aeolic'. Dindorf suggested γονὰς, Wecklein δρόcουc. Better are (1) **θηλὰc πορίcαc** (Broadhead) **οὖc** (Diggle; cf. 224, 234, 256): for this construction (ἀρνῶν picks up οὖc) cf. *IT* 736, *Su.* 201–2. (2) τροφὰc (Wieseler): perhaps ΣΙΤ became ΣΠ. Cf. 189. But elsewhere τροφή meaning θρέμμα has a possessive genitive (189n.), and ἀρνῶν here cannot mean the ewes. It is however possible that ἀρνῶν specifies τροφὰc 'brood . . . consisting of lambs' (cf. 189n.), or that τροφὰc stands alone and ἀρνῶν goes with θαλάμοιc (57n.).

57. θαλάμοιc: most commonly, and originally, of the inner rooms of a house as opposed to the μέγαρον or δῶμα. In *Od.* Pol. is away all day pasturing the flock, but leaves the lambs and kids in various pens within the cave (9.219–22): hence ἀρνῶν (?56n.) θαλάμοιc and ἀμερόκοιτοι (58; cf. e.g. S. *Phil.* 160 πετρίνη κοίτη of a cave).

58–9. Cf. *Il.* 4.434–5. **ἀμερόκοιτοι βλαχαί:** cf. A. *Sept.* 348 βλαχαὶ δ' αἱματόεccαι . . . ἀρτιτρεφεῖc κτλ.

60. αὐλὰν can mean a courtyard (in the country this usually contains animals, e.g. *Il.* 5.138), or a dwelling in general (e.g. S. *Ant.* 786), an ambiguity indicative of the open character of Greek houses. At *Od.* 9.239, 338, 462 there is an αὐλή. Cf. 345n. **ἀμφιβαίνειc:** ἀμφιβαλεῖc (Tr. 3) restores responsion with 46. But nowhere else is ἀμφιβάλλω intransitive referring to movement. Most of the attempts to emend ignore the fact that ἀμφι- prefixing verbs of motion (cf. περι-) suggests *encompassment*, which does not suit the desired movement of the ewe. This difficulty is perhaps removed by Jackson's—ἔτ' ἀμφινέμηι ποιηροὺc λείπουcα νομούc; — Αἰτναίων κτλ. (*Marginalia Scaenica*, 134), which seems however to make the satyrs averse to the ewe leaving the pastures. Read perhaps ἀμφίθυρον: cf. S. *Phil.* 159 οἶκον μὲν ὁρᾶιc τόνδ' ἀμφίθυρον πετρίνηc κοίτηc (and with αὐλάν here cf. ibid. 19 δι' ἀμφιτρῆτος αὐλίου). *Cyc.* was probably produced shortly after S. *Phil.*, and *Cyc.* 707 δι' ἀμφιτρῆτοc τῆcδε probably alludes to Philoctetes' cave (707n.; intro., §VI), an allusion which might seem too abrupt and improvised unless we read ἀμφίθυρον here. Certainly the consequent ellipse of the verb is difficult, particularly with the appendage of a participal clause (though cf. 61n.), and this may have elicited the corruption. But the ellipse of a verb of motion is surely natural enough in a shepherd's orders to his flock: cf. e.g. Theocr. 8.49–5 ὦ τράγε, τᾶν λευκᾶν αἰγῶν ἄνερ, ἐc βάθος ὕλαc / μυρίον—αἱ cιμαὶ δεῦτ' ἐθ' ὕδωρ Ἐριφοι- (also 4.46, 5.3, 100, 102). Nevertheless, the passage remains a crux.

61. λιποῦcα: λειποῦcα (Tr. 3) was to achieve responsion with 47. But inexact responsion in the base of aeolic cola is common (e.g. 44 = 58), and in this participial idiom meaning effectively 'away from' the aorist is standard (Stinton in *PCPhS* 21 (1975), 85): e.g. *HF* 787 πατρὸς ὕδωρ βᾶτε λιποῦςαι.

63-7. For the vigorous parataxis of these lines cf. Pratinas fr. 3 (satyric: 2n.).

63. τᾶδε ... τᾶδε (L) may be the remnant of an attempt to create responsion with 49 (49-50n.). Cf. 204, Stevens on *Andr.* 168. Headlam (in *CR* 15 (1901), 22) deleted the second τᾶδε, comparing 204-5, *Andr.* 168 οὐ γάρ ἐςθ' Ἕκτωρ τάδε, οὐ Πρίαμος οὐδὲ χρυςός; Eriphus fr. 6. But cf. *Hyps.* fr. 1.ii.9 οὐ τάδε πήνας, οὐ τάδε κερκίδος κτλ. Diggle's text makes a perfectly good iambic dimeter (for its context cf. *Hipp.* 161). The contrast between former joys and present sorrows, to be found also in the openings of some tragedies (29n., 80n.), has already been emphasized by Sil. (25-6). Cf. 76-7n.

65. The τύμπανον {*Ba.* 124 βυρcότονον κύκλωμα) resembles the tambourine, except that it is covered on both sides with hide (Wegner, op. cit. 40n., 65; *pace* Dodds on *Ba.* 59). At *Ba.* 120-34 the *thiasos* sings of its invention by the Korybantes; they gave it to Rhea, from whom the satyrs obtained it (Dodds on *Ba.* 59, 120-34; Seaford, art. cit. 63-7n., 90). In Attic vase-painting it appears only in the last quarter of the 5th cent. (Wegner, 228-9)—a time of popularity for oriental cults—and is almost always seen in the hands of Maenads: hence perhaps its association with Βάκχαι here. Cf. 205n. ἀλαλαγμοί: because for the Greeks musical instruments uttered cries, particularly in orgiastic religion (e.g. fr. 586.4; *h. hom.* 14.3), the same word ἀλαλάζειν can refer both to music (A. fr. 57.7 ψαλμὸc δ' ἀλαλάζει; *Hel.* 1352) and to ecstatic cries (*Ba.* 1133). And so the translation of γέγονα ... κύμβαλον ἀλαλάζον in Paul 1 *Cor.* 13.1 as '... a tinkling cymbal' is clearly insufficient. For the language of the drum in particular see A. E. Crawley, *Dress, Drink and Drums*, 249. Accordingly, ἀλαλαγμοί here seems to mean the confusion of the cries of the drums with human cries; cf. 40n.

66-7. Diggle follows Hermann in reversing the order of these lines, on the grounds that the water goes better with the wine than with the drums (*Ba.* 704-7). But perhaps we should not demand too much precision of the satyrs' idea of paradise. And the reversal introduces in 65 an isolated choriambic enoplian, as it precludes the division ἀλαλαγ / μοί.

66. Springs are part of the traditional *locus amoenus* (Schönbeck, op. cit. 44n., 10), and are associated both with the Nymphs (68; cf. e.g. *IA* 1294) and with Dionysos (*Ion* 1074; Dodds on *Ba.* 704-11).

67. χλωρός can mean 'fresh' (of cheese at Ar. *Ran.* 559), 'alive' (of branches at Hes. *Op.* 743; cf. *Od.* 9.320), and 'vigorous' (of γόνυ at

Theocr. 14.70). It also describes liquids which seem to possess their own life and vigour (blood: *Hec.* 127; S. *Trach.* 1055; tears: *Med.* 906, 922, *Hel.* 1189), and this is the point of χλωραί here. Vines may weep (Theophr. fr. 121) and wine may be the blood of the god (Timoth. 780 *PMG*). Of the latter notion there may be a suggestion both here and at Moero, p. 22 Powell, 2: βότρυ, Διωνύcου πληθόμενοc cταγόνι. The sense of movement (cτάζω) is probably present also in cταγόνεc, which is also used of tears (A. *Ag.* 888, *Cho.* 186; cf. E. *Su.* 79–82) and of blood (*Pho.* 1415, *Ba.* 767; A. *Ag.* 1122, *Cho.* 400; S. *OT* 1278). (The word χλωρόc is discussed at length, but without penetration, by E. Irwin, *Colour Terms in Greek Poetry*, ch. 2.)

68. At *Ba.* 556–9 the *thiasos*, oppressed by Pentheus, lament the absence of their lord: πόθι Νύcαc ἄρα τᾶc θηροτρόφου θυρcοφορεῖc θιάcουc, ὦ Διόνυc', ἢ κορυφαῖc Κωρυκίαιc; Nysa is a fictional mountain of no fixed abode, associated with the name Dionysos. At *Il.* 6.133 it is the scene of Lykourgos' pursuit of the nurses of Dionysos; and at *h. hom.* 1.9 it is near the limits of the poet's inkling of the world cχεδὸν Αἰγύπτοιο ῥοάων. Later we find it, as the scene of Dionysos' childhood, in Arabia (D.S. 1.15, 3.64), Libya (D.S. 3.66), Aethiopia (Hdt. 2.146), and Asia (Apollod. 3.4.3); see also *h. hom.* 26.3–5. **οὐδ' ἐν Νύcαι:** all that is visible (after Tr. 3) of the original reading of L is νυc. The correction is hard to read, but does begin with οὐ, and looks like οὐ νυcca. The apparent loss of εν may have been influenced by 65 and 67. οὐδ' is preferable (as introducing a new structure, with a verb expressed, as the last item of a series) to Duport's οὐκ.

69–70. Ἴακχον derives from ἰάχω (Frisk s.v.), and means either an enthusiastic cry or its divine personification, both associated especially with the Eleusinian mysteries (e.g. Hdt. 8.65; Nilsson, *Gesch. Gr. Relig.*, i 664). The repetition echoes the song of the initiates Ἴακχ' ὦ Ἴακχε (Ar. *Ran.* 316, etc.). The god Ἴακχοc is already in the 5th cent. identified with Dionysos (*Ba.* 725; S. *Ant.* 1154, fr. 959 Ἴακχοc on Nysa). Is the song or the god meant here? Probably the song: Ἴακχοc ὠιδή can mean 'Iacchos song'. If the god, then we should (despite *HF* 687, *IA* 1467, where there is no ambiguity) read ὠδαῖc (cf. *Antiope* 86 Page μέλπειν θεοὺc ὠδαῖcιν; Powell, *Coll. Alex.* 141.3 ἵνα Φοῖβον ὠδαῖcι μέλψητε; Ar. *Thesm.* 988), or Kassel's ὠιδᾶι. In either case it comes as a slight, and perhaps humorous, surprise that the recipient of the song (cf. *Tro.* 515 μέλοc ἐc Τροίαν ἰαχήcω) should be Aphrodite. This apparently divided allegiance (cf. *Ba.* 78–82) is not based on any general association of the satyrs with Aphrodite herself: however close her association with

Dionysos (Dodds, and Roux, on *Ba.* 402-3), Aph. appears with the satyrs before 400 BC only, so far as I know, on one Boeotian skyphos (Athens Inv. 1406; cf. Brommer *Satyroi* (Würzburg, 1937), 14-15). We should rather compare those Attic vase-paintings in which the satyrs are, in the presence of Dionysos, more concerned with nymphs or maenads (e.g. *ABV* 261.40, *ARV*² 182.6, 1145.36). Nevertheless, Aph. here is not a mere abstraction ('sex') any more than are the Ἔρωτες on her island at *Ba.* 405. For it is of the essence of the satyrs that their secular activities are also religious (9n., 39n., 81n., 495-502n.).

71. Hunting is a frequent metaphor for ἔρως (e.g. Archil. fr. 196a (West, *Delectus*), 47; *Tro.* 369, 979, *IA* 960, fr. 428; Ariphr. 813.5 *PMG*; Men. fr. 258; Pl. *Phdr.* 240a; Meleager 4620 Gow and Page). It is also an activity of Dionysos (e.g. *Ba.* 1189; Winnington-Ingram, *Euripides and Dionysus*, index s. 'hunting') and of the satyrs (A. *Dikt.* 814-20; S. fr. 154 (*Ach Erast.*), *Ichn.*). And so it is particularly suitable as a metaphor for the satyrs' imagined mountainside pursuit here. Cf. S. fr. 779 ἐγὼ δὲ χερςὶν ἄγραν βρίακχον (i.e. βάκχην), spoken no doubt by Sil. or a satyr (cf. A. *Dikt.* 801, where Sil. calls Danae an ἄγρα). Although ἂν refers to Aphrodite, this does not mean that the satyrs are to be envisaged as actually pursuing the goddess any more than are the maenads at *Ba.* 688 θηρᾶν καθ' ὕλην Κύπριν, or Dionysos at *Ba.* 459 τὴν Ἀφροδίτην καλλονῆι θηρώμενος. But the goddess is less of an abstraction here (cf. 69-70n.) than at *Ba.* 459, 688 (or at *Ion* 1103, *IA* 1159, 1264, *Pho* 399; *Od.* 22.444; Pi. *Ol.* 6.36), and the realized metaphor is incoherent, inasmuch as it implies that it is the goddess rather than the Βάκχαι that the satyrs are after. **πετόμαν:** cf. *Ion* 716-17. For the supernatural swiftness of maenads see Dodds on *Ba.* 1090-3. For maenads as birds see *Ba.* 748-50; Naevius frr. 30-2 W.

72. The satyrs' female companions are Βάκχαι here and at 64, νύμφαι at 68 and 430. Cf. 3-4n., 430n. In the ancient *Homeric Hymn to Aphrodite* the female companions of the cιληνοί are nymphs (262), as they are in 6th cent. Corinthian and Attic vase-painting (Edwards in *JHS* 80 (1960), 78-9). Towards the end of the 6th cent. the nymphs tend to be replaced by maenads (Edwards, 80-2). The merging identities of nymphs and maenads (Roscher, *Lex. Myth.*, s. Mainaden, 2244-5; both nurses of Dionysos: Henrichs in *HSCP* 82 (1978), 141) may reflect the maenads' conception of themselves as nymphs (just as men dressed up to become Dionysos' mythical satyrs): D.S. 4.3. **λευκόποcιν:** cf. *Ba.* 863. Βάκχαι went barefoot (Dodds on *Ba.* 664-7). and λευκός is frequent in tragedy of female flesh. The same emphasis occurs in black-figure vase-painting, where female flesh is commonly white.

73. Mortals may invoke a god as φίλος (e.g. A. *Sept.* 154, 159, 174; S. *Aj.* 14; *Pho.* 684, 1061; Ar. *Eq.* 1270). But here the relationship is more intimate: 81n., 435; S. *Ichn.* 76.

73–4. Ussher prints Diggle's earlier suggestion φίλος ὦ Βακχεῖε ποῖ οἰοπολεῖς; / ⟨ποτ'⟩ ξανθὰν χαίταν σείεις (anapaestic). But whereas φίλος ὦ would be unique in E. (despite delayed ὦ at *El.* 167, *Hel.* 1451, *Or.* 1246), ὦ φίλος is very common (*Andr.* 510, 530, 1204, *Su.* 278, *Tro.* 267, 1081, *IT* 830, *Rhes.* 367; cf. also A. *Dikt.* 807; West in *Glotta* 44 (1966), 143). 'O dear Hector' is ὦ φίλ' Ἕκτορ (*Tro.* 673). For the pathetic repetition cf. *Tro.* 1081 ὦ φίλος, ὦ πόσι μοι, *Andr.* 530 ὦ φίλος, φίλος, *Su.* 278. Βακχεῖε is Tr. 3 and so probably a metrical conjecture. P originally had Βάκχιε, which was then changed to Βακχεῖε, probably with reference to L (cf. G. Zuntz, *An Inquiry into the Transmission of the Plays of Euripides* (Cambridge, 1965), 140). Indeed, nowhere else is Βακχεῖος a noun (cf. e.g. Ar. *Thesm.* 988 Βακχεῖε δέσποτα). In *Cyc.* Βάκχιος occurs eleven times, always as a noun, and always (except at 446) guaranteed by the metre, whereas Βακχεῖος occurs not at all. ὦ φίλος ὦ φίλε Βάκχιε may be acceptable as an ibycean (for such in an aeolo-choriambic context see *IT* 1098, *El.* 151, 155, *Or.* 831, *IA* 169), although the final *brevis in longo* is unparalleled. A better analysis perhaps is anapaestic (cf. 74n., 75, 77–80), whether with metron-boundary after φίλε or (deleting ὦ φίλος) after Βάκχιε: cf. 74n., 75n.

74. **ποῖ οἰοπολεῖς** can be rendered anapaestic by such slight changes as ποῖ δ' ... (see apparatus), τί ποτ', or cυ ποῖ (postponed interrogative: 115, 129, 138, 502, 521, 549; Thomson in *CQ* 32 (1939), 147–52; correption in anapaests: 358, 360, 615; K-B i 197–8). οἰοπολεῖς does not mean that D. is necessarily alone (11), but that he is separated from his *thiasos*.

75. On the sea shore where he was captured by pirates D. appeared as a young man, καλαὶ δὲ περισσείοντο ἔθειραι κυανεαί (*h. hom.* 7.4–5). Originally no doubt of religious significance (cf. Apollo ἀκερσοκόμης and Pan ἀγλαέθειρος), D.'s long hair is in 4th cent. vase-painting part of his effeminacy. Already in *Ba.* the merely effeminate (235, 455, cf. Anacr. 422 *PMG*) and the religous aspect are dramatically opposed (493–4). **σείεις**: the shaking of the head is, in contemporary vase-painting, part of the Dionysiac dance: see Dodds on *Ba.* 862–5. σείων is probably a conjecture (Tr. 3) to restore the syntax. Conceivably the text may stand (with the question mark after οἰοπολεῖς) as a statement contrasting with 76. Better to read ... οἰοπολῶν / ξανθὰν χαίταν σείεις; (Nauck; cf. K-G ii 98), or ⟨ποῖ⟩ ξανθὰν χαίταν ϲείειϲ; (Murray), or simply ... ⟨καὶ⟩ ξανθὰν χαίταν ϲείειϲ; cf. *Ba.* 184–5 ποῖ δεῖ χορεύειν, ποῖ καθιϲτάναι πόδα / καὶ κρᾶτα ϲεῖϲαι πολιόν.

76–81. The metre of these verses is discussed by Diggle (art. cit. 39n., 45) and by Stinton (*JHS* 97 (1977), 138). 76 is a blunt choriambic heptasyllable (parodos n.). 77 in L (θητεύω Κύκλωπι) is a hexamakron with *brevis in longo*. But Stinton points out that the hexamakron is always clausular to threnodic anapaests (cf. Diggle in *PCPS* 20 (1974), 22–4), and accepts Headlam's (*CR* 16 (1902), 250) deletion of Κύκλωπι as a gloss (though not his rearrangement of the rest as choriambs): this gives θητεύω τῶι μονοδέρκται as a paroemiac, followed by anapaestic dimeter, monometer and colarion. If it is felt that there is insufficient pause after Stinton's proposed paroemiac, other possibilities are the transposition of θητεύω to after μονοδέρκται (Diggle, giving enoplia in 77 and 78) or to after Κύκλωπι (Fritzsche, printed by Diggle): this has the advantage of not breaking up the dimeters 79–80, but Κύκλωπι θητεύω would be an iambic dimeter with spondaic contraction, a verse which occurs elsewhere in E. only at *Alc.* 401 = 413 (context dochmiac), *Su.* 781 = 789 (iambo-trochaic), perhaps *IT* 400 = 415 (mostly aeolic), *Ion* 1509 (conceivably anapaestic; though cf. Dale, op. cit. 53n., 176), *Or.* 1447 (iambic). For the anapaestic close 81, see Dale, 60–1.

76–7. Poignantly contrasted are the two kinds of service, a τόπος perhaps of satyric drama (63n.; S. *Ichn.* 223 τίϲ μετάϲταϲιϲ πόνων; intro., §IV). Strabo numbers the satyrs among the δαίμονεϲ ἢ πρόπολοι θεῶν (10.3.7; cf. *Hel.* 570) (cf. the πρόϲπολοι of Bakchos in Limenius, *Delphic Hymn*, 44–6 (Powell, *Coll. Alex.*, p. 150) and in the song from Doura-Europos, 13 (*AJP* 69 (1948), 29).). Teiresias (*Ba.* 366) and the satyrs (709) desire to be slaves of Dionysos. Ion too is proud of being a slave οὐ θνατοῖϲ ἀλλ᾽ ἀθανάτοιϲ (*Ion* 133; cf. *Or.* 418, *Tro.* 450; S. *OT* 410; Pl. *Apol.* 23c; Wilamowitz on *HF* 823). The practice of dedicating slaves to a deity occurs in the 5th cent. (*Ion* 310, *Pho.* 221, etc.; Bömer in *AAWM* 1960/1, 149, 179; 1961/4, 275–91; W. H. D. Rouse, *Greek Votive Offerings*, 56, 102, 336; *IG* i³ 383.1.157). For the (later) practice of voluntary divine slavery see R. Reitzenstein, *Die Hellenistische Mysterienreligionen*[3], 192–215.

76. ἐγὼ...: cf. the ending κἀγὼ ... at 619, and in general Kranz, *Stasimon*, 120–3.

78. μονοδέρκται: cf. 21n., and Cratinus fr. 149. ἀλαίνων denotes (*pace* Ussher) not movement but exile: see Denniston on *El.* 202–4.

80. Does this phrase refer to the normal dress of the stage-satyr (the short skirt called περίζωμα) or to the satyrs' dress as shepherds in this play? If the former, then here is an indication of the original goatishness of the stage-satyrs (cf. A. fr. 207; S. *Ichn.* 367), which would provide a link between Aristotle's derivation of tragedy ἐκ cατυρικοῦ and one possible etymology of the word τραγωιδία. The περίζωμα is in contemporary vase-painting sometimes (e.g. on the Pronomos Vase: Plate III) shaggy and suggestive of a goat. (Pollux, *Onom.* 4.118, includes the goatskin in a list of what stage-satyrs wear; but he is writing well after the Hellenistic confusion of the satyrs with the goatlike Pans, and the Hellenistic adornment of processional satyrs in novel and luxurious styles.) Although χλαῖνα means 'cloak', τράγου χλαῖνα might conceivably, as a humorous description of the skin of a goat, refer to the περίζωμα. But the περίζωμα, with the phallus attached, represents satyric nudity, and it would be curiously metaphysical of the satyrs to complain thus of their own nature. Rather the satyrs, like Theocritus' rustics (3.25; 5.2, 10, 15; 7.15; Gomme and Sandbach on Men. *Epitr.* 229), are wearing goatskins because they are shepherds. The humorous point in τράγου χλαῖνα is then much better. The satyrs are wearing as a χλαῖνα (i.e. over their shoulders, not as περίζωμα) the χλαῖνα of a goat. The snobbery of the complaint (cf. Ar. *Nub.* 69–72) combines in a faintly ridiculous way with the sensitivity of the satyrs, as θῆρεc (624, etc.), to the implication that they are goats. In 5th cent. vase-painting satyrs sometimes wear the most unlikely costumes, and it may well have been a feature of the genre that in those plays in which the satyrs performed some unlikely function (intro., §IV) the joke was consummated by their adoption of the appropriate, or rather the inappropriate, dress. Furthermore, in the company of Dionysos in vase-painting the satyrs frequently wear over their shoulders (e.g. *ARV*² 182.6) the fawnskin (νεβρίc) and the leopard skin (πάρδαλιc) (cf. A. *Dikt.* 790 ὦ ποικιλόνω[το]ι; S. *Ichn.* 224–5; *Ba.* 111, 249). These skins are the badge of that service of Dionysos of which the satyrs are bitterly lamenting the loss. On the entrance of the shepherd-satyrs the audience would have been quick to notice their skins as not of leopard or fawn but of goat—an absurd but telling symbol of the μετάcταcιc πόνων. Yet another factor in the joke may have been the audience's memory of e.g. *El.* 184–6 cκέψαι μου πιναρὰν κόμαν / καὶ τρύχη τάδ' ἐμῶν πέπλων / εἰ πρέποντα κτλ. (also *Alc.* 818, *El.* 501, *Hel.* 416, 1079): the satyrs are implicitly claiming tragic status: cf. 29n.

81. cᾶc χωρὶc φιλίαc   echoes a religious formula: cf. the last line of

Ariphron's hymn to Ὑγίεια (813 *PMG*): cέθεν δὲ χωρὶc οὔτιc
εὐδαίμων ἔφυ, which Norden (*Agnostos Theos*, 157 n. 3, 159 n. 1) sees
as derived from cultic poetry, and gives further parallels; cf. also
frr. 391, 1025. But the mention of φιλία in the formula was no
doubt rare, inasmuch as φιλία generally (despite 73n., Pl. *Symp.*
188d) refers to relations between mortals (Aristotle denies that it
can obtain between man and god: *EN* 1159a4, *MM* 1208b30).
And so we have here again that combination of the profane and
the sacred that is symptomatic of the satyrs' status between man
and god (9n., 39n., 69–70n., 495–502n.). Cf. S. *Ichn.* 76. The φιλία
here is probably mutual (Dale on *Alc.* 279) and may be both
subjective (*Hipp.* 254) and objective (*HF* 1200).

82–95. These lines make a long announcement of the entry of
Odysseus and his men. Long entry-announcements in tragedy are
designed to increase apprehension and expectancy about the
entry (Taplin, *The Stagecraft of Aeschylus*, 297)—e.g. *El.* 962–87; S.
Phil. 201–18—sometimes by describing the person approaching
(A. *Su.* 176–83, 710–23; S. *OC* 310–23). This example, which may
be faintly paratragic, allows us to savour the humorous prospect of
the unlikely meeting not to be found in Homer.

83. **προcπόλουc:** the convention of giving orders to palace πρόcπολοι
(e.g. *Hipp.* 808, *HF* 332) is out of place at Pol.'s cave. But E. makes
no attempt (*pace* Lindskog, *Studien zum Antiken Drama*, 10) to make
them appear a symptom of his Pol.'s wealth and civilization
(intro., §VII), for we hear no more of them. They are rather no
more than a fleeting necessity, to look after the sheep while the
chorus dance, and perhaps dressed as satyrs. Most unlikely is that
they are the chorus themselves (cf. πρόπολοc 76, but ὦ τέκνα 82).
In general see G. Richter, *De Mutis Personis quae in Tragoedia atque
Comoedia Attica in Scaenam Producuntur* (Halle, 1934).

84. **ἀτὰρ δή** is rare. X asks a question or makes a request; Y answers
or assents, and with ἀτὰρ δή introduces his own question, which
may, as here, touch on the reason for X's question or request (*Tro.*
63, *Andr.* 883).

85. **πρὸc ἀκταῖc** means that the ship is in shallow water; cf. Thuc.
7.34 πρὸc τῆι γῆι ναυμαχεῖν. **ναὸc... cκάφοc:** this periphrasis, though
it does occur elsewhere (e.g. *IT* 742), has a particularly vigorous
life in this play: 362, 467, 505, 702. Cf. 98n.

86. For the metaphor cf. *Alc.* 498, *IA* 1260; A. *Pers.* 378, 383; S. fr.
775; Ov. *Met.* 13.2. On E. *Telephos* fr. 705 κώπηc ἀνάccων Aristotle
remarked (*Rhet.* 1405a30) ἀπρεπέc, ὅτι μεῖζον τὸ ἀνάccειν ἢ κατ'
ἀξίαν. In fact the metaphor may derive in part from an ancient

sense of ἀνάccειν as 'control' (e.g. in χειρῶναξ). But certainly in this context, and in the mouth of Sil., it seems designed to appear pompous.

88. φέρονται. (As late as Hermann's edition (1837) it was believed that the MSS. had φέρονταc). Paley printed Elmsley's φέρουcι, objecting to the middle. But the middle may convey no more than a slight suggestion that the action is performed for the advantage of the subject (K-G i 109). And Sil. is not uninterested in why the strangers have the pots. Cf. 191 φέρεcθε; Dodds on *Ba.* 1280; Hdt. 7.50.4; Xen. *Cyr.* 3.1.32; Men. *Dysk.* 448; and perhaps (*pace* Kells) S. *El.* 476 Δίκα δίκαια φερομένα χεροῖν κράτη (Δίκη attacks Injustice with hammer or staff: Paus. 5.18.2; Furtwängler, *Bronzefunde aus Olympia*, 95; for κράτη cf. S. *O T* 200–201).

89. We hear nothing about the desire for water after 97. Cf. Bond on *Hyps.* fr. 1 iv 29, where 'the request for water is shelved for more than 40 lines'.

89–90. Cf. *IT* 479 πόθεν ποθ' ἥκετ', ὦ ταλαίπωροι ξένοι; The phrase is amusingly heroic here. **τίνεc ποτ' εἰcίν** has been taken (Jacobs) to mean 'whoever they might be', on the grounds that there is no point in asking the chorus. But the question is rhetorical, as at 99. Exx. of τίc for ὅcτιc are given by Diggle on *Phaeth.* 46: each is, unlike here, the object of a verb.

90–3. Cf. the similar situation in Achaios' probably satyric *Kyknos* fr. 43 τοιοῦδε φωτὸc πρὸc δόμουc ἐλήλυτε.

91. τε γῆν: most editors retain L's cτέγην, which would mean the cave. But (1) ἐμβαίνειν with the accusative in E. means to step *onto* something (except *HF* 164 τάξιν ἐμβεβώc): as exx. I can be no fairer than cite those cited by Wieszner in *defence* of cτέγην: *Alc.* 1000 δοχμίαν κέλευθον ἐμβαίνων, *Hec.* 921–3 ναύταν ... ὅμιλον Τροίαν Ἰλιάδ' ἐμβεβῶτα (this must refer to the Greek encampment), *Rhes.* 214. Od. and his men are not on the roof of the cave. And to read εἰcβεβῶτεc would be no improvement, for neither are they *in* the cave. The point is that they have left their ship and are on land (*Hec.* 921–3). (2) ἄξενον cτέγην is unparalleled. But the ταλαίπωροι ξένοι of *IT* (89–90n.) arrive ἄγνωcτον ἐc γῆν, ἄξενον. (3) τε creates smoother syntax, and allows ἐμβεβῶτεc and ἀφιγμένοι to be taken more closely with ἵcαcι (hence presumably κἄξενον cτέγην Kirchhoff). (4) Without word-division the corruption would have been easy. And cτέγαc has already occurred at 29. (2) and (3) count also against Musgrave's γύην.

92. Κυκλωπίαν γνάθον: elsewhere in E. the adjective is always suggested by the prehistoric architecture of Mycenae (*HF* 15, 998, *Tro.* 1088, *El.* 1158, *IT* 845, *Or.* 965, *IA* 265, 534, 1501) and always, save at *IA* 265, without the article. And so there may be παρὰ προσδοκίαν in γνάθον: they have come to an ἄξενος γῆ where it is not the buildings that are Cyclopean but—a jaw! (cf. Κυκλώπιον τροχόν in S.'s satyric *Herakles at Tainaron*, fr. 227).

93. This line may seem merely to weaken the punch in Κυκλωπίαν γνάθον, and Wecklein was for deleting it (cf. 174, 341). But given the meaning of ἐμβεβῶτες (91n.), γνάθον requires ἀφιγμένοι (cf. 352). τὴν: the considerations in favour of L's τῶιδε at 30 cannot defend L's τήνδ' here: it is easier to refer thus to an absent Pol. (30n.) than to his absent jaw. τήνδε in the previous line would explain the corruption (cf. e.g. *IA* 599). And cf. S. *OT* 190 Ἄρεά τε τὸν μαλερόν.

94. ἥσυχοι seems to mean 'still' here rather than 'quiet'. Excited, prancing satyrs are frequent in vase-painting. Perhaps the chorus are in excited motion at the arrival of the strangers: cf. 213n.

95. πάρεισι with the simple accusative: cf. 106, *El.* 1278, *Ba.* 5.

96. Od. enters, presumably along the other eisodos from that used by the satyrs, though not necessarily (*pace* Ussher) from the left (Taplin, *The Stagecraft of Aeschylus*, 450), and not necessarily (*pace* Ussher) with all the twelve companions he had in Homer: given a Pol. of less than giant size driving the Greeks into the cave (346), the producer might prefer a smaller number. φράσαιτ' ἄν: for this form of the polite request see K-G i 233; esp. *IT* 513.

96–7. The double periphrasis νᾶμα ποτάμιον... δίψης ἄκος, absurdly pompous in the humble setting, immediately determines Od.'s status. On νᾶμα see Wilamowitz on *HF* 625.

97. δίψης ἄκος: cf. *Il.* 22.2 ἀκέοντό τε δίψαν; Pi. *Pyth.* 9.103 ἀοιδᾶν δίψαν ἀκειόμενον.

98. This verse illustrates a barely noticeable tendency in E. to repeat a rare word, phrase, or image that he has recently used. ὁδᾶν, to sell, occurs elsewhere in literature only at 12 and 133 of this play, ἐξοδᾶν only at 267. Sil. and Od. use the word independently of each other and in different contexts. So too with βορὰν ... κεχρημένοις Od. unknowingly picks up the same phrase in 88 (unless we read Wecklein's ἐφθαρμένοις: cf. 300, *IT* 276). Other exx. of the same habit are, in *Cyc.*, 10, 110, 282 (ἐξαντλεῖν), 85, 362, 467, 505, 702 (the σκάφος of a ship), 385, 473 (waggon-power as a measure of weight), 577, 602 (ἄκρατος), 276, 601 (ἐκπαιδ-), 107, 282, 351 (Τρωικοὶ πόνοι). To take another play: *HF* 18, 81 (εὐμαρίζειν), 445, 454 (the independent repetition of the image has an intensifying effect), 686, 871, 879 (χορεύω active), 819, 872 (πεδαίρω).

99. The consecutive resolutions in this line expresses a change of mood (203n.). ⟨ἕα·⟩: τί χρῆμα in E., as a reaction to a previously unsuspected sight, is elsewhere always preceded by ἕα and followed by 'I see ...': Stevens on *Andr*. 896; Kassel in *Maia* 25 (1973), 101. **Βρομίου πόλιν:** for the original audience this phrase might be tinged with a suggestion of the Athenian spring festival of the Anthesteria, in which it seems that satyrs participated (intro., §II); cf. *Ba*. 1295 πᾶσά τ᾽ ἐξεβακχεύθη πόλις.

100. τόνδε means little more than 'here': cf. 222 ἕα· τίν᾽ ὄχλον τόνδ᾽ ὁρῶ . . .;, *Alc*. 24 ἤδη δὲ τόνδε Θάνατον εἰσορῶ πέλας, *Hipp*. 1151, *Andr*. 494–5, *Su*. 980; Diggle in *ZPE* 24 (1977), 291–2. And so emendation (τοῖσδε, or οἷον for Σατύρων Hermann) is unnecessary.

101. Elsewhere this periphrasis is required by special circumstances (*El*. 552 ὅμως δὲ—χαίρειν τοὺς ξένους προσεννέπω, *Hipp*. 113; S. *Trach*. 227–8 χαίρειν δὲ τὸν κήρυκα προὐννέπω ... χαρτὸν εἴ τι καὶ φέρεις). Here, on the other hand, it expresses an elaborate formality consonant with the good manners that consist in addressing the oldest person first. And the same effect is created by the aorist (266, *Med*. 272 εἶπον τῆσδε γῆς ἔξω περᾶν, 'I hereby tell you ...'; K-G i 163–5; Kannicht on *Hel*. 330). The crafty Od. has no choice but to be scrupulously polite. But this, in the Βρομίου πόλις, makes him seem a little ridiculous. **προσεῖπα:** the form εἶπα is not found in Old Comedy or 5th cent. tragedy (cf. Theodektas fr. 6.8; Trag. adesp. 655.6), and so we should probably read προσεῖπον (Fix, Kassel, art. cit. 99n., 101). **γεραίτατον:** γεραίτερον Barnes. It is true that there are only two categories, the satyrs and Sil. And it is also true that the MSS often confuse the comparative and superlative: A. *Sept*. 568, 598, 657; *Med*. 68, 743; Men. *Dysk*. 128; Hes. *Th*. 34; Theocr. 15.139, 135; 17.4. (In fact this point works the other way, for it casts doubt on the apparent cases of comparative words denoting age used of the oldest of, not two, but several: Lys. 10.5, 13.67; Xen. *Cyr*. 5.1.6; P-Cambridge, op. cit. in., 18.) But a single old man in a gathering is the oldest in it. And although Sil. calls his sons παῖδες (16) and νέοι (28), in contemporary vase-painting their faces seem middle-aged, largely because balding; and Sil. their father is *very* old, a παπποσειληνός. Furthermore, Od. is anxious to please: cf. Dikaiopolis' worried ὦ Ἀχαρνέων γεραίτατοι at Ar. *Ach*. 286. A γεραίτερος is often simply an old man (e.g. *Ba*. 175, 207).

103. Cf. Ar. *Vesp*. 185: Οὔτις σύ; ποδαπός; Ἴθακος Ἀποδρασιππίδου, which may be paratragic. **Ἴθακος:** cf. 277 Ἰθακήσιοι, the Homeric term (e.g. *Od*. 2.25), which may be the result (so Wilamowitz, *Kleine Schriften*, i 302) of Homeric ignorance of how the Ithacans described themselves: see O. Kern, *Inschriften von Magnesia am*

Maeander, 36. According to Paganelli (*Echi Storicho-Politici nel Ciclope Euripideo* (Padua, 1979), 128–31) the mention of the Cephallenians here, subjects of a sympathetic Od., is to be connected with their support for the Athenians in the Sicilian expedition (Thuc. 7.31.2, 57.7; Ar. *Lys.* 394). Cf. S. *Phil.* 264; *Il.* 2.631, *Od.* 24.378.

104. Laertes married Anticleia when she was already pregnant with Odysseus by Sisyphos—a version of Od.'s parentage that is popular with his enemies in tragedy (A. fr. 175; S. fr. 567, *Aj.* 189. *Phil.* 417; *IA* 524, 1362; cf. Lycophr. *Alex.* 344; Ov. *Met.* 13.32). It must be disheartening and deflating for Od. to find that, epic hero though he is, his reputation for chatter and the unsavoury story of his parentage have preceded him to a faraway island, and that they should be well known even to Sil. Cf. the apparently contemptuous reception given by the satyrs to Hermes in S. *Inachus* (fr. 269c 21–4; Carden op. cit. 5n., 85). **οἶδ' ἄνδρα:** cf. Ar. *Ach.* 430 οἶδ' ἄνδρα, Μυσὸν Τήλεφον; *Od.* 4.551; Dem. 54.34. **κρόταλον:** cf. Hes. fr. 198 υἱὸς Λαέρταο πολύκροτα μήδεα εἰδώς; Ar. *Nub.* 260, 448. Od. in tragedy attracted abuse more appropriate to comedy: *Rhes.* 498 αἱμυλώτατον κρότημ' Ὀδυσσεύς; S. fr. 913 πάνσοφον κρότημα, Λαέρτου γόνος, *Aj.* 381, *Phil.* 927. **δριμύ** probably describes κρόταλον, not γένος. Nowhere else does δριμύς describe sound, but there is no reason why it should not: cf. διαπρύσιος of the sound of κρόταλα at *Hel.* 1308. If the remark of Aristophanes Byz. (ap. Eustath. ad *Od.* 3.20) that E. used δριμύ meaning συνετόν refers to this passage, then he has picked up the secondary reference. **γένος:** the line is quoted by the scholiast on S. *Aj.* 190 with γόνον. Cf. *IA* 1362 ἆρ' ὁ Σισύφου γόνος; S. fr. 913 πάνσοφον κρότημα, Λαέρτου γόνος. But the less obvious γένος makes good sense (cf. e.g. S. *Ant.* 1117; Nisbet and Hubbard on Hor. *Odes.* 1.3.27) and should be retained (*pace* Kassel, art. cit. 99n., 102).

105. αὐτός (οὗτος L): cf. *IA* 1362–3 (Κλ. ἆρ' ὁ Σισύφου γόνος; Αχ. αὐτὸς οὗτος), Ar. *Pl.* 82–3 (ἐκεῖνος ὄντως εἶ σύ; Πλ. ναί. Χρ. ἐκεῖνος αὐτός; Πλ. αὐτότατος), 704, *Eccl.* 328, *Ran.* 552; S. *Trach.* 287; Trag. adesp. 363; Men. *Asp.* 435; Lucian *Gall.* 4. οὗτος ἐκεῖνος occurs elsewhere so far as I know only in the third person: Ar. *Pax.* 240; Hdt. 1.32.7 (cf. τοῦτ' (or τόδ') ἐκεῖνο: Page on *Med.* 98; Headlam on Herodas 1.3). For the first person ὅδε is used: S. *Phil.* 261 (δδ' εἴμ' ἐγώ σοι κεῖνος), *OC* 138; Theocr. 1.120, and numerous exx. in Headlam on Herodas 1.3.

106. Cf. 95, and Pol.'s first words to his visitors in Homer (9.252): Ὦ ξεῖνοι, τίνες ἐστέ; πόθεν πλεῖθ' ὑγρὰ κέλευθα;.

107. Part of the Athenians' claim to occupy the left wing at Plataia is καὶ ἐν τοῖϲι Τρωικοῖϲι πόνοιϲι οὐδαμῶν ἐλειπόμεθα (Hdt. 9.27.4; cf. *Il.* 6.77–8, etc.; S. *Phil.* 248). The phrase Τρωικοὶ πόνοι occurs three times in the play (347, 603; cf. 282, 351) and nowhere else in E. (98n.); Paganelli, op. cit. 103n., 65. γε may stand (Denniston, *GP*, 133), against τε (Hermann) and τοι (Wecklein; cf. S. *Phil.* 245 ἐξ Ἰλίου τοι δὴ τανῦν γε ναυϲτολῶ, in a similar context).

108. Cf. *IT* 1066 γῆϲ πατρώιαϲ νόϲτοϲ; *Od.* 5.344–5 νόϲτου γαίηϲ Φαιήκων. **ἥιδηϲθα** and ἥιδειϲθα both occur in the MSS, e.g. at *El.* 926; see Veitch, *Greek Verbs*, 219; Dover on Ar. *Nub.* 329.

109. This is described in *Od.* 9.80–3. At *Od.* 10.48 Od. describes the effect of his comrades opening the ἀϲκόϲ of Aeolus: τοὺϲ δ᾽ αἶψ᾽ ἁρπάξαϲα φέρεν πόντονδε θύελλα.

110. Cf. *Or.* 504 νῦν δ᾽ ἐϲ τὸν αὐτὸν δαίμον᾽ ἦλθε μητέρι; S. *OC* 1337 τὸν αὐτὸν δαίμον᾽ ἐξειληχότεϲ. The impersonal sense of δαίμων (e.g. *Andr.* 974, *IA* 1136; Men. *Dysk.* 282) is discussed by Stevens on *Andr.* 98. He effectively identifies it with ϲυμφορά (comparing *Alc.* 551 with 561); but to me it seems likely that δαίμων preserves a connotation of the inexplicability in secular terms of the ϲυμφορά (cf. e.g. *Hec.* 721 ὥϲ ϲε πολυπονωτάτην βροτῶν δαίμων ἔθηκεν κτλ.). **πάπαῖ** probably expresses more grief (cf. e.g. *IA* 655)—Sil. remembers his sufferings—than surprise (cf. e.g. 572).

112. διώκων: cf. the less heroic statement at 14.

114. Sil. does not answer the second part of Od.'s question. But this is insufficient reason to emend 113 (κἀκ τίνοϲ καλοῦϲι νιν; Wieseler). **ὄχθοϲ:** Aetna is at 20 a πέτρα, at 95 a πάγοϲ. ὄχθοϲ and perhaps πάγοϲ, might be thought curiously humble words to use of such a huge and dominating mountain. Conceivably there is intended a slightly comic diminutive effect (cf. 266 Κυκλώπιον). But Mt. Cynthus on Delos (Κύνθιοϲ ὄχθοϲ: *IT* 1098; *h. hom.* 3.17) and Acrocorinth (fr. 1084 Ἀκροκόρινθον, ἱερὸν ὄχθον) are not inconsiderable, though admittedly much smaller than Aetna.

115–6. Cf. the chorus of Greek women among the Tauri: Ἑλλάδοϲ εὐίππου πύργουϲ καὶ τείχη ... ἐξαλλάξαϲ (*IT* 132).

116. ἐϲτ᾽ (εἰϲ᾽ L): neuter plural subjects may have verbs in the plural, but almost always either when they refer to living agents (e.g. 208), or when the plurality is important (Pl. *Crat.* 425a ἐξ ὧν τά τε ὀνόματα καὶ τὰ ῥήματα ϲυντίθενται; Xen. *An.* 1.4.4 ἦϲαν ταῦτα δύο τείχη; K-G i 65). Of the latter kind of exception there is no example known to me in drama. ἐϲτ᾽ is a better remedy than οὐκ· εἰϲ᾽ ἔρημοι κτλ., with δέ που in 115 (Duchemin): Od. is more likely to ask 'Where are the walls etc.?' than 'Are there walls etc.?', and the former gives 116 more force.

118. Cf. *Od.* 9. 112–15

> τοῖϲιν δ᾽ οὔτ ἀγοραὶ βουληφόροι οὔτε θέμιϲτεϲ,
> ἀλλ᾽ οἵ γ᾽ ὑψηλῶν ὀρέων ναίουϲι κάρηνα
> ἐν ϲπέϲϲι γλαφυροῖϲι, θεμιϲτεύει δὲ ἔκαϲτοϲ
> παίδων ἠδ᾽ ἀλόχων, οὐδ᾽ ἀλλήλων ἀλέγουϲι·.

But cf. ϲτέγαι (29), δόμοι (33, 129, etc.), 29n.. **ἔχοντεϲ**: οἰκοῦντεϲ (Nauck) may be right (corrupted by ἔχουϲι in 117?): cf. 22 Κύκλωπεϲ οἰκοῦϲ᾽ ἄντρα κτλ. In 324, and *Med.* 448 γῆν τήνδε καὶ δόμουϲ ἔχειν, the sense is different.

119. The question is a natural one (cf. Oedipus newly arrived in Colonus (S. *OC* 66) ἄρχει τίϲ αὐτῶν, ἢ 'πὶ τῶι πλήθει λόγοϲ;), and also allows an answer based on *Od.* 9.112–5 (quoted 118n.).

120. **μονάδεϲ**: νομάδεϲ (L) when applied to people means 'nomads', which the Cyclopes are neither in Homer nor here (22, 118). For μονάδεϲ (Schmidt in *Maia* 27 (1975), 291) cf. *Od.* 9.112–5 (quoted 118n.). This makes 120 answer 119, and gives point to ἀκούει δ᾽ οὐδὲν κτλ., and to Od.'s next question: see intro., §VII. For the corruption ('anagrammatism') cf. e.g. A. *Ag.* 218, 234, 1157, 1205, *Eum.* 727. Paganelli objects (*Mus. Crit.* 13–14 (1978–9), 197–200) that the Cyclopes have much in common with νομάδεϲ. But this does not make them νομάδεϲ. **οὐδείϲ κτλ.**: fourfold repetition (οὐδενὶ οὐδαμῆι οὐδαμῶϲ οὐδεμίαν...) occurs at Pl. *Parm.* 166a, threefold at Pl. *Tim.* 29e (for threefold repetition of other words see B. Gygli-Wyss, *Das Nominale Polyptoton* (Göttingen, 1966), 43). The apparent infringement of Porson's law, with οὐδείϲ (οὐδέν) in this position occurs also at 672, *Alc.* 671, *Pho.* 747, *Hyps.* fr. ap. Lydum (p. 48 Bond). 3, fr. 494.1; S. *OC* 1022—perhaps because the word was conceived of as οὐδὲ εἷϲ (P. Maas, *Greek Metre*, transl. Lloyd-Jones 1962, §135).

121–4. There is here an interesting deviation from the Homeric model. In Homer the Cyclopes neither plant nor plough, but cereals and vines grow automatically (9.109 ἄϲπαρτα καὶ ἀνήροτα). Why has Euripides deprived them of these benefits? Not just in the interests of realism, but because (1) he was familiar with the contemporary awareness of an earlier time in which man had neither agriculture not its benefits (see esp. *Su.* 201–5; D.S. 13.26.3; Isocr. *Paneg.* 28–32; Guthrie, *History of Greek Philosophy*, iii 60–84); (2) the effect of the wine on Sil. is the more amusing for his enforced abstinence, on Pol. for his complete ignorance; (3) the innovation is well suited to the satyric genre (intro., §IV).

121. With the parenthesis cf. *Hel.* 1579, *Tro.* 299, *Ba.* 649; Pearson on S. *Ichn.* 198; Fraenkel on A. *Ag.* 318; Bond on *HF* 222; Diggle, *Studies in the Text of Euripides* (1981), 116.

123. This question serves to introduce an important discrepancy with the Homeric model (121–4n.). As for its motive, Od. may conceivably be testing the value of his own wine as barter (cf. 160n.). But in fact it is a natural follower to his previous question: cf. *Ba.* 274–85 (esp. 279, 281) and Dodds' note. ῥοᾶϲ: Kalinka (in *SAWW* 1922/6, 10) observes that ἀμπέλου ῥοάϲ adds nothing, whereas ῥοαῖϲ (L) refers to the wine-making process. But the tautology, unlike ῥοαῖϲ, is elegant. At *Ba.* 281 ἀμπέλου ῥοῆϲ means simply οἴνου. The scribe was influenced either by the datives of the previous verse, or by the Ptolemaic practice of writing feminine accusative plurals -αιϲ (E. Mayser, *Grammatik der griechischen Papyri aus der Ptolemäerzeit*, i 1 (1970), 97).

124. ἄχορον: ἄχαριν (Tr. 2) is almost certainly a conjecture (cf. Tr. at A. *PV* 545). ἄχορον should stand: for the logic of τοιγάρ cf. 156. The satyrs' loss of their god and his wine and dancing is bewailed at 63–81, and was probably a τόποϲ of the genre. Cf. 121–4n.

125. In Homer Od. takes the fatal decision to stay in Pol.'s cave to find out whether the natives are ὑβριϲταί κτλ. or φιλόξεινοι κτλ. (9.174–6). περὶ: 'in their dealings with': cf. *Alc.* 1148 εὐϲέβει περί ξένουϲ, *Cres.* fr. 66 (Austin). 13, *Su.* 367.

129. Some editors, noting that Od. has heard nothing about this particular Cyclops, mark a lacuna after this verse. If some lines have dropped out, they may have contained a question as to why the satyrs have escaped such universal slaughter. But for this there are already in the text two good reasons (24–37, 220–1). It would be dramatically undesirable for Sil. to repeat here too much of the contents of the prologue. From 118, the sight of the cave, and 120 (with μονάδεϲ), Od. can infer the truth, as he now rapidly needs to do; αὐτὸϲ probably has the connotation 'master' (24n.). Critics tend to notice inconsistencies unimportant to the dramatist or audience: e.g. 31n., 160n. ἤ should be perispomenon here, at 111, and possibly at 117, though not at 119 or 121: see Herodian *Prosod.* ii Lentz, p. 112.

130. Similarly in *Hel.* (153–4) Helen tells Teucer that the (ξενοκτόνοϲ) king Theoklymenos is away hunting with hounds, which here express Pol.'s wealth. Αἴτνηι: Reiske's Αἴτνην may be based on the misconception of a break before θῆραϲ.

131. δρᾶϲον: L's δράϲειϲ is printed by Duchemin and Ussher. But οἶϲθ' οὖν ὃ δρᾶϲον occurs at *Hec.* 225, *Ion.* 1029, *Hel.* 315, 1233, *IA* 725, always followed, as here, by an order or request in the subjunctive or imperative mood. On the construction see K-G i

239; Kannicht on *Hel.* 315. The corruption to δράςειc is natural, and occurred in some MSS at *Hec.* 225; Ar. *Av.* 54, 80 (Renehan, *Greek Textual Criticism*, 5). In support of δράςειc there is only *IT* 759 ἀλλ᾽ οἶςθ᾽ ὃ δράςω, *Med.* 600 οἶςθ᾽ ὡς μετεύξηι κτλ. (μέτευξαι Elmsley), and Lucian *Herm.* 63 οἶςθ᾽ οὖν ὃ δράςειc (φράςω **M**). Only the Lucian is really parallel, and may be corrupt. **ἀπαίρωμεν:** from having its object (ναῦν) understood, the verb came to mean merely 'leave': *Tro.* 944 ἀπῆρας νηί.

132. δρώιημεν: cυνδρῶιμεν Dawes. But cf. Ar. *Nub.* 427 λέγε νυν ἡμῖν ὅ τι cοι δρῶμεν; S. *OT* 145 ὡς **πᾶν** ἐμοῦ δράcοντοc. The plural optative in -ιη- is defended at *Hel.* 1010, *Ion* 943, fr. 582, and here by Kannicht on *Hel.* 1010 (see also Pearson on S. fr. 222.7; Lautensach in *Glotta* 7 (1916), 106; K-B ii 72; Schwyzer, *Griech. Gramm.*, i 796 n. 3).

134. This remark is strictly inaccurate. But ἔcτι in 136 shows that we need the full stop after κρέαc (cf. *Ion* 1002, 1012). Sil.'s negative really refers to the absence of cereals, to which Od. replies καὶ τόδε ('meat too . . .').

136. τυρὸς ὀπίας: Pol. has cheeses in Homer (9.219). Sicilian cheese was admired in Athens (Ar. *Vesp.* 838, 896; Antiph. fr. 236: Hermipp. fr. 63.9; Philem. fr. 76; annon. ap. Athen. 658a). Curdling milk with ὀπόc (vegetable juice) occurs in a simile in Homer (*Il.* 5.902–3; cf. Arist. *HA* 522b2;). The ὀπόc used is from the fig tree (Athen. 658c; Varro *RR* 2.11.4; Columella *RR* 7.8; Pliny *NH* 23.63). **βοὸς γάλα:** Pol. in Homer milks his sheep and goats (9.223, 238, 244, etc.), but has no cattle. And there has been no mention in the play so far of cattle. Hence the conjectures (δῖον Nauck, δῖος Wieszner, πῖον Wieseler, etc.), among which we should include Διὸς preserved in Athen. 658c and Eustath. ad *Od.* 4.88. But cf. 218, 325, 389. The Greeks did not drink much milk, so notice was taken of the habit among barbarians (*Il.* 13.5; Hes. fr. 150.15; Hdt. 1.216, 3.23, 4.2; Columella *RR* 7.2; Pliny *HN* 11.96) and among shepherds (*El.* 169, fr. 146; Pol.'s boast at Theocr. 11.34–5, τὸ κράτιcτον ἀμελγόμενοc γάλα πίνω, is absurd). Homer specifies that Pol. drinks his milk unmixed (9.297 ἄκρητον), which suggests that Greek practice was to mix it (cf. the libations at *Od.* 10.519; *IT* 162; etc.). With the elimination of the automatic agriculture (121–4n.), E.'s Pol. lives in a purely pastoral economy, like Homer's Libyans (*Od.* 4.86–9; cf. Hdt. 4.186, 1.216 the Massagetai, also cannibal milk-drinkers), on cheese, milk and meat. But why did E. depart from Homer by giving Pol. *cow's* milk? Perhaps to emphasize the barbarism associated with milk-drinking: the Greeks preferred sheep's or goat's milk, and thought of other races as drinking βόειον (Galen 6.765; *RE* xv s. Milch, 1572). He *eats* cattle as well (325), because he is well-to-do.

138. It is for the sake of gold that Sil. and the satyrs undertake to track Apollo's cattle in S. *Ichn.* (51, 78, 208). And it appears that Sil. attempts to sell some ἑταῖραι to a visitor to Skiron's lair in E. *Skiron* (fr. 675).

140. Cf. 67; lack of wine may have been usual for the satyrs in captivity, although we hear of it elsewhere only at Ion. fr. 26. At Achaios fr. 9 the satyrs complain at having to drink it with water (cf. Ion fr. 27; Aristias fr. 4). Some editors punctuate after φίλτατ', which thereby becomes a vocative. But cf. *Ion* 1488 ὦ φίλτατ' εἰποῦσα; S. *Phil.* 1290 ὦ φίλτατ' εἰπών. The antecedent of οὗ is the πῶμα, which also constitutes the φίλτατα.

141. In Homer the wine that Od. gives Pol. has been given him by Maron, Εὐάνθεος υἱός, / ἱρεὺς Ἀπόλλωνος, ὅς Ἴσμαρον ἀμφιβεβήκει (9.197–8). In the same area as the Homeric Ismaros, in a part of Thrace famous for its wine (Archil. fr. 2; Pliny *NH* 14.6.54; Head, *Historia Numorum*, 248), was Maroneia, which belonged to the Athenian empire and in which, at least in the Roman period, Maron shared a cult with Zeus and Dionysos (Reinach in *BCH* 5 (1881), 93, and 8 (1884), 51). Already in Hesiod (fr. 238; cf. Eustath. ad *Od.* 9.198) Maron was the grandson (or the great-grandson) of Dionysos. E. emphasizes Dionysos' *fatherhood* of Maron here, not I think because he is inventing it *ad hoc* (*pace* De Falco in *Dioniso* 5 (1935–6), 110), but because it provides a useful link between the Homeric and the satyric worlds, and perhaps also because of a previous satyr-play on the παιδοτροφία of Maron (142n.). Maron is found later as Dionysos' companion (Nonn. 15.141, etc.), once even as his nurse (Fulgent., *Myth.* 2.12), the son of Sil. (Nonn, 14.99), and once the son of Dionysos (Satyros 631 FGH fr. 1.27). At Cratinos fr. 135 (probably from the *Odysseis*), wine is called 'Maron' (cf. *Cyc.* 412). Webster (*BICS* Suppl. 20, 157) suggested that a mid-4th-cent. vase-painting in Lipari (inv. 2297), in which Maron hands an ἀσκός to Odysseus, was inspired by this verse; but a more likely source of inspiration is Homer.

142. The antecedent of ὅν has been taken to be θεοῦ. If so, then Βακχίου in 143 specifies (σαφέστερον) the θεός, and in 142 Sil. refers to a well-known incident (4n.). But it is more likely that ὅν refers to Maron, who is the subject of 141 and 143. If so, Sil. refers to an incident unknown elsewhere, but which may well have been represented, or at least related (e.g. in Aristias' *Cyclops*?), in a previous satyr-play (Waltz, op. cit. 11–17n., 294; Sil. παιδοτρόφος: intro., §IV). The verse is reminiscent of what the nurse says at A. *Cho.* 750 ὅν ἐξέθρεψα μητρόθεν δεδεγμένη; *El.* 488, *Hyps.* fr. 60.10. But it is not necessarily paratragic. Satyric drama had its own moments of joy after suffering and its own παιδοτροφία (intro., §IV). Indeed, because tragedy developed ἐκ cατυρικοῦ (intro., §III) it may not be coincidental that the only positively low character in tragedy (except the doorkeeper in the consistently lighthearted *Helen*) is the τροφόc of another's child: the humble preoccupations of the nurse in A. *Cho.* may derive ultimately from the satyric παιδοτροφία (cf. esp. S. fr. 171).

144. **cέλμαcιν** (Dindorf) abolishes the trochaically divided tribrach, which occurs 85 times in Aristophanes (33 times in the second foot: J. W. White, *The Verse of Greek Comedy*, 40), but nowhere else in satyric drama. The satyric trimeter does allow itself certain of the licences of the comic (intro., §V). But we should not allow this to remain as an isolated example of another, particularly as the ν would have been easily lost, as at 511(n.). Even though (despite K-B i 227) there is no other case of synizesis in the 46 occurrences of νεώc in tragedy (28 in E.), synizesis of -εω- is common enough (e.g. 115, *Hipp.* 56, *Su.* 273, *El.* 234, *Ion* 1563, *Hel.* 1007, fr. 360.7; Diggle, op. cit. 12 1n., 93); and the same word can be one or two syllables in the same play (θεόν in *Ba.* 289, 1297), or even in the same line (231 θεόν ... θεῶν). **φέρειc:** at 88 the middle is appropriate (88n.). Here, on the other hand, Sil.'s interest is merely in the whereabouts of the wine.

145-54. Cf. the description of the wine in Homer (9.208-13):

τὸν δ' ὅτε πίνοιεν μελιηδέα οἶνον ἐρυθρόν, / ἓν δέπαc ἐμπλήcαc ὕδατοc ἀνὰ εἴκοcι μέτρα / χεῦ', ὀδμὴ δ' ἡδεῖα ἀπὸ κρητῆροc ὀδώδει, / θεcπεcίη τότ' ἂν οὔ τοι ἀποcχέcθαι φίλον ἦεν. / τοῦ φέρον ἐμπλήcαc ἀcκὸν μέγαν.

145. With the emphatic ὅδε cf. *Hipp.* 178 τόδε cοι φέγγοc, λαμπρόc ὅδ' αἰθήρ, *El.* 556. **ἀcκόc** (Radermacher) is better than L's ἀcκὸς (678n.). It has been objected to the paradosis that Sil. cannot be expected to see through a skin. Hence e.g. ὄνπερ εἰcορᾶιc (Hermann; for loss of εἰc- cf. *Tro.* 991, *El.* 1242, *IA* 171). But the contents of an ἀcκόc would normally be taken to be wine (e.g. the τραγωιδοί were given an ἀcκόc of wine: Burkert in *GRBS* 1966, 114). It is unnecessary even to take ὁρᾶιc as subjunctive like μάθηιc in 143.

146. The satyrs have of course a great capacity for drink. On a late-6th-cent. cup in Geneva (inv. 16908) a satyr has his head inside a large κρατήρ, ignoring a nearby cup (see also *ARV*² 677.13).

147. There are two things wrong with what is in L. Firstly, ναί is inappropriate. It can be used to implore someone to relent from a refusal (exx. in Barrett on *Hipp.* 605): *Hipp.* 605 ναί, πρός cε τῆcδε δεξιᾶc εὐωλένου and *Pho.* 1665 ναί, πρός cε τῆcδε μητρὸc Ἰοκάcτηc, Κρέον are the only exx. in tragedy. And it can, in reply to a negative statement, mean disagreement with it (e.g. 555), provided that what follows ναί contains the reason for that disagreement. ναί here is not happy in either of these categories. Nor can it imply agreement with 146 (Torraca in *Vichiana* 4 (1967), 87–91): 'Certainly; nor would twice as much' is unacceptably elliptical, and leaves 148 somewhat odd. Secondly, δίc τόcον κτλ. is without a verb, and obscure. And so it has been suggested that there is a lacuna (printed by Diggle) after 146, and that 147 refers to an ἀcκόc which renews itself by magic (Kassel, art. cit. 99n., 102, combines the two suggestions). This would be a useful device for providing the great quantity of wine to be drunk in the course of the play. Furthermore, such a τέραc suits satyr-drama (intro., §IV; Dodds on *Ba.* 705), and the con-trick suits Od. But in fact emendation may be unnecessary. Cerri (*RFIC* 104 (1976), 139–43) makes a good case for reading ναι (Blumenthal, Grégoire) which, given the absence of accents in the early texts, is not an emendation. νάειν is associated especially with flowing *water* (S. fr. 5 οἴνωι γὰρ ἡμῖν Ἀχελῶιοc ἄρα ναι; Pl. *Phdr.* 264d; etc.), and so with κρῆναι (*Il.* 21.197, *Od.* 6.292, etc). In saying 'there runs twice as much drink as flows from the skin' Od. means, according to Cerri, that to this wine you add two parts of water (cf. *Od.* 9.209; Anacr. 356 *PMG*; Alc. 346 L-P). ναι (of the mixed drink) contrasts with ῥυῆι (of the wine). Cf. Hes. *Op.* 595, where the water to be mixed with wine is called κρήνη αἰέναοc. Sil.'s reply (148) is sarcastic; but Od. then shrewdly offers a taste of the wine *unmixed* (149), and this removes Sil.'s misgivings (164). This is plausible, except that (despite e.g. *Med.* 504, 514, 588) 148 need not be sarcastic (Sil. is easily pleased), and πῶμα may refer to the mixture, not just the water. 147 still appears abrupt, but perhaps only to those unfamiliar with drinking language (152n.). If this interpretation is right, then there is a previously undetected irony in *Hec.* 392 καὶ δὶc τόcον πῶμ' αἵματοc γενήcεται, where Hecuba is offering to be killed along with her daughter.

148. The satyrs were associated with springs (e.g. Wide, *Lakonische Kulte*, 255); and Midas caught Sil. τὴν κρήνην οἰνοχοήcαc (Philostr. *Im.* 1.22); cf. S. fr. 5 (quoted 147n.).

149. Drinking unmixed wine was unusual among the Greeks. Cleomenes learnt it from the Scythians, and the habit was said to have made him mad (Hdt. 6.84). At Ar. *Eq.* 105 two slaves indulge in it. Perhaps it was the practice to *sample* wine unmixed (Euboulos fr. 138 quoted below). The wine, at least in Homer (9.209) if not here (147n.), is exceptionally strong; and Sil., after long abstinence, reacts strongly (156–74). For the construction βούληι cε γεύcω cf. e.g. *Pho.* 909 βούληι παρόντοc δῆτά coι τούτου φράcω; S. *El.* 80 θέλειc μείνωμεν; Latin *quid vis faciam?*; K-G i 221. For the double accusative cf. Euboulos fr. 138 οἶνον γάρ με ψίθιον γεύcαc / ἡδὺν ἄκρατον. For the form βούληι (βούλει L) see K-B ii 60; Murray *OCT* intro., x.

150. ἡ γὰρ affirms the reason for agreement: cf. *Hipp.* 90 καὶ κάρτα γ'· ἡ γὰρ οὐ cοφοὶ φαινοίμεθ' ἄν; Denniston, *GP*, 284. γεῦμα κτλ. sounds proverbial: 'a taste invites the purchase' (a rare metaphorical use of καλεῖν). *Anecd. Graec.* i 87, 31–3 Bekker on γεύεcθαι meaning ὀcφραίνομαι in *Cyc.* may be a misunderstanding of this passage.

151. Perhaps Sil. has already greedily grasped the ἀcκόc, so that καὶ μὴν expresses the polite emphasis with which Od. draws his attention to the ποτήρ (cf. 146n.). It may however express no more than in 141. **ἐφέλκω:** the word is often used by E. metaphorically (e.g. *Med.* 462). At *HF* 632 it refers to the physical contact of Herakles with his children: ναῦc δ' ὣc ἐφέλξω. A boat in tow is an ἐφολκίc. The cup may be attached to the ἀcκόc (or to Od.'s belt) by a string; and so he is 'towing' it. For the ἀcκόc as a ship cf. Herodas *Mim.* 8. 36–43; Slater in *AJA* 81 (1977), 556. **ποτήρ':** the usual form is ποτήριον. Dale suggests that ποτήρ, which occurs elsewhere only at *Alc.* 756, was coined by E. to mean a particularly large ποτήριον (*CR* 2 (1952), 132 = *Collected Papers*, 101).

152. ἐγκάναξον (ἐκπάταξον L): πατάccειν is to strike, but may be onomatopoeic in origin (Frisk, *Griechisches Etymologisches Wörterbuch* s. πάταγοc), and πάταγοc is a sound. And so with ἐκπάταξον Od. is being asked to strike the cup with the wine (not presumably the skin with his hand), perhaps with the suggestion of a splashing noise (cf. *Alc.* 798). But this requires a relation between ἐκ- (from the skin) and -πατάccειν (the cup) curious in itself and unparalleled in the two other occurrences of the compound (*Od.* 18.327 φρέναc ἐκπεπαταγμένοc; *AP* 9.309). Still, ἐκπατάccειν may be a variation, in the esoteric vocabulary of the symposium (571n.), on ἐκχέειν. For ἐγκάναξον cf. Ar. *Eq.* 105–6 ἄκρατον ἐγκάναξον μοι πολὺν / cπονδήν; Alciphr. 3.36. Wine striking the cup makes a καναχή. For the corruption ἐκ for ἐγ- cf. A. *Ag.* 332; S. *OC* 699. **ἀναμνηcθῶ:** the compound implies a conscious act of memory (cf. e.g. *El.* 351 with *Med.* 1246). And so unlike e.g. *Hec.* 244 μεμνήμεθ' ἐc κίνδυνον ἐλθόντεc, the (possibly coincident) participle πιὼν seems to refer to both past and present: 'so that I may remind myself (by drinking) of having drunk'; cf. V. *Aen.* 4.23 *agnosco* *veteris vestigia flammae.* Emendation is unnecessary (ἀναπληcθῶ Pitzalis).

153–4. We should compare the satyr Orochares, painted by the Berlin painter (*ARV²* 196; Arias and Hirmer, *A History of Greek Vase Painting*, nos. 150, 152), holding a cup of wine to his nose and apparently gazing intently at it. In *Od.*, even when Od.'s wine was mixed with twenty parts of water, ὀδμὴ δ' ἡδεῖα ἀπὸ κρητῆρος ὀδώδει / θεcπεcίη (9.210–11). And perhaps the horse in Sil. has a strong sense of smell: the Centaurs smelt Pholus' wine from the surrounding woods (Apollod. 2.5.4). But what is the point of 154? Sil.'s absorption in the mere odour of the wine, whether issuing from a pretence at connoisseurship or a genuine contentment after such long abstinence, is absurd. Od.'s question is not 'It *has* a fine bouquet, hasn't it?' (Ussher), but 'You *saw* it, did you?' (εἶδεc in emphatic position: see G. Thomson, *The Oresteia²*, ii 253; with γάρ cf. e.g. *Or.* 483, *Hel.* 311; S. *OT* 1029; Denniston, *GP*, 75, 77). I know of only two cases of καλόc describing a smell: Theocr. 1.149 θᾶcαι, φίλος, ὡc καλὸν ὄcδει, and Ar. *Av.* 1715–6 ὀcμή ... καλὸν θέαμα. And in both cases the smell is thought of as *visible*, as at Alexis fr. 222.3–4 ἅπαντεc ὀρχοῦντ' εὐθὺc ἂν οἴνου μόνον ὀcμὴν ἴδωcιν. Perhaps the (vulgar?) idea of a visible smell implicit in καλὴν ὀcμήν prompts the urbane Od.'s question, which is then made to look ridiculous by Sil.' literal reply. With αὐτὸc for αὐτήν (Jackson in *CQ* 36 (1941), 51; Paley's αὐτόν would have to refer to the ἀcκόc), Od. is merely asking Sil. whether he saw the wine (Od. has probably not yet proffered it 153n.), but Sil., either stupidly or facetiously, thinks of his own previous remark and takes Od. to mean 'Did you see the odour?'.

153. ἰδού presumably accompanies compliance with Sil.'s request (cf. 188, 212, 544, 562) rather than the proffering of the wine (cf. 570), which occurs probably at 155. παπαιάξ is an expression of surprise.

154. οὐ μὰ Δί': cf. Ar. *Eccl.* 556, where Blepyros responds thus to what seems to him a silly question.

156. Cf. A. fr. 278 Lloyd-Jones, almost certainly from the satyric *Prometheus Pyrkaeus:*]cι[α] δέ μ' εὐμενὴc χορεύει χάρις; the satyric fr. 33 of Achaios: ὁ δὲ cκύφος με τοῦ θεοῦ καλεῖ πάλαι κτλ.; Theocr. 7.153 (of the effect of Od.'s wine on Pol.): τοῖον νέκταρ ἔπεισε κατ' αὔλια ποccὶ χορεῦcαι; and Alexis fr. 222 (quoted 153–4n.). For the identity of god and wine see 519–28n.: to translate 'the wine' here would be inadequate; and παρακαλεῖ is not a metaphor.

157. ἄ, like other Greek exclamations, can express different emotions: cf. e.g. *HF* 1051, *Alc.* 526; S. *Ichn.* 176. The triple ἄ, because a rarity, may be a subtle expression of the anarchy of Sil.'s joy. Exclamations are common in satyric drama: e.g. S. *Ichn.* 88, 176, 213, *Inach.* frr. 269a.51, 269c.25; intro., §III (2). Presumably Sil. executes some dance steps (156 χορεῦϲαι) as he utters it.

158. μῶν: 'I ask 'μῶν x' *when I am reluctant to accept x as true* ... The reluctance sometimes weakens down into hesitation, and the particle then may mark the question as a guess' writes Barrett (on *Hipp.* 794), and cites this line as notable: 'Odysseus presumably both thinks x probable and approves of it'. μῶν οὐ (Wecklein; cf. *Med.* 733) would remove the anomaly. But the paradosis may stand. Od. has no reason to doubt that Sil. is pleased. μῶν τὸν κτλ. expresses mock surprise. Cf. 377n. διεκάναξε occurs only here; cf. 152n. (on ἐγκανάϲϲειν).

159. Cf. Rhianus, *AP* 12.93.9–10 (Gow and Page, *Hellenistic Epigrams*, 3216–7): τοῖον ϲέλαϲ ὄμμαϲιν αἴθει / κοῦροϲ κὰϲ νεάτουϲ ἐκ κορυφῆϲ ὄνυχαϲ, (also Gow and Page, *The Garland of Philip*, 3055). On ἐξ ὀνύχων see G. Williams, *Horace Odes* iii, 66. For ὥϲτε ... γε as strongly affirmative cf. 217; Denniston, GP, 134.

160. We do not have to explain the contradiction with 139 by supposing (Wilamowitz) that νόμιϲμα refers to the contemporary Athenian *silver* coinage (cf. 161 χρυϲίον). It is cunning of Od. to offer the money now that it is not necessary. But why should he offer it all? Probably for the sake of the humour in Sil.'s drunken indifference to everything except wine, which may, like Caliban's, derive in part from stories of Athenian merchants exploiting foreigners: the Celts of Diodorus' time (5.26) would sell a slave to foreign merchants for a cup of wine: cf. 164! (Cf. V. G. Childe, *What Happened in History*, 167). E. may also have had in mind the gold given to Od. by Maron (*Od.* 9.202). Currency is of course an anachronism. Cf. the attempt to sell prostitutes for coins in E. (satyric) *Skiron* (see 138n.). **μέντοι:** 'proceeding to a new item in a series': Denniston, *GP*, 407.

161. χάλα τὸν ἀϲκὸν means not 'undo the skin' (De Falco, *et al.*), but 'slacken the wineskin', i.e. 'pour out the wine' (cf. 55). The skin is already open. De Falco cites exx. (*Med.* 1314, *Hipp.* 808; S. *Ant.* 1186) of χαλᾶν with κλῆιθρα; but you do not open bolts, you loosen them. Opening an ἀϲκόϲ: *Od.* 10.47 ἀϲκὸν μὲν λῦϲαν; *Med.* 679 ἀϲκοῦ με τὸν προύχοντα μὴ λῦϲαι πόδα. Od. does not comply with the request (cf. 192).

162. Why should not Od. ask for *both* cheese and sheep (cf. 134–6)? That is after all what he gets (189–90). τυρεύμα καὶ (Wilamowitz) would solve the problem; but we would expect the plural (cf. 190, *El.* 496; the only other occurrence of the word is in the singular,

meaning 'intrigue', at com. adesp. 706K). τυρεύματ' ἤ may stand:
Od. is not insisting on one or the other, but saying in effect
(cautiously perhaps) 'whatever you have'. γε epexegetic in a
participial clause: Denniston, GP, 139.

163. Cf. in *The Tempest* the self-confidence of the slave Caliban after
his first-ever taste of strong liquor.

164–6. L has ἐκπιεῖν (164) and ῥῖψαι (*sic*, 166). But ἄν ... μαινοίμην
is doubtful as a stronger form of βουλοίμην ἄν. Hence Diggle's text,
which means 'I would go mad after a drink—giving away the
flocks and flinging myself into the sea' (ἀντιδούς and ῥίψας coincident with μαινοίμην ἄν: see Barrett on *Hipp.* 289–92); ἀμειβοίμην
(Wecklein); ἐκπιών ... μὴ ἀντιδούς ... ῥίψας, with μαίνεσθαι meaning the same as in 168 (Kirchhoff); μαιοίμην (F. W. Schmidt;
Kassel, art. cit. 99n., 104). But μαίομαι is not found in E. Kassel
thought μαίνεσθαι with the infinitive unparalleled: but cf. Aelian
fr. 244.26 Hercher ἑκάτερος δι' ἁρπαγῆς τὴν κόρην ⟨ἑαυτοῦ⟩ ποιή-
cασθαι ἐμάινοντο, also μέμονεν, μεμαώς etc. with the infinitive in
Homer; Hor. *Odes.* 1.15.27; Manil. 5.660. If the optative is
thought suspect (Kassel), then despite the aptness of ὡς ... γε
(247n.) there is something to be said for the easily corrupted
(through misapprehension of the point of ἄν) κἄν κύλικα μαίνομαι
(W. Schmid)—'I am mad with desire to drink, even if only a cup,
a single one': cf. e.g. S. *El.* 1483 κἄν cμικρὸν εἰπεῖν; Ar. *Vesp.* 92 κἄν
ἄχνην. κύλικα is in the emphatic position (rather than μίαν, which
adds little) because it means 'even a cupful (let alone the whole
ἀcκός)'. And from other exx. of the same τόπος (166–7n.) cf. Solon
fr. 33.6, where the *desideratum* is to be tyrant of Athens μοῦνον
ἡμέραν μίαν, ἀcκὸς ὕcτερον δεδάρθαι ... , and (for the καὶ) *Od.* 1.58
ἱέμενος καὶ καπνὸν ἀποθρώcκοντα νοῆcαι ἧς γαίης, θανέειν ἱμείρεται.

165. βοcκήματα in E. has a passive sense, meaning animals that are
fed (*Alc.* 576, *Ba.* 677, *El.* 494; cf. *Hipp.* 1356 ἐμῆς βόcκημα χερός):
188 ποιμένων βοcκήματα. Duchemin takes it as active, 'food', on
the pedantic grounds that Sil. would not confine himself to
animals (cf. 162). She compares S. *El.* 364 and (wrongly) A. *Su.*
620 (add A. *Eum.* 302; Ar. *Ran.* 892); but in all these cases βόcκημα
is in the singular and metaphorical.

166–7. These lines combine two τόποι: (1) 'Having achieved
such and such I will be happy to die' (164n.; numerous refs. in
Thomson on A. *Ag.* 539; also Agathias *Hist.* 2.31; Nonnus 4.148;
Ter. *Phorm.* 165). But the plunge from the Leucadian rock is not
simply a metaphor for death (as Dieterich, *Nekyia*, 28; Usener, *De
Iliadis Carmine Quodam Phocaico*, 41 (= *Kleine Schriften* iii 453); cf.
Wilamowitz, *Sappho und Simonides*, 32 n. 2), rather (2) a con-

sequence (Men. fr. 312; Athen. 619e), cure (Strabo 10.2.9 (452);
Ov. *Her.* 15.167–8; Serv. *ad Aen.* 3.274) and image (Anacr. 376
PMG, cf. 378) of the loss of self-control that Sil. would suffer ἅπαξ
μεθυϲθείϲ. **ῥίψαϲ** is intransitive: cf. Men. fr. 312 (of the Leucadian
leap); *Alc.* 897, *Hel.* 1325; Theogn. 176.

167. Raised eyebrows may express pride (e.g. Cratin. fr. 355; Men.
Sicyon. 160; Post in *AJP* 82 (1961), 101–2), and so, according to
Duchemin, Sil. amusingly claims here a certain dignity. But they
may also express strain or distress (Sil. has long been without wine
and sex): e.g. *Hipp.* 290, *IA* 648; Ar. *Ach.* 1069, *Vesp.* 655; Men.
Dysk. 423; and Straton's (*AP* 12.42.3) καὶ ϲτυγνὴν ὀφρύων λύϲειϲ
τάϲιν—the effect of a beautiful boy, comparable perhaps to that of
drink. But elsewhere the brow is merely relaxed (e.g. *Hipp.* 290
ϲτυγνὴν ὀφρὺν λύϲαϲα): καταβαλών is unique, and refers perhaps to
drunken sleep (cf. the drunken sleep of Sil. at V. *Ecl.* 6.14–5; and
Wecklein thought of the 'Barberini Faun'—a sleeping satyr, M.
Robertson *A History of Greek Art* i 534–5). It may be relevant that
the eyebrows of Sil. and the satyrs seem in 5th-cent. vase-painting
to be more emphasized than those of men.

168. Cf. *IA* 1251 μαίνεται δ' ὃϲ εὔχεται θανεῖν; Amphis fr. 26.

169. Ussher accuses Sil. of mistaken reasoning, 'since drinking does
not promote virility'. But it may stimulate and enhance sexual
pleasure: cf. Ar. *Eccl.* 948, fr. 596; Ion fr. 27 West, 9–10. Sil. of
course has no female to hand. Why then does he say what he does?
Partly because his excited imagination takes him back to happier
times. And the passage may well represent a satyric τόποϲ, vigorous enough to survive even where there are no women or nymphs
to justify it (cf. 464–5n., 477n.). Its survival was assisted by the
phallus, to which Sil. gestures with τουτί (2n.; S. *Ichn.* 151, fr. 421;
Ar. *Thesm.* 157): cf. Ar. *Vesp.* 1062, *Lys.* 863, 937. In Nemesianus
Ecl. 3, which has been taken to reflect the contents of S. *Dionysiskos*,
the newly invented wine arouses in the satyrs lust for the nymphs.
τ' ὀρθὸν: τοὐρθὸν L, which Brunck (on S. *Trach.* 1245) took to be
the origin of the corrupt Hesychian gloss τοὐθρὸν· τὸν ὄρθρον,
which he emends to τοὐρθὸν· τὸ ἄρθρον. But a more likely source is
fr. 206.4. ὀρθὸν here is predicative (at Ar. *Vesp.* 1062, *Lys.* 863, 937,
τοῦτο suffices to refer to the phallos).

170–1. Both these actions are performed by satyrs in vase-
paintings: μαϲτοῦ δραγμόϲ in *ARV*² 1155.6 (Amymone; Brommer,
*Satyrspiele*², fig. 15); λειμῶνοϲ ψαῦϲιϲ in *ARV*² 371.14 and 462.43
(maenads; Pfuhl, *Malerei und Zeichnung der Griechen*, figs. 427, 443).
S. fr. 484, from the satyric *Pandora*, refers perhaps to satyric
δραγμόϲ of Pandora's newly created μαϲτόϲ (*EM* s. βλιμάζειν· τὸ

τιτθολαβεῖν κτλ.). **παρεϲκευαϲμένου**, if correct, means probably in effect παρατετιλμένου (cf. Ar. *Thesm.* 590, *Lys.* 89, 151, *Ran.* 516, *Eccl.* 13; Bain in *LCM* 7.1 (1982), 7–10), but is curiously vague. Hence παρεϲκυθιϲμένου Wieseler (cf. *El.* 241, *Tro.* 1026). But this is odd with λειμῶνοϲ (cf. Ar. *Eccl.* 13). And because Sil. is probably thinking of maenads, who in vase-painting tend to *resist* satyric advances, the correct reading may be some form of -εϲκεπαϲμένου ('covered'; περι- Jacobs; παρ- Hermann; κατ- Wieszner).

171. λειμῶνοϲ: for the metaphor cf. Archil. fr. 196a (West, *Delectus*) 23–4 ϲχήϲω γὰρ ἐϲ ποη[φόρουϲ κ]ήπουϲ, and more exx. in *ZPE* 14 (1974), 106. It often includes fertility (e.g. Anacr. 346 *PMG* 1.7 τὰϲ ὑακινθίναϲ ἀρ]ούραϲ) but here the suggestion may be rather of a *locus amoenus*: cf. 65–70; *Od.* 5.72. **ὀρχηϲτύϲ** may contain a pun on ὄρχειϲ (J. Henderson, *The Maculate Muse*, 27).

172. εἶτ' ἐγὼ κυνήϲομαι L. Logical εἶτα commonly serves in rhetorical questions to draw precisely the wrong conclusion from what precedes it, thus illustrating emphatically the absurdity of that conclusion (e.g. *Alc.* 957, *Andr.* 666, *HF* 1381, *El.* 1044). The negative was presumably eliminated by a scribe unaware of the synizesis in ἐγὼ οὐ, or at least in an attempt to substitute crasis (cf. the similar corruption at S. *OT* 332, 1002). Should we read ἐγὼ οὐ κυνήϲομαι (Matthiae) or ἐγὼ οὐκ ὠνήϲομαι (Tyrwhitt)? ὠνήϲομαι seems to make better sense (cf. Ar. *Vesp.* 52 εἶτ' οὐκ ἐγὼ δοὺϲ δύ' ὀβολὼ μιϲθώϲομαι ...;), and would have been easily corrupted by the elimination of the negative: -κ would be retained to avoid hiatus (cf. *OT* 332), and then κωνήϲομαι is a *vox nihili*. But κυνήϲομαι should probably be retained. Satyrs treated drinking equipment as sex objects (439–40n., 553–5n.). The point here is that Sil.'s mind, in passing from sex to drink, enthusiastically confuses them, perhaps because there are in fact no females to hand. For the analogy between kissing and drinking see Gow on Theocr. 7.70. The middle form of the future, κυνήϲομαι, is unparalleled, but acceptable here.

173. ἀμαθίαν: a favourite reproach to man or god in E. (see Bond on *HF* 347; Verrall on *Med.* 223; cf. Dover, *Greek Popular Morality*, 122–3), suggesting insensitivity of conduct as much as stupidity or ignorance. It sometimes connotes social class: Ar. *Eq.* 193; Pl. *Symp.* 204a; cf. Ps. Xen. *Ath. Pol.* 1.5. Plato's definition (*Symp.* 204a), τὸ μὴ ὄντα καλὸν κἀγαθὸν καὶ φρόνιμον δοκεῖν αὑτῶι εἶναι ἱκανόν, suits Pol.'s complacent and sophisticated brutality (esp. 316–46.). But a closer parallel is Dionysos' description of Pentheus as ἀμαθήϲ (*Ba.* 480, 490): both Pol. and Pentheus are hostile to, and ignorant of, the joys of the *thiasos*; cf. 593 τὸν ἀπαίδευτον; *Suda* s.

LINES 174–181   137

ἀμαθής· ἀμύητος; Seaford in *CQ* 31 (1981), 254. Callimachus said
ναὶ Γᾶν οὐκ ἀμαθὴς ὁ Κύκλωψ (*Epigr.* 46.2) of Pol. transformed by
Theocr. (*Id.* 11).

174. κλαίειν κελεύων: this colloquialism occurs (with ἄνωγα) at 340,
701, and in Ar. (e.g. *Eq.* 433), but not in tragedy. After the over-
abstract ἀμαθίαν the second object ὀφθαλμόν goes to the opposite
extreme, making κλαίειν appear absurdly literal. μέсον (21n.) goes
closely enough with τὸν ὀφθαλμὸν not to require a second τόν.

175–87. Sil. now goes off into the cave, and returns at 188 with the
barter.

176. προсφέρεсθε is indicative probably, not imperative: cf. Xen
Anab. 5.5.19; Pl. *Phdr.* 252d, *Charm.* 165d cὺ μὲν ὡς φάсκοντος ἐμοῦ
εἰδέναι περὶ ὧν ἐρωτῶ προсφέρηι πρός με.

177. Cf. *Andr.* 628 χειρίαν λαβών, also of the capture of Helen after
the Trojan War. In both cases the original, physical sense of the
word seems uppermost (cf. *Andr.* 630).

177–87. The conventional attack on Helen (e.g. *El.* 213–4, *IT* 525;
Gorgias fr. 11.2) is funny at 280–1 because, although a τόπος, it is
uttered by Pol. (280–5n.); and it is funny here because the satyrs,
exotic creatures stranded in a faraway land, are disconcertingly
familiar with even the details of the conventional condemnation
(cf. e.g. *Andr.* 229 τῆι φιλανδρίαι, 630 προδότιν, *Tro.* 991–2 quoted
below), and because the punishment recommended is not the
usual one of death (*Hec.* 265–70, *Andr.* 628, *Tro.* 874–9, 1030) but
something more in keeping with satyric preoccupations. Such a
vulgar version of the τόπος, sounding almost like a condemnation
of a recent occurrence in the village, is close to self-parody. The
joke may derive from Sophocles' satyric Ἑλένης γάμος, in which
the satyrs attempted to rape Helen (Aristid. 2.399 Dindorf).
Other plays in which Helen and the satyrs may have appeared
together are A. *Proteus* and Cratin. *Dionysalexandros* (cf. the hypothesis in *P. Oxy.* 663; Körte in *Hermes* 39 (1904), 482–3) but in
neither can we be sure that they tried to rape her. It has been
conjectured that on an early-5th-cent. kyathos a warrior with a
drawn sword pursuing a woman, while a satyr is about to throw a
stone, refers to a satyr-play on the adventures of Helen (Karouzou
in *BCH* for 1949, 519, cf. Stesich. 201 *PMG*; Ghali-Kahil, *Les
Enlèvements et le Retour d'Hélène* (1955), 98). Helen was in fact saved
by those very charms which for the satyrs determine the form of
her punishment (*Ilias Parva* xvii; *Andr.* 627–31; Ibycus 296 *PMG*;
Ar. *Lys.* 155–6; Q. Smyrn. 13.388; Ghali-Kahil, op. cit.).

181. Wilamowitz (*Anal. Eur.* 225) regarded this line as interpolated,
on the grounds that the accusative τὴν προδότιν (182) has no

justification, and that γαμεῖν cannot be used in this sense (mere sexual intercourse) at this time. But there is no doubt as to whom τὴν προδότιν describes: it is in distant, emphatic apposition to αὐτήν (180). Cf. 492–3n., and e.g. *Tro.* 398 Πάρις δ' ἔγημε τὴν Διός. Archil. fr. cit. (171n.) 38 πολλοὺς δὲ ποιεῖτα[ι φίλους suppl. Merkelbach-West, might be supplemented with γάμους. Cf. Stesich. fr. 223 *PMG*, where Aphrodite makes the daughters of Tyndareus διγάμους τὲ καὶ τριγάμους.

182–4. Cf. e.g. Hor. *Odes.* 4.9.13–16. The account of the seduction in the *Cypria* may well have described the beauty of Paris and the splendour of his dress: cf. *Il.* 3.392 (also 39, 55), where Paris awaits Helen κάλλεῖ τε cτίλβων καὶ εἵμαcιν. But the earliest extant details of the encounter are in E. (*Tro.* 991–2 ὃν εἰcιδοῦcα βαρβάροιc ἐcθήμαcι / χρυcῶι τε λαμπρὸν ἐξεμαργώθηc φρέναc; A.'s attention is on the *consequences*: *Ag.* 403–87, etc.): for the consequent contradiction with Paris the simple shepherd see Stinton, op. cit. 40n., ch. IV. The seduction of Helen was always popular in art, and particularly in the luxuriously erotic vase-painting of *c.* 420–350 BC. But although *Tro.*, *IA*, and *Cyc.* were all written in the decade after 416 BC, the first extant paintings of Paris in gorgeous Phrygian dress with Helen are after 400 BC (Ghali-Kahil, op. cit. 177–87n., nos. 128ff.—nos. 138 and 147 are 5th cent., but not of Paris and Helen; W. Koch, *Paris vor Helena*, nos. 11–17). Attic exx. are *ARV*² 1341, 1416, and 1522.1, which is according to Beazley 'hardly Paris and Helen', perhaps because Paris appears ridiculous in his Phrygian costume. With this passage in mind Beazley might have judged differently, for the arrangement of the figures is the one usual for the scene. **θυλάκουc τοὺc ποικίλουc... κλωιὸν:** Greek men wore neither trousers nor necklaces (Bieber, *Griechische Kleidung*, 27). Persian men wore both (Hdt. 5.49.3–4; 8.113.3; etc.). Paris' dress is based not, it seems, on Homer, but on contemporary Persian practice: cf. esp. the ποικίλαι ἀναξυρίδεc of the Persian nobles at Xen. *Anab.* 1.5.8, and the Persians' θύλακοι ('bags') at Ar. *Vesp.* 1087. The ποικιλία of Paris' trousers is clearly visible on some of the vases mentioned above. And in one (*ARV*² 1341) he wears a necklace. Greek κλωιά were for prisoners and dogs (Wilson in *CQ* 25 (1975), 151); and so the term here is no less derogatory than θυλάκουc. **ἰδοῦcα** (183) has as object θυλάκουc (182) and νιν understood with φοροῦντα (184).

184. κλωιὸν: in MSS of 5th-cent. authors the word appears twice in the form κλοιόc (here and Eupolis fr. 159.16), and twice in the form κλωιόc (235; Ar. *Vesp.* 897). Corruption was likely to be towards the post-5th-cent. form κλοιόc (Mayser, op. cit. 123n., i

1.114; Meisterhans, *Grammatik der Attischen Inschriften* (1900), 65–6). **περὶ μέcον τὸν αὐχένα:** cf. Aristophanes' parody of Philoxenos (Ar. fr. 725; 827 *PMG*) μεcαύχενας νέκυας, of wineskins. If Philox. used μεcαύχην of hanged men, then it referred not presumably to the point midway between head and shoulders, but to the unrelenting clasp of the rope: the neck is in the middle of what goes all the way round it: cf. *Or.* 265 μέcον μ' ὀχμάζεις (of an Erinys with its arms round its victim); Ar. *Ach.* 1216; Theogn. 265. At Ar. *Lys.* 681 αὐχήν appears to have the *double entendre* penis (Henderson, op. cit. 171n., 114); if it does so also in S. fr. 756 ἀνακειμένωι μέcον εἰc τὸν αὐχέν' εἰcαλοίμην (uttered by a satyr burning with passion for Herakles: Athen. 23d), then μέcον can have the same sense as here, *Or.* 265, etc.: the satyr intends to leap on the reclining erect Herakles in an act of instantaneous rape. Cf. Ar. *Ach.* 1216 τοῦ πέους ἄμφω μέcου προcλάβεcθε (i.e. all the way round). This suggests that αὐχήν here too may contain the *double entendre* penis (and θυλάκους in 182 as scrotum?--Henderson, 27), in keeping with the spirit of 180–1, and with the satyrs' estimate of female lasciviousness at A. *Dikt.* 830 ἐcορῶc' ἤβην ἡμετέραν / γαθ]εῖ, γάνυται.

185. ἐξεπτοήθη: πτοεῖν describes Helen being seduced in Alc. fr. 283.3 (as a virtually certain supplement), and at *IA* 586. The stronger ἐκπτοεῖν is nowhere else erotic; but cf. *Tro.* 992, equally condemnatory of Helen: ἐξεμαργώθης φρένας. Cf. also Sappho fr. 22.13–4 ἁ γὰρ κατάγωγις αὔτα[ν / ἐπτόαιc ἴδοιcαν, where κατάγωγιc, a woman's dress, is comparable with θυλάκους and κλωιόν here.

185–6. ἀνθρώπιον λῶcτον λιποῦcα is very different in spirit from Sappho fr. 16.7–8 ... Ἑλένα [τὸ]ν ἄνδρα / τὸν [πανάρ]ιcτον / καλλ[ιποῖ]c' ἔβα κτλ. (cf. Alc. fr. 283.8; *Andr.* 603, *Or.* 99, etc.). The satyrs' patronizing diminutive must be seen against the generally unfavourable treatment of Menelaos in E. (Paganelli, op. cit. 103n., 82–3).

186–7. These verses may have been inspired partly by *Od.* 14.68 ὥc ὤφελλ' Ἑλένης ἀπὸ φῦλον ὀλέcθαι; but they certainly parody a Euripidean τόπος (*Med.* 573–4, *Hipp.* 616–50). Hostility to women was not of course confined to E. (cf. e.g. A. *Sept.* 187–8, 200), but he was notorious for it (P. Décharme, *Euripide et l'Espirit de son Théatre*, ch.4). Because Ar. *Thesm.* (see esp. 85, 389–90, 545) was produced probably not long before *Cyc.*, there may be something defensive about this self-parody (222n.); cf. fr. 657, where it is said to be silly to generalize about women.

186. μηδαμοῦ: μηδαμῶc Wecklein. Cf. the variants at *Tro.* 910, *Ba.* 46: in both cases it appears that -οῦ was corrupted to -ῶc. -οῦ should be retained here.

187. μὴ 'μοὶ is an obvious correction of L's μή μοι. Cf. 346n.

188–92. The attribution of these lines to Sil. is almost certainly correct. If the sheep of the parodos were real (parodos n.), then no doubt Sil. brought on real lambs here (tied together: 225n.).

188. βοcκήματα means animals (not as food, but as what is fed): 165n. ποιμνίων (Scaliger; ποιμένων L) would define the animals as sheep: cf. *Ba.* 677–8 βοcκήματα ... μόcχων. But the objections to ποιμένων—that it is a curious self-reference, irrelevant, and trite —reckon without the slightly absurd pomposity of Sil. (1n., 29n., etc.) as displayed e.g. in the periphrases of the next two lines. And in fact, unlike Κυκλώπων ... βοcκήματα (165), ποιμένων βοcκήματα brings out the original sense of βόcκημα: ἃ βόcκουcι (ποιμένεc): cf. fr. 27.5, *Andr.* 1101, *Hipp.* 1356.

189. ἀρνῶν τροφαί: does this mean (a) 'brood consisting in lambs' or (b) 'brood of sheep'? For (a) cf. Pl. *Leg.* 790d τὰ νεογενῆ παίδων θρέμματα, 56n. (?), and the fact that elsewhere these lambs are called ἄρνεc (224, 234, 256; *Od.* 9.226). But elsewhere genitive with τροφή is possessive: S. *Ichn.* 232 θηρὸc εὐναί[ου] τρο[φ] ῆc, *OT* 1 Κάδμου τοῦ πάλαι νέα τροφή. And ἄρνεc can mean sheep as well as lambs (*El.* 719, *IT* 196; etc.).

190. This kind of postponement of τε (cf. Pl. *Crat.* 403e τέλεοc coφιcτήc τε) is rare: Denniston, *GP*, 517.

191. cf. *Od.* 9.224–7, where Od.'s companions urge him, sensibly but unsuccessfully, to take the food and leave the cave. **φέρεcθε:** cf. 88n.

192. εὔίου: εὐίον Wecklein. But cf. S. fr. 255.2 βακχεῖοc βότρυc.

193. This line is generally attributed to Sil. (as Diggle) or to the chorus. But L's attribution to Od., though without authority, has something to be said for it. Sil. is preoccupied with the wine, but when addressed more decisive perhaps than is consistent with 193; and the plural δράcομεν probably refers to one of the two *groups* of satyrs and sailors. As for the attribution to the chorus, at 194 Od. is clearly addressing *Sil.*, and at 203–4 the chorus seem happily unaware of Pol.'s arrival. Against the attribution to Od. Hermann argued that he has not seen Pol. before, and so would not recognize him. But cf. 117, 126–30, 174, and the ease of recognition in Homer. He also argued that 194 seems to be an answer. L has γάρ, which there is no good reason to emend (τἄρ' Hartung, Diggle; slightly preferable is γ' ἄρ': see Lowe in *Glotta* 51 (1973), 34–63). A γάρ clause in dialogue may support implied assent ('Yes, for ...', 'No, for ...') to a statement or to a question which suggests its own answer (Denniston, *GP*, 73). But τί δράcομεν does not suggest its own answer (the nearest parallel would be *Alc.* 146–7—ἐλπὶc μὲν

οὐκέτ' ἐστὶ ζώζεσθαι βίον;—πεπρωμένη γὰρ ἡμέρα βιάζεται). Perhaps
with γάρ Od. gives his motive for saying τί δράcομεν (*GP*, 60; cf.
also 313; *GP*, 59).

195. In Homer Od. and his men are in the cave when Pol. appears at
the entrance, and so they naturally rush ἐc μυχὸν ἄντρου, where
they are nevertheless spotted (251). Here the idea is retained (cf.
407) merely as a suggestion by the cowardly Sil., which Od., who
must remain on stage, bravely rejects. γε has been suspected, but
makes excellent sense: 'where at least you will not be *seen*', implying that outright escape is impossible.

196. Cf. *IT* 1021 δεινὸν τόδ' εἶπας, ξενοφονεῖν ἐπήλυδας.

198–200. This brings out the contradiction inherent in *Od.* 9.263–7,
where Od. combines mention of the glory of the Trojan War with
supplication. Menelaos too in *Hel.* (808, 845, 863–4, 948–9)
regards the Trojan victory as requiring boldness from him among
the dangers of Egypt. For exx. of the idea that the vanquished
are demeaned by the subsequent cowardice of the victors see
Denniston on *El.* 184–9.

200. ὑπέςτην, a singular among plurals, expresses Od.'s egoism
(694n.) by effecting the contrast with μυρίον ὄχλον: cf. *Il.* 11.401–
75, where Od. fights single-handed a mass of Trojans.

201. εὐγενῶc: εὐκλεῶc Blaydes (cf. *Alc.* 292, *Hcld.* 534). But εὐγενῶc
may stand: cf. *Tro.* 727; S. *Aj.* 479–80 ἀλλ' ἢ καλῶc ζῆν ἢ καλῶc
τεθνηκέναι τὸν εὐγενῆ χρή. Further exx. of the thought: *Or.* 781; Ar.
Eq. 80–1; Men. *Dysk.* 379; and esp. *Or.* 1151–2.

202. L's πάρος εὖ cώcομεν is unmetrical. γ' εὖ (Tr. 3) lived on into
Duchemin's edition. But γε makes no more sense than εὖ. The
notion of success is sufficiently expressed in τὸν αἶνον cώιζειν. And
the phrase εὖ cώιζειν occurs neither in E. (the closest is *Su.* 313
τοὺc νόμους cώιζηι καλῶc) nor, so far as I know, anywhere else.
cυccώcομεν (alternatively cυν-: *IA* 1209, *Hel.* 1389; Men. *Sik.* 168;
but cf. *IG* 1³ 52 A 17 cυccεμαινόcθον), i.e. cὺν τῶι βίωι, would have
been easily corrupted (Σ to E; a possible loss of cυ- occurs at *HF*
825). cυccώιζειν, as far as I can discover, nowhere else takes an
abstract object; but given its rarity this may be insignificant. Cf.
on the other hand *Hcld.* 324–5 εὐγενὴc δ' ἂν' Ἑλλάδα cώιζειc
πατρώιαν δόξαν, *Su.* 313, 527, *HF* 507, *Ion* 20, 1323. And so best
perhaps is cώcομεν, preceded not by παρόντα (Wieseler)—at A.
PV 392 cῶιζε τὸν παρόντα νοῦν there is much more point to
παρόντα—but by πάροιθε. πάρος was likely to have replaced
πάροιθε, which seems to have disappeared after the 5th cent. BC
(except for the curious use at Theocr. 17.48), whereas πάροc is
found in non-literary papyri from the 3rd century BC to the 3rd

AD: (*P. Oxy.* 1121.36; *P. Petr.* ii 9.1.6; Kiessling *Wörterb. d. Gr. Urk.* Suppl. 1. 1940–66 s. πάρος). Cf. *Tro.* 1050 πάροιθε V, πάρος γ' P (with P representing the same tradition as L here: Zuntz, op. cit. 73–4n., 175).

203–5. Pol. now arrives with his club (210), though not necessarily with the hounds mentioned in 130. The satyrs are moving about the ὀρχήcτρα, conceivably because they have not heard 193–202 and are still celebrating the arrival of the wine, much more likely out of alarm, and possibly even to distract Pol. from their crime. At any rate, Pol. seems to be exaggerating, in the style of a sergeant-major.

203. Three tribrachs in succession do not occur in the spoken trimeters of tragedy (Descroix, op. cit. 7n., 152–5). They express agitation, as at 210, and Ar. *Ach.* 1054 ἀπόφερ' ἀπόφερε τὰ κρέα καὶ μή μοι δίδου. Cf. also *IT* 832. ἄνεχε πάρεχε: this formula occurs also at *Tro.* 308, Cassandra's first words as she arrives with two torches to sing a solitary wedding song, and at Ar. *Vesp.* 1326, Philokleon's first words as he arrives drunk and holding a torch with which he threatens the people following him. There are three interconnected problems: (1) What does the phrase mean in *Tro.* and *Vesp.*? (2) What does it mean here? (3) How close is its association with the wedding (and the κῶμος)? (1) The most natural meaning for the words is transitive: 'Hold up (the torches)! Hold them alongside!' And this is certainly how E. himself interpreted the wedding formula at *IA* 732–3 τίc δ' ἀναcχήcει φλόγα;—ἐγὼ παρέξω φῶc ὃ νυμφίοιc πρέπει (for ἀνέχειν of holding up a torch see also *Med.* 482, 1027, *Ion* 716, fr. 472.13; Thuc. 4.111; for παρέχειν *Od.* 18.317). It is true that in neither *Tro.* nor *Vesp.* is anybody else in a position to provide light (and Murray's φέρ', ὦ for φέρω in *Tro.* is unlikely); but Cassandra is creating the spirit, not the reality, of a wedding; and much the same may be true of Philokleon and his solitary κῶμοc. On the other hand Philokleon goes on to threaten with his torch those following him; and this suggests an *intransitive* meaning for the phrase (or with ὁδόν understood with πάρεχε). Cf. Ar. *Vesp.* 949 πάρεχ' ἐκποδών, 'make way'. (At Ar. *Av.* 1720 ἄναγε δίεχε πάραγε πάρεχε, from the wedding song, πάρεχε is no less ambiguous than here: Robert in *Hermes* 56 (1921), 307.) ἄνεχε meaning 'Back!' or 'Stop!' is unparalleled; but we should remember that παῦε is the only intransitive form of the active παύω, and that usages otherwise obsolete may be conserved in ritual language. (2) It is possible that Pol. is calling for light (the Greeks on the Richmond vase (Plate II) carry torches; cf. Arnott, op. cit. parodos n., 120–1; for the time-scheme see 213–14n.), but much more likely that he is calling a satyric confusion to order: the place of Philokleon's torch is taken by Pol.'s club (210–11, 213n.). Cf. the entrance of Ballio at Plaut. *Pseud.* 132 (to slaves) *Exite, agite exite, ignavi* (he goes on to beat them). The answer to (1) and (2) may be that the phrase was ambiguous even to the Greeks, the ancient call for torchlight coming to serve gradually also as a warning of the torchlight wedding procession moving through the street. (3) Does ἄνεχε πάρεχε necessarily suggest a wedding? A κῶμος is also a torchlight movement through the street (*RE* xi. s. Komos, 1294), and so may have adopted the warning phrase for its own use; and that would explain why Philokleon says it. But even in the mouth of Philokleon it may have been meant to suggest a wedding, for he has his arm round a flute-girl (Old Comedy finales as weddings: Cornford, *The Origins of Attic Comedy*, 56–66). As for its utterance by Pol. here, it is difficult to see the point of a suggestion either of a wedding (despite 511–18) or of a κῶμος (despite 492). One must reckon with the possibility firstly of self-parody (of *Tro.* 308), and of an attempt to achieve a ludicrous effect by contradicting Pol.'s grotesque appearance immediately with a civilized Greek formula, a herald of that combination of savagery and Greek sophistication which defines E.'s Pol. (intro., §VII). Finally, Duchemin gave the whole line to the chorus (L gives it to Sil.) on the grounds that ῥαιθυμία is inconsistent with τί βακχιάζετε; (204). But cf. Theopomp. 115 FGH 139; Phil. Jud. 2.461 (= E. fr. 687).

204. **τί βακχιάζετε:** cf. S. *Ichn.* 133 τί ποτε βακχεύεις ἔχων; **οὐχὶ Διόνυσος τάδε:** cf. 63. At *Andr.* 168 Hermione has reminded Andromache of her menial tasks: οὐ γάρ ἐσθ᾽ Ἕκτωρ τάδε κτλ. τάδε here means in effect 'here'. Διώνυσος (L) is the epic form, not found in tragedy or satyr-play. L has the same mistake at 590, where it is metrically impossible. Reading Διόνυσος (as at 139, 415, 436) we have to mend the metre (οὐ L). The emphatic οὐχὶ (Musgrave) is better than οὐχ ὁ (Porson): cf. esp. *HF* 857. If οὐχὶ became οὐ (cf. *Or.* 97, 107, *Med.* 257, 1096, fr. 242; S. *OT* 993), this would require the metrical change Διώνυσος. It was rare for the scribe of P to improve on L (Zuntz, op. cit. 73–4n., 138). But he was no doubt familiar with the normal form (e.g. 139) which he wrote both here and at 590.

205 τύμπανα (65n.), unlike κρόταλα, appear to be, at least in the 5th cent. **BC**, exclusively instruments of cult (Wegner, op. cit. 40n., 62–3, 64–5, 212–14). The two are associated in the cult of Dionysos and Kybele at *h. hom.* 14.3; Pi. fr. 70b.9–10 (cf. *Hel.* 1308–9; Sapph. fr. 44.25; Hdt. 2.60). And they are both played, in 5th-cent. vase-painting, by satyrs and maenads dancing in the company of their god (Wegner 212–14, 228–9; particularly striking is *ARV*² 371.14 by the Brygos painter). In the *theatre* of Dionysos, on the other hand, instruments other than αὐλός and lyre seem to have been exceptional (P-Cambridge, op. cit. 1n., 167): the τύμπανα in *Ba.* (124, 156) and presumably in S. *Tympanistai* (satyric?), and the κρόταλα in *Hyps.* (Schol. Ar. *Ran.* 1305–6). *Theatrical* satyrs appear along with αὐλός and lyre (esp. Pronomos Vase, Plate III; also Brommer, op. cit. 170–1n., figs. 2, 3, 6, 13, 20), but never with any percussion instrument. And so whereas Sil. may have actually heard ἀοιδαί βαρβίτων at 40, what is said at 65 and 205 is no doubt correct. Theatrical conditions coincide with the captivity of the satyrs in depriving them of the more exclusively orgiastic clapper and drum. χαλκοῦ: κρόταλα seem to have been more commonly of reed (Schol. Ar. *Nub.* 260), κύμβαλα of metal. On *Hel.* 1308, 1346 see Kannicht *contra* Dale.

206–16. The tasks expected here of the satyrs Pol. performs himself at *Od.* 9.244–9 (as here, before he sees the Greeks). The similarity with Homer brings out Pol.'s new sophistication.

206. Lengthening by position before βλ- is normal (K-B i 306), but an ultimate short lengthened by position in a longum of an iambic trimeter is somewhat rare (Maas, op. cit. 120n., §125). **βλαστήματα** is from the language of tragedy (*Hcld.* 1006, of human kind: A. *Sept.* 533; *Med.* 1099), here amusingly grandiose: cf. 41–8n., 188n.

207. τε: γε (L) in a question is unparalleled (except for the suspect A. *Ag.* 1115), and pointless here. Triclinius (Tr. 1, before P was copied) added (apparently *in rasura*) the compendious ending -τοις to μας-, and replaced the καὶ with χ (as at 2, 38, etc.). We cannot improve on this. But after the copying he added (Tr. 2) v to εἰσι (thereby covering L's question-mark) and ἢ before χύπὸ. This is because he thought that χύπὸ was a double short (cf. his similar mistake at *Su.* 344), and was furthermore misled by L's ἢ at the beginning of the line into believing that the two descriptions of the kids are mutually exclusive. But we should read ἢ (cf. **MS** ἢ for ἢ at 117, 129, 216). Here, as at 117 and 129, ἢ introduces 'a suggested answer, couched in interrogative form, to a question just asked' (Denniston, *GP*, 283). And in fact the second description completes the first, as at *Hcld.* 1003 κτείνοντα κἀκβάλλοντα καὶ τεχνώμενον, and as is clear from the τε in 208.

208. πλευρὰς: the feminine form of this word seems to have replaced the neuter in MSS at *Hcld.* 824, *Pho.* 1414, *Ba.* 740. Hence Elmsley's πλευροῖς. But the feminine form is common enough in E., and sometimes guaranteed by metre (e.g. *Hec.* 500). And there is nothing wrong with the accusative. τρέχουϲι: neuter plural subjects signifying living agents usually take a plural verb (K-G i 65).

209. πλήρωμα τυρῶν means the cheeses that fill (the baskets): cf. *Ion* 664 τῶν φίλων πλήρωμ' ἀθροίϲαϲ, *Med.* 203. ἐξημελγμένον seems curious only to those who buy their cheese: at *Od.* 9.247 Pol. puts *milk* into the baskets θρέψαϲ, having curdled it. Cf. 136.

210. Both here and at *IT* 1072 E. may have intended a pause to precede τί φάτε; see also S. *Phil.* 804–5, 951, Cf. *Hel.* 483 τί φῶ; τί λέξω, *Hel.* 471, 779; S. *Aj.* 757. τῶι ξύλωι: not the stocks (Ussher, comparing Ar. *Nub.* 592), but Pol.'s club. In Homer it lies in the cave (319), and Od. blinds him with it. Here however Pol. carries it (203n.) like a rustic (Theocr. 7.19) or Herakles (213–14n.). For beating with τὸ ξύλον see Ar. *Vesp.* 458, *Pax.* 1121; Men. *Sam.* 440; Plaut. *Poen.* 1319–20. Herakles clubbing the satyrs seems to have been an early theme of satyric drama (Buschor in *SBAW* 1943/5, 91–6; Brommer, op. cit. 170–1n., vases 78–83; 213–14n.); satyrs are sometimes spanked in vase-painting (Brommer, vases 155–7), and are threatened with physical punishment at A. *Theoroi* 77 and S. *Ichn.* 168. In fr. 693, from the satyric *Syleus*, (Herakles') ξύλον occurs *in sensu obscoeno* (cf. Ar. *Lys.* 553: *AP* 4.26); but despite 589 I do not detect a *double-entendre* here.

211. ἄνω καὶ μὴ κάτω is not (*pace* Denniston, *GP*, 2) like e.g. S. *OT* 58 γνωτὰ κοὐκ ἄγνωτα: for ἄνω is not equivalent to μὴ κάτω. The satyrs are looking at the ground (κάτω) in fear (S. *Ant.* 441; cf. *Ion* 582). ἄνω βλέπειν means to look not just up but upwards (Ar. *Av.* 175, cf. 178; Pl. *Rep.* 529b; Moschus 8.5; cf. Herodas 7.79). Pol. seems to be demanding that the satyrs look at him (cf. S. *Trach.* 402, *OT* 1121); but because he is bigger than they, and they are probably crawling away from him (213n.), this means they must look ἄνω (212–14).

212–19. L gives 212–13, 215, 217, 219 to Sil. But Pol. only sees Sil. after 221 (226–7); and cf. plural ἀπολέϲαιτε in 221.

212. ἰδού calls attention to the performance of the act requested: cf. 544, *Ba.* 1265.

213–14. raise the problem of the play's time-scheme. On the one hand the sheep have returned to the cave and the satyrs claim to be looking at the stars. On the other hand Pol. asks after his ἄριϲτον, which may mean breakfast or lunch but not an evening meal; and at 542 Sil. refers to the sunshine. In Homer the story is explicitly spread over more than twenty-four hours (*Od.* 9.234, 307, 344, 437). Several tragedies begin in darkness (Diggle on *Phaeth.* 63). And within A. *Cho.* we seem to pass from the evening of one day to the morning of the next (660–2, 710–11, 983–6, 1035); but this is harder to imagine in *Cyc.* because, although Pol. may have been out hunting all night (cf. Xen. *Mem.* 3.11.8, *Kyn.* 6.13, 12.7; Pi. *Pyth.* 9.20–5), and although there is no reason why ἄριϲτον should not be taken early in the morning before it is light, the Greeks arrive (apparently by daylight: 85–9) as the sheep are still being driven into the cave (82–5); so we cannot imagine night passing during the parodos. We can agree with the remarks of Arnott ('We leap from one part of the day to another with a freedom unparalleled in Greek Drama.' *GR* 8 (1961), 169) and of Pathmanathan, who doubts 'the legitimacy of seeking a logical time-sequence in a drama of this type' (*GR* 10 (1963), 128). But if E. had in mind no definite time-sequence, he has no reason to imagine this episode as enveloped in darkness. If so, then the sudden creation of darkness at 213 must be for the sake of a fleeting joke. But this is not the 'comic παρὰ προϲδοκίαν' suggested by Pathmanathan. Rather, Orion is not so representative of the stars in general that one need not ask why he is mentioned here: the answer is that the satyrs, amusing even when terrified, pretend to mistake Pol. for Orion. As for their claim to be seeing the stars in general (τἄϲτρα), either this serves merely to prepare the joke, or it must be removed by emendation (213n.). Orion resembles E.'s Pol. in many respects: as a giant, the son of Poseidon (Hes. fr. 148(a)), above all as a hunter wearing a skin and carrying a club (*Od.* 11.572–5; Arat. *Phaen.* 638; *ARV*² 261.25; *ABV* 168; G. Thiele, *Antike Himmelsbilder*, 30, 39, 120; Roscher, *Lex. Myth.* iii 1023). Cf. 130, 203n., 210n., 360n. For the cowering satyrs Pol. dominates the prospect, no less inescapable than the massive hunter in the sky. In *ARV*² 188.66 (early 5th cent.), inspired no doubt by a satyr-play, a row of satyrs crawls away terrified from Herakles, who stands with skin and club next to Dionysos, their heads and hands turned back and upwards defensively towards him. Pol. has just threatened the satyrs with his club (210n.), and they may well be performing exaggerated gestures of fear before it. Furthermore, Orion was blinded by Oinopion after a drunken assault on his daughter Merope (Hes. fr. 148(a)). The detail preserved by Servius (on V. *Aen.* 10.763) that Oinopion was assisted in this by the satyrs probably derives from a satyr-play (S. *Kedalion* ?). Just as Sil. in the prologue seems to recall previous satyr-plays (3–4n., 5–9n, 11–17n., 39n.), so too here both audience and satyrs may remember another monstrous hunter striding on to the stage with his club; and the suggestion of Orion may also be a subtle suggestion of what will happen to Pol. Orion also represents the same type as a frequent figure of satyr-play, Herakles. Both are somewhat ludicrous 'culture-heroes', hunters in the service of a king (Parthen. 20; Arat. *Phaen.* 640; Her. as hunter in E.'s satyric *Eurystheus* ?), who free the land from wild animals (Schol. Nik. *Ther.* 15), and are rewarded for their services by admission to heaven, the lecherous (Call. *Hymn. Artem.* 265; etc.; for Her. see fr. 693, from the satyric *Syleus*) fathers of fifty sons (Corinna 655 *PMG* 1.14; Apollod. 2.4.10). The Homeric Pol. is a giant, but he is neither lecherous nor a hunter with a club. In E. he has become both (130, 203n., 210n., 583-9), and his callous drunkenness (425-6) is described in terms similar to that of Herakles at *Alc.* 760 (cf. 217n.).

213. τᾶςτρα: for the crasis cf. *HF* 633, *Hel.* 254, etc. (the accentuation is necessarily arbitrary: K-B i 331, anm. 4). τά τ' ἄςτρα (Nauck, after Choeroboscus) is therefore unnecessary, but would have the advantage (with the comma placed after ἄςτρα) of removing the satyrs' claim to be seeing stars other than Orion (213-14n.; Musso in *Att. Acc. Scc. Tor.* 108 (1973-4), 538). **Ὠρίωνα:** the second syllable is long in Homer and Hesiod, where of course a cretic is impossible, short here and at *Ion* 1153.

215. At Men. *Perik.* 307 the ἄριςτον itself is εὐτρεπές. There is material in *Od.* 9 (esp. 373-4) for the conversion of Pol. into a comic glutton: cf. 213-14n., 356, 388, 410. **φάρυγξ** is more usually feminine, but masculine at e.g. Epich. fr. 21.

216-7. Both κρατήρ and πίθος are more appropriate for wine than milk. The Homeric Pol. puts his milk ἐν ἄγγεςιν (9.248). Cf. 388n.

217. Cf. the capacity of Herakles in Sositheos' satyric *Daphnis* (fr. 2.7-8): πίνει δ' ἕνα / καλῶν μετρητήν, τὸν δεκάμφορον πίθον. A πίθος is a large jar for storage. **ὅλον:** the word is rare in E. (*Pho.* 1131, fr. 1041). For its aptness here cf. e.g. Ar. *Ach.* 85-6 παρετίθει δ' ἡμῖν ὅλους ἐκ κριβάνου βοῦς.

218. μεμειγμένον means cows' and sheeps' milk mixed. Ussher's interpretation 'mixed with honey' misses the joke: this form of expression was associated with a kind of mixture too elevated even for an aristocratic dinner table (A. *PV* 116 θεόςυτος ἢ βρότειος ἢ κεκράμενη; *Hel.* 1137), let alone milk, and appears for comic effect in the culinary sphere in the Middle Comedy (Euboul. fr. 7; Alexis fr. 173; cf. Sosipat. fr. 1.52). Many have in fact seen here parody of A. *PV* 116 (refs. in Roos, op. cit. 9n., 171), which, referring to an ὀδμά, certainly invited it. For the possibility of a revival of the *PV* after 427 BC, and other possible echoes of the *PV* after that date, see e.g. Hahne in *Philol.* 61 (1907), 47; M. Griffith, *The Authenticity of Prometheus Bound* (Cambridge, 1977).

219. ὄν: ὧν Kaibel; ὅ γ' Causaubon; οἷον Paley. The aim has been presumably to allow 218 to refer to the γάλα (relative pronoun corrupted into case of apparent antecedent: *Hel.* 809, *Ion* 1014, *Andr.* 268, *Med.* 1281). But ὄν should perhaps be retained ('whichever πίθος you like...'): 218 may indeed refer to the πίθος. **μὴ 'μὲ** is a correction of L's interpretation μή με: cf. 187n., 346n., 361. **μόνον** expresses a reservation: Headlam-Knox on Herodas 2.89.

220–1. In L ἀπολέcαιτε has no object. ἐπεί γε in the tragedians is rare and never introduces a hypothetical sentence (181, *Hipp.* 955, *HF* 141, *Ion* 1353, *Hel.* 556; A. *Pers.* 386; S. *Trach.* 484). And so μ' ἂν for γ' ἂν is attractive: at *Alc.* 1036 L has corrupt γ' for μ' (BV). But the word preceding ἂν generally deserves emphasis. ἐπεί τἂν (i.e. τοι ἂν) ... ἀπολέcαιτε μ' ὑπὸ (W. Schmid) is supported by 198 οὐ δῆτ'· ἐπεί τἂν κτλ. (also S. *OC* 1366; Ar. *Ran.* 34). Read perhaps ἐπεί τἂν μ' ἐν κτλ., which leaves the second ἂν intact (cf. Wackernagel, *Indog. Forsch.*, i 399).

221. **cχημάτων** here means the gestures and movements of the dance (despite the technical sense in Plut. *Mor.* 747c): Lawler in *TAPA* 85 (1954), 148. Cf. Ar. *Pax* 323. Dancing is a novelty for Pol. (124), and the satyrs' is vigorous (37n.).

222. See intro., §VI; 186–7n., 203n., 225n. **ἔα:** see Dodds on *Ba.* 644. At *HF* 1172 Theseus says ἔα· τί νεκρῶν τῶνδε πληθύει πέδον; ten lines after his entry. And so we do not have to suppose with Ussher that Sil. has just brought on a torch (cf. 203n.).

223–4. At *Od.* 9.252 Pol.'s initial question to the Greeks, whence they came and whether they are pirates, is conventional (cf. *Od.* 3.71–4; *h. hom.* 3.452–5; Thuc. 1.5.2): they have eaten of his cheese (9.232), but he has not noticed it. Here, on the other hand, γέ τοι (Denniston, *GP*, 550) introduces the good reason Pol. has for thinking the Greeks thieves. The remainder of Pol.'s conventional question in Homer reappears in *Cyc.* at 275. **κατέсχον** means put in to shore: cf. 349, *Hel.* 1206 πόθεν κατέσχε γῆν;

225. **cυμπεπλεγμένουc** means that the sheep are tied up so as to be entwined together like wrestlers (Hdt. 3.78) or lovers (Pl. *Symp.* 191a): at *Od.* 9.427 Od. binds the rams *together* εὐcτρεφέεccι λύγοιcι. Worthy of mention is Blaydes' cώματ' ἐμπεπλεγμένουc (cώματα seems preferable, see K-G i 316, and may be corrupted to cῶμα at *IT* 1155), which would be paratragic (cf. *Hipp.* 1236; S. *OT* 1264), perhaps defensively so (222n.): Ar. *Thesm.* 1032 ἐν πυκνοῖc δεcμοῖcιν ἐμπεπλεγμένη parodies E. *Andromeda*.

226. '... and cheese-baskets all mixed up'; cυμμιγῶν (Halbertsma) would give worse sense.

227. Presumably the joke is that Sil.'s face is swollen with the wine

(V. *Ecl.* 6.15). His mask was certainly swollen in aspect and probably reddish: the satyr-masks appear reddish on the Pronomos Vase (Plate III), μιλτόπρεπτον at A. *Dikt.* 788 refers to Sil.'s φαλακρόν (on coloured masks see *Suda* s. Aeschylus; Pollux 4.141; O. Hense, *Die Modifizierung der Maske in der Griechischen Tragoedie* (Freiburg, 1902), 30–1), and in a mosaic from Pompeii (Bieber, *Denkm. z. Theaterwesen*, Taf. 49–50) a theatrical Silenos-mask is coloured reddish-brown, in contrast to the one next to it in the box. But the only kind of red and swollen face known to Pol. is caused by the ξύλον (124, 210). Probably Sil.'s pretence of agony (228) has already begun, and this allowed the audience to forget that his face is already familiar to Pol. Alternatively, Sil. has changed his mask (in general, see Hense, op. cit.) or smeared it with wine (cf. the cast *peruncti faecibus ora* at Hor. *Ars. P.* 277). There is nothing else to suggest that Sil. entered and has just returned from the cave: up to 222–7 he, like the Greeks with whom he has been bartering, is simply unnoticed. But a change of mask might conceivably have been effected between 174 and 188. **μέτωπον**: πρόcωπον L; it is the head (cf. 229 κρᾶτα) not the face that is bald (φαλακρόν); and for πρόcωπον replacing μέτωπον see the apparatus. On the other hand Sil.'s baldness *is* part of his *mask* (πρόcωπον). And πρόcωπον is used in the two other places (A. *Eum.* 990–1; S. *El.* 1297; Hense, op. cit., 4–5) where the tragedian seems to have the mask in mind. For φαλακρόν cf. A. *Dikt.* 788; S. fr. 171, *Ichn.* 368.

228. In cυγκεκομμένοc, 'beaten up', W. G. Arnott (in *Antidosis, Festschrift W. Kraus* (Vienna, 1972), 29) detects a play on the medical sense of cυγκοπή as any sudden collapse.

231. For the form of statement cf. *Alc.* 677. **θεόν** should be taken as monosyllabic and disyllabic in the same line, as at *Andr.* 1258, *Tro.* 1280, *Hel.* 560, fr. 292.7; S. *Aj.* 1129. In each case the disyllable falls outside, the monosyllable within, the first or third foot: see further Diggle in *PCPhS* 20 (1974), 31–6; Descroix, op. cit. 203n., 33.

232. ἐφόρουν: the imperfect expresses the idea that the Greeks ignored Sil.'s warning and continued to remove the goods. The choice of verb presumably expresses the same idea: φορεῖν τι is to have or carry something about with one, as Paris his necklace (185), an οἰνοχόος wine (*Od.* 9.10), or Phaedra her hands (*Hipp.* 316). Still, ἔφερον (Blaydes) deserves a mention: cf. φέρειν at 230 and the *middle* ἐξεφοροῦντο at 234: and φορεῖν may have replaced φέρειν in L at S. *OT* 1320.

233. γε: τε Kaibel; but see Denniston, *GP*, 157. **ἧcθιον**: ἐcθίειν

(Wieseler), to be taken with ἐξεφοροῦντο, would soften the lie by accusing the Greeks of a mere intention to eat the cheese. But the confusion of cheese-baskets (226), caused in fact probably by Sil.'s dropping them at 193, might lend credence to Sil.'s remark, which is no more mendacious than what he says next. At *Od.* 9.232 the Greeks do in fact eat of Pol.'s cheese.

234. ἐξεφοροῦντο gives the only third-foot anapaest in what remains of satyric drama. But there are anapaests in *Cyc.* in every other foot save the last (e.g. 229, 647, 566, 242). In Old Comedy anapaests occur in every foot save the last, and there is no reason why satyric drama should differ by excluding them from the third foot. And so Musgrave's ἐξεφροῦντο (cf. *Tro.* 652, *El.* 1033; Barrett on *Hipp.* 866–7; Macdowell on Ar. *Vesp.* 125) is unnecessary; it is also inept, for ἐκφρεῖν means to *let* out, whereas lambs tied up with withies are *carried* out.

235. Cf. 184n. For a collar applied preparatory to physical punishment see Xen. *Hell.* 3.3.11; Eupolis fr. 159.16. But there is a specific insult here: Solon enacted that dangerous dogs should wear the 'three-cubit collar', the κλοιὸν τρίπηχυ (Plut. *Sol.* 24), presumably because a large collar enabled them to be held at a distance (Xen. *Hell.* 2.4.41; cf. the slaves' καρδοπεῖον).

L's κάτα τὸν ὀφθαλμὸν μέcον (for omission of iota in κάιτα see e.g. 457, 563) makes no sense. And Murray's lacuna after 235 fails to remove the split anapaest, of which there are no certain exx. in the play (334n.). Duchemin read καὶ for κάτα; but eyes are not bound by collars. Most edd. print κατὰ τὸν ὀμφαλὸν μέcον (cf. *Ion.* 5, 462): the corruption to ὀφθαλμόν would have been influenced by 174. But this makes μέcον pointless; and κατὰ as in *Il.* 5.46 νύξε ... κατὰ δεξιὸν ὦμον does not occur in E. and is, so far as I know, confined to Homer. **κατὰ τὸν ὀφθαλμὸν μέcον,** 'in the sight of your central eye', is no real change inasmuch as κάτα is probably a mere interpretation of an unaccented text. Musgrave was right to compare κατ' ὄμμα còν (*El.* 910, *Rhes.* 421) and κατ' ὀφθαλμοὺς (fr. 410.3; Xen. *Hiero.* 1.14); see also van Leeuwen on Ar. *Ran.* 626, and modern Greek κατὰ πρόcωπον 'face to face'. None of these parallels contains the definite article, which is however demanded here by Pol.'s unusual single eye. The grotesque idea (cf. 174n.) of Pol.'s single central eye observing his own disembowelment (or, less likely, if we punctuate after μέcον not τριπήχει, his own collaring) is a clever combination of cruelty and contempt (stressed by the word order) for Pol.'s abnormality, calculated to drive Pol. wild.

237. ἀπολέψειν: 'peel off'; L's ἀποθλίψειν would suggest blood oozing from the flogged back, like juice from a grape (e.g. Nicander fr.

86). But θλίβειν (in the sense 'afflict') was familiar to Christian scribes from Biblical and Patristic Greek (Dover on Ar. *Nub.* 1376), and so the much less familiar ἀπολέψειν would be easily corrupted. Casaubon suggested ἀποδρύψειν, Fix ἀποτρίψειν.

238. cυνδήcαντεc: 'binding hand and foot', as Ajax does to the animals (S. *Aj.* 62 cυνδήcαc) before tormenting them. It cannot mean (Ussher) tying the pieces of Pol. up again.

239. ναὸc: ναὸc and νηὸc are variants at *Med.* 523, *Hec.* 1263, *Tro.* 691; at *IT* 1385 L has νηὸc, but generally ναὸc (e.g. 85); see G. Björck, *Das Alpha Impurum*, 242. **ἀποδώcειν** can mean 'sell' (Dover on Thuc. 6.62; Page in *WS* 69 (1956), 123), and so there is no need to read ἐμπολῶντεc (England) for ἐμβαλόντεc.

240. πέτρουc μοχλεύειν is part of the labour of building (Plat. Com. fr. 67). E. was impressed by the Cyclopes' work at Mycenae and Tiryns (92n.). Sil. makes his lie even less credible by seeming to forget that Pol. is supposed to have been disembowelled and so could hardly be expected to work. **ἢ 'c μυλῶνα** is Ruhnken's correction of L's ἢ πυλῶνα. πυλών is common in later Greek. The source of the error was probably the idea that καταβαλεῖν is parallel to μοχλεύειν (in fact ἢ is to be taken after ἀποδώcειν), together perhaps with a misunderstanding of κατα- (cf. Hdt. 4.146 cυλλαβόντεc δέ cφεαc κατέβαλον ἐc ἑρκτήν). Work in the mill was a punishment for slaves: see esp. Lysias 1.18 μαcτιγωθεῖcαν εἰc μυλῶνα ἐμπεcεῖν; Pearson on S. fr. 851; Austin on Men. *Asp.* 245.

241. οὔκουν (οὐκοῦν L) is required by Pol.'s angry impatience: cf. S. *OC* 897-8 οὔκουν (οὐκοῦν L rec.) τιc ὡc τάχιcτα . . . μολὼν κτλ.; A. *PV* 52; K-G ii 167; 632n.; *El.* 835-7 οὐχ . . . οἴcει τιc ἡμῖν κοπίδα;

241-2. κοπίδαc ... μαχαίραc: κοπίc occurs elsewhere only as a noun. But there is no need to emend: it is in fact (like πατρίc, cίνιc, νεᾶνιc, ἡμερίc, etc.) an adjective which usually dispenses with the noun associated with it. For the allied meaning of κοπίc and μάχαιρα (and pictures) see Sparkes in *JHS* 95 (1975), 132.

242-3. At *Od.* 9.251 Pol. lights a fire, just before he sees the Greeks. It appears that his threatening orders here are not carried out, and are forgotten in the ensuing debate, for Pol. eventually lights the fire himself (383), and puts the wood on it (383-4). Both **ἀνάψειc** here and ἀνέκαυcε in 383 mean (*pace* Ussher) to *start* a fire, not to make an existing one blaze up (cf. e.g. Hdt. 4.145.2).

243. ἐπιθεὶc: i.e. on the hearth (cf. 384). **ὡc:** 'inasmuch as', as at 247. L's ὢ occurred probably by haplography.

244-6. At *Od.* 9.291-3 Pol. eats the Greeks like a lion, leaving nothing: τοὺc δὲ διὰ μελειcτὶ ταμὼν ὁπλίccατο δόρπον. ἤcθιε δ' ὥc τε λέων ὀρεcίτροφοc, οὐδ' ἀπέλειπεν κτλ. In comedy, on the other hand, he has become a gourmand (Epich. fr. 82), and cooks the Greeks like fish (Cratin. fr. 143; cf. Antiphanes frr. 132, 133). E. was at 358 (n.) influenced by Cratinus' string of culinary terms. But here the tone is different again. Pol.'s cookery is also a sacrifice (cf. 334–5, 361–71, 395n.; Philox. *PMG* 823). However, in a comic fragment (Athenion fr. 1. ap. Athen. 660e) a μάγειρος claims that the institution of sacrifice and ὀπτᾶν (roasting or grilling) rescued man from primaeval cannibalism. Boiling was thought to have been invented after ὀπτᾶν ([Aristotle] *Probl.* 3.43 Bussemaker); and so the common practice exemplified here (cf. 404), first to ὀπτᾶν parts of the sacrificial animal and then to boil the others (M. Detienne, *Dionysos Slain*, 74–9) seems to have been regarded as embodying cultural history (Detienne, 79). And so Pol. is here distinguished not only from the animals, with which he is explicitly compared in Homer: the elegant antithesis (cf. 218n.; Sotades fr. 1) puts him at the highest level of civilization. Pol. is in his sacrifice both savage and sophisticated (and in fact both ἀνθρωποφαγία and ὀψοφαγία are perversions of the sacrificial meal: cf. Plut. *Mor.* 644b): this unity of opposites pervades the play (intro., §VII). The horror of the cannibalism is intensified by the careful, civilized sacrificial practice, as at Hdt. 1.119; Ov. *Met.* 1.228–9, 6.645–6; Accius 220–1; Sen. *Thy.* 765–7, 1060–5. And in this way the extra irony is felt that Pol. should be giving his ξένοι a meal (*Od.* 7. 159–76; 14.158, 414; etc.; 346n.). All this bears on the textual problem in 245. L's text does not make sense; and there have been numerous replacements of ἔδοντος and of τῶι κρεανόμωι, all based on no more than ingenuity and knowledge of Greek. The importance in public sacrifice of κρεανομία, the distribution of meat, is revealed in numerous inscriptions: F. Puttkammer, *Quo Modo Graeci Carnes Victimarum Distribuerint*, Diss. Königsberg, 1912. And κρεανομία had its place also in Dionysiac mystic ritual (Theocr. 26.24). And there is of course nothing unusual about a private meal being also a sacrifice (Ar. *Lys.* 1062; Plut. *Mor.* 696e): the meal in Achilles' tent in *Il.* 9 involves sacrifice (219–20), and Achilles carves (217 ἀτὰρ κρέα νεῖμεν Ἀχιλλεύς). τῶι κρεανόμωι here must be retained, and referred to Pol. At 359 the chorus describe his work as κρεοκοπεῖν μέλη ξένων, and two lines later insist μὴ 'μοὶ μὴ προσδίδου· μόνος μόνωι κτλ. Now προσδίδωμι is used frequently for the distribution of meat by a sacrificing priest (LSJ s.v. II). Pol. is μόνος μόνωι κρεανόμος. This is of course perverse (cf. Lycophr. *Alex.* 203: the snake at Aulis is cὺν μητρὶ τέκνων νηπίων κρεανόμος). And it is part of a greater perversity. For ἔδοντος we should read διδόντες (Heath). The grim irony of 346 (ἴν' ἀμφὶ βωμὸν cτάντεc εὐωχῆτέ με) is that the ξένοι, rather than being feasted (346n.), are themselves to feast Pol. (e.g. Ar. *Vesp.* 341 μ' εὐωχεῖν ἕτοιμόc ἐcτι), and with their own flesh. The irony of **διδόντεc δαῖτα τῶι κρεανόμωι** is similar but contains an extra twist: properly the κρεανόμοc gives the company their meat, but here the relationship is reversed. The scribes of course failed to understand the subtlety, and changed first perhaps to διδόντοc (to go with ἄνθρακοc): the ἔ of ἔδοντοc seems to have been written by Tr 1., or possibly by the scribe of L, and to have replaced two erased letters: it may therefore represent a conjecture by Tr. or a variant in Λ (L's model).

244. **πλήcουcι**: πλήcωcι Scaliger; but the matter-of-fact indicative πλήcουcι seems appropriately callous. **ἀπ' ἄνθρακοc**: on Greek roasting and grilling see Sparkes in *JHS* 82 (1962), 129.

246 provides a second object for διδόντεc, in antithesis to the meat cooked by dry heat: the tougher parts of the body, which for easier digestion require softening (τήκειν) by boiling: 404n.

247. **ὡc ... γε**: also at 168, 336, 439, in each case to emphasize a hedonistic justification of the attitude or intention just expressed, as also at *Alc.* 800. **ὀρεcκόου**: cf. Archil. fr. 278; A. *Sept.* 532; Barrett on Hipp. 1276. The corruption was phonetic.

248. Heroes kill lions (Herakles in Nemea, Alkathoos in Megara, Achilles at Pi. *Nem.* 3.44; cf. 213–14n.); but for Pol. to *eat* them as well seems meant to be a ridiculous form of gluttony, suggested perhaps by the corresponding passage in *Od.* 9, in which he eats *like* a λέων ὀρεcίτροφοc (292). Not comparable is Cheiron feeding Achilles lion cπλάγχνα (Apollod. 3.13.6; cf. Stat. Achill. 2.382–4). Despite Theocr. 1.72 there were probably no lions in Sicily in the 5th cent. BC.

248–9. λεόντων and ἐλάφων are to be taken more closely with ἅλιc than with θοινωμένωι, a verb which in E. takes the accusative when meaning 'feed on' (377, 550, *El.* 836, fr. 792); cf. *Hel.* 1446 ἅλιc δὲ μόχθων κτλ., *Alc.* 334, *Hec.* 278, *Su.* 1148, *HF* 1394, *Hel.* 143, 589, 1099, *Pho.* 1748.

249. χρόνιοc is used in a similar context, though with a slightly different meaning, of the Greek strangers arriving in the Taurian land at *IT* 258.

250. For the sentiment cf. *Or.* 234; Ar. *Eccl.* 583–5. The γε expresses assent (Denniston, *GP*, 130). ἐκ is frequent in E. and elsewhere to express the change of something into its opposite, not only where we would say 'from' (e.g. *Hcld.* 939) but also where we would say 'after' (e.g. here and *Hec.* 55).

251. **οὖν**: αὖ L. αὖ distinguishes emphatically what it follows from something else preceding. Hence it may follow ἕτεροc or ἄλλοc: e.g. Ar. *Thesm.* 664; A. *Ag.* 1280 ἥξει γὰρ ἡμῶν ἄλλοc αὖ τιμάοροc, which are crucially different in word-order and tense; and αὖ here is an odd word to follow γὰρ. οὖν on the other hand would strengthen γὰρ (Denniston, *GP*, 446; also *Med.* 533, *Hipp.* 666, *El.* 290, *Ion.* 1614, *Ba.* 922). αὖ seems to have replaced οὖν in MSS at *Med.* 306, *Or.* 1149. Here perhaps ὄν became by haplography οὐ, which was then emended to αὖ.

252. τά c' ἀφίκοντο in L does not scan. We must find an error which also caused the obviously similar corruption in 288. Murray's conjecture, printed by Diggle, assumes that in both cases (cf. also *El.* 413) coὐc- (i.e. coι ἐc-) was misinterpreted as coὐc. But the crasis was almost certainly not written into the MS (Zuntz, op. cit. 73–4, 129; see esp. 561, *Ba.* 1257, *IA.* 828); and it may anyway be too violent even for satyric drama: 561 coὐcτίν is less violent, and paralleled in tragedy (A. *Eum.* 913, *Cho.* 122; *IA* 828; etc.); and ἐγὼ οὐ (334; S. *Ichn.* 15) is also paralleled in tragedy (334n.). There is therefore something to be said for οἴκουc coὐc (Heimsoeth) in both places: perhaps οἴκουc was thought incompatible with 118 (cf. 597); and then coὐc had to be adapted to ἄντρα here, but at 288 could be taken with φίλουc. For the form of 252 so emended, cf. *Hipp.* 101, *IA* 1460. But cf. 288n.

253–76. Such active participation of four agents in a single scene is unparalleled in tragedy (G. F. K. Listmann, *Die Technik des Dreigesprächs in der Griechischen Tragödie* (Giessen, 1911), 63–5).

256. ἄντ' οἴνου cκύφου appears to be an unwise half-truth (164; cf. 161, 192), inasmuch as it is in Od.'s interest to make the bargain seem fair. But this is overriden by his desire to divert Pol.'s anger onto the despicable Sil.

257. ἀπημπόλα denotes the transaction, ἐδίδου the action. The reality of the bargain is affirmed. πιεῖν λαβὼν: cf. 412, 561; K-G ii 16.

258. ἑκὼν ἑκοῦcι: cf. *Od.* 3.272, 5.155; A. *PV* 19, 218, 671, *Su.* 227, *Sept.* 1033; S. *Ant.* 276, *Trach.* 198, *Phil.* 771, *OC* 767, *OT* 1230; *Andr.* 357, *Hcld.* 531, *Hipp.* 319, *Or.* 613, fr. 68.2. The frequency of this expression in tragedy may derive from the law courts: ἂν μὲν ἑκὼν παρ' ἑκόντοc κτλ. (Dem. 21.44) describes a fair contract, as Od. does here. τούτων: cf. e.g. S. *Trach.* 1278. τούτου Schechter (in *AJP* 86 (1965), 281): i.e. Sil.; cf. *Ion.* 1295.

259. φηcιν λέγει: cf. 210; S. *Trach.* 346; Hdt. 2.22 λέγει ... οὐδέν, φαμένη κτλ.

260. κατελήφθη: there are no certain exx. of a 'tragic' character uttering a 'comic anapaest' in what survives of satyric drama (intro., §V). Furthermore, this compound occurs in the tragedians only at *Hipp.* 1161 (in a different sense). Passive of simple λαμβάνω with a participle is standard in E. (e.g. *IT* 101, *Med.* 381, *Ion.* 1113). And so there is much to be said for γ' ἐλήφθη (Heath); cf. *Hipp.* 955 ἐπεί γ' ἐλήφθηc in a very similar context. Loss of γ' would require a remedy. The fact that 304 may contain a metrical phenomenon illicit in tragedy (see apparatus) carries little weight (304n.).

261. Cf. κακῶc ὄλοιο at A. *Theoroi* 38. **γ' ἄρ'**: γάρ (L) nowhere else strengthens a wish, except in the phrase εἰ γάρ (Denniston in *CR* 44 (1930), 214). And so Denniston gave κακῶc ... ψεύδομαι all to Od., which thereby represents the same spirit of 'vicarious self-sacrifice' as 269. But Sil.'s superstitious cowardice (268n.) is inappropriate for Od., who is telling the truth. In fact the joke is that he neatly turns Sil.'s mendacious indignation into a compelling declaration of his own veracity; cf. Plaut. *Pseud.* 38 Cal.: *At te di deaeque quantumst* Ps.:—*Servassint quidem.* Read γ' ἄρ' (cf. Lowe in *Glotta* 51 (1973), 34–64; Denniston, *GP*, 127), as in Ar. *Thesm.* 887 κακῶc τ' ἄρ' ἐξολοῖο κἀξολεῖ γέ τοι (MSS), where the preparatory τε is clearly undesirable.

262–5. Several deities are more effective than one in oaths. A usual number was three (Dover on Ar. *Nub.* 1234; Handley on Men. *Dysk.* 666–7; Fraenkel on A. *Ag.* 1432), although e.g. Agamemnon at *Il.* 3.276–80 used five. The extravagant variety of choice invited parody: Ar. *Nub.* 627, *Av.* 194; Antiph. fr. 296 μὰ γῆν, μὰ κρήνας, μὰ ποταμούς, μὰ νάματα. Poseidon here is well chosen: he is Greek, but also Pol.'s father, and oaths by him in Ar. seem stronger than most (e.g. *Eq.* 338, *Pl.* 396). But the consequent train of sea-creatures sinks into bathos, ending in ἰχθύων τε πᾶν γένοc with an artful parody of the practice of concluding with 'all the gods', as at *Med.* 746–7 ὄμνυ πέδον Γῆc, πατέρα θ' Ἥλιον πατρὸc / τοὐμοῦ, θεῶν τε cυντιθεὶc ἅπαν γένοc (see further Fr. Jacobi, *ΠΑΝΤΕΣ ΘΕΟΙ* (Halle, 1930); parodies also at Ar. *Av.* 863–6, *Thesm.* 270–4). For ending a list in bathos cf. e.g. Ar. *Av.* 721, 733; S. (sat.) fr. 1130.

265. μὰ θ' L. But μὰ repeated in oaths is always in asyndeton (Stinton, art. cit. 76–80n., 138). We seem to require an article (cf. 262–5); but **μὰ θαἰερὰ** gives a split anapaest in the second foot (cf. 334n.); θαἰρὰ (i.e. τὰ ἱρά) would avoid this problem, but ἱρόc in tragedy is rarely transmitted (A. *Pers.* 745; S. *OC* 16) and never demanded by the metre. μὰ κῦμα θ' ἱερὸν (Jackson) is not supported by the (exceptional) *Hipp.* 1206. μὰ διερὰ (Wecklein) is not impossible. Best after all is perhaps τά θ' (Hermann), for although the new category—sea and sea-creatures—seems to require as-

yndeton, Sil. may be adhering, slightly ridiculously, to the triple
formula (262–5n.; e.g. Ar. *Nub.* 627 μὰ τὴν Ἀναπνόην, μὰ τὸ Χάος,
μὰ τὸν Ἀέρα).

266. ἀπώμοσα: for the performatory aorist see K-G i 165; Kannicht
on *Hel.* 330.

266–7. The diminutives with repeated ὦ are redolent of comedy:
Ar. *Ach.* 475, *Eq.* 726, *Nub.* 746, *Vesp.* 1512, *Pax.* 1198, *Av.* 1271,
Lys. 872, *Ran.* 582, *Eccl.* 1129. In Achaios' *Linos* (fr. 26) the satyrs
called Herakles ὦ κάλλιστον Ἡρακλεί⟨διον⟩; cf. 185, 316. The
word κυκλώπιον at Arist. *HA* 533a9 means the white of the eye: but
a *double entendre* (Wetzel, op. cit. 16–17n., 69; cf. *Andr.* 406, *Or*
1082) seems doubtful.

267. ἐξοδᾶν: cf. 12n. ἐγώ is very emphatic: cf. Dem. 52.12 ἤθελον...
ἦ μὴν ἐγὼ τοῦ πατρὸς ἀκούειν.

268. To invoke destruction on *oneself* if lying (e.g. S. *OT* 644, 663) is
more convincing than invoking it on others. And the emphatic
formula κακὸς κακῶς (*Med.* 805, 1386, *Tro.* 446, 1055; etc.) compounds the ineptitude, reminding us of Sil.'s real estimate of his
sons (S. *Ichn.* 147 κάκιστα θηρῶν, 153, etc.; Lyc. *Mened.* fr. 2 παῖδες
κρατίστου πατρὸς ἐξωλέστατοι), which with οὓς μάλιστ' ἐγὼ φιλῶ he
is at pains to conceal. What makes his cowardice even more
contemptible is that offspring were often included in the oath
invoking self-destruction (Ar. *Thesm.* 349; Dem. 23.67–8, 47.70;
Antiphon 5.11; Aeschin. 3.111; Lycurg. *Leocr.* 79; *SIG*³ 578.49).
Similar ἀπροσδόκητα are A. *Dikt.* 799–800 Sil.(?) εἰ μή σε χαίρω
π[ροσορῶν] / ὄλοιτο Δίκτυς; Ar. *Thesm.* 1051, *Ran.* 588; Catull.
44.20.

270–2. The dishonesty of Sil. is grotesque enough to provoke a
moral stand even from the satyrs.

272. The satyr would have done better to swear by his own head,
but succumbs to the spirit of retaliation. μὴ ἀδίκει: for the synizesis
cf. e.g. *Hel.* 832. The words seem addressed to Pol.

273. The honesty of Od., the master of deceit, is no match for the lies
of Sil., whose position of trust, like the Paphlagonian's in Ar. *Eq.*, is
a measure of his master's insensitivity. Rhadamanthys is one of the
judges of the dead, and renowned for his justice (Pl. *Leg.* 624b;
etc.).

275–6. The disjointed nature of Pol.'s questions, which has dis-
turbed some editors, in fact derives from *Od.* 9.252–3 Ὦ ξεῖνοι τίνες
ἐστέ; πόθεν πλεῖθ' ὑγρὰ κέλευθα; / ἤ τι κατὰ πρῆξιν ἢ μαψιδίως κτλ.;
But the formal similarity emphasizes the difference in mood.
Simonides' πόλις ἄνδρα διδάσκει (fr. 15; cf. Pi. fr. 198a; S. *OC* 919;
Thuc. 2.41) could hardly be a Homeric sentiment. Here it exp-

resses Pol.'s incongruous (cf. 118, 120, 213–14n., 244–6n.) urbanity.

277. For the ellipse of the first person of the copula (rarer than of the third) see Denniston on *El.* 37; cf. *Hel.* 87.

280–5. The urbane Pol. knows even the condemnatory τόπος (*Andr.* 602–6, *Tro.* 368, 781; etc.; A. *Ag.* 1455–7; *Od.* 11.438, 14.68; cf. 177–87n.; Paganelli, op. cit. 103n., 92–5). A similar joke was made out of Od.'s meeting with Sil. (104n.). Cf. also *IT* 1174 Thoas: Ἄπολλον, οὐδ' ἐν βαρβάροις ἔτλη τις ἄν (matricide).

280. Both μετελθεῖν (*IT* 14) and ἁρπαγή (A. fr. 283 Lloyd-Jones. 5; Hdt. 5.94; cf. *Hel.* 50, *El.* 1041, 1065, *IA* 75, 1266, 1381) refer elsewhere to the same events.

280–1. With the double accusative cf. *Or.* 423 μετῆλθον c' αἷμα μητέρος θεαί.

282. ἐξηντληκότες: this word occurs in this sense outside E. only at Men. fr. 74.3. Of the six exx. in E. three are in this play (10, 110, 282): cf. 98n.

283. For the postponed γε cf. *Tro.* 1191 αἰσχρὸν τοὐπίγραμμά γ' Ἑλλάδι: Denniston, *GP*, 150–1.

285. This kind of ascription of responsibility to the gods (e.g. *Il.* 19.86; *Held.* 989) might be met in E. with awareness of the possibility of its abuse, as when Hekabe retorts to Helen ὁ còc δ' ἰδών νιν νοῦς ἐποιήθη Κύπρις (*Tro.* 988); cf. Gorg. *Hel.* 6. Od. may seem discomforted (cf. 105), and glib, but not entirely mendacious: Zeus wanted by the Trojan War to relieve the earth of its surfeit population: *Hel.* 38–40, *Or.* 1639–42: *Cypria* I; cf. *Il.* 1.5, 3.164–5; *El.* 1282, fr. 1082.

286. Does Od. cunningly convert information derived from 262 into an honorific address here and an argument at 290–5? I doubt the audience would make this connection, as the identity of Pol.'s father is not a recondite piece of information.

288. There is nothing wrong with φίλους (ξένους Kirchhoff): Od. has an interest in claiming φιλία, as at 176. But L's còc … φίλους is unacceptable, and ἄντρα requires qualification. Cf. 252n.: there is much to be said for οἴκους còc here too, even though it gives -ους four times in a row.

290. Does the context require ships (νεῶν L) or temples (ναῶν Canter; Attic νέως, 'temple', occurs in tragedy only at A. *Pers.* 810)? Temples might seem more important to the god, and their preservation a more natural boast (*Erechth.* fr. 360.15 ὡς θεῶν τε βωμοὺς πατρίδα τε ῥυώμεθα). But of course temples to Poseidon and harbours were closely associated, particularly no doubt by the mariner. All the places mentioned by Od. have temples to

Poseidon as well as harbours: and he seems in fact to have both in mind: ἱερᾶc (292) suggests a temple, λιμήν (292) and καταφυγαί (295) harbours. (μυχὸιc (291n.) and κευθμῶνεc (293n.) refer to caves or inlets.) ἕδρα may refer to the harbouring of ships (S. *Aj.* 460), but much more commonly to the habitation of a deity; and cf. καθίδρυται in Pol.'s reply (318n.). Although Poseidon is the saviour or lord of ships (*h. hom.* 22.5; Pi. *Pyth.* 4.207; Lycophr. *Alex.* 157), Od. needs to say that the Greeks have benefited the god himself, not the ships under his protection; and so harbours are not to his purpose, still less the periphrasis νεῶν ἕδραc. ναῶν ἕδραc means 'temples for him to dwell in': cf. *Andr.* 303 τυράννων ἔcχεc ἂν δόμων ἕδραc, *Hel.* 797. The scribe, thinking of ships, changed ναῶν to what seemed the orthodox form (cf. *Rhes.* 43 νεῶν O; ναῶν Murray).

291. ἐρρυcάμεcθα is the Euripidean form (*Alc.* 11, *Ion* 1298, 1565 *IA* 1155); εἰρυcάμην occurs in Homer, with short υ (*Il.* 4.186; etc.). For ῥύομαι with the infinitive see *HF* 197, *Or.* 599. **γῆc ἐν Ἑλλάδοc μυχοῖc:** μυχοὶ γῆc or χθονόc in E. are recesses in the earth, particularly Hades (*Su.* 545, 926, 1206, *HF* 37, *Tro.* 952, fr. 865). *IA* 660 ἐν Αὐλίδοc μυχοῖc (and 1600) refers to the recess of a natural harbour, *Andr.* 1265–6 παλαιᾶc χοιράδοc κοῖλον μυχὸν / Cηπιάδοc to a cave. At *Peirith.* 30–1 (Page, Loeb *Select Papyri*, iii 124) Herakles says of his search for Cerberus Εὐρώπηc κύκλωι / Ἀcίαc τε πάcηc ἐc μυχοὺc ἐλήλυθα: Page translates μυχοὺc 'farthest ends', a sense for which I can find no parallel (for the closest see West on Hes. *Th.* 1015). Perhaps Herakles means 'caves'. The actual entrance to the Underworld was the cave at Taenarum, the first place on Od.'s list. Both the cave there (292n.) and the one at Malea (293n.) seem to have been associated with Poseidon. And with μυχοὺc at 297 Od. seems to mean Pol.'s cave (cf. 480, *Hel.* 424). On the other hand, there is no evidence of sacred caves at Sounion (293) and Geraistos (295). And the translation 'farthest point' would suit all the four places mentioned (three are at extremities of the Greek mainland, the other of Euboia: Scylax *Per.* 46.57; Pliny. *NH* 4.15; Plut. *Mor.* 601a), and perhaps also Aitna (297–8) as the 'farthest point' of Greece. In fact the phrase may be deliberately ambiguous. The repetition of γῆc Ἑλλάδοc μυχοί (297) seems a rhetorical trick designed to conceal the absence of any service the Greeks have done Pol.: in fact, almost all Od. knows of Pol. is that he is Poseidon's son and lives in a cave.

292. The ancient harbour-town of Taenarum possessed a temple of Poseidon and a cave 'nearby' (Strabo 8.5.1); Pausanias (3.25.4) referred to a ναὸc εἰκαcμένοc cπηλαίωι (the cave said to be the entrance to the Underworld) with a statue of Poseidon in front. R. M. Woodward (in *BSA* 14 (1907–8), 249–53; confirmed by Waterhouse and Hope Simpson in *BSA* 56 (1961), 123–4) found an oblong building just outside (and perhaps leading into) a natural cave. ἱερᾶς (ἱερεύς L): cf. Pi. *Pyth.* 4.44 Ταίναρον εἰc ἱερὰν. Given the proximity of temple to harbour (Woodward, art. cit.), ἱερός is also possible. Certainly the adjective cannot be (*pace* Ussher) predicative like ἄθραυcτος.

293. Malea is the eastern of the three long southern promontories of the Peloponnese. Demosthenes established an Athenian presence there in 413 BC on his way to Sicily (Thuc. 7.26). **Μαλέαc τ' ἄκραc κευθμῶνεc** (ἄκροι L). κευθμών in E., and generally elsewhere, means a cave (*Hel.* 24) or recess in the earth (*Hec.* 1, *Hipp.* 732). λιμήν (292) and καταφυγαί (295) suggest that κευθμῶνεc too refers (uniquely) to a sheltered inlet of the sea (cf. S. fr. 371). On the other hand γῆc ἐν Ἑλλάδοc μυχοῖc (291n.) suggests that κευθμῶνεc might have its normal meaning of caves or recesses in the earth: cf. e.g. A. *Eum.* 805, where the Furies are to have ἕδραc τε καὶ κευθμῶναc ἐνδίκου χθονόc. And in fact Pausanias (3.23.2) refers to the populous area under Cape Malea as containing a harbour called Nymphaeum, a statue of Poseidon 'and a cave, very near the sea, and in it a fresh-water spring'. The only natural harbour in the area is at Hagia Marina, four miles west of the cape itself; and the spring in the cave has been found there too. That the cave was sacred to Poseidon is suggested by the spring (cf. Pausan. 2.2.8; 8.7.2; 8.8.2; 8.10.4; RE xxii. 1.504, 511; Roscher *Myth. Lex.* s. Poseidon 2818, 2832) as well as by the statue of Poseidon. Here too then, as at Taenarum (292n.), the harbour was close by a cave sacred to Poseidon. Perhaps with κευθμῶνεc E. was thinking both of the cave and of the shelter provided by the harbour (cf. the possible ambiguity of 291). What then does L's ἄκροι mean? In its literal sense ἄκροc almost always means some (extreme) part of what it describes (the only exception known to me is Sappho 105(a) ἄκρον ἐπ' ἀκροτάτωι, of the apple on the branch). So ἄκροι here probably cannot refer to the position of cave or harbour at (or near) the end of the promontory (nor to it being high up, for the cave is anyway 'very near the sea'). On the other hand, ἄκροc never refers to the *inmost* part (apparent exceptions: on 506 see 505–6n.; on *Hipp.* 255 see Barrett; on *Ba.* 203 see Roux, and Barrett loc. cit.). Pausanias (loc. cit.) refers to the cape as τὴν ἄκραν τῆc Μαλέαc. For ἄκραc cf. *El.* 442 Εὐβοῖδαc ἄκραc (with Denniston's note); Pi. *Pyth.* 4.174 ἀπ' ἄκραc Ταινάρου; S. *Trach.* 788. And notice Pol's reply (318): ἄκραc δ' ἐναλίαc ... τί τάδε προυστήϲω λόγωι; **Coυνίου**: Coυνίωι Musgrave, troubled presumably by the double genitive. But cf. Ταινάρου, Μαλέαc; *Ion* 12 Παλλάδοc ὑπ' ὄχθωι τῆc Ἀθηναίων χθονὸc; S. *Trach.* 1191, *Phil.* 489.

294. ὑπάργυροϲ πέτρα: less than 500 yards north of the harbour at Sounion are the southernmost traces of the ancient silver-mines centred on Laurion. Cf. *Rhes.* 970. It may be that at the time of the production of *Cyc.* these mines were effectively in the hands of the Spartans based at Dekeleia (Thuc. 6.91, 7.27: cf. 8.4; Xen. *Hell.* 2.2.7, *Vect.* 4.43–4).

295. καταφυγαί probably expresses not remoteness (Ussher), but the fact that Geraistos is the only harbour in its area. Nestor put in there after crossing the Aegean, and sacrificed to Poseidon (*Od.* 3.177–8). Strabo (10.1.7) calls the temple of Poseidon there ἐπιϲημότατον τῶν ταύτηι.

296. L's text presents three difficulties: (a) δύϲφρων is curious describing ὀνείδη. (b) δίδωμι cannot mean (Musgrave) 'forgive', and so the sentence as a whole does not make sense. (c) It does not scan: given (a) and (b), the extremely rare opening choriamb (V. Schmidt, *Sprachliche Untersuchungen zu Herondas* (1968), 69) can be discounted. Suggestions have included various transpositions of 296 and a lacuna after 295. But Murray's view that 320 may answer something lost in Od.'s speech underestimates Pol.'s sophistication (cf. Kassel in *Rh. Mus.* 98 (1955), 286). And it is anyway dangerous to resort to lacuna or transposition when what survives is nonsense in itself. δύϲτλητ' (Heimsoeth), δύϲφημ' (Wecklein), δυϲφροϲιν (Kirchhoff), and δύϲφορά γ' (Parisinus 2887; cf. S. *OT* 783 δυϲφόρωϲ τοὔνειδοϲ ἤγον) meet difficulties (a) and (c). As for (b), οὐκ ἐδώκαμεν has been replaced by e.g. οὐ μεθήκαμεν (Wecklein) and ἐξεπράξαμεν (Kirchhoff). But ὄνειδοϲ in E. requires scrutiny: of the 17 or 18 cases in which it means 'disgrace' or 'matter for disgrace' it is 11 times predicative (e.g. *Andr.* 410 ἐμοὶ δ' ὄνειδοϲ μὴ θανεῖν ὑπὲρ τέκνου), and even the remaining cases tend to impute disgrace rather than merely refer to it: e.g. *Pho.* 1732 Cφιγγὸϲ ἀναφέρειϲ ὄνειδοϲ (cf. *Andr.* 621–2, 784?, *Hcld.* 301?, *IA* 999, *Ion* 593, *Tro.* 846). This favours Méridier's τά θ' Ἑλλάδοϲ—δύϲφορά γ' ὀνείδη—Φρυξὶν οὐκ ἐδώκαμεν, which also provides an antecedent for ὧν in 297. But γε (Tr. 2) is almost certainly a mere metrical conjecture. And although of the 11 cases in E. of predicative ὄνειδοϲ 5 are appositional (*Andr.* 1241, *Hcld.* 72, *HF* 129, *Med.* 514, *Pho.* 821), of these only *HF* 129 is plural, and this, unlike here, is in apposition to a plural. In fact of the 7 other cases of the plural all save *Andr.*

622 (and perhaps 784) refer to verbal rebukes (as would e.g. Schenk's ὀνείδη ... ἐκτετίκαμεν here), a sense unsuitable here. Furthermore all these appositional cases specify to whom the ὄνειδος attaches, and (except *HF* 129) in the dative; and this vagueness in Méridier's text is magnified beyond toleration by the reference of the apposition to a hypothetical negation of the main clause. Precisely what E. wrote seems beyond recovery; but all the requirements are met by e.g. τά θ' Ἑλλάδος, / δύσφορον ὄνειδος Φρυξίν, ἐξεσώσαμεν, 'We saved Greece, an intolerable disgrace for the Phrygians' (Seaford in *CQ* 25 (1975), 207) or τά θ' Ἑλλάδος / δύσφορον ἂν ἦν ὄνειδος ὡς προὐδώκαμεν, 'It would be an intolerable disgrace to have betrayed Greece' (cf. *Hcld.* 463; Hdt. 9.7; Φρυξίν as intrusive gloss). In both cases the original corruption would derive from the desire to give τά a noun (cf. the corruption of τὰ Τρώων at *El.* 1077). Od.'s argument in 290–8 requires the (false) premise, suggested by the Persian wars (297n.), that the Trojans were intent on conquering Greece. If any reference to an ὄνειδος is thought an odd way of expressing this, we might read τά θ' Ἑλλάδος / δύσφροσιν ὀνάσθαι Φρυξὶν οὐκ ἐδώκαμεν (R. Mathewson).

297. The Trojans were of course not a threat to Sicily. And Sicily at this time could not be called part of Greece. Od.'s desperate rhetoric is reminiscent of the vain Greek appeal to the Syracusans in 480 BC (Hdt. 7.157), which alluded to the Trojan War (Hdt. 7.159; 7.161.3); also, more importantly, of that contemporary Athenian pride in the achievement of having saved Greece from the Persians (Thuc. 1.73; 5.89; etc.) by which in 415/4 BC the Athenian ambassador to Kamarina in Sicily (Thuc. 6.83.) justified Athens' empire, and which, after their defeat, the Syracusan Nikolaos, according to Diodorus (13.25.2), mentioned in his plea for mercy for them. And the Athenians could try to justify their presence in Sicily by kinship with some of its Greek inhabitants (Thuc. 3.86.4; 6.6.1). **κοινοῖ:** κοινοῦ L, Duchemin. But the imperative would be rhetorically inept; and cf. Nikias before Syracuse calling the allies κοινωνοὶ μόνοι ἐλευθέρως ἡμῖν τῆς ἀρχῆς ὄντες (Thuc. 7.63.4). **μυχοὺς:** cf. 291n.

298. Aitna had erupted in 425 BC (Thuc. 3.116). **Αἴτνηι:** Αἴτνης (Hermann) would remove the apposition; but cf. Thuc. 3.116.1 ὑπὸ τῆι Αἴτνηι τῶι ὄρει, on which however Gomme remarks that τῶι ὄρει distinguishes it from the city of the same name and was perhaps added later.

299. νόμοις and εἰς in L are simple corruptions. But L's **ἀποστρέφηι** makes better sense than ἐπιστρέφηι (Reiske), which Theogn. 440

does almost nothing to support. Cf. *IT* 801 μή μ' ἀποστρέφου, *Hel.* 78; S. *OC* 1272; these cases refer to the addressee turning away from the speaker: hence Kayser's φίλους (cf. 288) for λόγους. But λόγους ἀποστρέφηι may stand, either as metaphorical (*Su.* 159 τὸ θεῖον ... ἀπεστράφης; Ar. *Pax* 683), or, more likely, with Pol. physically turning away (cf. 319). Od. then has to resort to the simpler point; but the antithesis between νόμος and λόγος does not mean that λόγοι here means words in general: cf. *Hel.* 832 φέρ', ἢν δὲ δὴ νῶιν μὴ ἀποδέξηται λόγους, *Med.* 773.

300. ἐφθαρμένους: *El.* 234 φθείρεται Denniston translates 'goes miserably'. He gives exx. of φθείρεσθαι connoting motion, and takes ἐφθαρμένους here and at *IT* 276 ναυτίλους δ' ἐφθαρμένους to denote ejection from the ship. But the Greeks have not been ejected from their ship (85), and *Hel.* 774 ἅλιον ἐφθείρου πλάνον means Menelaos travelling *in* his ship. And the idea to be included with the motion is not subjective 'misery', but (objective) waste: Od. means that they have been physically wasted by their time at sea.

301. πέπλους: πέπλοις L; but nowhere else does ἐπαρκεῖν meaning 'supply' take the dative of the thing supplied. Cf. e.g. Pl. *Protag.* 312a αὐτοῖς ἀλληλοφθορῶν διαφυγάς ἐπήρκεσε; A. *Ag.* 1170.

301–2. Kassel (op. cit. 99n., 105) suggested the loss after 301 of e.g. τούτων δίκαιόν σου τυχεῖν ἡμᾶς, ἄναξ. But the ἱκέτας (300) are so central to 300–301 that the break in construction seems acceptable, and may even express indignation.

304–7. The theme of Greek bereavement caused by the Trojan War occurs at *Andr.* 307–8, 611–13 (verbally similar), 1037–46, *Hec.* 322–5, 650–6; cf. also *Su.* 35, 170; A. *Ag.* 430–1, *Pers.* 580.

304. ἅλις δὲ: ἅλις γε Bothe. But cf. *Alc.* 334, 1041, *El.* 73, *Hel.* 143, 1446. Cf. also *Hec.* 278 τῶν τεθνηκότων ἅλις, *Rhes.* 870. **ἐχήρωσ' Ἑλλάδα:** of the strictly comparable infringements of Porson's law in tragedy, i.e. those involving elision of a word of more than two syllables, S. *Aj.* 1101 is easily emended, *Hcld.* 529 and S. *Phil.* 22 less so (but see R. D. Dawe, *Studies in the Text of Sophocles*, iii 122). For the sense cf. *Il.* 5.642 χήρωσε δ' ἀγυίας.

305. πιοῦσα: the same image occurs at A. *Eum.* 980, *Sept.* 736, 821; S. *OT* 1401. It may derive from, and suggest, the idea of sacrificial blood flowing into the earth to be drunk by the dead or Death (*Hec.* 536, *Alc.* 845, 851; W. Burkert, *Griechische Religion der archaischen und klassischen Epoche* (1977), 107–8). **δοριπετῆ** occurs elsewhere only at *Andr.* 653 and *Tro.* 1003, in both cases of the Trojan War.

306–7. ἔκτισε (Kayser, for ὤλεσεν) would make ἀνάνδρους and ἄπαιδας predicative (cf. *Andr.* 612); ἄπαιδας would then presumably be understood as predicative with πατέρας, for I know of no example in Greek literature of grief turning the hair white. Retain ὤλεcεν, with ἀνάνδρουc and ἄπαιδαc proleptic: cf. *Med.* 435 τᾶc ἀνάνδρου κοίτας ὀλέcαcα λέκτρον (with Page ad loc.); ἄπαιδαc is then felt with πολιούc τε πατέρας (*Andr.* 613, *Su.* 35,170).

307. παῖδάc τ' ἀπάτορας Wecklein; but cf. *Andr.* 613 πολιούc τ' ἀφείλου πατέρας εὐγενῆ τέκνα, *Su.* 35, 170.

308. ἀναλώcειc means simply 'consume', as at Pl. *Protag.* 321b. πικράν: λίχναν (Musgrave) would destroy the joke: a δαὶc πικρά would normally be unpleasant for the eater (cf. 589; Ar. fr. 597 πικρότατον οἶνον τήμερον πίει). Here, on the other hand, Od. means unpleasant for the eaten—although there may also be a veiled warning to Pol.

309. ποῖ τρέψεταί τις; is a shadow of the kind of argument used by Orestes at *Or.* 598–9 ποῖ τις οὖν ἔτ' ἂν φύγοι, / εἰ μὴ ὁ κελεύcαc ῥύcεταί με μὴ θανεῖν; *Hcld.* 593–5.

310. Cf. A. fr. 258 μαργῶcηc γνάθου; Phrynich. fr. 5.4; *Od.* 18.2.

311–2. Warnings against ill-gotten gains are numerous in Greek literature (e.g. Hes. *Op.* 352; Theogn. 466; Antiph. fr. 270). Verbally similar is 'Men.' *Mon.* 301 κέρδος πονηρὸν ζημίαν ἀεὶ φέρει.

313–15. Elsewhere E. combines the savagery of the Homeric Pol. with its civilized opposite, in a grotesque sacrifice. Here too Sil.'s advice reminds us on the one hand of *Od.* 9.292, where Pol. eats everything ('like a lion'), and on the other hand of sacrificial practice: the tongue had a special place in the sacrifice (*Od.* 3.341; Ar. *Pax* 1060, *Av.* 1705; Men. fr. 292.5). It was sometimes offered to Hermes (Athen. 16b; Ar. *Plut.* 1110), and frequently prescribed as the priest's γέρας (e.g. 4th cent. BC inscr. *SIG*³ 599; see further Stengel, *Opferbräuche*, 176–7, and op. cit. 469–71n., 114). The remark also (1) makes Od.'s eloquence amusingly counter-productive; (2) reverses amusingly the tragic convention of short choral comment between the ῥήcειc of the ἀγών, which is usually neutral and often conciliatory (*Alc.* 673–4, *Or.* 542–3; S. *Aj.* 481–4; etc.); (3) may evoke such expressions as ἴcχε δακὼν cτόμα cóν (cf. A. fr. 397; Ar. *Ran.* 43; Men. *Sam.* 356); (4) may reflect actual belief (cf. satyric superstition at 646): cf. Philostr. *Apoll.* 1.20, 3.9; Frazer, *The Golden Bough*, V ii ch. 12; Ar. *Ran.* 357?; (5) seems to prefigure the parasite of later comedy.

314. ἢν δὲ (ἤν τε L): of the 201 cases of ἐάν and ἤν in E. listed in Allen-Italie only four others are followed by τε; of these *Su.* 499 and *Hel.* 1394 express the thought 'whether or not . . .', as at *Andr.* 432 ἤν τε κτανεῖν νιν ἤν τε μὴ κτανεῖν θέλῃι; and the remaining case (fr.

340.2) is no more than a variant. There are on the other hand 44 cases of ἦν followed by δέ, in only a minority of which it picks up a μέν. Cf. e.g. *Hel.* 479–80 καιρὸν γὰρ οὐδέν' ἦλθεc. ἦν δὲ δεcπότηc λάβηι cε. For confusion of τε and δέ see 30, 390.

315. κομψός in E. is almost always derogatory (e.g. *Su.* 426, *Tro.* 651). In Plato, Dodds remarks on *Gorg.* 493a, it often 'conveys a hint of irony'. **λαλίcτατοc:** λαλητικόc Nauck; but the superlative occurs at e.g. *Men.* fr. 164. 1; perhaps also at S. *Ichn.* 135 (Sil. of the satyrs).

316. This form of statement had been used for the simple attribution of divinity (Hes. *Op.* 764) or description of popular allegiance (A. *Cho.* 59 τὸ δ' εὐτυχεῖν, τόδ' ἐν βροτοῖc θεόc κτλ.). The sophistic movement of the late-5th century (see esp. Prodicus B5 D-K; W. K. Guthrie, *A History of Greek Philosophy*, iii ch. 9) may be behind a third use: sophisticated attribution of divinity (e.g. *Pho.* 506, *Hel.* 560; S. fr. 922; Wilamowitz, *Glaube der Hellenen*, i 18), tending towards persuasive redefinition of divinity, particularly when it appears to be exclusive (e.g. frr. 941, 1018). Exclusivity is explicit here and at Ar. *Nub.* 365 αὗται γάρ τοι μόναι εἰcι θεαί τἄλλα δὲ πάντα φλύαροc. Similar sentiments about money are at *Pho.* 439, frr. 142, 325, 580; S. fr. 28; Theogn. 669, 717; Pi. *Isthm.* 2.11; Pytherm. 910 *PMG*; cf. Pl. *Ep.* 8.355b. Plato complained of the widespread ἔρωc πλούτου, which excludes concern for everything except daily gain (*Leg.* 831c): cf. 336–8; Bond on *HF* 671–2. **πλοῦτοc:** πόλτοc Vitelli; 'Quid, obsecro, Cyclopi cum divitiis?' (Wilamowitz, *An. Eur.*, 228). In fact E. assimilates Pol. to the contemporary πλούcιοc (intro., §VII). **ἀνθρωπίcκε:** the word implies a dismissive attitude also at Pl. *Phdr.* 243a; Ar. *Pax* 751; but here the diminutive is particularly appropriate: Od.'s arguments may be dismissed precisely because he is so much smaller than Pol.

317. For equally villainous dismissal of mere λόγοι see *HF* 238–9, *Tro.* 905; cf. Alexis fr. 25.8–9; see further Paganelli, op. cit. 103n., 26–30. **εὐμορφία:** L's εὐμορφίαι is not necessarily wrong.

318. ἐναλίαc: ἐναλίουc Wecklein; but the feminine form is frequent in the MSS of. E. (two-termination only at *Hel.* 526); cf. Diggle, art. cit. 20n., 123. **αἱc** (ἃc L): at Hdt. 2.42 (ἵδρυνται ἱρόν) ἵδρυνται is transitive; but ἄκραι here are not the temples. Cf. *SIG*³ 1020.5 (Halikarnassos, 1st cent. BC) Ποcειδεῶνοc τοῦ καθιδρυθέντοc ὑπὸ κτλ.

319. προυcτήcω λόγωι: 'put forward as a pretence' (LSJ II 3) 'in your speech' (*Hcld.* 253) probably, rather than 'put at the front of your speech' (reading λόγου?); the latter would suit the crushing display of Hellenic rhetorical technique with which Pol. answers

Od.'s points in order (see next note; also *Su.* 517; S. *Aj.* 1097); but προΐϲτημι in this sense is unparalleled. Cf. Lykos' sneer at *HF* 155 τοῖϲδ᾽ ἐξαγωνίζεϲθε.

320–2. These lines have been taken as evidence of a lacuna in Od.'s speech, in which he mentions Zeus. But the brute is sophisticated enough to draw out the implication of 299–301 (cf. 354): ξένε (320) picks up ξένια (301) and shows that he has in mind Ζεὺϲ ξένιοϲ. Cf. *Od.* 9.266–78. And so Pol. answers three of Od.'s points in the order in which they were presented: 318–19 = 290–8, 320–341 = 299–301, 342–4 = 301. For this technique in tragedy see Duchemin, *L'ΑΓΩΝ dans la Tragédie Grecque* (1968), 173–5.

320–1. Cf. Ov. *Met.* 13.842–3, 857. Such sentiments, as Kadmos points out to Pentheus (*Ba.* 337–40), do not go unpunished. Cf. 332–3n. There may also conceivably be parody of the sentiment later represented in *Hellenistic Epigrams* 3660–1 (Gow and Page) τὸν γὰρ ἀπαυδήϲαντα πόθοιϲ καὶ ἔρωτα δαμέντα / οὐδὲ Διὸϲ τρύχει πῦρ ἐπιβαλλόμενον (cf. 3670–1, 854–9, 870–5): cf. 327–8n.

321. ὅτι: we should perhaps read ὅ τι: cf. *IA* 525 οὐκ ἔϲτ᾽ Ὀδυϲϲεὺϲ ὅ τι ϲε κἀμὲ πημανεῖ, *Ba.* 506. Pol. does not fear Zeus' thunderbolt, nor does he fear him in any other way.

322. If τὸ λοιπόν is the subject of μέλει (Ussher), it may refer either to what is frightening about Zeus besides his thunderbolt, or to what remains of Od.'s argument (at 319 Pol. has dismissed his first point: cf. Pl. *Rep.* 444e τὸ λοιπὸν ἤδη ἡμῖν ἐϲτι ϲκέψαϲθαι, πότερον ...). But in its numerous occurrences in E. (e.g. 709) τὸ λοιπόν is always adverbial meaning 'in the future'. Pol. meets the implication in Od.'s speech (299–301, 311–12) that Ζεὺϲ ξένιοϲ will punish him in the future. The subject of μέλει is Zeus (cf. 605, *Ba.* 424; A. *PV.* 938), as also of ἐκχέηι in 323 (as often of ὕει).

323–31. At Theocr. 11.44–8 a less unattractive Pol. tries to entice Galatea with a description of the delights of his Aitnaean cave. And at Theocr. 9.15–21 Menalcas boasts of the delights of his Aitnaean cave, among them perfect protection against the weather: cf. Semon. fr. 7.25–6; Ar. *Vesp.* 773, *Pax* 1131). The passage is reminiscent also of Antisthenes' satisfaction with his lot at Xen. *Symp.* 4.37–8.

324. ἔχων (Reiske) is an economic cure for the syntax. But greater smoothness would be achieved by retaining L's ἔχω and reading καὶ μόϲχον Boissonade) in 325 (οὖ ... Musgrave; ἧι ... Reiske). ϲτέγν': ϲτεγάν' Blaydes; ϲτεγνόϲ does not occur in tragedy: cf. ϲτεγανόϲ at fr. 472.6; A. *Ag.* 358; S. *Ant.* 114.

325. μόϲχον: cattle, which in Homer he does not possess, are an aspect of Pol.'s wealth (316n.).

326. ἐν ϲτέγοντι L. The most plausible replacements are (1) εὖ ϲτενῶν τε (Jacobs); cf. *Il.* 16.163 περιϲτένεται δέ τε γαϲτήρ. But ϲτενόω is rare, occurring once (uncertainly) in the 5th cent. (Hp. *VM* 22); in the atticizing Libanius (VII p.19.15 Foerster) τὴν γαϲτέρα ϲτενοῦντι has the opposite sense to that required here. (2) εὖ ϲάττων τε with κἀιτ' ἐκπιών in 327 (ϲάττω Schenkl); cf. 563, Ar. *Eq.* 354–5 θύννεια θερμὰ καταφαγών, κἀιτ' ἐκπιὼν ἀκράτου / κτλ. For ϲάττων see Pherecr. fr. 161. ειτεκ is easily corrupted to επεκ. (3) Best is **εὖ τέγγων** (Reiske); cf. 574, Alc. fr. 347 τέγγε πλεύμοναϲ οἴνωι. The passage seems to allude anyway to Alcaeus (329n.). **ἐπεκπιών** κτλ. then (327) specifies the general τέγγων (cf. Pl. *Ap.* 31a κρούϲαντεϲ ἄν με, πειθόμενοι Ἀνύτωι), surprising the civilized (Alc. fr. 338; 329n.) expectation of wine with barbarous (136n.) milk; and the joke is compounded by the amphora (327), which was normally for wine (cf. 216–17n., 388n.). And cf. *Od.* 9.297 ἐπ' ἄκρητον γάλα πίνων (i.e. on top of the human flesh). There might also be in τέγγων an obscene *double entendre* brought out by πέπλον κρούω (327–8n.).

327. ἀμφορέα: it is unnecessary (cf. 5th foot anapaest in e.g. 242) to assume synizesis here in εα, but desirable, for there are no other 'comic' anapaests in the ἀγών.

327–8. πέπλον κρούω ... κτυπῶν refers not to farting (Ar. *Nub.* 293 ἀνταποπαρδεῖν πρὸϲ τὰϲ βροντάϲ) but (hyperbolically) to masturbation, sharing with Cat. 32.10–11 (*Nam pransus iaceo et satur supinus* / *Pertundo tunicamque palliumque*) three elements: (1) *pransus ... satur*; Pol. has just eaten an entire animal. Cf. Petr. *Sat.* 112 *scitis quid plerumque soleat temptare humanam satietatem*; E. fr. 895 ἐν πληϲμονῆι τοι Κύπριϲ, ἐν πεινῶντι δ' οὔ; Hierocl. in *CA* 9–10. (2) *Pertundo tunicamque palliumque*; πέπλον κρούω. Martial 11.16.5 *ah quotiens rigida pulsabis pallia vena.* For κρούω *in sens. obsc.* see Ar. *Eccl.* 990. The κτύποϲ is no more surprising than the ϲτέρνων κτύποϲ of mourning (*Su.* 87; etc.). (3) *iaceo ... supinus*; γαϲτέρ' ὑπτίαν; Hor. *Serm.* 1.5.85–6 *tum immondo somnia visu nocturnam vestem maculant ventremque supinum.* At *Od.* 9.371 Pol. ἀνακλινθεὶϲ πέϲεν ὕπτιοϲ (cf. V. *Aen.* 3.624). But in E. he is no longer a mere creature of fable, and so after dinner he turns naturally enough to sex (cf. 582–9), combining defiance of Zeus with another aspect of his self-devotion. Cf. Euboul. fr. 120 on the womanless Greeks masturbating at Troy. K. J. Dover (*Greek Homosexuality*, 97) notes a tendency in art and literature for masturbation to be associated with slaves, satyrs or foreigners. And cf. 320–1n.

329. βορέαϲ occurs at e.g. Thuc. 2.96.4, although the more usual Attic form is βορρᾶϲ (e.g. Cratin. fr. 207). Hesiod too (*Op.* 518–20) realized the importance of staying at home when the north wind blows. E. may have had in mind a poem of Alcaeus (fr. 338) recommending in foul weather fire, wine, and a soft woollen pillow (Burzacchini in *QUCC* 3 (1979), 65-8). Here milk is substituted for the wine and skins for the pillow.

331. For the *nominativus pendens* cf. *IT* 947 with Platnauer's note (K-G ii 106; Schwyzer ii 403; Diggle, op. cit. 121n., 107).

332-3. These verses combine traditional arrogance (*Su.* 499 Capaneus swore to destroy Thebes θεοῦ θέλοντος ἤν τε μὴ θέληι: cf. A. *Sept.* 427-8) with intellectual modernity: Aristophanes' Socrates replaces Zeus with ἀνάγκη (*Nub.* 367, 377, 405; cf. esp. *Tro.* 886). For the importance of ἀνάγκη as a cosmological principle at this time see Dover on Ar. *Nub.* 377; Guthrie, op. cit. 316n., index s. necessity; Paganelli, op. cit. 103n., 36. These lines are quoted by Plutarch (*Mor.* 435b), and by Athenagoras (*Suppl.* 25), who reverses their sense, citing them to illustrate πρόνοια τοῦ θεοῦ. Athenag. has φύουca for τίκτουca, perhaps quoting from memory and remembering the more obvious word (cf. fr. 898.12). τίκτειν in this sense: A. *Cho.* 127, *Su.* 674, fr. 44.4.

334. ἀγὼ οὕτινι θύω (L) gives a 'split anapaest' (i.e. a word extending from a previous foot and ending with a resolved element), which is found nowhere else (235n., 265n., 343n., 410n.) in satyric drama and is uncommon even in Old Comedy (Maas, op. cit. 120n., 111; White, op. cit. 144n., 47). To suppose correption in θύειν (Ar. *Ach.* 792) gives a trochaically divided tribrach, again unknown in satyric drama and rare even in Old Comedy (White, 41). Men. *Asp.* 219 begins εἶτ' οὐκέτι θύουc' (see Austin ad loc.). But Menander's trimeter appears to be looser in this and similar respects than the satyric (Handley, intro. *Dyskolos.* 56-9, 63-6; Gomme and Sandbach, intro. *Menander*, 37-9). And Pol.'s ῥῆcιc is elsewhere metrically indistinguishable from tragedy. Read perhaps ἀγὼ οὔτι θύω (Hermann; ὧν οὔ τι θύω Paley). For the synizesis cf. S. *Ichn.* 9 ἐγὼ οὐκ; Jebb on S. *OT* 332. Perhaps a scribe, not understanding the adverbial οὔτι, made it parallel with ἐμοί.

334-5. Pol.'s religion is another subtle synthesis of opposites (213-14n.). On the one hand he is the monster of legend, the son of Poseidon (231, 262, 290), who does not deny the existence of Zeus and the gods (231, 320-1, 328). And on the other hand, as a sophisticated modern, he redefines divinity (316n., 332-3n., 337n.). But because he is also still Homer's asocial monster, the redefinition involves the absurdity of a sacrifice to his own belly (cf. 244-6n.). The result is a parody of contemporary redefinitions of deity.

335. Cf. *Alc.* 1136 μεγίϲτου Ζηνόϲ; A. *Cho.* 245 πάντων μεγίϲτωι Ζηνί; *h. hom.* 23.1; Eupolis fr. 172 κοιλιοδαίμων; Paul. *Phil.* 3.19 ὧν ὁ θεὸϲ ἡ κοιλία; Alexis fr. 25.6–9; Epimen. B1 D-K; Anaxandr. fr. 39.4–5 ... ἐγὼ δὲ θύω τοῖϲ θεοῖϲ. τὴν ἔγχελυν μέγιϲτον ἡγεῖ δαίμονα; com. adesp. 1274. **τῆι μεγίϲτηι** gives a humorous ambiguity, seeming as it does to qualify γαϲτρί.

336–40 appear to combine a perverted traditional wisdom (336–8n.) with continuing (316n., 332–3n.) parody of sophisticated new ideas: (1) hedonism: e.g. Kallikles at Pl. *Gorg.* 491e8 δεῖ τὸν ὀρθῶϲ βιωϲόμενον τὰϲ μὲν ἐπιθυμίαϲ τὰϲ ἑαυτοῦ ἐᾶν ὡϲ μεγίϲταϲ εἶναι καὶ μὴ κολάζειν, ταύταιϲ δὲ ὡϲ μεγίϲταιϲ οὔϲαιϲ ἱκανὸν εἶναι ὑπηρετεῖν δι' ἀνδρείαν καὶ φρόνηϲιν, καὶ ἀποπιμπλάναι ὧν ἂν ἀεὶ ἡ ἐπιθυμία γίγνηται. Parody also at Alexis fr. 271, where it is argued that the ϲώφρων (337n.) will concentrate on drink, food, and sex: cf. also Alexis fr. 25. On ἀλυπία (338) see Bond on *HF* 503–5; Guthrie, op. cit. 316n., 290–1. (2) Hostility to νόμοι: e.g. Kallikles again (quoted 338–9n.); Guthrie, op. cit. 316n., ch. 4.

336–8. Cf. the courtesan Laïs τὸ καθ' ἡμέραν ὁρῶϲα πίνειν κἀϲθίειν μόνον (Epikr. fr. 2.6–7). It seems to have been traditional wisdom to live each day without suffering (Alcman fr. 1.37–9; *Hec.* 627–8, *HF* 503–7), as pleasantly as possible (Pi. *Isthm.* 7.40; *Ba.* 423–6, 910–11, *HF* 503; S. frr. 356, 593; trag. adesp. 95; cf. Petr. *Sat.* 99; see further Bond on *HF* 503–5). This may entail eschewing concern with wealth (*Teleph.* fr. 714; cf. *El.* 429–31, fr. 196), though not for Pol. (316), whose wealth is of a primitive, immediate kind. On the other hand, and despite *Ev. Matth.* 6.34 ἀρκετὸν τῆι ἡμέραι ἡ κακία αὐτῆϲ, to live merely in the present is to be ignorant of where tomorrow's meal is to come from (*Pho.* 401; Diogen. Sinop. fr. 4). And the νόοϲ (*Od.* 18.136) and θυμόϲ (Archil. fr. 131) of mankind is whatever Zeus makes it ἐπ' ἦμαρ. Cf. Semon. Amorg. fr. 1.1–5; H. Fränkel in *TAPA* 1945, 131–45 (repr. in his *Wege und Formen Frühgriechischen Denkens*). This may lend slight irony to the brutishness of Pol.'s extreme redefinition of Zeus here.

336. τοῦ πιεῖν γε καὶ φαγεῖν L. (1) **τοὐμπιεῖν** (Reiske) is probably right. For ἐμπίνειν with a convivial sense see Theogn. 1129; Epicharm. fr. 35.7; Ar. *Pax* 1143, 1156, *Eccl.* 142. (2) τε (Duchemin) for γε is clearly wrong: 247n. (3) κἀμφαγεῖν (Reiske) may be right. ἐμφαγεῖν does not occur before the 4th cent. BC, and tends to be used not, like ἐμπινεῖν, in a convivial context, but to mean 'swallow'. But perhaps that sense suits Pol.'s uncouthness. Cf. Renehan, *Studies in Greek Texts*, 20. There is comparable corruption at Xen. *Cyr.* 7.1.1. Paganelli, art. cit. 120n., 201, supports Heath's ἐκπιεῖν. **τοὐφ':** Duchemin believes this τὸ picks up the τὸ of τούμπιεῖν, and compares *El.* 429 τῆς ἐφ' ἡμέραν βορᾶς. But in fact the phrase τοὐφ' ἡμέραν is adverbial, as at fr. 835 τοὐφ' ἡμέραν κακόν τι πράςςων; Diog. Sinop. fr. 4.

337. Cf. the modern redefinition at *Tro.* 886 Ζεύς, εἴτ' ἀνάγκη φύςεος εἴτε νοῦς βροτῶν, fr. 877; 316n., 332–3n. **τοῖςι ςώφροςιν:** this is paradoxical: cf. Pl. *Rep.* 430e κόςμος πού τις . . . ἡ ςωφροςύνη ἐςτὶν καὶ ἡδονῶν τινων καὶ ἐπιθυμιῶν ἐγκράτεια . . . ; cf. 336–40n.; Pl. *Ep.* 8.354e θεὸς δὲ ἀνθρώποις ςώφροςιν νόμος, ἄφροςιν δὲ ἡδονή.

338. λυπεῖν...αὐτόν: cf. *Hel.* 1286 τρύχουςα ςαυτήν, fr. 174, and Diggle in *Prometheus* 2 (1976) 83, on *IT* 483; S. *Aj.* 589.

338–9. Cf. Kallikles at Pl. *Gorg.* 483b: ἀλλ' οἶμαι οἱ τιθέμενοι τοὺς νόμους οἱ ἀςθενεῖς ἄνθρωποί εἰςιν καὶ οἱ πολλοί; cf. 336–40n. At *Od.* 9.106 the Cyclopes are ἀθέμιςτοι. **ποικίλλοντες:** making (unnecessarily) complicated by embroidery; of νόμοι again at Pl. *Leg.* 927e, and of the effect of some unknown power on human life at Plut. *Mar.* 23. For the derogatory sense see esp. *Su.* 187 (and Collard's note). Cf. also *PMG* 818 (Pol. to Od.).

340. Barnes added δὲ after τὴν. Jackson (*Marginalia Scaenica*, 235) added δὲ after ψυχήν, because an unusual position might effect the loss. But it seems that such postponement occurs only for metrical reasons. And there is anyway nothing wrong with the asyndeton. Asyndeton often creates emphasis: we must ourselves supply mentally the unexpressed logical relation of the phrase or sentence to what precedes it, and may thereby become more conscious of that relation than if it had been expressed. And the relation here (of predictable contrast) is sufficiently suggested by the emphatic position of τὴν ἐμὴν ψυχήν: cf. S. *Ant.* 1334 μέλλοντα ταῦτα· τῶν προκειμένων τι κτλ., *Aj.* 470 οὐκ ἔςτι ταῦτα· πεῖρά τις ζητητέα κτλ.; K-G ii 342.

341. οὐ παύςομαι κτλ.: a nobler credo is expressed in the same way at *HF* 673–4. **κατεςθίων γε ςέ** (τέ ςε L; ξένους Herwerden; κατεςθίω τε ςέ Kirchhoff). There is much to be said for τε ςέ (Fix): the smoothness of δρῶν εὖ κατεςθίων τε prepares for the callous abruptness of ςέ.

342–4. The incident at *Od.* 9.355–70 of Pol.'s cruel ξεινήιον to Od.—eating him last—reappears in the play in miniature at 548–51, but without the word ξένιον (Sil. calls it γέρας 551) which occurs here instead, in a piece of irony alien to Homer but typical of tragedy (*Hel.* 480 θάνατος ξένιά ςοι γενήςεται, *Or.* 1109 Ἅιδην νυμφίον κεκτημένη).

343–4. L's δυςφόρητον in 344 makes no sense. Hence Scaliger's **διαφόρητον,** 'torn in pieces' (cf. *Ba.* 739, 746, 1210), and Palmer's δυςρόφητον. All these words are *hapax legomena*, except that Hsch.

has δυσφόρητον· δυσβάστακτον· This is Pol.'s reply to 301–3, and
ἀμφέξει alludes to 301 (Duchemin). Read δυσφόρητος. Pol. offers
Od. a fine inherited garment of bronze (Ar. *Thesm.* 165 καλῶς
ἡμπέσχετο), but Od. will not enjoy wearing it. The *hapax legomenon*
is less surprising where the notion is almost unique (cf. *Il.* 3.57;
Pi. *Nem.* 11.16; A. *Ag.* 872; A. R. 1.691, 1326). For the function of
δυσ- cf. δύσνυμφος, δυσφόρμιγξ and δύσγαμος, which may be all
Euripidean inventions. φορεῖν, like ἀμπέχειν, often refers to wearing armour. But δυσφόρητος no doubt also retains the abstract
sense of δυσφορεῖν (cf. ἀφόρητος). This then is another of Pol.'s
grim but subtle ironies, and again the copyist has failed to understand it (244–6n.). And the same is true of the corruption in 343:
Jackson (op. cit. 340n., 91) removed the split anapaest (235n.,
334n.) and the pointless γε by reading τόνδε χάλκον (λέβητα as
intrusive gloss). The cauldron is bronze (392; cf. *Su.* 1197); and a
cauldron in Homer can be called simply χαλκόν (*Od.* 8.426,
13.19). δυσφόρητος, by restoring the full force of Pol.'s irony, also
adds point to πατρῷον τόνδε χαλκόν, which could refer to cauldron
or armour. Both cauldron and armour are acceptable ξένια (*Od.*
13.19; *Il.* 10.269), but not when combined in a single object.

345–6. It appears from εἴσω that αὔλιον means the cave (as at S.
Phil. 19, 954, 1087, 1149). Why does Pol. call himself (or his belly:
335) the god in the cave? And why does the βωμός appear only
here in the play? Thirdly, why, despite this βωμός, is the sacrifice
ἀποβώμιος (365)? The key to all these problems is the altar in the
middle of the ὀρχήστρα, what Pratinas' satyrs called the Διονυσιὰς
θυμέλη (fr. 3.2). Burkert (in *GRBS* 7 (1966), 87–121) correctly
emphasizes the importance of the sacrifice of the goat at the θυμέλη
in the origins of tragedy, and discusses the influence of this origin
on the conception of killing, expressed as sacrifice, in extant
tragedy (e.g. A. *Ag.* 1433; *Med.* 1054). But he ignores the essentially conservative (intro., §III) satyric drama, which in fact
provides the missing link in his argument. Pol.'s sacrifice of the
Greeks (244–6n., 365) takes place at an altar (like Medea's in
vase-painting: Burkert, 118). And it is almost as if it has to be
explained (by its exceptional nature) why the sacrifice does not
take place at the altar the audience can see in the ὀρχήστρα. The
satyrs, as they dance presumably around this altar, reject participation in the hideous sacrifice (361–2n.), which they call
ἀποβώμιος, 'away from the altar' (365n.). τοῦ κατ' αὔλιον θεοῦ is in
emphatic position: the sacrifice will take place (not outside here at
the θυμέλη, but) at the god *in the cave's* altar, which is introduced
fleetingly for this purpose (it may have been already familar to the

audience from a previous satyric *Cyc*.: intro., n. 157), and achieves the same subtle horror as the κρεανομία of 244–6(n.). At the same time the request to the new arrivals to go inside for the sacrifice is appropriate, like the more cryptically ironical words of Klytaimnestra to Kassandra at A. *Ag.* 1036–8 εἴcω κομίζου ... / ἐπεί c' ἔθηκε Ζεὺc ἀμηνίτωc δόμοιc / κοινωνὸν εἶναι χερνίβων, πολλῶν μετὰ / δούλων cταθεῖcαν κτηcίου βωμοῦ πέλαc (cf. 1298), and the unconsciously ironical words of Aigisthos at *El.* 787–92: ἀλλ' ἴωμεν ἐc δόμουc / ... λούτρ' ὡc τάχιcτα τοῖc ξένοιc τιc αἱρέτω, / ὡc ἀμφὶ βωμὸν cτῶcι χερνίβων πέλαc. Cf. 346n., 469–71n. And there is a further irony. We are reminded of the household altar of Zeus ἑρκεῖοc or κτήcιοc (*Od.* 22. 334–5; *Il.* 11.772–4; Athen. 189e; Hdt. 6.67–8; *HF* 922; etc.; Robert, *Hell.* 10.34 (Zeus ἐναύλιοc)). Cf. A. *Ag.* 1036–8 (quoted above). Pol. implicitly substitutes himself (or his belly, 335) for Zeus (cf. 320–1, 337, 579–80n.). Finally, it may also be relevant that Pausan. (2.2.1) saw at Corinth, the mother city of Syracuse (cf. intro., §VII), an ancient Κυκλώπων βωμόc.

345. τοῦ ... θεοῦ (Blaydes): τῶι ... θεῶι (L) can hardly mean 'in honour of the god' here: perhaps a scribe, misunderstanding its early (emphatic) position, took it with ἕρπετε.

346. βωμὸν (κῶμον L): cf. e.g. *El.* 792 quoted 345–6n. **εὐωχῆτέ:** εὐωχία, feasting, is part of the sacrifice: Hdt. 1.31.5 ἔθυcάν τε καὶ εὐωχήθηcαν, 5.8; Ps. Xen. *Ath. Resp.* 2.9. The Greeks are to feast Pol. (Ar. *Vesp.* 341 μ' εὐωχεῖν ἕτοιμόc ἐcτι), but with their own flesh (244–6n.). This will be a reversal of the normal sacrifice not just because the ξένοι will be eaten rather than eat (*El.* 791–2 quoted 345–6n.; *Od.* 14.158, 414 ἵνα ξείνωι ἱερεύcω; etc.), but also because the 'god' will get the meat. **με** is preferable to 'ἐμέ (cf. 187n., 219n., 341n., 361): the irony is concentrated in εὐωχῆτε (244–6n.), and there is no contrast between the pronoun and τῶι κατ' αὔλιον θεῶι.

347–55. The Greeks submit without a fight; and so Od.'s declaration at 201–2 was bravado, or he did not anticipate Pol.'s power. In the Oxford production of 1976 it seemed best to have Pol. herding Od.'s men into the cave with his club (213–14n.) while Od. speaks, and then returning for Od.; Sil. enters voluntarily either here (following the wine perhaps: cf. 431) or (less likely) at 316. Presumably Pol. also takes the cauldron (343 τόνδε) into the cave (399).

347–8. Cf. *Od.* 1.12 πόλεμον τὲ πεφευγότεc ἠδὲ θάλασσαν.

348–9. Cf. Achaios fr. 43, from the probably satyric *Kyknos*: τοιοῦδε φωτὸc πρὸc δόμουc ἐλήλυτε. **ἀνδρὸc ἀνοcίου:** cf. 26n., *Ba.* 613.

349. ὠμὴν: cf. Pl. *Leg.* 718d ὠμὴ ψυχή. L's γνώμην would, with καρδίαν, constitute a variation on the Homeric κραδίη καὶ θυμός, but is unlikely. Another possibility is γνάθον (cf. 92). **κατέϲχον** must with ἀλίμενον have its nautical sense.

352. There is no need for emendation (e.g. κινδύνου βάθη Musgrave). Translate '. . . and onto the foundations of danger'. βάθρα, like κρηπίϲ (frequently metaphorical: *HF* 1261; A. *Pers.* 815; etc.), is used of the foundation of an altar (e.g. *Tro.* 16–17 πρὸϲ δὲ κρηπίδων βάθροιϲ / πέπτωκε Πρίαμοϲ Ζηνὸϲ ἑρκείου θανών). Od.'s powerful image is close to the reality (346): it is of the sacrificial victim standing on the very base of the altar, and so near to death.

353–5. A. M. Dale points out (*Maia* 15 (1963), 312 = *Collected Papers* 182) that the 'challenging-nouthetetic' address from mortal to god, 'at the close of a scene, just before going off at a climax of the action, is typical of Euripides' latest plays'. Cf. 599–607, fr. 136, *Hel.* 1093–1106, 1441–50, *IT* 1082–8, and especially *Pho.* 84–7. Cf. the satyric A. *Dikt.* 782–4. Similarly placed prayers (but without the challenge) are *Hipp.* 522–4, *Pho.* 586–7, 782–3, *Or.* 1242–5, *Phaeth.* 268–9; A. *Sept.* 69–77, *Ag.* 973–4; S. *Trach.* 200–201, *OT* 149–50, *El.* 1376–83, *Phil.* 133–4. The challenging-nouthetetic is found elsewhere in E. (e.g. *Hec.* 488–91), also in Homer (e.g. *Il.* 12.164; *Od.* 9.529).

353. **φαεννὰϲ** (φαεννῶν L) Kassel, comparing *Pho.* 84–5 ὦ φαεννὰϲ οὐρανοῦ ναίων πτυχὰϲ Ζεῦ, *El.* 726; but cf. Pi. *Ol.* 1.6 φαεννὸν ἄϲτρον, where Pindar is thinking of the sun.

354. εἰ δὲ ταῦτα (Wecklein) is unnecessary. For αὐτὰ see Diggle on *Phaethon* 52.

355. **τὸ μηδὲν ὢν θεόϲ** meaning 'a worthless god' has no parallel in E.: θεόϲ should be taken rather with νομίζηι (cf. 667, *Hcld.* 166–7 γέροντοϲ οὕνεκα, τύμβου, τὸ μηδὲν ὄντοϲ, *El.* 370, *Tro.* 613, fr. 332.8), to which it would be bound more closely by reading **Ζεῦ** (easily corrupted after νομίζηι; cf. 354). In addressing Zeus Od. is doubting neither his existence nor (therefore) his divinity (cf. *HF* 342, *Hec.* 488, *Pho.* 86). He is rather saying that (if Zeus ignores what is happening) the honour paid to him as a god is paid in vain: νομίζηι tends to the sense 'honour' or 'respect' (521; Lys. 12.9. οὔτε θεοὺϲ οὔτ' ἀνθρώπουϲ νομίζει) rather than simply 'believe' (Pl. *Symp.* 202d Ἔρωτα οὐ θεὸν νομίζειϲ;). On τὸ μηδὲν see Barrett on *Hipp.* 638–9.

356–74. There are two important questions about the form of this song.
    (1) Do 356–60 and 368–74 correspond? Astropha are frequent

in late Euripides (A. Sachs, *De Tragicorum Carminibus Astrophis . . .*
(Berlin, 1909), 39–41), and isolated choric astropha (i.e. unac-
companied by monody, lyric dialogue or verses corresponding
with each other) occur at *Hipp.* 1268–81, *Hec.* 1024–33, *Su.*
918–24, *Ion* 1229–43, *El.* 585–95 (also A. *PV* 687–95, *Cho.*
152–63; S. *Trach.* 205–24; for Ar. see White, op. cit. 144n., 334).
Satyric drama is a special case. In keeping perhaps with the satyric
mood, short astrophic choral songs seem to have been more
common than in tragedy. They occur at 608–23, 656–62; S. *Ichn.*
64–78, 177–202; whereas corresponsion occurs certainly at
41–8 = 55–62, 495–502 = 503–10 = 511–18; S. *Ichn.* 243–
50 = 290–7, and probably 329–38 = 371–9; and in the fragments of A.'s satyric *Prom. Pyrk.* there are two stanzas probably in
corresponsion (Lloyd-Jones, appendix to *Loeb Aeschylus* ii 565),
each followed by an identically worded ἐφύμνιον. And so on
general grounds we might expect either corresponsion or astropha
here, except that 361–7 seem to form a separate unit in sense and
perhaps also in metre, and there is no parallel to three consecutive
astrophic stanzas. This suggests corresponsion. True, no line as it
stands corresponds with its supposed counterpart, and a line is
missing at the end of the 'antistrophe'. But the discrepancies are
easily removed (356n., 358n., 372–3n., 374n.). And the similarity
of content extends (if we accept Hermann's transposition: 372–
3n.) even to corresponsion of the same word: ἐφθά (358) = ἐφθά
(373), βρύκειν (358–9) = βρύκων (372); cf. e.g. *Alc.* 461 = 471,
464 = 474, 909 = 932. I will therefore, perhaps wrongly, assume
corresponsion.

(2) Should 361–7 be repeated after the antistrophe? The repetition would have been easily lost. Such losses may have occurred
in our MSS of drama, but there is no certain instance: I have
argued against the repetition of 49–54 (parodos n.); and there is
no need to repeat A. *Ag.* 1455–61 or 1537–50 (see Fraenkel), or
Cho. 807–11 or 827–30. A lament is repeated at A. *Ag.* 1513–20,
part of the Furies' binding song at A. *Eum.* 341–5, a prayer at *Ion*
141–3, and refrains at *Ba.* 897–901, 1011–16. And there is the
repeated refrain, already mentioned, of A.'s satyric *Prom. Pyrk.* On
the other hand, a lyric mesode between strophe and antistrophe
occurs at *El.* 125–6, 150–6, *Hec.* 177–96 (for mesodes in general
see Münscher in *Hermes* 62 (1927), 154). The case for repetition is
not strong, but it is stronger than in the parodos: 361–7 express a
heartfelt desire, almost a prayer, of which repetition would be
dramatically apt.

Metrical Scheme

356–60 = 370–4.

— · — · / — ᴗ — ⸜	trochaic dimeter
	(see note 1 below)
— ᴗ — ᴗ / — ᴗ — ᴗ	trochaic dimeter
— ᴗ — ⸜ / — ᴗ —	trochaic dimeter (catalectic)
— ᴗ ᴗ / — ᴗ ᴗ / — ᴗ ᴗ / — ᴗ ᴗ / — ⸜	dactylic pentameter
	(see note 2 below)
— — / — —	? dactylic dimeter
	(see note 3 below)
⸝⸝ ᴗ — ᴗ / — ᴗ ⸝	trochaic dimeter (catalectic)
360. ᴗ ᴗ — ᴗ ᴗ — / ᴗ ᴗ — ᴗ ᴗ —	anapaestic dimeter
361–7.	
— · — — / — ᴗ —	? trochaic dimeter (catalectic)
	(see note 4 below)
ᴗ — ᴗ — / ᴗ — ᴗ — / ᴗ — ᴗ —	iambic trimeter
— ᴗ — ᴗ / — ᴗ — ᴗ	trochaic dimeter
— ᴗ — ᴗ / — ᴗ —	trochaic dimeter (catalectic)
365. ᴗ ᴗ — ᴗ ᴗ — / ᴗ ᴗ — ᴗ ᴗ —	anapaestic dimeter
⸝ — — — / — ᴗ ᴗ —	choriambic dimeter B
ᴗ — ᴗ — / ᴗ — ᴗ —	iambic dimeter

Notes

(1) 356–7 I take as (see comm.)

Εὐρει / ου λάρυγγος
ὦ Κύκλωψ ἀν / αστομοῦ τὸ
χεῖλος ὡς ἔ / τοιμά coι

and 368–70 as (see comm.)

Νηλής, / τλᾶμον, ὅcτιc
δωμάτων ἐφ / εcτίουc ἱκτ-
ῆραc ἐκθύ / ει ξένουc

(alternatively, read φάρυγοc in 356 with ὅc in the antistrophe: Dale, op. cit. 53n., 89). For the initial spondee (double syncopation) cf. 612, 619, 622, *Hel.* 350; S. *OC.* 1747; A. *Ag.* 150, *Cho.* 603; Ar. *Lys.* 659–60. The tone is comic, and word-overlap between trochaic dimeters (with relatively free responsion) is frequent in Ar. (Dale, 87–90).

(2) This colon occurs in an iambo-trochaic context at *Phaeth.* 97 (cf. Dale, 34); A. *Ag.* 165 = 174.

(3) χναύειν βρύκειν = 372. If this is another trochaic dimeter,

then the double syncopation in each metron is unparalleled (the closest known to me is S. *OC* 1747). True, the grotesque sense suits the kind of emphasis arising elsewhere from double syncopation of the iambic metron (e.g. S. *OT* 1332 τλάμων; Dale, 85). Better though is a dactylic (*Pho.* 795; Ar. *Lys.* 1264) or even an anapaestic (cf. 360) analysis.

(4) Or an iambic dimeter, with double syncopation in the first metron. Or if we allow word-break in μόνος (362), 361–2 are trochaic. On such ambiguity see Dale, 94.

356. The form φαρυγ- occurs throughout the MSS of Homer and comedy, except at Cratin. frr. 186.3, 257; Telecleides fr. 1.12; Ar. fr. 614. And in these cases (except Cratin. fr. 257), as elsewhere in this play (410, 592), metre requires the restoration of φαρυγ-, which is specified by Herodian (1.45.4; 2.598.1 Lentz) as the Attic form. φαρυγγ- is the later form (Nik. *Alex.* 363) and should not be printed either here or at Cratin. fr. 257. It can be replaced here with **φάρυγος** (215, 410, 592; Epich. fr. 21.2; *Od.* 9.373), or with λάρυγγος, which gives corresponsion (368–71n.) as well as a smooth and paralleled colon (see above) and would be easily corrupted to the more familiar (especially after the classical period) word. Cf. 158; Euboul. fr. 139.2 ἀνόςιοι λάρυγγες.

357. ἀναςτόμου: ἀναςτομοῦ (Wilamowitz), middle, is perhaps preferable.

358. The apparent hiatus between coι and ἐφθά presents no difficulty, as there need be no synapheia. With Hermann's admirable supplement ἄπο ⟨θερμά⟩ / χναύειν cf. 244 5. **ὀπτὰ καὶ:** ὀπταλέ' (Kirchhoff) and ὀπτὰ κρέ' (Barnes) are attempts to remove a supposedly unreal distinction between ὀπτά and what is ἀνθρακιᾶς ἄπο. But Pol. has ὀβελοί (303, 393): cf. Poseidonius ap. Athen. 151e (fr. 67 Edelstein-Kidd) ὀπτὰ ἐπ' ἀνθράκων ἢ ὀβελίcκων. Anyway, E.'s aim is not precision but a sense of culinary abandon, as at Cratin. fr. 143 φρύξας, ἑψήσας, κἄπ' ἀνθρακιᾶς ὀπτήσας; Ar. *Ach.* 1005: 244–6n.

359. κρεοκοπεῖν (κρεωκοπεῖν L): cf. A. *Pers.* 463, where κρεοκοποῦcι and κρεωκοποῦcι are variants. Synizesis of -εω- is common enough (144n.): but see Porson, *praef. Hec.*, p. 6; Lob. *Phryn.* 693–5. For the sense, 'cut up meat', cf. 244–6n.

360. ἐν means, as Diggle rightly observes (art. cit. 39n., 45–6), that Pol. is dressed in a goatskin (*Ba.* 249 ἐν ποικίλαιcι νεβρίcι; S. *Trach.* 613; Pi. *Isthm.* 6.37; etc.; cf. Theocr. 7.132 ἐν ... βαθείαιc ... χαμευνίcιν); a rug would require ἐπ', and we should retain ἐν (330, 385–6). But the goatskin cannot be (*pace* Diggle) like the fleecy garment worn by Sil. (intro., § I), which, designed (originally at least) to represent body-hair, is no less unique than his mask. Rather an ordinary animal-skin, such as the skin in which (partially draped over him) Pol. is reclining on the Richmond vase (Plate II), is appropriate *dress* for Pol. (213–14n.). The point of the satyrs' remark is not (*pace* Diggle) envy (8on.), but the combination in Pol. of refinement (κλινομένωι) and crudity. κλινομένωι (καινόμενα L): Λ was read as Α (cf. A. *Ag.* 1418), and then agreement with μέλη introduced. Diggle (art. cit. above) suggests as an alternative κλινόμενος (comparing, for the anacolouthon, 330–1; K-G ii 105–7), which would allow 360 to be repeated unchanged after 374.

361–2. Why do the satyrs reject with such vehemence meat which they are hardly likely to be offered (31, 244–6n., 325–6, 345–6n.)? The rejection by the *thiasos* of participation in cannibalism occurs also at *Ba.* 1184 (there is even a striking verbal parallel: 368–71n.), and may well be a τόπος (more at home in *Ba*, where flesh *has* been offered) deriving ultimately from the sacrifice forming part of the ritual of initiation (Seaford in *CQ* 31 (1981), 274; Bremmer in *Studi Storico-Religiosi* 2 (1978), 16–17; cf. W. Burkert, *Homo Necans* (1972), 151, and in *GRBS* 7 (1966), 106).

361. προcδίδου is a verb frequently used of the distribution of meat by the sacrificing priest (LSJ s.v. II); cf. 244–6n.

362. For γέμιζε (Wecklein) cf. 505; Men. *Per.* 546; Ev. Luc. 15.16; Themist. *Or.* 23 (293d); for the image: 505–6n.; Dionys. Com. fr. 2.41; Plaut. *Pseud.* 1306, *Cist.* 121. cκάφοc is properly the hull of a ship, as at 505.

363–4. For μὲν ... δὲ linking verbs in anaphora, in clauses of identical rhythm, see Diggle, op. cit. 121n., 55 (*Rhes.* 906–7; A. *Pers.* 694–5, 700–1).

365. There are three problems. (1) ἔχει (L) gives poor sense and poor metre. Restorations of the anapaest have been e.g. παρέχει (Wilamowitz), ἀνέχει (Spengel), ἔχει ἀθυcίαν (Murray). Best is ἀνάγει (Jackson in *CQ* 35 (1941), 37; and, independently, J. Casabona, *Recherches sur le vocabulaire des Sacrifices en Grec*, 306): the phrase θυcίαν ἀνάγειν occurs at Hdt. 2.60, 5.119; 6.111; 2 *Macc.* 1.18; *Act. Ap.* 7.41; cf. esp. Phil. *VM* 2.31 θυcίαc ἀθύτουc ἀνήγαγον. (2) What does ἀποβώμιοc mean? Hsch. defines it as ἄθεοc; both Aristoph. Gramm. (ap. Eustath. ad *Od.* 12.252) and Hsch. refer it to sacrifices occurring away from the altar; and in the (possibly spurious) Arcadian inscr. *IG* v ii 403 it refers to a statue. This does not mean that there was a special ἀποβώμιοc category of actual sacrifice. It expresses here horror (A. *Eum.* 305 καὶ ζῶν με δαίcειc οὐδὲ πρὸc βωμῶι cφαγείc), meaning roughly ἀνίεροc, but with the

extra implication that the sacrifice would defile the altar in the
ὀρχήςτρα (345–6n.). (3) The syntax. (a) ἀποβώμιος refers surely to
the θυςία, not to Pol.; either then we must abstract the nominative
from θυςίαν, which has been attracted into the case of the preceding relative (e.g. *HF* 840 γνῶι μὲν τὸν Ἥρας οἷος ἐςτ' αὐτῶι χόλος),
or we should actually read θυςία (Hartung) as retaining the
(nominative) case appropriate to the main clause even though
enveloped in the relative (e.g. *Ion* 1307 τὴν cὴν ὅπου coι μητέρ' ἐςτι
νουθέτει). (b) θυμάτων goes more naturally with ἀποβώμιος than
with the distant and virtually tautologous (despite Pl. *Rep.* 394a ἐν
ἱερῶν θυςίαιc) θυςία. Translate '. . . sacrifice which is away from the
altar [i.e. unholy] in respect of the victims'. Cf. *Pho.* 324 ἄπεπλος
φαρέων, *El.* 310 ἀνέορτος ἱερῶν.

368–71. L has νηλὴς ὦ τλᾶμον ὅςτις δωμάτων ἐφεςτίους ξενικοὺς
ἱκτῆρας ἐκθύει δόμων. Wecklein took ξενικοὺς δόμων as originally a
gloss, written one word over the other at the end of the line, on
δωμάτων ἐφεςτίους and deletes ὦ (*JClPh.* Suppl. vii, 328). This,
with Kirchhoff's ξένους, gives the arrangement printed above
(356–74n.). True, τλῆμον (or τλᾶμον) in E. is almost always
preceded by ὦ. But in all such cases it means 'O suffering one'.
Here it means shameless or reckless, as at S. *OC* 978 μητρὸς δέ,
τλῆμον, οὐκ ἐπαιςχύνει γάμους, *Ant.* 229 τλήμων (leg. τλῆμον?),
μένεις αὖ; and above all (361–2n.) at *Ba.* 1184 τί; μετέχω, τλᾶμον;
Cf. *Hcld.* 763 ξένους ἱκτῆρας; A. *Su.* 365 δωμάτων ἐφέςτιοι ἐμῶν,
Eum. 577.

368. νηλὴς: cf. *Od.* 9.287 (of Pol.) ὁ δὲ μ' οὐδὲν ἀμείβετο νηλέϊ θυμῶι.

372–3. Hermann was right to transpose these lines: ἔφθα cannot be
hot from the coals. This also makes for correspension.

373. μυcαροῖcί τ' (-οῖcιν L) restores the point to τε in ἐφθά τε.

374. Hermann's deletion of ἀνθρώπων before θέρμα as a variant for
ἀνθράκων restores the trochaic dimeter. Correspension would require a lacuna after 374, which Haupt filled in with δαcυμάλλωι ἐν
αἰγίδι κλινόμενος.

375. The drama requires that Od. have the opportunity, denied
him in Homer, to reappear from the cave. He is still carrying the
ἀcκός (145, 412, 446, 482n., 510).

376. Expressions of amazement in E. are usually *comparative*: e.g. *IT*
837 ὦ κρεῖccον ἢ λόγοιcιν εὐτυχοῦcα μου ψυχά, 900, *Su.* 844, *Hipp.*
1217, *Hec.* 714, *Ba.* 667. This is exceptional (the closest known to
me is Plaut. *Menaechmi* 1046 *Haec nihilo esse mihi videntur setius quam
somnia*), because not entirely serious: the joke is that Od. is right. In
the action of 5th-cent. tragedy people do not deliberately cook and
eat other people. Placed by satyric drama in a world brutally

incompatible with his own, the Od. of tragedy can only compare it with the μῦθος βροτῶν that it is. And with this observation he places himself to some extent outside the story, rather like Cratinus' Od., who gives the impression of having read it: (fr. 141) τῆ νῦν τόδε πῖθι λαβὼν ἤδη, καὶ τοὔνομα μ' εὐθὺς ἐρώτα. Cf. (on *Hel.*) A. Pippin Burnett, *Catastrophe Survived*, 92. **οὐδ' ἔργοις:** οὐκ (Kirchhoff) is wrong; οὐδέ may hold apart incompatibles: e.g. S. *OT* 1434 πρὸς cοῦ γάρ, οὐδ' ἐμοῦ, δράcω; Denniston, *GP*, 191.

377. μῶν: see 158n. At 31 the surprise expressed by μῶν is genuine, at 158 ironical. Here too there may be irony: Od. is beside himself, but the satyrs are more familiar with Pol.'s cannibalism (93, 126, 359, etc.). Cf. S. *Ichn.* 203 πάτερ, τί cιγᾶιc; μῶν ἀληθ]ὲc εἴπομεν.

379. Despite various conjectures (e.g. cταθμήcαc for ἀθρήcαc Pierson, cf. fr. 376.2; κἆιτα βαcτάcαc Blaydes) the sense in L cannot be improved. The γε is assentient. Pol. selects by looking at (ἀθρήcαc) the fattest Greeks, and then tests his selection by running his hands over them (ἐπιβαcτάcαc). On βαcτάζω see Fraenkel on A. *Ag.* 35, Dale on *Alc.* 19; ἐπι- (hapax legomenon) adds the idea of extension over a surface, as in e.g. ἐπαλείφω, ἐπάργυροc. Cf. the Megarian at Ar. *Ach.* 766 ἄντεινον (sc. τὴν χεῖρα) . . . ὡc παχεῖα καὶ καλά.

380. Cf. Cratin. fr. 143: (Pol.) . . . ὃc ἂν ὀπτότατόc μοι ἁπάντων ὑμῶν φαίνηται, κατατρώξομαι, ὦ cτρατιῶται. **εὐτραφέcτατον:** (ἐντρεφέc-τατον L). Several editors have preferred εὐτρεφέcτατον. But the MSS of E. have elsewhere only the form εὐτραφήc (*Med.* 920, *IT* 304). Scribes would be familiar with the root τρεφ-, and hence the corruption here and at A. *Sept.* 309; Theophr. *CP.* 1.81.1.

382. For χθόνα (L) read cτέγην (Musgrave). Perhaps an original loss of the sigma lead to replacement of τε γῆν (on grounds of syntax) with χθόνα. Despite 29 (cτέγαc) the Cyclopes are ἄντρ' ἔχοντεc, οὐ cτέγαc δόμων (118), and so πετραίαν here is not merely decorative.

383–5. Either E. or Sil. (he is still onstage at 313–15) has ignored Pol.'s orders at 242–3 (n.). And 388 seems inconsistent with 216–17.

383. μέν: for μέν ... ἔπειτα (386) cf. 3–5; Denniston, *GP*, 376. **ὑψηλῆc:** cf. *Il.* 14.398 περὶ δρυcὶν ὑψικόμοιcι. **δρυὸc** here probably means 'oak', as apparently at Theophr. *Hist. Plant.* 3.8.2 (he distinguishes various kinds); *Ba.* 110, 685, 703, *HF* 241 δρυὸc κορμοὺc (though cf. Bond's note); S. *Trach.* 1195). By δρῦc· πᾶν ξύλον Hsch. (cf. schol. *Il.* 11.86) means presumably that δρῦc may refer to any kind of tree (615 olive, cf. 455; S. *Trach.* 766 pine), not that it refers to all kinds at once (as it seems to only when associated proverbially with πέτρα: LSJ s. δρῦc). True, at *Od.* 9.233–4 Pol. brings in simply ὄβριμον ἄχθος ὕλης ἀζαλέης. But this messenger-speech is on the whole more detailed than its Homeric model.

385. 'Of about a weight which would require three carts to carry it.' At *Od.* 9.241–2 it is said that twenty-two ἄμαξαι could not move the stone in the cave's entrance; this stone E. must omit if Od. is to reappear.

392. See 392–3n. below. ἐπέζεϲεν: ἐπέϲτηϲεν Lobeck (corruption perhaps by 'dictation interne'): ἐπιζεῖν is nowhere else transitive, save perhaps at *IT* 987, and ζεῖν is more often than not intransitive.

387. ἔϲτηϲεν (L) suggests a ϲτιβάϲ already made, which would spoil the effect of crudity; ἔνηϲεν Reiske: ἔϲτειψεν Wieseler (cf. S. *Phil.* 33). With ἔϲτρωϲεν (Pierson) cf. e.g. *Su.* 766, *Med.* 41, 380; *Od.* 19.599; ἔϲτρωϲεν was corrupted also at *HF* 366.

388. κρατῆρα: it is one of the indications of Pol.'s civilized savagery that he fills a κρατήρ, a bowl for the mixing of water and wine, with milk: cf. 216–17n., 326n. The same irony does not attach to the ϲκύφοϲ κιϲϲοῦ (390), which rustics might indeed fill with milk (fr. 146.2, *Alc.* 756; Theocr. 1.143). δεκάμφορον occurs elsewhere only in Sositheos' satyric *Daphnis*, in which Lityerses drinks a δεκάμφορον πίθον of wine a day (fr. 2.7–8): cf. Pol. at 216–17. But inasmuch as on the whole an amphora is smaller than a πίθοc but larger in volume than a κρατήρ (cf. Hdt. 1.51.2), Pol.'s κρατήρ is the more startling, and could hardly appear on stage in such dimensions (503n.).

389. μόϲχουϲ here means milch-cows, as at *IT* 163 (cf. *Ba.* 735–6); cf. 218, 325. ἐϲχέαϲ: ἐγχέαϲ (Herwerden) is the commoner word (e.g. 556, 568). But cf. Hdt. 4.2 (on the Scythians) ἐπεὰν δὲ ἀμέλξωϲι τὸ γάλα, ἐϲχέαντεϲ ἐϲ ξύλινα ἀγγήια κοῖλα κτλ. More difficult is the choice between εἰϲ- (L) and ἐϲ- (Wecklein): Kannicht, *Helena*, i p. 108; Collard, *Supplices*, i p. 42. For the coincident aorist see Barrett on *Hipp.* 289–92.

390. ϲκύφοϲ... κιϲϲοῦ is an iambic periphrasis for the κιϲϲύβιον in which Od. hands Pol. his wine at *Od.* 9.346 (cf. *Alc.* 756; fr. 146; Timoth. 780 *PMG*; Dale in *CR* 2 (1952), 132 = *Collected Papers*, 102). This one though belongs to Pol. ϲκύφοϲ in the MSS of E. is more often masculine (256, 556, *Alc.* 798, *El.* 499, fr. 379) than neuter (390, 411, fr. 146), and should probably be emended to masculine at fr. 146 (Wecklein in *Philol.* 63 (1904), 156). But we should allow E. the inconsistency here (47n.). The Richmond vase (Plate II) shows Pol. with a (one-handled) cup.

392–3. In the order of lines given in L ὀβελούϲ is a strange object for ἐπέζεϲεν (or ἐπέϲτηϲεν: 392n.), and the suspicion is increased by πυρί ending both verses. A natural order of events is given by reading 392 after 385 (Paley, Diggle: he lights the fire, then puts the cauldron on to boil) or after 395 (Hartung: he prepares his roasting then his boiling instruments, the same order as in 403–4). The latter is preferable, as providing an explanation of the corruption: after writing 391 the scribe's eye passed from one πυρί to the next, three verses further down, and the consequently omitted lines (393–5) were then inserted with an inversion mark ignored by a later scribe. ὀβέλους κτλ. can then go with παρέθετο (390), as it can also with Diggle's line-order.

394. Spits of wood probably suggest rustic or primitive conditions (h. hom. 4.121; V. Georg. 2.396). **ξεστοὺς δὲ δρεπάνωι:** necessary because παλίουρος wood is thorny (Theophr. HP 1.5.3). **τἆλλα** (Scaliger; L's γ' ἀλλὰ is uncial corruption) provides the contrast with ἄκρους μέν. **κλάδων** (Scaliger) or κλάδους (Kirchhoff) must replace κλάδωι (L and Athen. 650a).

395. **cφαγεῖα** are bowls for catching blood in a sacrifice. But, unlike the cauldron and the spits (392, 393, 399, 402n.), Pol. does not in the event use cφαγεῖα. In fact the blood seems to flow into the cauldron (see below). Probably then Αἰτναῖά τε cφαγεῖα is a (corrupt) grim periphrasis for the cauldron: Pol. uses it as a vast (Αἰτναῖον) cφαγεῖον (cf. Ar. Pax 73 Αἰτναῖον μέγιστον κάνθαρον; E. Fraenkel, Beobachtungen zu Aristophanes, 53–7). The problem is connected with those of 398–9: ῥυθμῶι τινι (L) is obscure, and 399 lacks a verb. With ῥυθμῶι θ' ἐνί Diggle suggests (in CQ 21 (1971), 46–8) the loss after 399 of a line containing ἔρριψε, taking presumably ῥυθμῶι θ' ἐνί ... ἔρριψε ... ἐξέρρανε as filling out the details of ἔσφαζε. But cφάζειν means to kill with a blade (the exceptions are metaphorical), usually by cutting the throat, and frequently in sacrifice. It can refer neither to boiling someone nor to beating his brains out. Certainly there is an imbalance between 399 (τὸν μὲν κτλ.) and 400–402 (τὸν δὲ κτλ.). After τὸν μέν the scribe's eye may, as Diggle suggests, have passed too quickly to τὸν δέ. But perhaps in copying 400–402 he realized his error and wrote the omitted lines in the margin, whence they were later inserted wrongly (once again the scribe misses the grim irony: 244–6n., 343–4n.) in the text (as 395 and 398) and adjusted to their context. And so perhaps E. wrote something like

τὸν μὲν λέβητος ἐς κύτος χαλκήλατον,
cφαγεῖον Αἰτναῖον γε, πελέκεως γνάθοις
ἔσφαζ'· ἑταίρων τῶν ἐμῶν, ῥυθμῶι τινι,
τὸν δ' αὖ κτλ.

This operation may appear complicated, but would not require three hands of the sophisticated giant. For epexegetic γε with a noun in apposition see Denniston, *GP*, 138–9; for its position cf. 163, 283. *Tro.* 1191 αἰϲχρὸν τοὐπίγραμμά γ' Ἑλλάδι. The emendation has important advantages: (1) It creates more orderly syntax, and balance between τὸν μὲν κτλ. and τὸν δὲ κτλ. (2) It makes sense of 395. (3) ἔϲφαζε (or read perhaps Barnes' ἔϲφαξε) detached from 400–402, to which it cannot refer, now makes excellent sense: with ἐϲ κύτος κτλ. cf. *Pho.* 1010 ϲφάξας ἐμαυτὸν ϲηκὸν ἐϲ μελαμβαθῆ; A. *Sept.* 43 ταυροϲφαγοῦντες ἐϲ μελάνδετον ϲάκος (cf. Ar. *Lys.* 188–9); Hdt. 3.11.2 ἔϲφαζον ἐϲ τὸν κρητῆρα, 4.62.3; Xen. *Anab.* 2.2.9; more exx. in P. Stengel, *Opferbraüche der Griechen*, 120. (4) 403–4 are allowed to mean what they seem to mean, that the ϲάρξ of *both* men is roasted and their μέλη boiled (246n., 402n.). (5) ῥυθμῶι τινι (L) is perfectly acceptable: cf. Plut. *Mor.* 67f ἰατροῦ ϲάρκα τέμνοντος εὐρυθμίαν τινα δεῖ … τοῖς ἔργοις ἐπιτρέχειν; Austin *CGF*, fr. 292.22 ϲευτλίον ῥυθμόν τιν' εἶχε; Nonnus 13.156 οἷς τινι ῥυθμῶι κύκλα ποδῶν μεμέλητο. But what point does ῥυθμῶι τινι have here? At *Od.* 9.289–92 Pol.

> cùν δὲ δύω μάρψας ὥϲ τε ϲκύλακας ποτὶ γαίηι
> κόπτ'. ἐκ δ' ἐγκέφαλος χαμάδις ῥέε, δεῦε δὲ γαῖαν.
> τοὺς δὲ διὰ μελεϊϲτὶ ταμὼν ὁπλίϲϲατο δόρπον.
> ἤϲθιε δ' ὥϲ τε λέων ὀρεϲίτροφος, οὐδ' ἀπέλειπεν.

E. clearly has this passage in mind here (φῶτε ϲυμμάρψας δύο … παιών … ἐγκέφαλον ἐξέρρανε; cf. also fr. 384). But the cannibalism has been made even more horrible by being combined with the civilized institutions of sacrifice and cookery (Athenion's μάγειρος boasts that it was the invention of sacrifice-cookery that brought men *out* of the age of cannibalism: see further 244–6n.). Indeed the Ἀιδου μάγειρος (397n.) carries out his previously expressed intentions of (a) performing a sacrifice (244–6n., 334–5, 346n.)—he uses the λέβης as a grotesque ϲφαγεῖον—and (b) using both dry and wet heat (244, 246): tougher meat requires boiling (Athen. 656a = Philoch. *FGH* 328 F 173; cf. Arist. *Meteor.* 381b), and so he roasts the ϲάρκες (403) and boils the (tougher) μέλη (404). (The same horrible sophistication in cooking human flesh occurs at Hdt. 1.119.3; Accius frr. 187–9 Warmington; Ov. *Met.* 1.228–9, 6. 645–6; Seneca *Thy.* 1060–5; Clem. *Protr.* 2.18.) Combining artfully the Homeric savagery with the civilization of sacrifice, E. makes Pol. kill one of the men as in Homer and sacrifice the other. This is the contrast, between two kinds of horror, expressed by ῥυθμῶι τινι and reinforced strongly by δ' αὖ in 400 (cf. e.g. *El.*

1104), a contrast trivial enough to us but significant to an audience familiar with the religious and psychological necessity of articulating the killing of animals as sacrificial ritual (W. Burkert, *Homo Necans, passim*). For the τινι cf. *Tro.* 470: the gods are not on Hecuba's side, ὅμως δ᾽ ἔχει τι cχῆμα κικλήcκειν θεοὐc (the sense of ῥυθμόc here is close to cχῆμα: LSJ s. ῥυθμόc II-VI: nowhere in E. does ῥυθμόc refer simply to motion: *El.* 772 τίνι ῥυθμῶι φόνου ... ; *Hcld.* 130, *Su.* 94). It must be admitted, however, that the postponed genitive ἑταίρων τῶν ἐμῶν is hard to parallel: *Hel.* 1126–8 is lyric and therefore almost irrelevant, and *El.* 1357–9 exemplifies the postponed genitive narrowing the range of ὅcτιc, whereas the identity of the men here is not in doubt. Perhaps the repetition issues from O.'s incredulity: 'he sacrificed them--yes, my comrades!' If this is thought unacceptable, then 395 should be left where it is, to follow 392 postponed (392-3n.), with cφαγεῖον κτλ. qualifying λέβητα (392), and πελέκεων γνάθοιc still hopelessly corrupt (πελέκεων an intrusive gloss replacing cὺν χἀλκου? cf. 343-4n.). **πελέκεων γνάθοιc:** read perhaps πελέκεωc: he needs only one; the plural may have been wrongly inferred from γνάθοιc, which means in fact the double axe: cf. S. *El.* 195–6 οἱ παγχάλκων ἀνταία γενύων ὡρμάθη πλαγά (other exx. of the metaphor at fr. 530.5–6; S. *El.* 485; A. *PV* 64, 726). For cutting the victim's throat (cφάζειν) we expect the knife. The axe was used in sacrifice, but for striking cattle on the back of the neck (*Il.* 17.520; *Od.* 3.449; A. R. 1.429; V. *Aen.* 2.224), and so, like the λέβηc used as cφαγεῖον, it indicates Pol.'s monstrosity.

396. θεοcτυγεῖ expresses the abnormality of Pol.'s sacrifice; but like θεομιcήc and θεοφιλήc, it is ambiguous. Despite 605, it is probably passive here (i.e. 'hated by the gods', not 'hating the gods'), as it seems to be at *Tro.* 1213 (of Helen). Or perhaps it implies mutual hatred. The word occurs also at 602; S. *Inach.* fr. 269a.22; Neophron fr. 2.4; *Ep. Rom.* 1.30; and Pollux 1.20: in no case is either sense clearly preferable. The only other compound ending -cτυγήc, βροτοcτυγήc, occurs twice—of δνόφοι and of the Gorgons (A. *Cho.* 51, *PV* 799).

397. "Αιδου: δίδου (L) derives from a misreading of Λ as Δ (similar corruption at e.g. A. *Cho.* 474, *Su.* 254). "Αιδου μαγείρωι: "Αιδου meaning 'hellish' (*Hec.* 1077, *HF* 1119, *IT* 286, fr. 122; A. *Ag.* 1115, 1235) is applied to nouns which already have some connection with death (that is one reason why Fraenkel's defence of μητέρα at A. *Ag.* 1235 is mistaken): e.g. at *Hec.* 1077 Polymestor can refer to the Trojan women as maenads out of hell (βάκχαιc "Αιδου) tearing apart his children, because maenads did (sup-

posedly) tear apart the young (Seaford in *CQ* 31 (1981), 263; cf.
HF 1119, where there is the extra point that Herakles is possessed).
And in fact Ἅιδου here means more than just 'hellish'. The
μάγειρος sacrifices (Athen. 659d–661c; *SIG*³ 1024.14; etc.: A.
Giannini in *Acme* 13 (1960), 135–216; H. Dohm in *Zetemata* 32
(1964)). But this sacrifice (395n.) is not to the (Olympian) gods; in
fact it is hateful to them (θεοςτυγής, 396n.). The victims are
human and the only purpose is eating (similarly the killing of
Polymestor's children has no ritual purpose), and so inasmuch as
it is nevertheless imagined as a sacrifice, the only recipient can be
Hades, whose realm is hateful to the Olympian gods (W. Burkert,
Griechische Religion in der archaischen und klassischen Epoche (1977),
310); the θεοςτυγής at S. *Inach.* fr. 269a.22 is probably Hades
himself: Seaford in *CQ* 30 (1980), 23–9). This idea is assisted by
the apparent popular conception of the infernal eating of corpses,
as by the canine Hekate (Attic bf. lekythos, Athens NM 19765;
Vermeule, *Aspects of Death in Early Greek Art and Poetry* (1979), 109),
or by the demon Eurynomos, who like Pol. eats everything (save
the bones: Pausan. 10.28.7; cf. *Od.* 9.292–3; Hes. *Th.* 311, 773; V.
Aen. 8.297). And the same idea may underly Aristias fr. 3 (probably satyric) Ἅιδου τραπεζεύς, ἀκρατέα νηδὺν ἔχων, and S. *El.*
542–3 (A. Dieterich, *Nekyia*, 46–54). **δύο:** δύω (L) occurs at *Od.*
9.311, 344; but that is not enough to defend it here: the same
corruption occurs at e.g. *El.* 1033, *Or.* 1401, 1536.

398–402. See 395n.

400. 'The tendon at the end of the foot' is where the foot joins the leg:
E. may have been influenced in this detail by Herakles' treatment
of Lichas at S. *Trach.* 779–81: μάρψας ποδὸς νιν, ἄρθρον ἧι
λυγίζεται / ῥιπτεῖ πρὸς ἀμφίκλυστον ἐκ πόντου πέτραν· / κόμης δὲ
λευκὸν μυελὸν ἐκραίνει. Cf. also *Il.* 1.591; *Il. Parv.* fr. 19.4;
Sositheos, *Daphnis* (satyric) fr. 3.

401. In *Od.* (9.289) Pol. strikes his victims simply ποτὶ γαίηι, in Virgil
however, as here, *ad saxum* (*Aen.* 3.625); cf. S. *Trach.* 780 (quoted
400n.). **cτόνυχα:** γ' ὄνυχα (L) may derive from the similarity of Γ
and the compendium for ϲτ: cf. 506 γαςτρὸς L; cταcτρὸς P.

402. καθαρπάζειν occurs in E. only at *Andr.* 813 ('seize from'), 1122
('seize down') and elsewhere only at Ar. *Eq.* 856 ('seize down' or
'away') and Strabo 16.2.37 ('carry off'). These senses do not fit
here. But such conjectures as καθαρμόσας (Murray) and κἀιτ'
ἀναρπάσας (Blaydes) do not meet the difficulty that Pol. has spits to
do the roasting (393), and must anyway first cut (from both
victims: a colon must follow ἐξέρρανε) the parts for roasting from
the parts for boiling (404), as in other exx. of the τόπος (395n.):

e.g. Hdt. 1.119.3 cφάξας αὐτὸν καὶ κατὰ μέλεα διελὼν τὰ μὲν ὤπτησε, τὰ δὲ ἥψησε τῶν κρεῶν (also Ov. *Met.* 6.644–5; Sen. *Thy.* 1060, 1062; Clem. *Protr.* 2.18). Even in Homer, where it seems unnecessary (395n.), τοὺς δὲ διὰ μελεϊστὶ ταμὼν ὁπλίσσατο δόρπον (9.291). Surely what Pol. does with the μάχαιρα here is to cut up the bodies (hence λάβρωι), whether we read διαρταμῶν (Paley; cf. A. *PV* 1022–3), διαρπάσας (Paley), or καταικίσας, καταμέρισας, καῖτα κατατεμὼν. A scribe may have reproduced ἁρπάσας from 400, or perhaps it was inferred from 403 that Pol. was using his knife as a toasting fork. καθαρπάσας λάβρωι μάχαιραν Meurig-Davies (in *CR* 63 (1949), 49); καθαρπάσας λάβρον μάχαιραν Ussher, who attempts to give καθ- a point by imagining the knife kept on a ledge! But E. would not have left to the imagination the spitting *and* the cutting-up. And Meurig-Davies' point that λάβρος nowhere else describes a weapon is insensitive: see Bond on *HF* 253; A. *PV* 1022–3.

404. μέλη are tougher than cάρκες (403), and so are best boiled (246n., 402n.). The point of the distinction between boiling and roasting is easy digestion (Arist. *Meteor.* 381b); and both τήκειν (246) and ἕψειν can refer to the act of digestion itself (Hp. *Acut.* 28, cf. *Aff.* 49).

406. κἀδιακόνουν: καὶ διήκονουν (L) is the later form. Rutherford (*New Phrynichus*, 86) favours the double augment κἀδιηκόνουν.

407–8. For the simile cf. *Il.* 22.141; Bond on *HF* 974. In Homer the Greeks are in the cave when Pol. arrives: (236) ἡμεῖς δὲ δείσαντες ἀπεσσύμεθ' ἐς μυχὸν ἄντρου. E. of course had to alter this sequence of events. Cf. *Hec.* 1066.

407. ἄλλοι (ἄλλοι L) is required by the sense: 678n. **πέτρας:** δέμας (Wecklein) is suggested by A. *Pers.* 209–10 πτήξας δέμας παρεῖχε, which is however very different in sense. And cf. e.g. S. *OC* 1169 cχὲς οὗπερ εἶ.

410. φάρυγος (φάρυγγος L) avoids a split 'comic' anapaest (334n.). At 502 too L has φάρυγγος where φάρυγος is required by the metre. Cf. *Od.* 9.373 φάρυγος; 356n. **ἀνέπεσε:** cf. 326; *Od.* 9.296–8, 371. **αἰθέρ':** ἀέρ' Scaliger; ἀτμὸν Nauck. But cf. 629, where, as here, the elevated word is intended to amuse. And the quotation in Athen. (23e) for what it is worth (see below), has αἰθέρ'. **ἐξανεῖς:** ἐξιεῖς L; Athen. (23e) quotes the line with ἐξανιεῖς (whence Porson's ἐξανεῖς: for the coincident aorist see 389n.), i.e. with a 'comic' anapaest, of which there is no other certain ex. in Od.'s lines (260n.). Furthermore, Athen. also has φάρυγγος (giving another 'comic' anapaest), which is certainly wrong: see above, and 356n.

412. Μάρωνος: 141n.; cf. Cratin. fr. 135: Pol. οὔπω 'πίον τοιοῦτον οὐδὲ πίομαι Μάρωνα. αὐτῶι τοῦδε (αὐτοῦ τῶιδε L): cf. 446. Probably the case of αὐτῶι was assimilated to Μάρωνος. πιεῖν: cf. 257n.

413. τοῦ: παῖ Aldina (cf. 286); but cf. *Ion* 1619 ὦ Διὸς Λητοῦς τ' Ἄπολλον, *IT* 1230.

414. Ἑλλάς: in the Sicily of the Cyclopes there are no vines (124). Unlike at *Od.* 9.348, Od. seems to be speaking the language of a clever Greek trading with barbarians. Cf. 160n.

415. θεῖον...πῶμα: cf. *Od.* 9.205 θεῖον ποτόν of this same drink. κομίζει: cf. [Men.] *Monost.* 539 χθὼν πάντα κομίζει.Διονύcου γάνος: cf. *Ba.* 261, 382–3, fr. 146.3; A. *Pers.* 615; Ar. *Ran.* 1320; Philox. Leuc. 836c4 *PMG*.

416. ἔκπλεως is stronger than ἔμπλεως (Dobree): 'full up' rather than 'full'; cf. 247.

417. Cf. *Od.* 9.353 ὁ δὲ δέκτο καὶ ἔκπιεν. ἄμυcτιν means not just 'a long draught' (LSJ) but 'a draught which empties a full cup' (from μύω); cf. 421, 575. τ' (Barnes) cannot be bettered.

418. ἄρας χεῖρα: the occurrences of this gesture in ancient literature are listed by C. Sittl, *die Gebärden der Griechen und Römer*, 13. It signifies here admiration, not (*pace* Ussher) a request for another cupful.

422. οἶνος: οἶνος L; 678n.; cf. *Od.* 21.293 οἶνός σε τρώει, where however the wine is less specific. For οἶνος rather than ὄινος see K-B i 220.

424. Cf. Ar. *Ran.* 844 καὶ μὴ πρὸς ὀργὴν σπλάγχνα θερμήνηις κότωι. Charlesworth (*CR* 40 (1926), 4) argues that Ar. has taken the verse from A., to whom it is addressed, and that E. here parodies the same verse by the change of κότωι to ποτῶι (cf. 218n.).

425–6. These verses represent a τόπος of satyric drama: cf. fr. 907; Trag. adesp. 418.5–6; anon. on Herakles in A. *Syl.* (p. 575 Nauck) ἤσθιε καὶ ἔπινεν ἀίδων. In the prosatyric *Alc.* the drunken singing of Herakles, warmed by wine (758 ἐθέρμην': cf. ἐθέρμαινον here in 424), contrasts with the laments of the servants for Alkestis (759–63; cf. esp. ἄμους' ὑλακτῶν). The scene in Pol.'s cave is strikingly similar, except that Pol. so far from considering it αἰσχρὸν παρὰ κλαίουσι θοινᾶσθαι ξένους (Herakles at *Alc.* 542) is himself by his θοινᾶσθαι the cause of their weeping. For Pol. and Herakles see 213–14n. Cf. also Theogn. 1041–2 δεῦρο σὺν αὐλητῆρι· παρὰ κλαίοντι γελῶντες / πίνωμεν, κείνου κήδεσι τερπόμενοι (cf. 1217–18).

425. συνναύταις: συν ναύταις L, as at 705 (n.), but not at 708.

426. ἐπηχεῖ, present, is better than ἐπήχει (L), imperfect: cf. ἄιδει in 425.

429. φεύγειν differs from φυγεῖν in implying permanence in the separation: cf. 194 ποῖ χρὴ φυγεῖν (interest is in the act of getting away) with *Tro.* 400 φεύγειν μὲν οὖν χρὴ πόλεμον ὅστις εὖ φρονεῖ. ἄμεικτον describes the inhospitable Kyknos at *HF* 393, and the centaurs at S. *Trach.* 1095. Cf. Bond on *HF* 393.

430. L's δαναίδων is pointless (despite the satyric attempt on the Danaid Amymone in A. *Amym.*). For **Ναΐδων** cf. Pratinas fr. 3.4 ἀν' ὄρεα cύμενον μετὰ Ναϊάδων (cf. 68) and A. fr. 278 (Lloyd-Jones), both almost certainly sung by satyrs. At Pi. fr. 156 Sil. is Ναΐδοc ἀκοίταc. Cf. also *Hipp.* 550, *Hel.* 187.

432. κἀποκερδαίνων implies that Sil. is deriving from the wine both disadvantage (*Hec.* 518) and advantage. To enjoy the full benefit of the wine is to be completely helpless. Drinking tends to develop its own vocabulary (English is no exception). Earlier commentators, failing to appreciate the irony, wanted to emend.

433–4. Animal similes occur in satyric drama at A. fr. 210(?), *Theoroi* 44; S. *Ichn.* 127, 128, 367, frr. 113, 363, 848.

Both Duchemin and Ussher take πτέρυγαc with λελημμένοc: 'his wings caught in the cup as if in bird-lime.' But in fact birds are caught in lime by their feet, and flap with their wings. And the flow of the trimeter gives us πτέρυγαc ἁλύει (cf. fr. 908.7–8 ψυχὴν ἀπολύειν MS; ἁλύειν Bergk). Sil.'s mouth is clasped to the cup, and his body is in incoherent motion (cf. *Od.* 9.398 Pol. ἔρριψεν … χερcὶν ἁλύων) on one spot. For the lime metaphor cf Luc. *Cat.* 14; (erotic) *AP* 5.96; etc.

435–6. Od.'s appeal is well suited to the mood of his audience: cf. φίλον with 73–4, 81, 436 with 76–7.

437. *Rhes.* 464 εἰ γὰρ ἐγὼ τόδ' ἦμαρ εἰcίδοιμ', ἄναξ; and Ar. *Pax* 346 (merely εἰ γὰρ ἐκγένοιτ' ἰδεῖν ταύτην με τὴν ἡμέραν) suggest that there is no element of apodosis in ὢ φίλτατε either here or at *Or.* 1100 ὢ φίλτατ', εἰ γὰρ τοῦτο κατθάνοιμ' ἰδών. For assentient γάρ in a wish see Denniston, *GP*, 92.

439–40. With the widowed penis cf. the orphaned penis at Ar. *Lys.* 956 πῶc ταυτηνὶ παιδοτροφήcω. At A. *Dikt.* 824–32 the satyrs (or Sil.) suppose that Danae's long sexual abstinence has made her lascivious. For ὡc … γε see 247n. But these lines present several problems: (1) the first syllable of cίφωνα must be long (Meleager *AP* 5.151 = Gow and Page, *Hellenistic Epigrams*, 4167; Ar. *Thesm.* 557; Juvenal 6.310). (2) The active χηρεύομεν with accusative of respect (cίφωνα) is so far as I know unparalleled (cf. the middle at *Alc.* 1089). It cannot be (LSJ) transitive. (3) 440 in L gives no sense and does not scan. Hence e.g. Hermann's ὡc διὰ μακροῦ γε τὸν φίλον cίφωνα δὴ / χηρεύομεν τόνδ' οὐκ ἔχοντα καταφυγήν, Diggle's (suggested tentatively in correspondence) ὡc διὰ μακροῦ γε τὸν

φίλον χηρεύομεν (or χηρεύομαι) / cίφωνα, τῶιδε δ' ἔχομεν οὐχὶ
καταφυγήν ('our dear cίφων has long been widowed, and we have
no place for it to go'), and West's ... καταρραγήν, 'means of
discharge' (in *BICS* 28 (1981), 68). But one might expect the
enthusiastic prospect of liberation (rather like 168–72: 169n.; cf.
68–72, 430) provided by Headlam's ὡc διὰ μακροῦ γοῦν, οἵ γε τόνδε
τὸν φίλον / χηρεύομεν cίφων', ἔχοιμεν καταφαγεῖν (*CR* 15 (1901),
22), with διὰ μακροῦ meaning 'after a long interval': cf. Ar. *Lys.*
904 κατακλίνηθι μετ' ἐμοῦ διὰ χρόνου, *Vesp.* 1252 ἵνα καὶ μεθυcθῶμεν
διὰ χρόνου. But ἔχοιμεν καταφαγεῖν gives poor sense and a fifth foot
dactyl (unparalleled in tragedy and satyr-play). Perhaps then we
should read something like ὡc διὰ μακροῦ γ' ἄν, ὅc γε τόνδε τὸν
φίλον / χηρεύομαι cίφων', ἔχοιμι καταφυγήν. An entirely satisfactory refuge would be provided by a nymph (68, 430n.). Cf. *Alc.*
1089 χηρεύcηι λέχοc, *Su.* 267 ἔχει γὰρ καταφυγὴν θὴρ μὲν πέτραν κτλ.
The factors producing corruption may have been (1) the introduction of plural forms χηρεύομεν and ἔχοιμεν from 437 ἴδοιμεν
(wrongly of course: cf. 211–2, 465; A. *Theor.* 23, 30–1); (2) *simplex
ordo* (cf. e.g. A. *Ag.* 1064 κακῶν κλύει φρενῶν; κακῶν φρενῶν F; G.
Thomson in *CQ* 14 (1965), 161) causing the transposition of
cίφωνα; (3) consequent attempts to mend the metre. Whatever
the true reading, commentators have missed the humour of the
ambiguity of cίφων, which means a 'siphon, used for drawing wine
out of a cask or jar' (LSJ), and refers here also to the visible, erect
phallus of the chorus-leader (2n.). In 5th-cent. vase-painting the
satyrs sometimes actively confuse the pleasures of wine and sex, as
if the distinction was irrelevant to such forthright, hedonistic
creatures: e.g. on *ARV*² 76.65 (Epictetus, in Tarquinia) a satyr
sexually assaults an ἀcκόc (cf. *ARV*² 85.21, an amphora), and on
*ARV*² 446.262 (Douris, in the British Museum) a satyr balances a
cup on his erection. At 165–174 only one of the twin pleasures of
wine and sex has been offered to Sil., but he intends nevertheless to
indulge in them both (see esp. 172n.). And 439–40, like 172,
cunningly suggests them both (cf. Juvenal 6.310; Hipponax fr.
56), as also perhaps A. fr. 108, from the satyric *Kerykes*: cτενόc-
τομον τὸ τεῦχοc.

441. τιμωρίαν: at *Od.* 9.299–305 Od. restrains his impulse to kill the
sleeping Pol., because he knows that only the giant can move the
great stone from the entrance to the cave. Here, on the other hand,
because Od. must be free to emerge from the cave (375n.), there is
no stone. Indeed, with Pol. asleep (454, 627) the Greeks might
have all crept out to freedom (though this may well not have
occurred to the audience). And so the blinding here must be

presented largely as a matter of vengeance, which requires that Pol. be actually persuaded to remain in the cave (445, 451, 531–40).

442. θηρὸς refers to humankind at *Or.* 1272, *Pho.* 1296. **πανούργου:** κακούργου Wecklein; but cf. *Alc.* 766 πανούργον κλῶπα, in a passage similar to this (425–6n.).

443–4. The satyr relates the novel experience to a characteristically satyric one: cf. 104; S. fr. 331. **Ἀσιάδος ... κιθάρας:** this is called Asiatic in tragedy only by E. after 423 BC (*Erecth.* fr. 370, *Hyps.* 64.101), which prompts Webster (*The Tragedies of Euripides*, 18) to see in the epithet a compliment to the Milesian Timotheos. Cf. Rogers on Ar. *Thesm.* 120.

445. ἐπὶ κῶμον: ἐπίκωμος Wecklein (and ἐπίκωμον at 508). But cf. Ar. *Plut.* 1040 ἔοικε δ᾽ἐπὶ κῶμον βαδίζειν; Xen. *Symp.* 2.1; Antiphanes fr. 199; Machon 112 Gow; Athen. 621c. For the double preposition cf. e.g. Apollod. Caryst. fr. 5.21 ἐπὶ κῶμον εἰς Κόρινθον. For ἐπίκωμος cf. only Aristias fr. 3 (397n.).

447–65. This passage seems to represent a satyric τόπος, in which the satyrs make guesses at the nature of a εὕρημα, which when revealed fills them with vigorous delight (464–5n.).

447. δρυμοῖσί νιν: ῥυθμοῖσί νιν L. There is something to be said for ῥυθμῶι τινι (Dobree): the satyrs' absurd idea of perfect τιμωρία (441) is to pay .Pol. back in kind: ῥυθμῶι τινι σφάξαι corresponds with ἔσφαζ᾽... ῥυθμῶι τινι (398), and πετρῶν ὦσαι κάτα (448) with Pol.'s other method (400–402). Cf. 395n. Nevertheless, δρυμοῖσί is more likely (cf. *Hipp.* 1128), giving an antithesis with πετρῶν. For ἔρημον Kassel suggests ἐρήμοις, comparing A. fr. 304. 10 δρυμοὺς ἐρήμους.

448. κάτα: κάτω (L) with genitive does not mean 'down from': e.g. *Alc.* 45 κάτω χθονός means 'below the earth'. Cf. *IT* 1429–30 ἢ κατὰ στύφλου πέτρας ῥίψωμεν, ἢ σκόλοψι κτλ.; Hdt. 8.53.2 οἱ μὲν ἐρρίπτεον ἑωυτοὺς κατὰ τοῦ τείχεος κάτω. At *Hcld.* 592 L has κάτα and Stobaeus (probably rightly) κάτω.

449. προθυμία:ἐπιθυμία (L) occurs elsewhere in E. only at *Andr.* 1281 (a sexual context). προθυμία means 'intention', as at e.g. *Alc.* 51 ἔχω λόγον δὴ καὶ προθυμίαν σέθεν, 1107.

450. πῶς δαί after the rejection of a suggestion: *Hel.* 1246; Macdowell on Ar. *Vesp.* 1212.

451–3 anticipate 531–42, where the emphasis is however on prestige (532) and prudence (534, 538) rather than as here (453) pleasure: cf. 532n.; Pol. is of course quite used to having a kind of solitary κῶμος at home (322–8).

454. The god is absent, but in a sense also present (156, 526).

Βακχίου νικώμενος: genitive of comparison, by analogy with ἡττώμενός τινος, ἥττων τινος (K-G i 392): cf. *Med.* 315, *Tro.* 23; A. *Su.* 1005; S. *Aj.* 1353; Ar. *Nub.* 1087.

455-9. This plan is simpler than in *Od.*, where the stake, after being sharpened, is then hardened and hidden in the dung (9.328-9); cf. 591-2n.

455. In *Od.* Pol. is blinded by a stake cut from his own vast club of olive wood (9.319-20). E. has substituted a mere branch of olive, perhaps because Pol.'s club had been seen to be too small (203n., 213-14n.; cf. 472 μέγας), perhaps also because he wanted Pol. to be carrying it in the next episode.

456. ἐξαποξύνας: the addition ἐξ- is Tr.1, and so probably has the authority of Λ (intro., §VIII). The compound, though not found elsewhere, 'is of a type favoured by E. (e.g. ἐξαπάλλασσω *Hlc.* 1108, *IA* 1004, ἐξαπόλλυμι *Hcld.* 950, *Tro.* 1215, ἐξυπεῖπας (*hapax*) *Ba.* 1265, and many compounds with ἐξανα-). Tr. is more likely to have drawn on some authority than to have invented this *hapax*' (Zuntz, op. cit. 73-4n., 54; see also Bond on *HF* 18). At *Od.* 9.326 Od. gives the club to his companions (ignored here: 469-83n.), ἀποξῦναι δ' ἐκέλευσα (ἀποξῦcαι P²W), and when they have made it smooth, ἐγὼ δ' ἐθόωσα παραστὰς ἄκρον. The ἐξ- is apt here, as expressing completion.

458-9. βαλῶ...ὄμματ' is preferable to βαλὼν ... ὄμματ' (L), not because it restores ὄμμα (cf. 470), but because ἄρας ... βαλὼν in asyndeton is too harsh. For the corruption cf. *Alc.* 847.

459. ὄψιν, ὄμμα: ὄμμα is more concrete than ὄψις: cf. e.g. *IA* 233-4 τὰν γυναικεῖον ὄψιν ὀμμάτων ὡς πλήςαιμι.

460-1. This is an abbreviated version of the simile at *Od.* 9.383-6, where Od. blinding Pol. with the help of his companions is compared to a man drilling a hole in a ship while his assistants turn the drill around with a strap. Here Od. ignores his companions again (456n.), so that the satyrs may be allowed to help (464-83n). The metaphor is more at home in a narrative (*Od.* 9.383-6) than in the outlining of a plan of action: cf. 591-2n., 608-10n. For the function of the holes drilled (for cords to hold together planks) see Morrison and Williams, *Greek Oared Ships*, 199.

461. κωπηλατεῖ refers to the motion to and fro which propels the drill around its axis, imparted here by two straps (cf. *Od.* 9.385).

462. κυκλώcω: 'turn around' (active) is more commonly κυκλέω than κυκλόω (e.g. *El.* 561, *Or.* 632; many instances could be either); and at *Or.* 1379 the MSS are divided between the two forms. But κυκλήcω (Musgrave) is unnecessary, and would damage the word-play (Κύκλωπος, 463). **φαεςφόρωι**: the high-sounding epithet is cruelly chosen, for the torch will introduce more light. *Cf. Pl. Tim.* 45b τῶν δὲ ὀργάνων πρῶτον μὲν φωςφόρα ξυνετεκτήναντο ὄμματα.

464–5. Clever though the plan is, the satyrs' joy seems excessive. And the plural εὑρήμαςιν is surprising: εὕρημα in E. is frequent, and normally singular: in the exceptions (*Ba.* 59 τυμπανα, Ῥέας τε μητρὸς ἐμά θ' εὑρήματα, *Hec.* 250 πολλῶν λόγων εὑρήματα) there is a good reason for the plural. As at 169–74, satyric abandon stands out rather oddly from its context. I suspect that both passages represent satyric τόποι (cf. 169n.; intro., n. 122). With μαινόμεςθα, which suggests that they break spontaneously into dance (cf. 157n.), cf. the satyrs as μαινόμενοι (*Ba.* 130) in the context of the tympana as εὑρήματα.

464. ἰοὺ ἰού: the scholiast on Ar. *Pax* 317, and the *Suda* s. ἰού, stipulate ἰού for suffering and ἰοῦ for joy. But this is probably a convenient guess.

465. Wilamowitz (on *HF* 222) punctuates γέγηθα, μαινόμεςθα, τοῖς. But a comma merely after γέγηθα would be better: cf. *Pho.* 1193 ἔθνηιςκον, ἐξέπιπτον ἀντύγων ἄπο, *Su.* 529. **μαινόμεςθα:** for this sense see Ar. *Ran.* 103, 751; S. *El.* 1153.

466. καὶ cέ: possible is καί cε (see Schwyzer, *Griech. Gramm.*, ii 187); but cf. e.g. *Hcld.* 281. **φίλουc:** despite its position between cέ and the γέρων Sil., this probably refers to Od.'s companions (cf. 478, 650; *Od.* 9.63) rather than to the other satyrs. Od. thinks first of those present, whom he addresses through their leader (cέ), and then those in the cave.

467. ἐμβῆςαc is transitive, with double accusative: cf. *Hcld.* 844 ἱκέτευςε... ἐμβῆςαι νιν ἵππειον δίφρον, *IT* 742 ναὸς εἰςβήςω ςκάφος (sc. αὐτόν). The accusatives in 466 also form the object of ἀποςτελῶ (468).

468. διπλαῖςι κώπαιc seems to mean 'with two banks of oars'. What one expects Od. to say is 'full speed ahead'. Probably E. imagines Od.'s ship to be the two-banked penteconter, which was replaced during the 7th and 6th cent. BC by the three-banked trireme (L. Casson, *Ships and Seamanship in the Ancient World*, 59, 81). Pindar (fr. 259) and Thuc. (1.14) supposed that the Greek ships at Troy were penteconters. Cf. also *Hel.* 1412, *Hyps.* fr. 1.ii.23, *IT* 1124 (and *IT* 408 δικρότοιςι refers, *pace* Platnauer, to the double bank: cf. Casson, 133, cf. Xen. *HG* 2.1.28; Morrison and Williams, op. cit. 460-1n., 194–5; Casson, 59 n. 82). Only occasionally would all three banks of a trireme be used at once (Morrison and Williams, 309); and the same may have been true of the two banks of a penteconter.

469–75. The satyrs' enthusiastic offer to help, and their subsequent cowardice (635–55), represents a stock joke: πιϲτοὶ λόγοιϲιν ὄντεϲ ἔργα φεύγετε (S. *Ichn.* 152). If it had occurred to anyone that Od. is unwarrantedly ignoring the companions who assisted him in Homer (9.331–5, 380–5), and on whom he eventually has to rely here too (650), then E. might have replied that they are still cowering terrified in the recesses of the cave (407–8n., 456n.).

469–71. What is the point of the simile? The key to the general sense is in φόνου . . . κοινωνεῖν (Diggle prints πόνου, 471n.). In a description preserved by Porphyry (*de Abst.* 2.29, p. 159 Nauck) of the first ever sacrifice, those who assist the man who actually strikes the blow κοινωνήϲουϲιν τοῦ φόνου. The satyrs want to participate (necessarily in a secondary role) in the blinding, somewhat like Electra in the killing of her mother (*El.* 1225 ξίφουϲ τ' ἐφηψάμαν ἅμα in a sacrificial context: cf. 1222, *Or.* 1235). But what specific element of the sacrifice provides the parallel to helping hold the torch? As part of the preparation for a sacrifice a burning torch was dipped into water (the χέρνιψ), which was then sprinkled over altar, onlookers and victim (Ar. *Pax* 959 with schol.; *HF* 928–9; Athen. 409b; Hsch. s. δάλιον; Stengel, op. cit. 313–15n., 16, 17, and *die Griechischen Kultusaltertümer*³, 109; cf. *IT* 54, 58, 622, *IA* 955; Ar. *Lys.* 1129). There are two considerable advantages in supposing that this is what E. had in mind here. (1) The description of the blinding in Homer is embellished by two similes in quick succession. Od. here has just reproduced one (460–1n.), and we now expect the other, the simile of the smith dipping hot metal into cold water (*Od.* 9.391–4). In fact it seems that E. has substituted his own, similar (a burning brand dipped in water) but in fact closer to the reality (a brand rather than metal) and (perhaps as a satyric τόποϲ: Seaford in *CQ* 31 (1981), 273–4) drawn from the ritual: both Pol.'s cannibalism (245n.) and the τιμωρία for it are expressed as sacrifice. (2) φόνου . . . κοινωνεῖν (471) becomes particularly apt. Participation in the sacrifice might be expressed (partly at least) through contact with χέρνιψ: A. *Ag.* 1037–8 Klytaimnestra to Kassandra . . . κοινωνὸν εἶναι χερνίβων, πολλῶν μετὰ / δούλων ϲταθεῖϲαν κτηϲίου βωμοῦ πέλαϲ (here the irony, missed by the commentators, was that the victim was sprinkled as well as the onlookers: cf. *IA* 675, 1518), *Eum.* 656; S. *OT* 240; *El.* 792, *Or.* 1602; etc. But the torch plunged into the eye of Pol. will be wet not with the χέρνιψ but with blood (*Od.* 9.397 πεφυρμένον αἵματι πολλῶι). And so φόνου here seems to mean not just sacrificial killing (which in reality the blinding is not) but also gore. Cf. *IT* 644–5 κατολοφύρομαι ϲὲ τὸν χερνίβων ῥανίϲι μελόμενον αἱμακταῖϲ (metaphorical!); A. *Sept.* 44 θιγγάνοντες χερςὶ ταυρείου φόνου (an oath). Just as in the sacrifice the burning torch is plunged into the χέρνιψ, which is then sprinkled over the onlookers to express their participation (as well as to cleanse them), so in the reality the burning brand will be plunged into Pol.'s eye, and then it will be withdrawn covered with blood, contact with which will express the satyrs' participation. The difficulties of this interpretation are as follows. Firstly, there is no evidence that the δαλός in the sacrifice was held by more than one person. This may however have been the case (cf. e.g. Ar. *Pax* 961); and we should anyway perhaps not demand precise correspondence in every detail, given the general aptness of the simile. Secondly, and more seriously, what does ἐκ cπονδῆς θεοῦ (469) mean? That is the reading of L, and it means 'after a libation' (cf. Hdt. 1.50.2 ἐκ τῆς θυςίης; *Hipp.* 109). But the torch-ritual did not occur after a libation. With the text as it stands the libation might be the one poured after a meal or symposium, and so before the κῶμος, in which torches are carried. The satyr is then amusingly claiming some experience with the torch (cf. 443n.). But this seems unlikely. And so the following emendations must be considered: (a) ὥςπερ ἐν cπονδαῖς θεοῦ (Reiske). cπονδή elsewhere in E. is always in the plural. cπονδαῖς here might have a general sense covering θυςίαι, as perhaps at *Ba.* 45–6 cπονδῶν ἄπο ὠθεῖ με (cf. Burkert, op. cit. 397n., 122–3). In the mystic ritual performed by the βαςίλιννα at the Dionysiac Anthesteria (intro., §II) were a secret sacrifice, and the administration at the altar of an oath to the fourteen γεραιραί before they handled the sacred objects (πρὶν ἅπτεςθαι τῶν ἱερῶν): [Dem.] 59.73,78. Conceivably the satyrs are thinking of their experience of the god's mysteries (intro., §II): the ingenious δαλός, appropriately perhaps for a εὕρημα (447–65n.; intro., §IV), is imagined as a ἱερόν: i.e. a traditional feature of the *thiasos* has been adapted to the Cyclopeia (intro., n. 172). (b) **ὥςπερεὶ cπονδῆς θεοῦ.** This was suggested by Reiske, apparently without knowledge of D. Chr. 34(17).34 οἱ δ' ἐκ παρέργου προςίαςιν ἁπτόμενοι μόνον τοῦ πράγματος, ὥςπερ οἱ cπονδῆς θιγγάνοντες κτλ., or of Aeschin. 2.84 τῶν ςυμμάχων τοὺς ὥςπερ ςυνεφαπτομένους τοῖς cπένδουςι τῶν ἱερῶν. Both passages attest the existence of a secondary role, effected by physical contact of some sort, in the cπονδή. And in the passage of D. Chr. it is a metaphor. Perhaps then, reading ὥςπερεὶ cπονδῆς, we may take the satyr to mean that his contact with the torch will be merely formal, like the (semi-proverbial?) contact of those who merely touch, or grasp hold of (cf. *Ion.* 1187), the cπονδή. However, this seems perhaps inconsistent with the enthusiasm of 473–5. And it loses the attractive torch-ritual metaphor. Θιγγάνοντεc in D. Chr. might suggest that with cπονδῆc he was thinking of the χέρνιψ (cf. e.g. *Or.* 1602 εὖ γοῦν θίγοιc ἄν χερνίβων); and the χέρνιψ might be thought of as a cπονδή (cf. Plut. *Mor.* 435c, 437a, 438a, *Alex.* 50; schol. Ar. *Pax* 960; Stengel, op. cit. 313–15n., 34–9); but θεοῦ counts against this equation here. (c) It appears therefore that there may be deep corruption. cπονδή may be an intrusive gloss (on a difficult passage). But I can do no better than ἐκ τῆc χέρνιβοc (cf. Ar. *Lys.* 1129) or ἐc τὴν χέρνιβα (cf. *HF* 929).

471. πόνου (Nauck; χοροῦ Wecklein); φόνου L. True, Pol. is not to be killed; and πόνοc is corrupted to φόνοc at *HF* 1279; probably also at *IT* 1046; S. *Aj.* 61, *OC* 542. But cf. 469–71n., and the phrase κοινωνεῖν φόνου at *Andr.* 915, *El.* 1048, *Or.* 1591.

472. μέγαc: cf. 615n.; at *Od.* 9.322–5 Pol.'s club is as big as the mast of a large ship, and from it Od. cuts the length of an ὄργυια (about six feet). οὐ replaces ὅν (L), which would give the unwanted meaning 'catch' (*Or.* 1189, 1346). And cf. 471 δαλοῦ, and Ar. *Lys.* 313 τίc ξυλλάβοιτ᾽ ἄν τοῦ ξύλου:

473. The figure is derived from *Od.* 9.241–2, where it is said that twenty-two ἄμαξαι could not move the stone from the entrance to the cave. E. has already used it at 385 (cf. 98n.). ἀραίμην: cf. *Or.* 3; Ar. *Ran.* 1406.

474. Blaydes suggests τὸν κακῶc ὀλουμένου ὀφθαλμὸν. But cf. *Held.* 874–5 τοῦ κακῶc ὀλουμένου Εὐρυcθέωc.

475. A similar simile occurs at Ar. *Lys.* 475; A. R. 2.134 (bees). S. fr. 778 ἤ cφηκίαν βλίccουcιν εὑρόντεc τινά may refer to the satyrs (cf. 443–4n.). ἐκθύψομεν (Hertlein) is the future of ἐκτύφω: cf. 655, 659; Ar. *Vesp.* 457 cὺ τῦφε πολλῶι τῶι καπνῶι (sc. τοὺc cφῆκαc); A.R. 2.134 (bees καπνῶι τυφόμεναι). Neither ἐκθρύψομεν (L; a *hapax legomenon*) nor ἐκτρίψομεν (Tr. 3), nor ἐκθλίψομεν (Scaliger, supported by Pearson in *CR* 38 (1924), 13) gives such good sense.

476. For the juxtaposition of plural and singular cf. 427–8, 465. νυν: the enclitic νυν (Bothe) associates easily with imperatives, and should perhaps be read here rather than νῦν, even though Od. might just as well say 'be quiet *now*' (he goes on to explain why words are no longer necessary) as 'be quiet then'.

477–8. Wecklein suggests κελεύcω and (in 478) πίθεcθε. Fraenkel on *Ag.* 1054 notes that although πειθ- has replaced πιθ- in the MSS at A. *Ag.* 206, *PV* 274, πείθου is guaranteed by the metre at Men. fr. 929. And the present tense here is quite acceptable.

477. τοῖcιν ἀρχιτέκτοcι: the word is somewhat surprising in this context, and so is the plural (does he mean himself and his companions?). At Ar. *Pax* 305 the chorus of farmers tell Trygaios φράζε κἀρχιτεκτόνει, in a scene with several points of resemblance with this one (cf. 429–30 with *Pax* 340–5; 437 with *Pax* 346; 439 with *Pax* 570; 472 with *Pax* 437, 465; and 476 with *Pax* 309). And so the oddity of language may be symptomatic of a τόπος (cf. 464–5n.) of comedy and satyr-play, the collective task (A. *Dikt.*, *Theoroi* 18–9; S. *Ichn.*; Ar. *Pax* 459–519), the performers of which may be summoned by an indiscriminate appeal for help to the inhabitants of the country (intro., §IV, A. *Dikt.* 18–20; S. *Ichn.* 39–49; Ar. *Pax* 296–300; cf. *P. Oxy.* 2256 fr. 72; A. *Theor.* 72–4; Ar. *Plut.* 223, 253–6).

478–9. Cf. Pylades explaining to Orestes that he does not want to seem προδοὺς cεcῶcθαι c' αὐτὸc εἰc οἴκουc μόνοc (*IT* 679). But we need not suppose self-parody. The concern Od. shows for his companions in Homer (*Od.* 9.421) is made more heroic here by the circumstance, necessary to the drama, that Od. could if he wished escape without returning to the cave.

480–2. These lines were defended by Wetzel (op. cit. 16–17n., 99) as deliberately making Od. ridiculous. Zwierlein (in *Gnomon* 39 (1967), 451) replied that Od. is nowhere else in the play comic, and added four points in favour of deletion: (1) καὶ is odd between φύγοιμ' ἂν and ἐκβέβηκα. (2) ἐκβέβηκα does not mean 'I have slipped away'. (3) ἄντρου μυχῶν is inept: cf. ἄλλοι in 407. (4) The interpolator seems to have used material from 407, 478–9, which was originally perhaps a marginal explanation of ἐγὼ γὰρ κτλ. (478–9). (1) and (2) seem to carry little weight. But the impression of hesitation, which is certainly out of place, the repetition (ἀπολιπὼν φίλουc . . . ἀπολιπόντ' ἐμοὺc φίλουc and μόνοc cωθήcομαι . . . cωθῆμαι μόνον), and the lameness of the lines form, taken together, a decisive case for deletion. The interpolator probably wanted to make explicit (esp. 480) the discrepancy with Homer (478–9). On the other hand, the lines are included by Biehl in his numerical analysis of the trimeters (in *Hermes* 105 (1977), 159–75), in which (along with other apparent correspondences of varying impressiveness) he notes that in the one episode in the first half of the play there are the same number of trimeters (274) as in the remaining episodes (excluding 663 as spoken ἔνδοθεν). But it is doubtful that his analysis has decisive implications for textual criticism.

482. There is no reason to suppose that Od. returns to the cave in order to emerge again with Pol.

483–518. Triclinius (Tr. 3) assigned 483–6, 488–94, 495–502 and 511–18 to semichoruses, perhaps rightly (cf. 632–4n.). In the anapaests he may well have been influenced by the admonition cίγα cίγα (488). But that may be (despite S. *Ichn.* 103; Cratin. fr.

144) a *Selbstanrede*: cf. *Su.* 271, *HF* 119, 819, *Tro.* 1235. Verses 483-94 are anapaestic dimeters, with the penultimate line a monometer (493; cf. *Med.* 1114) and the final line catalectic. Anapaests may have been chosen to convey a martial spirit (483n.). At 495 the mood of the play changes sharply to the komastic, rather as in the prosatyric *Alc.* (after 746, when in the Oxford production of 1971 the silence lef by the departing funeral procession was broken by a Heraklean belch ἔνδοθεν). The spirit of the refined κῶμος is conveyed immediately by the simple mono-strophic anacreontics κατὰ cτίχον (cf. Anacr. 356, 395, 396 *PMG*; on the ending of each stanza see 501-2n.) with which the satyrs accompany the emergence (491) of Pol., and which are taken up (503-10) by Pol. himself. They have no real parallel in tragedy. Satyric drama is open to the simplicity and monostrophic com-position of everyday songs (Parodos n., 356-74n., 656-62n.). Indeed, Rossi (in *Maia* 23 (1971), 21) points out that this song is a pastiche of several 'biotic' songs (the μακαρισμός, the cκόλιον, the κῶμος, the παρακλαυcίθυρον, the ὑμέναιος), with the result that the various festive songs of the πόλιc are centred on a figure, Pol., who is outside the πόλιc. (The song is not a ὑπόρχημα (Duchemin): see Dale in *Eranos* 48 (1950), 14-20 = *Collected Papers*, 34-40.)

483. 'Come, who is to be stationed first, and who after the first . . .?' The expression may have had a military or nautical connotation. Cf. 632.

484. κώπην can mean 'oar' and so has been taken here as a nautical metaphor (cf. 483n., 460), but may rather simply preserve its primary meaning 'handle'. ὀχμάcαι: cf. 29-30 πληροῦν . . . τέταγμαι. Still, ὀχμάcαc (L) is not unacceptable: for the three participles ταχθεὶc . . . ὀχμάcαc . . . ὥcαc in asyndeton see K-G ii 104.

485. βλεφάρων: cf. *Od.* 9.389 πάντα δέ οἱ βλέφαρ' ἀμφὶ καὶ ὀφρύαc εὗcεν ἀϋτμή.

487. |ᾠδὴ ἔνδοθεν|: Taplin argues (in *PCPhS* 23 (1977), 121-32) that Greek dramatists did not write stage directions. Certain παρεπιγραφαί indicating sounds do not seem inferable from the text (A. *Eum.* 117, 120, 123, 126, 129, *Dikt.* 803; Ar. *Thesm.* 129, 276-7); but Taplin makes a good case for taking even these as later additions. This one, on the other hand, though inferable from the text, is possibly E.'s.

489. μουcιζόμενοc: this rare verb (Theocr. 11.81 (also of Pol.), 8.38), and the unique middle ('doing the musical', Paley), may be intended to appear faintly ridiculous.

490. The satyrs pretend ironically that Pol. is to be punished like an unsatisfactory pupil (492-3), for his poor singing: cf. Pl. *Hipp.*

Maj. 292c οἴει ἂν ἀδίκως πληγὰς λαβεῖν, ὅστις διθύραμβον τοσουτονὶ
ᾄσας οὕτως ἀμούσως πολὺ ἀπῆισας ἀπὸ τοῦ ἐρωτήματος; and Men.
Sam. 427 οἰμώξεται σκαιὸς ὤν. The reality is suggested by the
secondary reference in κλαυόμενος to the wound in Pol.'s eye
(517n., 701n.). **ἀπωιδός:** ἀοιδὸς Herwerden; ἀπωιδὸν Stahl; ἀπωιδὸς refers elsewhere to the sound rather than to what makes the
sound (e.g. Luc. *Icar.* 17 ἀπωιδὰ φθεγγομένων), but should nevertheless probably be retained here. **καὶ κλαυόμενος:** κατακλαυόό-
μενος (Hermann) might give more punch to the syntax. But the
simple verb is regular in this sense (e.g. 554).

491. μελάθρων: Philoktetes calls his cave μέλαθρον at S. *Phil.* 1453.
Cf. Pi. *Pyth.* 5.40 κυπαρίσσινον μέλαθρον. Πέτρινος was used of
buildings, but Pol.'s dwelling is of course not as grand as πέτρινα
μέλαθρα might suggest.

492. κώμοις: for the various senses of κῶμος see Rossi, art. cit.
483–518n., 12. At 445, 451, 497, 508 it has the specific meaning of
a revelling excursion. But here it seems to mean 'revelling songs',
and it is to be taken with παιδεύσωμεν not ἀπαίδευτον: cf. Ar. *Thesm.*
988–9 ἐγὼ δὲ κώμοις σε (Dionysos) φιλοχόροισι μέλψω. Pol. is to be
dissuaded from going out on a κῶμος (451). The chorus will
educate him instead with κῶμος-songs at home (see esp. 502n.,
511–18n.), in what Rossi calls a 'κῶμος-mancato'.

492–3. νιν (νυν Diggle, comparing 568, *Or.* 1281): the third pronoun followed by apposition (τὸν ἀπαίδευτον) occurs in Hom.,
Soph., and elsewhere (K-G i 658), but according to Breitenbach
(*Untersuchungen zur Sprache der euripideischen Lyrik*, 258) nowhere else
in E. But cf. 181n. It may perhaps be apt here, as throwing weight
onto τὸν ἀπαίδευτον (as 182).

494. πάντως here means not 'in every way' (i.e. intellectually blinded
as well, according to Duchemin) but 'anyway': the satyrs may or
may not achieve the difficult task (requiring perhaps violence:
490n.) of παιδεύειν τὸν ἀπαίδευτον. But it is a poignant certainty
that Pol. will in any case be blinded. Cf. *Or.* 1163–4 'I
want to harm my enemies, as I am in any case (πάντως) about to
die.'

495–502. For this form of expression, μακαρισμός, see Norden,
Agnostos Theos, 100, n. 1; Dirichlet, *De Veterum Macarismis* (Giessen,
1914); Snell in *Hermes* 66 (1931), 75; Dodds on *Ba.* 72–5. C. de
Heer, ΜΑΚΑΡ-ΕΥΔΑΙΜΩΝ-ΟΛΒΙΟΣ-ΕΥΤΥΧΗΣ (Amsterdam,
1969), distinguishes between μάκαρ and words of similar meaning.
Even when applied to men μάκαρ never entirely loses its religious
connotation. Now whereas ἔρως (500–503) is frequently the
object of μακαρισμός (Dirichlet, 41–3), the same cannot be said

for secular εὐωχία, wine and the κῶμοc (the closest cases are in comedy: Ar. *Ach.* 1008–10, *Eccl.* 1129, *Ran.* 85). This passage is remarkable as combining the ideal of wine and sex with the solemn formula characteristic of the mysteries: cf. *Ba.* 72–4 μάκαρ ὅcτιc εὐδαίμων τελετὰc θεῶν εἰδὼc βιοτὰν ἁγιcτεύει κτλ (cf. Seaford, art. cit. 469–71n., 253); Richardson on *h. hom. Dem.* 480. (εὐιάζειν too (495) is a religious practice: S. *Ichn.* 227, *Ant.* 1135; *Ba.* 67, 1034.) But this does not mean that the satyrs are indulging in parody, as Rossi believes (art. cit. 483–518n., 21). Rather the contradiction expresses the unique nature of the satyrs: intermediate between man and god, and separated from their god only by accident, the satyrs can on the whole take a more crudely hedonistic view of bliss than the mystic initiate. For the earthly pleasures of the κῶμοc are essentially religious (9n., 39n., 69–70n., 81n.; intro., §III (3)). This is not to say that sometimes even human initiates could not take a similar view (Pl. *Rep.* 363c; F. Graf, *Eleusis und die Orphische Dichtung Athens* (1974), 94–103). Finally, cf. the μακαριcμός at *Ba.* 902–11, which occurs at a similar point in the action (Seaford, art. cit. 469–71n., 260).

495. μάκαρ ὅcτιc (Hermann): cf. *Ba.* 72 μάκαρ ὅcτιc εὐδαίμων κτλ. The corruption was probably by dittography.

496. πηγαῖc is instrumental, to be taken with ἐκπεταcθείc (497). For the idea cf. *HF* 892–3 τᾶc Διονυcιάδοc βοτρύων ἐπὶ χεύμαcι λοιβᾶc.

497. Ussher understands φρέναc or θυμόν, and thinks that the verb is from ἐκπέτομαι, 'your heart agog for'. But for the form he can cite only φρένας ἐκπεπεταcμένος, a variant for ἐκπεπαταγμένος at *Od.* 18.327. In fact the verb is ἐκπετάννυμι, 'spread out'. Wilamowitz (*HF* 890n.) saw an image from wrestling (cf. 454, 678, *HF* 887, *Med.* 585, *Ba.* 202), and read ἐπίκωμοc: this gives 'laid out by the wine as he goes on his way in the κῶμοc, embracing a friend [for support]'. But if we retain L's ἐπὶ κῶμον, the metaphor is more likely nautical, anticipating the corresponding line (505) in the next strophe: 'he proceeds to the κῶμοc with the wind in his sails as a result of the wine . . .': cf. 507–8; Plut. *Mor.* 590c (ψυχήν) ὥcπερ ἱcτίον ἐκπετaννυμένην; *IT* 1135. If on the other hand we take ἐκπεταcθείc literally, we might read ἐπὶ κῶαc (e.g. *Od.* 3.38, 16.47) or ἐπὶ κώδι' (e.g. Pl. *Prot.* 315d), supposing an uncial corruption (AC-ΔI-M) assisted by 445 or 508; cf. 330; and, for ἐπὶ cf. e.g. 352; *Il.* 8.422 ἐπὶ θρόνον . . . ἕζετο. This gives 495–502 as a single scene, in which the reveller has a man on the rug and a woman on the bed as well: there would then be more point to τίc in 502. (ἐπὶ κώμωι (Ussher) gives epic correption (cf. 360), which is impossible here: Maas, *Greek Metre*, §129.)

498. If 497 refers to movement, then the action described here may express, besides affection, the drunken need for support: cf. the drunken Hephaistos with his arm round a satyr for support in *ARV*[2] 1145.36 (= Arias and Hirmer, *A History of Greek Vase Painting*, no. 198). Perhaps Pol. emerged from the cave supported by Sil. (cf. 539, 585).

499–500. δέμνια seems to mean 'bed' rather than 'couch', but the Greeks used the same item for both purposes (G. M. Richter, *The Furniture of the Greeks, Etruscans and Romans* (1966), 52). The scene seems to be that frequently depicted in vase-painting (B. Fehr, *Orientalische und Griechische Gelage*, 32, 34, 43, 90, 104, 115, 119), a man on a couch with a courtesan (cf. Alexis fr. 293). It is imagined either (if 497 refers to being spread out on the couch) as simultaneous with 497–8—i.e. he has both man and girl with him (502n.), or (if 497 refers to the movement ἐπὶ κῶμον, and despite 502n.) as just another typical moment of the revel. The problem is aggravated by a textual difficulty in 499: (1) A pre-penultimate long is unparalleled in anacreontics κατὰ στίχον. (2) The paradosis gives very complicated syntax, in sharp contrast to the rest of the song. (3) ξανθὸν ... βόστρυχον cannot be the object of ἔχων: 501 surely refers to the man, and we would anyway expect ἐχόμενος and the genitive (this tells also against μαστόν (Hartung) and τε κᾶπον (Wecklein)): cf. Ar. *Pax* 863 τῶν τιτθίων ἔχωμαι. Hermann's τε κάλλος and Dindorf's δεμνίοισι τ' ἄνθος would have to mean 'being as beautiful [blooming] as a ἑταίρα'. Possible is ἐπὶ δεμνίοισι τ' ἀνθέων / χλιδανὴν ἔχων ἑταίραν (cf. 582) or even χλιδανῆς ἐρῶν ἑταίρας: for spondaic ἀνθέων cf. e.g. *Med.* 843; for exx. of beds of flowers (roses), especially in an erotic context, see Nisbet and Hubbard on Hor. *Odes* 1.5.1. (e.g. Lucian *Asin.* 7): cf. also Ar. *Eq.* 403; Archil. fr. 196a(West, *Delectus*).42–4; also Anacreon 396 *PMG*. For flowers depicted in this situation see Fehr, op. cit., 79, 94, 100; *ARV*[2] 336.10, 402.12, 467.118. For the genitive cf. e.g. Ar. *Ach.* 992 στέφανος ἀνθέμων, Schwyzer, *Griech. Gramm.*, 2.129, and Pol.'s bed at 386–7 φύλλων ἐλατίνων ... εὐνήν. The ξ may derive from a gloss ἐξ ἀνθέων. But if δέμνιον is thought too concrete ('bedstead'), another possibility is that if there was a mention of the rug in 497 (n.), ἐπὶ δεμνίοισι was originally a gloss on it.

500. χλιδανᾶς (Diggle; χλιδανῆς L); but rather than introducing Doric forms here and at 504 (ἥβης L) in convivial (Ionic) Anacreontics (cf. e.g. Anacreon 395 *PMG* χαρίεσσα δ' οὐκέτ' ἥβη), it might be better to read νύμφη in 515.

501–2. (509–10, 517–18). 'The pure ionic dimeter as the penultimate phrase in anacreontics is characteristic of Anacreon himself' (Dale, op. cit. 53n., 126): cf. *PMG* 395. With the final clausula cf. *Ba.* 72, 536 = 555. The synapheia between 501 and 502 suggests a pentameter, but the strong break after 509 a final trimeter.

501. μυρόχριστος λιπαρός L; better perhaps than **λιπαρόν** (Scaliger) is μυρόχριστον λιπαρός (Musgrave): cf. *Od.* 15.332 λιπαροὶ κεφαλὰς καὶ καλὰ πρόσωπα. Men often put unguents on their hair in the κῶμος: *RE* iA. 1854–6 (s. Salben); Nisbet and Hubbard on Hor. *Odes* 1.4.9.

502. Θύραν τίς οἴξει μοι; alludes to the παρακλαυσίθυρον, the song sung by the κωμάζων outside his beloved's closed door (483–518n.; cf. e.g. Ar. *Eccl.* 962; the rustic ex. in Theocr. *Id.* 3; F. O. Copley, *Exclusus Amator*). But this does not preclude (as Copley, op. cit., 146) a sexual *double entendre*: cf. Ar. *Eccl.* 990: ὅταν γε κρούσῃς τὴν ἐμὴν πρῶτον θύραν (the door or gate as a sexual image: J. Taillardat, *Les Images d'Aristophane*, 70–1, 77; Headlam on A. *Ag.* 609; Wills in *CQ* 20 (1970), 113; Archil. fr. 196a(West, *Delectus*).21). Indeed, it seems that the satyrs are subtly dissuading Pol. from going out on his κῶμος (451, 492n., 508, 511–18n.), by saying effectively: 'The question "who will open the door for me?" is most pleasantly asked by someone who has a girl [and a man? 497n.] on the couch with him, not by somebody actually standing in the street outside a door.' Cf. 511–18n. τίς may express (497n.) a choice between the φίλος ἀνήρ (498) and the ἑταίρα (500–501); cf. 581–4n. (The satyrs exhibit both homosexuality and heterosexuality: intro., n. 109.)

503. Pol. has emerged from the cave (491) with a cup (411, 556) and accompanied by Sil. (431, 539), who may be carrying a large mixing-bowl (388, 545). Entries within a lyric structure are rare: see Taplin, *The Stagecraft of Aeschylus*, 174. Pol. probably performs some clumsy dance steps, although Schol. Theocr. 7.153 ἐξ Εὐριπίδου μετήνεγκε τὸ χορεῦσαι τὸν Κύκλωπα may be a guess. Pol. certainly danced in Philoxenos' *Cyclops* (Ar. *Plut.* 290; *PMG* 819); cf. Hor. *Sat.* 1.5.63, *Epist.* 2.2.124. **παπαπαῖ:** the form πα πα πᾶ (L) is found elsewhere only at S. *Phil.* 746 (apparently), in the wild expression of pain ἀπαππαπαῖ παπᾶ παπᾶ παπᾶ παπαῖ. παπαῖ, on the other hand, is frequent as an expression of grief (e.g. *Alc.* 226) or surprise: e.g. 572, where Pol. says παπαῖ, σοφόν γε τὸ ξύλον τῆς ἀμπέλου; and cf. 153 παπαιάξ, ὡς καλὴν ὀσμὴν ἔχει. And so there is a good case for παπαπαῖ (Hermann) here. For the extended form cf. Ar. *Thesm.* 1191 ὃ ὃ ὃ παπαπαπαῖ, ὡς γλυκερὸ τὸ γλῶσσα. **πλέως** κτλ.: εἰμί is omitted: see Denniston on *El.* 37; K-G i 40; Bond on *HF* 628.

504. ⟨δὲ⟩ (Tr. 3) is an acceptable conjecture; δέ may have been lost because phonetically identical in later Greek with δαι-. **ἥβαι** (ἥβης L; read perhaps **ἥβηι**: 500n.): for the sense cf. Pi. *Pyth.* 4.295 cυμπocίαc ἐφέπων θυμὸν ἐκδόcθαι πρὸc ἥβαν πολλάκιc (the joy associated with youth). But if δαιτὸc ἥβη is thought curious, consideration should be given to **ἥδη** (Stephanus): δαιτὸc then goes with γεμιcθείc; and cf. the sense and position of ἥδη at Anacr. 432 *PMG* κνυζή τιc ἥδη καὶ πέπειρα γίνομαι cὴν διὰ μαργocύνην.

505–6 mean literally 'loaded as to my hull [cκάφoc], like a cargo-ship [ὁλκὰc ὥc], right up to the deck at the top of my belly', or simply 'loaded like a cargo-ship hull . . .' (cf. A. *Ag.* 661 ναῦν τ' ἀκήρατον cκάφoc). And so ὁλκάδoc (Wecklein in *RhM* 36 (1881), 142) is unnecessary (for the position of ὥc cf. *HF* 869 ταῦρoc ὥc ἐc ἐμβολήν). γεμιcθείc, though a commonplace in this sense (362n.; Pherecr. 143; Meleag. 4616 (Gow and Page) κωμάζω δ' οὐκ οἶνον ὑπὸ φρένα πῦρ δὲ γεμιcθείc), is here part of a vivid image, the cargo-ship full of wine. We are reminded, despite the carefree tone, of the horror of 362. For **ἄκραc** see 293n.

507. φόρτoc, 'cargo', continues the metaphor of 505–6, whereas χόρτoc (L) gives little sense. A ὁλκάc is literally a ship that needs towing. But Pol. is drawn along (ὑπάγει) by his own cargo, the wine; cf. Antiph. fr. 3 ὅλην μύcαc ἔκπινε.—μέγα τὸ φορτίον (Diggle, art. cit. 39n., 43 n. 3; W. Schulze, *Kleine Schriften*, 713); and *Alc.* 798 . . . μεθορμιεῖ cε πίτυλoc ἐμπεcὼν cκύφου, where the noise of wine is compared to the noise of oars. **εὔφρων:** εὐφρocύνη, caused by the wine, is transferred to the wine itself: cf. *Il.* 3.246 οἶνον ἐΰφρονα; Xenophan. fr. 1.4 κρατὴρ . . . μεcτὸc ἐΰφρocύνηc; Fraenkel on A. *Ag.* 806; Kazantzakis, Ζυρβᾶc, 148: (the abundance of food so carefully prepared, the glowing brazier . . .) πόco ἁπλὰ καὶ γρήγορα μετουcιώνουνταν cὲ μεγάλη ψυχικὴ εὐφρocύνη. The idea is particularly apt here, inasmuch as the wine is the subject of ὑπάγει.

508. ἐπὶ κῶμον: ἐπίκωμον Wecklein; but cf. 445n.; and ἐπί in the next line supports ἐπί here too (cf. 511, 512). **ἦρoc ὥραιc:** cf. Ar. *Nub.* 1008 ἦρoc ἐν ὥραι. *Cyc.* was performed in springtime, at the Great Dionysia (P-Cambridge, op. cit. 1n., 41); and this was also the opening of the sailing season (Theophr. *Char.* 3): cf. 505–7.

510. The original reading of L is illegible; but most likely it was as P (φέρε ξέν'). After P had been copied Triclinius (Tr. 3) rubbed most of this out and substituted ξεῖνε φέρ'. It is no doubt a metrical conjecture, and Zuntz rejects it: perhaps E. 'preferred the metrical variation as being suitable to the popular style of the song' (op. cit. 73–4n., 53). But the conjecture is in fact acceptable. ξεν- and ξειν- are variants at fr. 132; S. *OC* 174. And elsewhere the song is

metrically pure (499–500n.), as are the very similar songs of
Anacreon at *PMG* 356, 395, 396.

511–18. The song now passes from the κῶμος to the wedding
(511–12n., 512n., 513n., 517n., 515 νύμφα). The transition is not
as arbitrary as it may appear, inasmuch as the post-prandial
torchlit movement through the streets, with the object of sexual
union at its destination, was common to both. And for the drunk
bridegroom see Theocr. 18.11; Plut. *Lyc.* 15. Furthermore, the
allusion to the wedding is in keeping both with the satyric genre
(intro., §IV; esp. A. *Dikt.* 821–3) and with the allusion to the
mysteries in the first verse (495–502n.), as the two rituals are
closely associated (both are τελεταί; and see Dem. 18.259; Plut.
Prov. 16; Firm. Matern. *De Err. Prof. Rel.* 104). In their previous
verse the chorus seemed to be implying that to have sex available
at the symposium itself is preferable to having to go out on a κῶμος
for it (502n.). Here they add the necessary complement, that it
is indeed available in the cave (515–16). Furthermore, if there
is a sexual *double entendre* in δροcερῶν ἔcωθεν ἄντρων (516; so
Henderson, op. cit. 171n., 27), it picks up the similar ambiguity in
θύραν (502n.). The point is to reverse Pol.'s intention to go out ἐπὶ
κῶμον (451, 508).

511–12. Complimenting the bridegroom was a feature of the
wedding-song: Sappho frr. 111, 112, 115, 116; Ar. *Pax* 1349;
Catull. 61.190–2; Sen. *Med.* 82–92. And with καλὸν ... καλὸc
cf. the hymenaeal μετ᾽ ἐμοῦ καλή / καλῶc κατακείcει at Ar. *Pax*
1330–1.

511. Cf. 533. ὄμμαcι (L) was corrected by Triclinius (Tr. 2): cf.
144n., *Pho.* 1115.

512. καλὸc (Scaliger; καλὸν L) is probably right. Possible too is
ἐκπερᾶιc (Heath; cf. 518, 514), or the imperative ἐκπέρα
(Scaliger). This may allude to the emergence of the bridegroom
after the feast at the bride's house, before the procession to his own;
whereas in Sappho's hymenaeal fr. 111 ἴψοι δὴ τὸ μέλαθρον ...
γάμβροc + εἰcέρχεται ἴcοc + Ἄρευι seems to refer to an entry.

513. With τίc (L) the satyrs may be suggesting that (whereas Pol.
has a νύμφα waiting for him) nobody loves *them*; or alternatively
the line is spoken by Pol. With unaccentuated τιc they suggest that
Pol. has erotic designs on them (cf. 585–9; Stinton in *JHS* 97
(1977), 138–9.). But of course the clause may well be incomplete:
remedies for the metre have included καλὸc ὢν (Musgrave),
παπαπᾶ (Murray), κελαδῶν (Diggle). The line may allude to wedding banter (cf. Sappho frr. 110a, 111; Theocr. 18.9–15; Ar. *Pax*
1336–57; Hsch. s. κτυπιῶν).

514–5. Diggle prints what is in L. Murray thought ἀμμένει a correction; but it seems in fact to be Triclinius' (Tr. 3) clarification of an obscure compendium, and this is confirmed by the fact that P (copied before Tr. 3) has ἀμμένει. But the paradosis is hopelessly corrupt, both in metre and sense. Presumably the irony apparent in 516–18 begins here: cf. the irony of *Hec.* 1281 φόνια λουτρά c' ἀμμένει (cf. *Ba.* 964, *Ion* 578; Seaford in *CQ* 31 (1981), 272 n. 191; also S. *Trach.* 527 τὸ δ' ἀμφινεικητὸν ὄμμα νύμφας ἐλεινὸν ἀμμένει). But if so, then Diggle's λύχνα δ' ἀμμένειν ἐάσον·/ ῥόδα, φῶc, τέρεινα νύμφα (in *Maia* 24 (1972), 345–6: cf. Alcaeus fr. 346; he lists previous conjectives) fails to provide a *sous-entendre*; and conjectures which retain δάϊα or have χρόα as the object of λύχνα δ' ἀμμένει (e.g. λύχνα δ' ἀμμένει πάλαι còv/χρόα καὶ τέρεινα νύμφα) are too explicit, failing to provide an ostensible meaning to cover the *sous-entendre*. To meet these requirements Stinton (*JHS* 97 (1977), 139) proposed λύχνα δ' ἀμμένει còv ὄμμα,/χρόα χρώc, τέρεινα νύμφα (cf. the conjugal burning at *Su.* 1019–21, Evadne cῶμά τ' αἴθοπι φλογμῶι πόcει cυμμείξαcα, φίλον χρῶτα χρωτὶ πέλαc θεμένα; Theocr. 2.140), 'with τέρεινα νύμφα in apposition, in the first place to χρῶc, more remotely (with *sous-entendre*) to λύχνα'. But given the relative simplicity of the uncorrupted parts of the song, perhaps we should read something like

> λύχνα c' ἡμμέν' ἀμμένει καὶ
> ῥοδόχρωc τέρεινα νύμφα.

ἡμμέν' ἀμμένει (Dindorf) would be easily corrupted by haplography (and δ for c in minuscule: e.g. 690, *Ba.* 600; A. *Cho.* 182), and attempts to emend would follow. E is fond of -χρωc adjectives (e.g. μελάγχρωc, πολιόχρωc, χιονόχρωc); ῥοδόχρωc describes the bride in Theocritus' epithalamium (18.31), its *sous-entendre* here the red-glowing stake (457; the bride at Greek weddings was veiled), and this gives a point to cτεφάνων δ' οὐ μιὰ χροιά (517). Of the λύχνα the *sous-entendre* is the fire. λύχνα were a signal for the evening revel (Alcaeus fr. 346), and necessary both in a cave (fr. 421) and in the bridal-chamber (Musae. 275–6). But all this is highly conjectural. Given the hymenaeal context, the irony would be better suited by a torch (δάϊc; cf. e.g. Schol. *Pho.* 344), which some have seen lurking in δάϊα (e.g. λύχνα δ' ἀμμένει cε δάιδων (Wecklein).

516. The cειληνοί make love in caves at *h. hom.* 5.262; (cf. *Ion* 17; etc.). **δροcερῶν** may allude to the blood of Pol.'s recent victims (cf. *IT* 443 δρόcον αἱματηράν; Stinton in *JHS* 97 (1977), 139), but is more likely a sexual *double entendre* (511–18n.).

517. Cf. 559. The bridegroom wore a ϲτέφανοϲ (*ARV²* 527.73, etc.; Plut. *Mor.* 771d) of many colours (Ar. *Av.* 159–61 with schol.; Ov. *Fast.* 4.869; schol. Ar. *Pax.* 869), and his house and bed were similarly decorated (W. Erdmann, *Die Ehe im Alten Griechenland*, 257). Cf. also *PMG* 818. The *sous-entendre* consists in the many colours of Pol.'s wound (cf. *Od.* 9.388–90, 397 πεφυρμένον αἵματι πολλῶι). The grotesque idea may derive from the bloodying of crowns worn by sacrificial victims (Stengel, op. cit. 469–71n., 108), or from the association in the dirge (A. *Ag.* 1460–1; Bion 1.35, 41, 66, 75) of the funeral crown with blood.

518. ἐξομιλήϲει, as a neutral verb, suits the irony. Cf. S. *Aj.* 1199–1201 ἐκεῖνοϲ οὔτε ϲτεφάνων / οὔτε βαθειᾶν κυλίκων / νεῖμεν ἐμοὶ τέρψιν ὁμιλεῖν; Plut. *Mor.* 79c (= *PMG* 593) ἄνθεϲιν ὁμιλεῖν; Hp. *Medic.* 3 ὁμιλεῖν ... τῶι νοϲοῦντι μέρει (bandages etc.), *Art.* 1. The ἐξ- conveys perhaps a hint that this will not be casual consorting.

519–28. For the identity of Dionysos and wine cf. 156, 454, 67n., Dodds on *Ba.* 284; Handley on Men. *Dysk.* 946; Burkert, *Homo Necans*, 249; Seaford, art. cit. 514–5n., 273.

521. Most editions take this line as a single question. But then, as Ussher points out, τίϲ has to mean ποῖοϲ, and Pol. assumes without being told that Βάκχιοϲ is a god. And so for τούτου (520) Hermann reads θεοῦ, and for τίϲ (521) Ussher reads τιϲ (comparing *Od.* 9.142). But these difficulties are better overcome by printing a question mark after τίϲ, also perhaps by giving θεὸϲ νομίζεται to Od. (Wieseler): for the resultant verse form cf. *IA* 1460. The isolated ἀντιλαβή would be no more unnatural than at *Hel.* 1514, *Ba.* 189. For the postponed interrogative τίϲ see G. Thomson in *CQ* 23 (1939), 148: 'When a word is taken up by one speaker from another ... the repeated word usually becomes emphatic in Greek and accordingly is placed first.' Cf. *Ba.* 470–1 καὶ δίδωϲιν ὄργια. Penth.: τὰ δ' ὄργι' ἐϲτὶ τίν' ἰδέαν ἔχοντά ϲοι;, where the context is strikingly similar: information about Dionysos is imparted to an ἀμαθήϲ (173, *Ba.* 480, 490) who is to be destroyed; see further Seaford, art. cit. 514–15n.; *Ba.* 274–85. The commentators have remarked on the more obvious parallel with Bdelykleon's education of his father (Ar. *Vesp.* 1122–64). Similar scenes may have occurred elsewhere in satyric drama: cf. Ion *Omphale* fr. 24; Achaios *Hephaistos* fr. 17, *Linos* (education of Herakles in music?); A. *Lykourgos* (wine-drinking?: intro., n. 66); S. *Ach. Erast.*, *Krisis* (rustic educators of Paris? cf. Hygin. *Fab.* 91. 3); anon. *Mathetai* (Trag. adesp. 5g).

523. Pol.'s belch in Homer (*Od.* 9.374; cf. V. *Aen.* 3.622–3) provides material here for an irreverent joke.

524. This is of course a lie: 422n., *Ba.* 860–1 (Seaford, art. cit. 514–15n., 261).

525. Correlated or contrasted terms may gravitate together at the beginning of the sentence, thereby necessitating the postponement of the interrogative: Thomson, art. cit. 521n., 148; e.g. *El.* 977 ἐγὼ δὲ μητρὸς οὐ φόνου δώcω δίκαc;

526 refers to the liquidity of the wine, and so to its easy adaptability to any container: εὐμενήc (Kirchhoff) is unnecessary. Cf. *Ba.* 477–8.

527. cῶμ': to emend (δῶμ' Pierson; πῶμ' Bernadakis; c' ὧδ' Nauck) is to spoil the joke: skins were worn only by the lower orders (8on.). E. may also be thinking of the irony that in fact Dionysos does wear animal skins (νεβρίc and πάρδαλιc).

528. ἠ (Blaydes) is perhaps better than ἦ (129n., 207n.).

529. Wecklein sees a sexual joke in ἀcκόν here and at 510, and compares *Med.* 679 (cf. also Archil. fr. 119). This seems unlikely. True, without it the remark seems ponderous and pointless; but that is true of stichomythia sometimes, and of débuts in drunkenness frequently. Still, there may be some point now lost.

531. Cf. 445, 507–9. προcδοῦναι: cf. 245n., 361n.

532. At 452–3 Od. planned to invoke ἡδονή rather than τιμή. Cf. 540–2.

534. is quoted at Athen. 36d as a single line (πληγὰc ὁ κῶμοc λοίδορόν θ' ὕβριν φέρει), and so perhaps from memory, which would account for its discrepancies. For the thought cf. Panyas. fr. 13; Epich. fr. 148; Ar. *Vesp.* 1253, *Eccl.* 664; Euboul. fr. 94; Alexis fr. 156; Isaeus 3.13; Headlam on Herodas 2.34 gives exx. of violent κῶμοι; cf. 39n.

535. Duchemin, and Stanford (*Ambiguity in Greek Literature*, 105), see here an allusion to the famous Οὖτιc joke. This is over-subtle. In fact the allusion occurs at 548–50.

536. Rossi (art. cit. 483–518n., 30) considers this line a parody of the proverb οἴκοι μένειν χρὴ (or δεῖ) τὸν καλῶc εὐδαίμονα (fr. 793.1; A. fr. 317; Pearson on S. fr. 934). But a better *parody* would have been οἴκοι μένειν χρὴ τὸν καλῶc πεπωκότα. ὦ τᾶν: cf. Panyas. fr. 13.10 ἀλλὰ πέπον, μέτρον γὰρ ἔχειc γλυκεροῖο ποτοῖο, / cτεῖχε παρὰ μνηcτὴν ἄλοχον, κτλ.

537–8. It is ironic that it is Pol., after his first experience of wine, who displays Hellenic urbanity in his desire to sally forth ἐπὶ κῶμον after drinking (Headlam on Herodas 2.34), from which he must be dissuaded by his Greek educators.

538. δὲ…γε is common in lively interchanges in drama (Denniston, *GP*, 153). And so αὖ for ἂν (Reiske) is unnecessary.

539. Pol. shows the same misplaced trust in Sil. as at 273–4.

541 is surely spoken by Od. (Mancini in *SIFC* 7 (1899), 448). Both καὶ μήν and καὶ ... γε (542) express assent (Denniston, *GP*, 157-9, 353-5). But if Pol. assents here, 542-3 are unnecessary. In fact he assents at 544, after a crescendo of persuasion. **γ' οὐδᾶς:** τοὐδᾶς (L) is defended by Kassel (art. cit. 99n., 105); cf. Hipponax fr. 118.5 τοὺς. **ἀνθηρᾶς χλόης:** ἀνθηρᾶι χλόηι Kirchhoff; but the genitive is perhaps defensible, either with λαχνῶδες (on the analogy of e.g. *Od.* 5.72-3 λειμῶνες μαλακοὶ ἴου ἠδὲ σελίνου θήλεον; S. *El.* 895-6 περιστεφῆ ... ἀνθέων, *OC* 16 βρύων δάφνης) or with οὐδᾶς (cf. *Od.* 4.124 τάπητα ... μαλακοῦ ἐρίοιο; Hdt. 1.93 ἡ κρηπίς ἐστι λίθων μεγάλων).

542. For the thought cf. Alcaeus fr. 347, for πρὸς ἥλιον Ar. *Vesp.* 772. Cf. also the expression πρὸς τὸ πῦρ πίνειν (Ar. *Ach.* 751, *Pax* 1131; Pl. *Rep.* 372c, 420e). For the problem of the time of day raised by this line see 213-14n.

543. Cf. Ar. *Vesp.* 1208-9 ἀλλὰ δευρὶ κατακλινεὶς προσμάνθανε / ξυμποτικὸς εἶναι καὶ ξυνουσιαστικός (Bdelykleon to his father). **κλίθητί:** cf. fr. 691, from the satyric *Syleus*: κλίθητι καὶ πίωμεν. **μοι** means effectively 'next to me'; cf. δευρὶ κατακλινεὶς quoted above. Greek painting shows pairs of men at symposia reclining in a close proximity to each other which is sometimes amorous, as in the famous tomb-painting from Paestum (see e.g. M. Napoli, *La Tomba del Tuffatore* (Bari, 1970)), and which may be Sil.'s undoing here (581 τόνδ' ἔχων).

544. **ἰδού** was added *extra metrum* (Tr. 1), almost certainly from the MS from which L was copied. It was then apparently overlooked by the scribe of P (Zuntz, op. cit. 73-4n., 55). Cf. εἶεν *extra metrum* after Ar. *Eq.* 1237, ἰοὺ ἰού *extra metrum* at 464, 576. ἰδού accompanies obedience to a command at 562, *Ba.* 934; Ar. *Ran* 200-201 (more exx. given by Amati in *SIFC* 9 (1901), 139).

545. **ἐμοῦ:** coῦ Wecklein, on the grounds that Sil. and Pol. are facing each other (543 μοι; 547 ἐς μέσον). But I imagine that Sil., as οἰνοχόος (560), keeps on the move. In fact this passage, up to 565, appears to represent a piece of traditional satyric slapstick. A number of vase-paintings from the earliest years of satyric drama show the satyrs serving Dionysos and Herakles at the symposium, and making a nuisance of themselves (Buschor, art. cit. 210n., 84, 91-6; cf. 213-14n). For drinking directly from the κρατήρ (547) see 146n. ἀλλοτριοφάγοι in S. fr. 329 probably refers to the satyrs, but as parasites no doubt rather than food-stealers. **τίθης:** τιθεῖς L. The two forms are variants at *Alc.* 890, *Andr.* 210; at *Ion* 741 L has τιθεῖς, elsewhere τίθης (in the compound προστίθης)

546. L has καταλάβηι, but of this verb the middle would be better here. The confusion between βαλ- and λαβ- occurs elsewhere, e.g. at *IT* 637 (between L and P). With καταβάληι, παρίων (Reiske) is better than L's παρών.

548–51. Od.'s famous trick is essential in Homer (*Od.* 9.355–70, 403–12), but here prepares for nothing more than satyric taunting (672–5). The abruptness of its introduction may owe something to previous dramatists: cf. Cratin. fr. 141 quoted 376n.; 342–4n.

549. Οὖτιν has, as a name, a recessive accent. **ἐπαινέcω** may be future, or aorist subjunctive.

550. ὕcτερον: ὕcτατον Hermann, comparing πύματον at *Od.* 9.369. For the confusion of comparative and superlative see 101n.

551. Some editors reproduce L's attribution of this line to Od., because Sil. is drinking and so neither capable nor desirous of drawing attention to himself. But (1) Sil. is unable to resist the quip (cf. 250–2, 313–15), which (2) assists the action (Pol. turns to Sil., and notices the theft of wine); (3) Od. is unlikely to refer to himself as τῶι ξένωι.

552. Sil. may have done what Pol. asked him at 547, but the conversation between Pol. and Od. allowed him to drink more wine. **οὗτος** here means 'hey, you!', as at e.g. *Alc.* 773.

553–5. For the satyric confusion of drinking objects and sex objects see 172n., 439–40n.

555. οὐ (Diggle, art. cit. 39n., 48); but L's ναί may be right: Sil. affirms what he implies in 553, and contradicts Od.: 'Yes, by Jove, (he does love me) since he says he is in love with me for my good looks.' Cf. Ar. *Eq.* 338 X. οὐκ αὖ μ' ἐάcειc; Y. μὰ Δία X. ναὶ μὰ Δία; Pearson on S. *Ichn.* 112–13.

556. There should be no punctuation after cκύφον: 'pour, and give me the cup only when it is full' (πλέων in emphatic position).

557. Sil. presumably buries his head in the large κρατήρ, like the satyr depicted on the Geneva cup (146n.). Despite 147 (n.) the wine may in fact be unmixed (558n.).

558. ἀπολεῖc: understand με (cf. ἀπολεῖc at Ar. *Nub.* 893, 1499, *Pax* 166, *Eccl.* 775, *Plut.* 390, etc.), and perhaps also (as *sous-entendre*) τὸν οἶνον: cf. Aristias fr. 4 ἀπώλεcαc τὸν οἶνον ἐπιχέαc ὕδωρ (from his satyric *Cyclops*). In Achaios fr. 9 it seems that one satyr asks μῶν Ἀχελῶιος ἦν κεκραμένος πολύς; and another replies ἀλλ' οὐδὲ λεῖξαι τοῦδε τῶι γένει θέμις; **οὕτως:** 'without further ado', as at S. *Ant.* 315 εἰπεῖν τι δώcειc, ἢ cτραφεὶς οὕτως ἴω;, *Phil.* 1067; *Alc.* 680. **οὐ μὰ Δί':** ναί (L) 'is strangely combined with a following negation' (Paley), and is defensible only as part of the slapstick: Sil. buys time by agreeing to Pol.'s request, but then immediately, in order to take another gulp, qualifies his agreement (cf. 560n.). But probably we should read οὐ.

559. **ϲτέφανον:** wearing a crown of leaves was standard practice in drinking sessions: see e.g. the vase-painting referred to 545n.; *Alc.* 796, 832. Nevertheless, the audience might remember 517 (n.). **τ' ἔτι** (L) is a scribal interpretation, but better than τέ τι (Nauck).

560. **οἰνοχόοϲ … οἶνοϲ:** i.e. ὁ οἰνοχόοϲ … ὁ οἶνοϲ. L has rasura before μὰ (the Byzantines thought that μά is long: Wilamowitz, *Anal. Eur.*, 12). As a supplement editors prefer Hermann's **οὔ**; but there is much to be said for ναί (Aldina): it is comic that Sil. should agree with Pol., but then introduce a more powerful consideration (cf. 558n.). Cf. ναί, ἀλλὰ at Aeschin. *Ctes.* 28, 84.

561. **ἀπομακτέον,** '[your mouth] must be wiped [of wine]', is Cobet's correction of L's ἀπομυκτέον. The latter means 'your nose must be wiped [of mucus]'. Certainly, mucus can run onto the mouth and its surrounding hair (562): Plaut. *Asin.* 796 *tu labellum abstergeas* (compared by Kassel, art. cit. 296n., 279). And it is true that Clement (*Paed.* ii 7.60.1) mentions ἀπομύττεϲθαι παρὰ πότον (along with τὸ ϲυνεχὲϲ ἀποπτύειν καὶ τὸ χρέμπτεϲθαι βιαιότερον) as a sign of ἀκοϲμία and ἀκραϲία. But because there is no reason to suppose that Pol. is suffering from a running cold ἀπομυκτέον can be defended only as an imaginative delaying tactic by Sil., who has experience as a nurse (intro., §IV). **coὺϲτὶν ὡϲ,** i.e. ϲοι ἐϲτὶν ὡϲ (Dodds on *Ba.* 1256–7). In L's ϲοι ὡϲ there is, *pace* Murray, no gap between ϲοι and ὡϲ. δ' ὅπ' above the line is Tr. 1 (Zuntz, op.cit. 73–4n., 55), but as a metrical change is likely to be conjectural (Zuntz, 197), and provides no support for ϲοὺϲθ' ὅπωϲ (Paley). **λήψηι πιεῖν:** see 257n.

562. Cf. Pentheus' response to the demeaning attentions paid him by Dionysos: *Ba.* 934 ἰδού, ϲὺ κόϲμει.

563. Cf. Philokleon being instructed by Bdelykleon (Ar. *Vesp.* 1210): πῶϲ οὖν κατακλινῶ; φράζ' ἁνύϲαϲ. Bd. εὐϲχημόνωϲ. **νυν:** Tr. 2 deleted the accent and, presumably as a further designation of the enclitic, added δή over the word: cf. W. J. W. Koster, *Autour d'un Manuscrit d'Aristophane Ecrit par Demetrius Triclinius,* (Groeningen, 1957), 234–5. **ἔκπιε:** for this form of the imperative cf. Men. fr. 151.

564. **οὐκ ἐμέ** has been taken to mean that Sil. has finished the wine and so is no longer drinking; but this would be better expressed by οὐκέτι, which Nauck reads. In fact the line probably means: 'as you see me drinking—and as now' (he drinks probably from the large κρατήρ: cf. 388, 545, 557n.) 'I am no longer to be seen' (Diggle in *PCPS* 22 (1969), 333). Cf. 577 ἐξένευϲα μόγιϲ. For ἐμέ after enclitic με cf. *Andr.* 752–4 and other exx. cited in Diggle in *Maia* 24 (1972), 348. Alternatively read οὐχί με (the emphatic negative is apt).

565 ἡμύcτιcα means that Sil. has succeeded in emptying the κρατήρ (?564n.) at a single draught. Compare the speed with which the slave Demosthenes drinks the stolen wine at Ar. *Eq.* 118–24.

566. L's λαβών was probably an attempt to create syntax after TE had become ΓΕ. Cf. Ar. *Eq.* 106 λαβὲ δή καὶ cπεῖcον ἀγαθοῦ δαίμονοc.

567. Cf. 519–20. Od. accepts the lowly office of οἰνοχόοc with a dignified periphrasis.

568. Pol. may have displayed the same impatience in Epicharmos' *Cyclops*: fr. 83 φέρ' ἐγχέαc εἰc τὸ cκύφοc.

569. Of the ellipse of οἶνον (cf. 573) Gow on Theocr. 18.11 gives exx.

571. ἐκθνήιcκειν regularly means to become as dead (through fainting or uncontrollable laughter). To say that Pol. *should* swoon with (cυν-) the drink is a compressed way of saying that he should drink the whole cup at one draught (570, 575), even if it renders him unconscious (as it may well) as the drink runs out ('dies'). The compressed version was probably a drinking saw (152n.), used here perhaps for the *double entendre* in -θανεῖν, and may indeed seem perfectly logical to anyone who has been challenged to drink a pint of beer ἀμυcτί. Cf. 577 ἐξένευcα μόγιc, 677n.

572. It seems that Pol. may be projecting his new mental state onto the wine (313–15n., 507n.). But there may also be a suggestion of the wine as Βάκχιοc (519–27, 575; cf. 67, 156, 454; cf. Diphilos fr. 86 ὦ πᾶcι τοῖc φρονοῦcι προcφιλέcτατε / Διόνυcε καὶ cοφώτατε; *Ba.* 395), perhaps also of the ξύλον as a club: cf. 571 cυνεκθανεῖν; 210n.; Arnott, op. cit. 228n., 28.

574. Cf. 326; Alcaeus fr. 347 τέγγε πλεύμοναc οἴνωι. **ἄδιψον** is proleptic (575n.), rather than meaning (Paley) 'when not thirsty [i.e. not waiting until you are so]'. Cf. alpha-privative adjectives proleptic at *Med.* 435; A. *Pers.* 298; S. *Ant.* 881, *OC* 1200. **ὕπνον**: cf. *Ba.* 282–3, 385; Ar. *Vesp.* 9; Hor. *Od.* 3.21.4. **βαλεῖ** (Musgrave; βαλεῖc L) is rightly supported by Fraenkel on A. *Ag.* 1172.

575. At 572 Pol. has clearly just drunk some of the wine. And so either he did not do what Od. asked him in 571, and left some wine in the cup, or he did drink it all and Od. has now refilled it. If the latter, then ἢν δ' ἐλλίπηιc τι ('but if you leave any in it') may refer to the ἀcκόc rather than to the cup. **ξηρανεῖ**: the thought seems to be that Dionysos makes the liquid a necessity: cf. 574 τέγξαc; and the contradictory 524.

576. **ἰοὺ ἰού**: cf. 464n. Od. has succeeded in persuading Pol. to drink a lot of wine quickly.

577. ἐξένευca μόγιc: 'I just managed to swim out': the death implied in 571 might indeed feel like drowning, inasmuch as the drinker runs out of breath. Cf. Petr. *Sat.* 21.6 *vino etiam Falerno inundamur*; 677n.. **ἄκρατοc ἡ χάριc:** cf. 602; S. fr. 941.4–5 ἵμεροc ἄκρατοc. There is probably also a play on οἶνοc ἄκρατοc: despite 557 (n.) the wine may be unmixed (558n.). Cf. e.g. *Hellenistic Epigrams* 3668 (Gow and Page) ἄκρητον μανίην ἔπιον.

578–80. This vision should be compared with Pentheus', another victim of Dionysos, at *Ba.* 918–22. They both form part of a pattern of Dionysiac initiation: 495–502n.; Seaford, art. cit. 514–15n., 273. Cf. also the vision in the mysteries of Isis described by Apuleius (*Met.* 11.23): *deos inferos et deos superos accessi coram et adoravi de proxumo*; A. Dieterich, *Eine Mithras-Liturgie*, 10–20: εἶτα ἄνοιξον τοὺc ὀφθαλμοὺc καὶ ὄψει ἀνεωγυίαc τὰc θύραc καὶ τὸν κόcμον τῶν θεῶν ὅc ἐcτιν ἐντὸc τῶν θυρῶν. It is possible that ἐξένευcα in 577 was chosen with the mystic theme in mind: escaping from the sea was an image of Dionysiac initiation: *Ba.* 902–3 (Seaford art. cit. 514–15n., 260); cf. Philodam., *Paean in Dion.* (Powell, 165–9), 35–6; and Apuleius again (11.15). 578 also reflects traditional popular belief about the original mixture of earth and sky (fr. 484, 898; A. fr. 44; Hes. *Th.* 116; D.S. 1.7.1; A.R. 1.496; cf. also fr. 687, from the satyric *Syleus*).

579–80. This vision does not overthrow Pol.'s assumption that he is a god no less powerful than Zeus (231, 320). Such is Pol.'s egoism that rather than adoring the throne of Zeus (578–80n.), he seems to believe that it is occupied by himself: for he takes his cup-bearer Sil. to be Ganymede the cup-bearer of Zeus (586n.).

581–3. Pol.'s mystic vision of the gods now takes on a sexual content (not inappropriately: 511–18n.). The κῶμοc will end in sex after all, and indeed in precisely the choice of male or female apparently alluded to at 502 (581–4n.). And there is irony in the fact that the satyrs are more often the perpetrators than the victims of rape (intro., §IV).

581–4. Pol. is so monstrous (327–8n.) that he takes the satyrs to be αἱ Χάριτεc and Sil. to be Ganymede; cf. Pentheus seeing Dionysos as a bull at *Ba.* 920–2, and Orestes seeing Elektra as a Fury at *Or.* 264–5. Sil. is hairier and even more brutish than his sons, and so he appears to Pol. as less female. This presents Pol. with a dilemma (502n.), which he resolves in favour of τὰ παιδικά, i.e. Ganymede. We need therefore in 581 the question mark after φιλήcαιμι (Wilamowitz), and perhaps also πῶc (Herwerden) for οὐκ. Pol. will get better relief (ἀναπαύcομαι κάλλιον) with 'Ganymede' than with 'the Graces'. (L's νὴ τὰc Χάριταc is odd after their appearance two lines earlier, and νή is not found elsewhere in E.: the emergence of NH from ΚΑΛΛΙΟΝΗΤΑϹ left ΚΑΛΛΙΟ, which required emendation: cf. 101n.) This change also requires punctuation after ἅλιϲ (Wecklein, comparing S. *Aj.* 1402): 'Stop! [to the Graces, who are tempting him] I prefer Ganymede...' Otherwise ἅλιϲ ἔχων has to be understood with τὰϲ Χάριτας, which ruins the sense. κάλλιϲτον ἤ (Paganelli in *Emerita* 49 (1981), 142) is impossible (cf. Stevens on *Andr.* 7).

582. Γανυμήδη: Γανυμήδην L; both forms are found (-ην e.g. Xen. *Symp.* 8.30; Dem. 61.30; -η Pl. *Leg.* 636c); the epic form is -εα (*h. hom.* 5.202; Theocr. 12.35; etc.; cf. *Il.* 5.266 -εοϲ). ἀναπαύϲομαι: the verb occurs in a sexual context also at Machon 286, 328 Gow; Athen. 603a; Plut. *Pomp.* 36, *Alex.* 2.

583–4. In this respect Pol. resembles the Celts, who (Athen. 603a) τῶν βαρβάρων καίτοι καλλίϲταϲ ἔχοντεϲ γυναῖκαϲ παιδικοῖϲ μᾶλλον χαίρουϲιν. Cf. also Trag. adesp. 355 Χ. πρὸϲ θῆλυ νεύει μᾶλλον ἢ ἐπὶ τἄρϲενα; Υ. ὅπου προϲῆι τὸ κάλλοϲ, ἀμφιδέξιοϲ, which is in fact more likely comic than satyric (Plaut. *Miles* 1113, *Truc.* 152–3); cf. 502n. Pol's somewhat abstract statement, and the poignant πωϲ, may have had an aristocratic flavour. Homosexuality was an aristocratic taste: Pl. *Symp.* 181b; Ar. *Eq.* 735–40; Com. adesp. 12–14; K. J. Dover, *Greek Homosexuality*, 142, 149–51; V. Ehrenberg, *The People of Aristophanes*, 77–8, 134.

584. τοῖϲ θήλεϲιν: ταῖϲ Zuntz (op. cit. 73–4n., 56); but cf. *HF* 536 τὸ θῆλυ γάρ πωϲ μᾶλλον οἰκτρὸν ἀρϲένων, *Hipp. 410* θηλείαιϲι 'females'; τὰ θήλεα in Aristotle (e.g. *Hist. An.* 509a30).

585. ὁ Διόϲ does not mean "son of Zeus", in the sense of being his descendant by way of Dardanos (586)' (Ussher), but rather Zeus' cup-bearer or catamite: cf. Hdt. 4.205 Φερετίμηϲ τῆϲ Βάττου (wife); Andok. 1.17 Λυδὸϲ ὁ Φερεκλέουϲ (slave); Philetair. fr. 9 ἡ ... Διοπείθουϲ ... Τέλεϲιϲ (hetaira). It is nevertheless just conceivable that Γανυμήδηϲ is an intrusive gloss on ἐρώμενοϲ (Arist. *Pol.* 1303b23 τὸν ἐρώμενον αὐτοῦ; Athen. 128b).

586. ἐκ τοῦ Δαρδάνου L. But Ganymede was not snatched from his great-grandfather (*Il.* 20. 219–32) Dardanus, for which ἐκ would be anyway inappropriate. τῆϲ Δαρδάνου (Hermann) means either the land of Dardanos (*Hcld.* 140 τῆϲ ἐμαυτοῦ, *Ion* 1297?), or the city called Dardanos (Hdt. 5.117; 7.43), near which, according to Strabo (13.1.11), some said that Ganymede was seized (by Zeus). The alternative place recorded by Strabo is Harpagia (cf. ἁρπάζω here) on the borders τῆϲ Κυζικηνῆϲ καὶ τῆϲ Πριαπηνῆϲ: hence Naber's ἐκ τοῦδ' Ὀρθάνου, Orthanes being, as Strabo goes on to remark, one of the Attic deities resembling Priapos. The joke would then be that Pol. pulls Sil. into the cave by his phallos (cf. *ABV* 97.25), with a pun on ἐκ (cf. e.g. ἐκ χειρὸc ἄγειν, LSJ s. ἐκ I 6). This might be less awkwardly achieved by ἐκ τῆc 'Ορθάνου (γῆc). But τῆc Δαρδάνου has a point: Pol. makes clear thereby that he is thinking of himself as Zeus. Sexual rivalry (328) has become identification, making the oath μὰ Δία absurd.

588. With L's πεπωκότα we must take κἀντρυφᾶιc as placed διὰ μέcου (cf. 121: for ἐντρυφᾶν absolute cf. Plut. *Alc.* 23). Better is **πεπωκότι** (Scaliger): cf. Alciphr. 1.35; Plut. *Them.* 18.7. The corruption was caused by the case of τὸν ἐραcτήν. Pol. means 'although I am drunk', not 'because . . .'. He has acquired the spirit of the κῶμοc (cf. 168–72), to the detriment of one of his instructors. Some editors give the line to the chorus, as a cruelly ironic reply.

589. **πικρότατον**: the wine, though desirable, is the cause of Sil.'s sufferings: cf. *Hec.* 772 πικροτάτου χρυcοῦ φύλαξ, *Med.* 399, *IA* 955, *Ba.* 357; Ar. fr. 597; Rogers on Ar. *Thesm.* 853. There may also be an obscene secondary reference to cπέρμα.

590. Nowhere else, so far as I know, are the satyrs the children or the descendants of Dionysos. In s-drama generally (A. *Dikt.* 805; S. *Ichn.* 153; etc.), as in *Cyc.* (13, 16, 27, 82, 84, 272, 431, 597), they are the sons of Sil., as Od. himself knows (431). But παῖδεc can have an imprecise sense (cf. e.g. Pl. *Rep.* 407e οἱ παῖδεc 'Αcκληπιοῦ), which suits Od.'s purpose here: cf. Tyrt. 11.1–2 ἀλλ' 'Ηρακλῆοc γὰρ ἀνικήτου γένοc ἐcτέ, θαρcεῖτε. It would be inept, in reminding the satyrs of their noble birth (εὐγενῆ), to mention their actual father. **Διονύcου**: cf. 204n.

591–2. This *prediction* derives from the *description* at *Od.* 9.372–4. Od., as at Cratin. fr. 141, appears to have read his Homer. Cf. 460–1n., 608–10n. In Homer Pol.'s vomiting in his sleep is followed immediately (καὶ τότε) by Od. putting the μοχλόc in the ash to heat. Here, on the other hand, the stake is already hot: cf. 455–9n.

591. **τῶι δ' ὕπνωι**: cf. *HF* 1043 τὸν ὕπνωι παρειμένον, and Bond's note. τῶι seems awkward, despite S *OT* 974 τῶι φόβωι παρηγόμην, and despite the possibility of reading Ὕπνωι (cf. 601); hence ὥcθ' (Hermann), ἔνθ' (Hartung), τῆιδ' (Blaydes).

593. **παρευτρέπιcται** (594n.) seems to go with δαλὸc, and so L's ὠθεῖ (caused probably by ὠθήcει in 592) cannot be replaced by an indicative. Hence καπνούμενοc (Murray): anything burning is being turned into smoke (*Tro.* 8, 586); πνέων Diggle (*PCPhS* 15 (1969), 34).

594. '[The torch] has been prepared, and there is nothing else [left to do] but to blind Pol.' This ellipse (cf. *Andr.* 746) is preferable to the violent change οὐδὲν ἀργὸν ἤ (Wecklein; cf. *Pho.* 766; S. *OC* 1605). Nauck suggests πᾶν εὐτρεπές. δεῖ δ᾿ οὐδὲν ἄλλο, Kirchhoff πάντ᾿ εὐτρέπισται κοὐδὲν ἄλλο. But παρευτρεπίζειν occurs in a similar context at *IT* 725.

596. Exx. of this τόποc are listed by Groeneboom on A. *PV* 242, Headlam-Knox on Herodas 6.4 and 7.108; add *Med* 1279–80, *HF* 1397, *Alc.* 981. Hardness of heart is of course usually a defect, though not at e.g. *HF* 1397. On satyric boasting see 1n., 635–55n.

598. ἀπάλαμνον: Arnott (art. cit. 228n., 28) sees an obscene overtone 'without hands'.

599–607. Cf. 353–5n., and especially *Ba.* 849–61.

600. Cf. Ar. *Eccl.* 1 Ὦ λαμπρὸν ὄμμα, a parody of an address to the sun. εἰπὼν ἀπαλλάγηθι (Pl. *Gorg.* 491c) means 'tell me and have done with it.' What Od. says here means 'have done once and for all' not so much with 'burning' as with 'your evil neighbour': i.e. γείτονος κακοῦ is felt with ἀπαλλάχθητι. Od. cleverly points out to Hephaistos, whose forge is in Aitna (Pi. *Pyth.* 1.25; A. *PV* 365–7; at Call. *Hymn.* 3.46–8 and V. *Aen.* 8.416–23 the Cyclopes work at Hephaistos' anvils), the identity of their interests.

601. At Hes. *Th.* 212, 756–63 Sleep and Death are the children of Night. Sleep is carried in her mother's arms (cf. Paus. 5.18.1—the Kypselos chest), and remains unknown to the Sun.

602. ἄκρατοc suggests the sleep produced by unmixed wine: at 577 it describes the χάριc of the unmixed wine, and occurs elsewhere in E. only at 149 (of the wine). **θηρὶ: καὶ τοὺc διὰ κακίαν δὲ τῶν ἀνθρώπων ὑπερβάλλοντας οὕτως ἐπιδυcφημοῦμεν** (Aristotle on θηριώδηc, *EN* 1145a32; cf. 1148b22). **θεοcτυγεῖ:** see 396n.

603–4. With the thought cf. 198–200, 347–9, 694–5. **πόνοιc:** a regular word in E. for the Trojan War: e.g. 107, 282, 347, 352, *Hel.* 603, etc.

604. L has ναύταc, the last three letters being written (probably Tr. 2) *in rasura*. Almost certainly L had ναῦc, which was copied in P. ναύταc was quite likely a conjecture, but a good one. The construction διὰ μέcου makes the sailors seem of secondary importance: cf. Ar. *Ran.* 587–8 πρόρριζος αὐτός, ἡ γυνή, τὰ παιδία, κάκιcτ᾿ ἀπολοίμην; *HF* 773–5, *Hyps.* fr. 60.13–14; Sil. 6.277–8; West on Hes. *Op.* 406; K-G 1 80. And so ναύταc τε καὐτὸν (Beck), αὐτοῖcι ναύταιc (Pierson) are unnecessary. See apparatus.

605. Cf. 322, 331; *Od.* 9.115 οὐδ᾿ ἀλλήλων ἀλέγουcι, 275 οὐ γὰρ Κύκλωπεc Διὸc αἰγιόχου ἀλέγουcιν. **ὑπό:** cf. *Alc.* 737, *Med.* 487 (Medea killed Pelias) παίδων ὑπ᾿ αὐτοῦ. To attribute the prospective destruction of the Greeks to Hephaistos and Sleep acting through Pol. is of course unfair.

606–7. For the thought cf. *Hec.* 488–9, fr. 901. τύχη may be dispensed or controlled by the gods (e.g. S. *Phil.* 1317; *HF* 1393, *Hcld.* 935, fr. 554), or it may be itself a δαίμων (e.g. A. *Ag.* 664; S. *OT* 1080; *Ion* 1512–14, *IA* 1136), and τὸ εὐτυχεῖν may be regarded by men as θεός τε καὶ θεοῦ πλέον (A. *Cho.* 60); cf. Paus. 4.30.5, 7.26.8).

607. Od. probably now enters the cave, to check the δαλός (631, 457–8).

608–23. Short astrophic choral songs seem to have been more common in satyric drama than in tragedy (356–74n., 656–62n.). The colometry of this song is uncertain (hence the odd linenumbering). Dale (op. cit. 53n., 46) takes πρασσέτω (617) with the following colon; but it seems to fall more naturally into the *preceding* trochaic rhythm, giving a catalectic trochaic trimeter (as 612, 622) with syncopation in the second metron (S. *El.* 1284). Another possibility is to take μαινομένου ... κακῶς and κἀγὼ ... θέλω as (enoplian) prosodiac compounds (A. *Eum.* 387–8, *Cho.* 591–2; Dale, 175–6). For the initial double syncopation in a catalectic trochaic trimeter (612 ἤδη, 622 Κύκλω-: Murray printed them as separate cola) see 356n.; Ar. *Lys.* 659. For the catalectic dactylic tetrameter (617, 620) see Dale, 42–3. For the spondee formed by a single word as an introduction to dactyls (619 κἀγὼ: this too Murray printed as a separate colon) cf. A. *Pers.* 864–906; Dale, 43–4.

Metrical Scheme

608	$-\cup-.\,/-\cup-\cup$	trochaic dimeter (with syncopation)
	$-\cup-\cup/-\cup-.$	catalectic trochaic dimeter
610	$-\cup\cup/-\cup\cup/-\cup\cup/-\cup\cup$	dactylic tetrameter
	$-\cup-\cup/-\cup-.$	catalectic trochaic dimeter
	$-.-./-\cup-\cup/-\cup-.$	catalectic trochaic trimeter (with initial double syncopation)
615	$-\cup\cup/-\cup\cup/-\cup\cup/-\cup\cup$	dactylic tetrameter
	$-\cup-\cup/-\cup-.\,/-\cup-.$	catalectic trochaic trimeter (with syncopation)
	$-\cup\cup/-\cup\cup/-\cup\cup/-$	catalectic dactylic tetrameter
	$\underset{\smile}{\cup}-\cup-/\cup-\cup-$	iambic dimeter
620	$--/-\cup\cup/-\cup\cup/-\cup\cup/-$	spondee and catalectic dactylic tetrameter
	$\cup-\cup-/\cup-\cup-$	iambic dimeter
	$-.-./-\cup-\cup/-\cup-.$	catalectic trochaic trimeter (with double syncopation)
	$--\cup-/\cup-\cup-$	iambic dimeter

608–10. 'The tongs will grasp fiercely the throat of the guest-eater.' There has been no mention of such an action. What then do the satyrs mean? Elsewhere in the play the absurd impression is given that Od., like every Athenian, remembers striking passages of the Odyssey (376n., 460–1n., 591–2n.), notably the shipwright whirling his auger (460–1n.). Here the joke is a little more complicated. The satyrs appear to remember that other great simile from the Homeric narrative, the simile of the smith dipping burning metal into cold water (391–3). But they have also confused simile and reality into a single picture, as perhaps only they could do. καρκίνος of a smith's tongs: Athen. 456d; *AP* 6.92.

610. ξένων δαιτύμονος L; **ξενοδαιτύμονος** Hermann, rightly: cf. 658, 244–6n., *HF* 391 Κύκνον ξεινοδαῖκταν. πυρὶ γὰρ: Musgrave's πυράγρα, 'fire-tongs', is inept, and based apparently on the illusion that the subject of ὀλεῖ must otherwise be ὁ καρκίνος. It could be δαλός (Reiske); but it is better to punctuate after κόρας (cf. *Hipp.* 440 ψυχὴν ὀλεῖς): this gives more point to ἤδη, and allows δρυὸς ἄσπετον ἔρνος to be appositional.

611. κόρας: the plural is surprising: but cf. 463, 21n.

615. κρύπτεται ἐς σποδιάν: κρύπτεται in E. means 'is hidden', rather than 'is being hidden' (*HF* 263, *Hel.* 606, *Or.* 1107. *Pho.* 336). The δαλός is already in the fire (593–4), and Od. is merely checking to see whether it is διάπυρος (631, 457–8). The ash comes from *Od.* 9.375. ἐς σποδιάν means 'in the ash', with an implication of previous motion (cf. Hdt. 8.60.2 Σαλαμὶς ... ἐς τὴν ἡμῖν ὑπέκκειται τέκνα τε καὶ γυναῖκες): in later Greek the implication of motion, being lost from εἰς (Luke 11.7 τὰ παιδία μου μετ' ἐμοῦ εἰς τὴν κοίτην εἰσίν), may be created by the context, as is true of Greek today. **δρυὸς:** see 383n.; the stake is of olive (455). **ἄσπετον:** E. may have in mind the description of Pol.'s vast club (*Od.*, 9.319–25) from which in Homer Od. cuts the stake.

616–8. Already the satyrs are showing signs of cowardice (cf. 635–55). Just as elsewhere Dionysos seems to be an agent in events in the form of wine personified (156, 524, 575), so here too the wine is personified, as Maron (141n., 412), and asked to perform the blinding (cf. 647–9). And so Kirchhoff's ἴτ' ὦ, μόρον πράσσετ' ὦ is inept (656–62 are κελεύσματα: 655). For πρασσέτω alone cf. A. *Ag.* 1669; Ar. *Thesm.* 216; Men. *Dysk.* 746 (Kassel in *Gnomon* 33 (1961), 138).

618. πίνειν κακῶς is presumably to suffer from the bad effects of drinking, and so makes a cruel understatement here. Cf. Theogn. 533 χαίρω δ' εὖ πίνων, 509 οἶνος πινόμενος πουλὺς κακόν.

619–23. As at the end of their first song, the satyrs' thoughts turn to their god, whom they now have a prospect of rejoining.

620–1. φιλοκιccοφόρον: cf. the satyrs' words in Pratinas fr. 3.16 θριαμβοδιθύραμβε κιccόχαιτ' ἄναξ. ποθεινὸν εἰcιδεῖν: Dionysos is longed for both now and at the moment of reunion (*Hel.* 540 ὡc ποθεινὸc ἂν μόλοιc).

622. Pol. lives in an ἐρημία (22, 116). But the word suggests also the satyrs' separation from Dionysos: at *Ba.* 609, in a scene based on mystic initiation (Seaford, art. cit. 514–15n., 258), the maenads greet the unexpected return of Dionysos: ὡc ἐcεῖδον ἀcμένη cε, μονάδ' ἔχουc' ἐρημίαν.

623. In the same way Strepsiades reacts to the prospect of τὸν πάντα χρόνον μετ' ἐμοῦ ζηλωτότατον βίον ἀνθρώπων offered him by the Clouds: (Ar. *Nub.* 466) ἀρά γε τοῦτ' ἄρ' ἐγώ ποτ' ὄψομαι; the expression may be associated with mystic initiation (cf. Seaford, art. cit. 514–15n., 268 n. 149): cf. 622n. Cf. also the end of a choral ode at *El.* 485–6 ἔτ' ἔτι φόνιον ὑπὸ δέραν ὄψομαι αἷμα χυθὲν cιδάρωι.

624. In the same way Trygaios has to quieten the exuberant chorus, before their dangerous task, at Ar. *Pax.* 309, 318 (cf. 477n.). θῆρεc expresses slight exasperation at their dangerously noisy song and dance. Cf. Kyllene at S. *Ichn.* 221–2 θῆρεc, τί τόνδε χλοερὸν ὑλῶδη πάγον / ἔνθηρον ὁρμήθητε cὺν πολλῆι βοῆι; (also 147).

625–6. The sequence οὐδὲ…οὐ…οὐδὲ appears to be unique; but there is no need to read οὔτε in 625: cf. Ar. *Eccl.* 452. The asyndeton expresses urgency.

627. ἐξεγερθῆι cannot but suggest the actual waking of Pol.; τὸ κακόν, on the other hand, cannot but suggest the disaster were he to be aroused before being blinded (ἐξεγείρειν metaphorical: *El.* 41).

628. ἁμιλλᾶcθαι tends to mean resisted effort (Kannicht on *Hel.* 546–8): πρὸc αἰθέρ' ἐξαμίλληcαι κόραc (*Hyps.* fr. 764.1) seems to refer to the straining of the eyes almost out of their sockets (Bond; cf. Diggle in *Dionysiaca* (ed. R. D. Dawe et al., Cambridge, 1978), p. 176 n. 34). Here the stake will have to be pressed home and twisted hard. *Or.* 431 ἐξαμιλλῶνταί cε γῆc suggests that ὄμματοc here (627) might mean 'from the eye'. But more probably ὄμματοc ὄψιc is to be taken together (459, *IT* 1167, *Or.* 513, *IA* 233). For the distinction between ὄμμα and ὄψιc see 459n. C. Willink has suggested (in correspondence) ἐξαμαυρωθῆι.

629. The satyr replies somewhat grandly (αἰθέρα: cf. 410n.) that they have their mouths shut. This will exclude utterance (624), coughing (626), and perhaps even breathing (625). In Euboul.

fr. 10.7 κάπτοντες αὔρας, ἐλπίδας σιτούμενοι the point is different.

630. νυν is enclitic, and short (*Or.* 1281).

631. καλῶς: 'nicely', as at *El.* 965.

632–4. These lines, and the division of the chorus which seems to accompany then (635–42n.), are no doubt procrastinatory in spirit. They may nevertheless represent a feature of the genre: cf. 483, and the division of the tracking chorus at S. *Ichn.* 100–105. E. may also have had in mind *Od.* 9.331–4, where lots are drawn to select Od.'s assistants in the blinding.

632. οὔκουν: see 241n.; Denniston, *GP*, 431, 435. πρώτους: i.e. at the front of the stake: cf. 483–6.

633. καυτὸν is closer than καυστόν to L's καὶ τὸν, and has inscriptional support (LSJ). τὸ φῶς: cf. the Virgilian version: (*Aen.* 3.635) *telo lumen terebramus acuto.*

633–4. τὸ φῶς Κύκλωπος: for the word order see Denniston-Page on A. *Ag.* 637.

634. κοινώμεθα: cf. 471 κοινωνεῖν, 469–71n. The audience may be reminded of the satyrs' participation in some labour in other plays, e.g. in dragging ashore Danae and Perseus in A. *Dikt.* (see further intro., §IV). If so, this emphasizes their cowardice here. Still, for the chorus to enter the cave would break theatrical convention (cf. 205n.).

635–55 illustrate the truth of Sil.'s accusation at S. *Ichn.* 151–2 εἰ δέ που δέηι, / πιστοὶ λόγοισιν ὄντες ἔργα φεύγετε (cf. S. *Kedalion* fr. 328), and of Nonn. *Dion.* 14.123 νόςφι μόθοιο λέοντες, ἐνὶ πτολέμοις δὲ λαγωοί. In their first appearance in literature the satyrs are οὐτιδανοί (Hes. fr. 123). And perhaps their boasting in S. fr. 1130 was later in the play belied by their cowardice. Cf. 1n.; Hermippus fr. 46.

635–42. The attribution of these lines in L is clearly astray. It seems that the satyrs are divided into two or three groups, perhaps with one group further from the entrance to the cave (635) than the others. Cf. S. *Ichn.* 100–123. Clearly 635–6 and 637 are spoken by two groups (or rather by a representative from each) X and Y. Y's δέ answering X's μέν is a joke: X knows that his will not be the only excuse. 638–9 probably belongs to X (see ἑστῶτες in 639, 636), possibly to a third group Z. ἑστῶτες ἐσπάσθητε; (640) is almost certainly Od. 640–1 must belong to whoever spoke 638–9 (X or Z), as it answers Od's question (καὶ ... γε: cf. e.g. 670) with another, more plausible excuse. 642 is clearly Od.'s.

635. μακρός ἐστι cannot mean 'he is distant', and so μακρότεροι (L) must be replaced by **μακροτέρω** (Matthiae) or μακροτέραν

(Cobet); μακρότερον (Musgrave) seems to refer more frequently to motion.

636. ὠθεῖν: ἢ ὠθεῖν Blaydes (with synizesis: K-B i 228); but the simple infinitive is defended by *Hcld*. 744 κακὸς μένειν δόρυ; Hdt. 6.109 ὀλίγους εἶναι ϲτρατίηι τῆι Μήδων ϲυμβάλλειν; K-G ii 10.

637. δὲ... γε is common in drama 'in lively retorts and rejoinders' (Denniston, *GP*, 153): e.g. S. *O T* 372 τυφλὸς ... εἶ — Σὺ δ' ἄθλιός γε.

638-9. Cf. Hdt. 6.134 τὸν μηρὸν ϲπαϲθῆναι.

640-1. At Ar. *Ran*. 192 Xanthias makes an excuse for not having fought at sea: μὰ τὸν Δι' οὐ γὰρ ἀλλ' ἔτυχον ὀφθαλμιῶν.

641. ἡμῖν: Duchemin defends ἡμῶν (L) as emphatic: a satyr draws attention to himself or to his group. But there is no question of a *new* speaker here (635–42n.). **κόνεος:** cf. e.g. πόλεος corrupted to πόλεως at *El*. 412, *Andr*. 138; see K-B i 442.

642. ἄνδρες (Matthiae, i.e. οἱ ἄνδρες), allows the verse to fall into two clauses joined by καί. But read **ἄνδρες:** '[They are] worthless men, worth nothing at all, these allies.' κοὐδὲν is an exasperated climax: cf. Thuc. 7.68 ὡς δὲ ἐχθροὶ καὶ ἔχθιστοι ... ἴϲτε. For predicative οὐδὲν cf. 667.

643. οἰκτίρομεν: αἰϲχύνομαι Blaydes, presumably to create consistency with the singular βούλομαι in the next line. But cf. e.g. 465.

644. Cf. Solon fr. 27.1–2 παῖς μὲν ἄνηβος ἐὼν ἔτι νήπιος ἕρκος ὀδόντων / φύϲας ἐκβάλλει πρῶτον ἐν ἔπτ' ἔτεϲιν.

646. An Orphic ἐπωιδή would be apt here, as persuading the inanimate δαλός to move (*IA* 1212; etc.). Among the satyrs' boasts in S. fr. 1130 is the claim ἔνεϲτι δὲ μαντεῖα πάντα γνωτὰ κοὐκ ἐψευϲμένα (13–14). The inadequacy of Orphic song is recognized at Diogen. Sinop. fr. 7.10–12; *Alc*. 965–70.

647. ὥϲτ': ὡς L; Diggle (*Studies on the Text of Euripides*, 7–9) makes a powerful case for ὥϲτε here and in the other three passages of E. in which ὡς with the infinitive is the only attested reading (*Alc*. 358, *El*. 667, *IT* 300).

648. μονῶπα: cf. 21n. **παῖδα γῆϲ:** at *Od*. 1.71–3 Pol. is the son of Poseidon (as here: 21, 286, etc.) and of the nymph Θόωϲα. But in Hesiod (*Th*. 139–46) the Cyclopes (Βρόντη, Στερόπη, and Ἄργη) are the children of Heaven and Earth. The choice of Earth here may express apprehension at Pol.'s size, as the giants were of course the offspring of Earth (5n.).

649. Od. seems to have known the satyrs' reputation (635–55n.) no less than they knew his (104n., 450); cf. Kyllene's ἀλλ' αἰὲν εἶ ϲὺ παῖς (S. *Ichn*. 366). **ἤδη:** for the form see Rutherford, *The New Phrynichus*, 236–7.

652–3. Cf. *Od.* 9.376–7 ἔπεccί τὲ πάντας ἑταίρους / θάρσυνον. The satyrs' cowardice coincides with dramatic convention in keeping them in the orchestra. On the Richmond vase (Plate II) the blinding is performed by Od.'s men, while the satyrs hover on the sidelines. ἀλλ' οὖν: cf. *Alc.* 363 ('I can't bring you back from the dead') ἀλλ' οὖν ἐκεῖcε προcδόκα με. ἐπεγκέλευε: cf. *El.* 1224–5 ἐγὼ δέ γ' ἐπεκέλευcά coι ξίφους τ' ἐφηψάμαν ἅμα; 469–71 n.

654. ἐν τῶι Καρὶ ὑμῖν ὁ κίνδυνος (Pl. *Lach.* 187b) is explained by the scholiast (Archil. fr. 216): παροιμία, ἐπὶ τῶν ἐπιcφαλέcτερον καὶ ἐν ἀλλοτρίοις κινδυνευόντων. Κᾶρες γὰρ δοκοῦcι πρῶτοι μιcφορῆcαι, ὅθεν καὶ εἰc πόλεμον αὐτοὺς προέταττον. 'We will run our risks vicariously.' Cf. S. fr. 540 (satyric *Salmoneus*) Καρικοὶ τράγοι.

655. κελευcμάτων: at *Andr.* 1031 the MSS are divided between κέλευμα and κέλευcμα; elsewhere in E. they have only κέλευcμα, which should be retained. κέλευμα is the older form (for the intrusive sigma cf. K-B ii 272–3). ἕκατι: cf. *Hel.* 1182 πόνου γ' ἕκατι, 'as far as my efforts are concerned'; A. *Pers.* 337.

656–62. With the exception of 495–518 the choral songs have become progressively shorter, so that the pace increases as we approach the climax (cf. A. *Ag.*). Rossi (art. cit. 483–518n., 22) calls the song a κέλευcμα (477, 652, 653, 655), by which he means the call of the κελευcτής giving time to the rowers. But the κέλευcμα and its cognates are not confined to the sea. Indeed the satyric song in S. *Ichn.* is called κέλευμα ... κυνηγετῶν (231), and κελεύcματα in general may have been a feature of the genre (intro., §IV): the τόπος wins new life from each new situation, and to introduce a third (nautical) element would be a deleterious complication. Although Od.'s companions are sailors, there appears to be nothing nautical about the song.

Metre. The scheme below, based on the text of L, is not without severe difficulties. It seems to fall into two halves, divided by 659, with 660–2 repeating roughly the pattern of 656–8. But the word-overlap between the choriambic dimeter (656) and the dochmiacs (657) is suspicious. And the colarion ἐξοδυνηθείς in 661 (paralleled only by e.g. A. *Sept.* 152 ὦ πότνι' Ἥρα; cf. Dale, op. cit. 53 n., ch. 7) can be made into a dochmius best by Kirchhoff's ἐξ ὀδύνης cυθείς, which gives inferior sense. Alternatively, dividing ἐξοδυνηθ / είς, we have dochmius and choriamb (cf. Barrett on *Hipp.* 1275) followed by (662) a pherecretean (as 658). Diggle's suggestion (see 656–7 apparatus) creates out of 656–8 one iambic followed by two choriambic cola; and with μὴ 'ξοδυνηθ / είς 661 (see apparatus) also becomes a choriambic dimeter.

Metrical Scheme

656	∪∪∪–– –∪∪–	choriambic dimeter B (with resolved base: cf. *Ion* 495). On ἰὼ ἰώ see Dodds on *Ba.* 580, 582.
657	–––∪–|–∪∪–∪–	two dochmii?
658	–––∪∪––	pherecretean
659	–∪–|–∪–	two cretics
660	∪–– –∪∪–	choriambic heptasyllable (blunt)
661	–––∪–|–∪∪––	dochmius and anonymous colarion?
662	––∪∪––	reizianum

656. Interjections introducing satyric songs occur at S. *Ichn.* 88, 176, 213, *Inach.* fr. 269c.25.

656–7. For the triple imperative cf. *Or.* 1302 φονεύετε, καίνετε, ὄλλυτε; A. *PV* 58; also the satyrs at Pratinas fr. 3. 10–12 παῖε ... φλέγε.

657–9. ἐκκαίετε ... καίετε. For 'the iteration of a compound verb in a succeeding clause or sentence by the simple verb alone, but with the semantic force of the compound' see Watkins in *HSCP* 71 (1966), 115–19; Renehan, *Greek Textual Criticism*, 78–85; Diggle in *GRBS* 14 (1973), 265.

658. θηρὸς: see 442n. ξενοδαίτα: cf. 610n., A. *Ag.* 124 λαγοδαίτας.

659. Murray retained L's τυφέτω καιέτω: 'incantatio est: cf. v. 616.' But even if 616–18 might be called an 'incantatio', 656–62 is a κέλευσμα (653, 655; cf. 656–7). On ὢ see 52n.; A. *Cho.* 942 ἐπολολυξάτ' ὤ; ἐπολολυξάτω M.

660. Αἴτνας: L's ἔτνας is phonetic corruption (cf. e.g. A. *Ag.* 75). Pol. is Αἰτναῖος at 366. μηλονόμον: this word occurs elsewhere only at Choerilus Ep. fr. 3 Kinkel and in *Suda* s. μηλοβοτήρ. E. has the form μηλονόμας at *Alc.* 572. But μηλονόμον may stand here (cf. μελισσονόμος, αἰγινόμος).

661. τόρνευ' ἕλκε. To express the twisting of the stake in Pol.'s eye Od. has used (460–1n.) the Homeric image of the auger spun round by thongs. The satyrs now use another technological image, derived from the circular motion of the lathe (τόρνος). The present imperative ἕλκε does not mean 'keep on ... pulling it out again' (Ussher), which would prolong unnecessarily and dangerously the rotary motion. Nor does it refer exactly to this rotary motion, *pace* Dodds on *Ba.* 1067. The Athenian potter's lathe was turned by a lower wheel persistently pulled round by an assistant with his hands (*ABV* 362 n. 36; *ARV*² 1092.76; Caltagirone Crater, Beazley, *PBA* 30 (1944), pl.5.1). ἕλκε probably refers to

this pulling on the wheel, which is of course comparable to the
pulling on the thongs to turn the auger in the earlier image. So too
at *Ba.* 1067 ἕλκει probably refers not to circular motion (*pace*
Dodds) but to the tangential pull of the pole-lathe on the pole:
Willink in *CQ* 59 (1966), 237–40. And the τόρνευμα δεινὸν ποδός of
HF 978 expresses the manner in which Herakles' movement
causes his son to move in a circle around the pillar to escape him.

662. μάταιον is not an understatement, but has the same strong sense
as at A. *Eum.* 337, where it refers by implication to matricide (cf.
A. *Su.* 229, 762; S. *Trach.* 565).

663. Pol. emerges into the entrance of the cave (668), presumably
after his initial ὤμοι. Did he have a new or altered mask?
References in tragedy to someone's altered facial appearance (e.g.
S. *OT* 1297–1306; *Hec.* 1117: cf. 670 here) are discussed by Hense
(op. cit. 227n.). They do not prove that tragic masks were altered
or changed, because the words may have been designed to stimulate the imagination of the audience. But Hense is probably right
in believing that alteration did occur. As the play was written for a
single performance at the Dionysia, there was no need for an
unmodified mask for the second night. In the Oxford production
of 1976, on the other hand, the mask was simply turned upside
down, so that Pol.'s gory mouth became his wounded eye. To
besmirch the mask with gore would give a special point to 517–18
(517n.).

663–8. 663, 665 and 666–8 are very similar to *Hec.* 1035, 1037 and
1039–40 (the blinding of Polymestor): cf. also A. *Ag.* 1343–5; S.
El. 1415–16; *Med.* 1007–9; and the parody at Ar. *Plut.* 934–5. See
further Seaford in *JHS* 103 (1983), 169. *Hec.* 1036 confirms the
attribution of 664 to the chorus leader (rather than Od.).

664. resembles the joyful reaction of the chorus of *HF* to Lykos' cry
within the palace (751–2) τόδε κατάρχεται μέλος ἐμοὶ κλύειν φίλιον
ἐν δόμοις (cf. also *Antiope* 51–2 Page), and exemplifies an irony of a
kind frequent in tragedy: X and Y are directly opposed in mood,
and yet the description of X in terms of Y is uncannily apt: cf. e.g.
345–6n., *Pho.* 1489 βάκχα νεκύων; A. *Ag.* 1188–91. The παιάν was
often a song of victory (A. *Sept.* 635; *RE* xviii 2348): the similarity
between exuberant cries of pain and of joy allows the satyrs to call
Pol.'s cry of pain a song of triumph for their own victory. The same
ambiguity in the παιάν is exploited elsewhere: A. *Sept.* 868–70
Ἀΐδα τ' ἐχθρὸν παιᾶν' ἐπιμέλπειν, *Ag.* 645, *Cho.* 151; *Alc.* 424 (see
Dale's note), *Tro.* 578. Cf. also 443–4. αὖ is Markland's correction
of L's ὧ: cf. *Hipp.* 232 τί τόδ' αὖ παράφρων ἔρριψας ἔπος;, *Ba.* 479, *IT*
972. αὖ also improves the paratragedy (663–8n.): cf. ὤμοι μάλ'

αὖθις at *Hec.* 1037; A. *Ag.* 1345; S. *El.* 1416; *Med.* 1009 αἰαῖ μάλ'
αὖθις. The satyr encourages Pol. to conform to the τόπος. He does
so (665), but without the αὖθις, which (with αὖ here) would be
superfluous.

665. ἐξολώλαμεν Nauck; but cf. *Pho.* 127 ὡς γαῦρος, ὡς φοβερὸς
εἰςιδεῖν.

667. οὐδὲν ὄντες: 355n., 642. At *Od.* 9.515 Pol. says that he knew a
prophecy that he would be blinded by Od., but did not expect an
ὀλίγος τε καὶ οὐτιδανὸς καὶ ἄκικυς.

668. φάραγγος: a cleft, i.e. the cave. Standing in the gateway of the
cave Pol. will fit his hands (in the gateway): cf. Ar. *Ran.* 1201–4
ἐναρμόττειν ἅπαν ... ἐν τοῖς ἰαμβείοισι. Alternatively read φάραγγι
τῆιδε (i.e. this cleft): cf. *HF* 179 πλευροῖς ... ἐναρμόσας βέλη, *Pho.*
1413. τῆςδε: with L's τάςδε the blind giant might be reassuring
himself of the existence of his own hands as he stretches them
across the entrance. ταῖςδε (Kirchhoff) creates two exits, which
would make Pol.'s strategem pointless, his specification of the exit
covered foolish, and 679–690 unnecessary. Clearly there is only
one frontal (706–7n.) exit from the cave.

669. τί χρῆμα 'why?' is according to Denniston (on *El.* 831) confined
to E., and according to Stevens (*CQ* 31 (1937), 191) a colloquialism. Cf. *Held.* 646 τί χρῆμ' ἀϋτῆς πᾶν τόδ' ἐπλήςθη ςτέγος...;.

670. It is quite wrong to suppose that 'the poet introduces a note of
compassion for the monster' (Ussher). Rather, the audience's
enjoyment of his misery is heightened by paratragedy (663–8n.,
683n., 687n.).

672–5. Cf. 548–51n.; *Od.* 9.398–414.

672. L's ἀπώλεςεν is almost certainly wrong: the third foot anapaest
is not illegitimate (234), but easily avoided here; and at 681 L has
ἐςτήκαςιν, which gives an (illegitimate) fourth foot dactyl.

673. μ' ἐτύφλου Wieseler; cf. 672 ἀπώλεςε ... ἠδίκει. But the present
τυφλοῖ expresses the present importance of the result of the action:
cf. e.g. S. *Ant.* 1173–4 τεθνᾶςιν ... καὶ τίς φονεύει;, and above all
Pol. at *Od.* 9.408 Οὖτίς με κτείνει.

674. †ὡς δὴ cύ†: we cannot mentally supply e.g. λέγεις, nor can the
phrase be simply interrupted and unfinished. Hence Diggle (art.
cit. 39n., 49–50) proposed that καὶ πῶς κτλ. interrupts ὡς δὴ cύ ...
ςκώπτεις, listing as exx. of interruptions having 'no connection in
syntax, and little connection in sense, with the words they inter-
rupt' *Alc.* 892, *HF* 1051–2, *Ion* 558, *Tro.* 1310; S. *Aj.* 981. To this
Stinton cogently objects (*JHS* 97 (1977), 140) that in such cases
the first speaker has always said something significant, and that
ςκώπτεις is better by itself (Ar. *Plut.* 973; Men. *Dysk.* 54; cf. Men.

Phasma 90; Ar. *Ran.* 58; Austin on Men. *Sam.* 596). He suggests therefore πῶc δῆτα; or πῶc φῄιc cύ; (e.g. *Su.* 756, *El* 575; Ar. *Av.* 319, *Plut.* 268, *Nub.* 1443). The meaning then is that at first the slow-witted Pol. fails to understand the joke: 'καί then has some point; it picks up πῶc, and answers the implication "I am blind".' But the καί has a point perhaps even in Diggle's version (Denniston, *GP*, 309–10), the real weakness of which is that there is no motive for the interruption: for this there is no support in his parallels, in all of which the interruption is an unrestrained expression of grief (save *Ion* 558–9, but here the interruption is clearly prompted by what Ion says). Read perhaps πῶc; ἴδε cύ: πῶc; is common in E (e.g. 108); and cf. S. *Phil.* 519 ὅρα cύ. This gives point to cύ (the satyr can see); the iota would be easily lost, and δή would then mend the metre.

676. For the enclitic με following a subordinate clause see Barrett on *Hipp.* 1154–5.

677. Cf. *Od.* 9.516 ὀφθαλμοῦ ἀλάωcεν, ἐπεί μ' ἐδάμαccατο οἴνωι. **μιαρόc** as a term of abuse occurs in satyric drama (fr. 673; S. *Ichn.* 197), and frequently in comedy, though not in tragedy (except possibly at S. *Ant.* 746). **κατέκλυcεν** (Canter; κατέκαυcεν L) implies a simple corruption (A for Λ); κατακλύζειν, to deluge, is used metaphorically at *Tro.* 995, *Or.* 343; cf. 577n., 571n. Possible also is κατέκλαcεν (Musgrave), which makes good sense of the assentient γὰρ in the next line: cf. Theocr. 25.146–7 κατὰ δ' αὐχένα νέρθ' ἐπὶ γαίηc κλάccε βαρύν περ ἐόντα.

678–9. 678 may well be spoken by the chorus. But if it is spoken by Od., this motivates the urgency (πρὸc θεῶν) of Pol.'s question. Biehl (art. cit. 480–2n., 166) leaves it with Pol. (as in L) on the basis of apparent numerical correspondences between trimeters within this episode. But cf. 480–2n.

678. Cf. 497n.; wine as agent: 156, 454, 524, 616. For the form of the line cf. *Hcld.* 4 πόλει τ' ἄχρηcτοc καὶ cυναλλάccειν βαρύc. **οἶνοc:** cf. ἄλλοι at 407 (ἄλλοι L), ἄνηρ at 591 (ἄνηρ L), 145, 422.

680. ἐπήλυγα, a hapax legomenon, may be either noun or adjective (cf. e.g. ἔπηλυc).

681–90. The slapstick of this scene resembles Ar. *Thesm.* 1217–26, *Ran.* 285–7, as well as blind-man's buff (χαλκῆ μυῖα: Pollux 9.123; Eustath. ad *Il.* 21.394). The entrance of the cave is too wide to be blocked by Pol.'s body; whereas in Homer the Greeks can escape only under the sheep, which would be difficult to stage.

681. ἐκ χερόc Blaydes; but cf. A. *PV* 714 λαιᾶc δὲ χειρὸc; Hdt. 4.34 ἀριcτερῆc χειρόc (also 5.77).

682. The phenomenon of two changes of speaker (ἀντιλαβαί) in a single iambic trimeter occurs elsewhere in E. only at *Alc.* 391, *HF*

1420 (both containing farewells), *Alc.* 1119 (as here, accompanying ridiculous movement), and the corrupt *HF* 1418. In S. even the three ἀντιλαβαί at *Ichn.* 205 are paralleled in tragedy at *Phil.* 753 (and *OC* 539 = 546).

683. κακόν γε πρὸς κακῶι is paratragic: cf. e.g. *Hipp.* 874 οἴμοι τόδ᾽ οἷον ἄλλο πρὸς κακῶι κακόν; S. *OC* 595. τὸ κρανίον: τοῦ κρανίου Blaydes: cf. e.g. Ar. *Ach.* 1180 τῆς κεφαλῆς κατέαγα. But cf. also e.g. cτάμνου κεφαλὴν κατεαγότος (Ar. *Plut.* 545): κρανίου is accusative of respect.

684. διαφεύγουcί presumably includes Sil. and the uneaten Greeks (466) as well as Od. γε: the satyr agrees with Pol., and points out yet another κακόν (cf. 640, 670).

685. 'Was it not somewhere here, over here, that you said [they are escaping]?': cf. *Rhes.* 689 οἶcθ᾽ ὅποι βεβᾶcιν ἄνδρεc; Od. τῆιδέ πηι κατείδομεν. And for the double τῆιδε cf. 49, *Pho.* 1720–1, *Phaeth.* 177; S. *OC* 1547. Pol. then picks up πηι with πῆι γάρ; (686). Alternatively, the words in L can be given some sense as οὐ τῆιδ᾽; ἐπεὶ τῆιδ᾽ εἶπαc;, '[Are they] not [escaping] here? for [it was] here you said [they were escaping]?'. West (in *BICS* 28 (1981), 68) punctuates οὐ τῆιδέ πηι· τῆιδ᾽ εἶπαc; 'Not anywhere this way—did you mean this way?'. οὔ ταύτηι λέγω: this (and περιάγου κτλ. 686) may be spoken by a different satyr, placed πρὸς τάριcτερά (cf. 635–42n.). That would give more point to ταύτηι.

686. περιάγου, κεῖcε: περίαγουcί cε (L) probably found its way into the text only after περιάγω with accusative became normal for 'go around' (e.g. Ev. Matth. 9.35 καὶ περιῆγεν ὁ Ἰηcοῦc τὰc πόλειc πάcαc), helped perhaps by the confusion of Κ and ΙC (e.g. A. *Eum.* 177, *Cho.* 897).

687. οἴμοι γελῶμαι is paratragic (as 683): cf. S. *Ant.* 839; A. *Eum.* 789, 819. So too ὦ παγκάκιcτε in 689: cf. e.g. *Med.* 465.

688. ἀλλ᾽ οὐκέτι: *Hel.* 1230–1 must almost certainly be read as (see Dale's note) Θε. τί κερτομεῖc με, τὸν θανόντα δ᾽ οὐκ ἐᾶιc; Ελ. ἀλλ᾽ οὐκετ᾽· ἤδη δ᾽ ἄρχε τῶν ἐμῶν γάμων. Helen says 'I will not taunt you any more.' Here too ἀλλ᾽ οὐκέτι negates κερτομεῖτε. In both cases the point is that the accusation of κερτομία is now beside the point because the situation has radically changed. Od. has now escaped to safety.

692. μ᾽ ὁ φύcαc (Nauck) sacrifices the assentient γε in L, but creates more regular word-order: see apparatus; E. Bruhn, *Anhang zu Schneidewin-Nauck Sophokles*, 91. ὠνόμαζ᾽: for the imperfect see Fraenkel on A. *Ag.* 681; Carden, op. cit. 5n., 83.

693–5. Cf. 422, *Od.* 9.477 καὶ λίην cέ γ᾽ ἔμελλε κιχήcεcθαι κακὰ ἔργα. In Homer (479) Od. regards the inevitability of Pol.'s punishment as the justice of the gods, whereas here he ascribes it to his own stature gained at Troy (cf. 198–202, 304–9, 347–52, 603–4).

694. καλῶc: ironical: cf. *Med.* 58: S. *Ant.* 739. L's κακῶc is defensible:
cf. 618 ὡc πίηι κακῶc '... with a bad issue'. A. Pallis compares
modern Greek τοῦ κάκου 'in vain' (*CR* 19 (1905), 36; cf. N.
Bachtin, *Introduction to the Study of Modern Greek*, ch. IV).
διεπυρώcαμεν: L's διεπυρωcάμην may be an unconscious repetition
from the end of the previous line (Jackson, *Marginalia Scaenica*,
226). On the other hand, in other references to the glorious
exploits at Troy Od. always uses the singular of the verb (200, 347,
352), as suits his conception of himself. And there is nothing wrong
with the middle here (Od. did not personally light the fire: see, if
proof be needed, *Tro.* 1260–4), or with the end-rhyme—άμην
(Carden on S. *Inach.* fr. 269a.(P. Oxy. 2369)25–6).

695. Cf. *Alc.* 733 εἰ μή c' ἀδελφῆc αἷμα τιμωρήcεται. **ἐτιμωρηcάμην:**
Od. is more concerned with revenge than in Homer, where the
point of the blinding is to escape from the cave. This change of
emphasis arises out of the change of medium. Although Od. has
implied that his companions are trapped in the cave (478–9), a
totally sealed cave is of course dramatically impossible: 441 n.

696–700. At *Od.* 9.506–21 Pol. describes the oracle, and at 528–35
he goes on to pray to his father Poseidon to prevent Od. coming
home, or at least that ὀψὲ κακῶc ἔλθοι. But here the future sufferings of Od. are made part of the prophecy, the whole of which is
condensed into four lines. Compare the equally abrupt prophecies
uttered by the blinded Polymestor, and the dismissive responses
thereto, at the end of *Hecuba*.

699. ἐθέcπιcεν: The ν is probably a conjecture (Tr.2). L has ν
ephelkustikon at the end of 306, 431, 676, 677.

701. Of the twenty or so colloquialisms in *Cyc.* that do not occur in
tragedy (intro., §V), κλαίειν c' ἄνωγα (174 n.) is the only one
uttered by Od. However, the exception is unreal: Od. is echoing
Pol.'s earlier rebuff to himself (338–40 οἳ δὲ τοὺc νόμουc ἔθεντο ...
κλαίειν ἄνωγα). He then adds καὶ δέδραχ' ὅπερ λέγω (L; Paley's
λέγειc destroys the point): 'and I *have done* what I say', i.e. unlike
you I do not need to rely on mere prophecy, I have actually made
you κλαίειν (Pol.'s eye is bleeding: 490 n., 174 n.). Paley remarks
that ἐγὼ δὲ in the next line implies some person other than Od. as
the subject of λέγ-. But with 701 Od. has dealt with Pol.; in 702 he
turns to his own much happier state. At *Hec.* 1048 the chorus ask
Hecuba whether she has managed to overpower Polymestor: ...
καὶ δέδρακαc οἷάπερ λέγειc;.

703. ἐπὶ κτλ.: 'over the Sicilian sea and to my homeland': cf. *Il.*
2.159–60 οὕτω δὴ οἶκόνδε φίλην ἐc πατρίδα γαῖαν / Ἀργεῖοι φεύξονται
ἐπ' εὐρέα νῶτα θαλάccηc. Ithaka is in fact in the πόντοc Cικελόc (cf.

Zuntz, *The Political Plays of Euripides*, 66, on *El.* 1374), and so εἰс (Schumacher) for L's ἔс τ' may be right.

704. ce (Tr. 1; γε L) may well derive from the MS from which L was copied. τῆcδ' ἀπορρήξαc πέτραc has been suspected: τήνδ'... πέτραν Kirchhoff (cf. *Od.* 9.481 ἀπορρήξαc κορυφὴν ὄρεοc μεγαλοῖο; Ov. *Met.* 14.182); τάcδε ... πέτραc Murray (at *Od.* 9.537 Pol. has a second shot; cf. Theocr. 7.152; Nonnus 39.219). But for the genitive cf. Ar. *Pax* 30 παροίξαc τῆc θύραc; Xen. *Hell.* 5.4.8. τῶν ... ὅπλων καθελόντεc; K-G i 345.

705. cυvναύταιcι (cὺν ν- L): cὺν is not used with the plural in this locution: see Owen on *Ion* 32; Page on *Med.* 164. The same slight corruption occurred at 425. Cf. 708. For the construction cf. e.g. *Hipp.* 1340-1 κακοὺc αὐτοῖc τέκνοιcι καὶ δόμοιc ἐξόλλυμεν.

706-7. δι' ἀμφιτρῆτοc τῆcδε: 'through this [rock?—see 707n.] bored at both ends'; i.e. the cave has an exit at the back leading ἐπ' ὄχθον. At *Od.* 9.481, 537 Pol. hurls massive stones into the sea at the departing Greeks. Clearly this cannot be done on the stage. E. neatly solves the problem with an idea derived probably from S. *Phil.*, which may well have been produced in the previous year (intro., §VI): Pol. is taken offstage into the cave, so as to go through an entrance at the back to the hilltop overlooking the sea. The elliptical (707n.) use of the unexpected ἀμφιτρῆτοc is best explained as a burlesque of S. Phil. 19 δι' ἀμφιτρῆτοc αὐλίου (Phil.'s cave; cf. 16, 17-18, 159, 952); the word occurs nowhere else. So Dale (*WS* 69 (1956), 104-6 = *Collected Papers*, 127-9): 'it may be objected that the nightmare of the Cyclops' closed cave is thereby spoilt; not more, however, than by the earlier necessity of letting Odysseus out on to the stage (426-7) to give his narrative speech.' Cf 6on., 345-6n.; Zwierlein in *Gnomon* 39 (1967), 453 n.2.

707. προcβαίνων ποδί: πέτραc Kirchhoff; but this creates an ugly repitition of τῆcδε ... πέτραc after 704. The ellipse of the noun (probably πέτραc understood from 704, or perhaps αὐλῆc: Schmidt in *Maia* 27 (1975), 292) has a special point (706-7n.). For the sense of προcβαίνων ποδί, 'climb', Schmidt compares *h. Hom.* 3.520 ἄκμητοι δὲ λόφον προcέβαν ποcίν; *El.* 489-90 ὡc πρόc-βαcιν τῶνδ' ὀρθίαν οἴκων ἔχει [sc. Elektra] / ῥυcῶι γέροντι τῶιδε προcβῆναι ποδί, 1288, *Hec.* 1263; S. *Aj.* 1281, *El.* 456; Stesich. *PMG* 185.5; *Il.* 5.745; etc; see also Diggle, op. cit. 121n., 36-7.

708-9. Whereas the service of Pol. is incompatible with the service of Dionysos (63-72, 76-7n.), the service of Od. will bring the satyrs to τὰ βακχίου μέλαθρα (429-30). τὸ λοιπὸν goes only with Βακχίωι δουλεύcομεν: cf. *Hel.* 1449-50 μίαν δέ μοι χάριν δόντεc τὸ λοιπὸν εὐτυχῆ με θήcετε. For the satyrs as sailors see 11-17n.. The play ends, as it began, with the thought of Dionysos.

INDEX

(with special reference to satyric drama)
References are to the page numbers